BAPTISM OF THE SWORD

JACK WINDRUSH
BOOK 12

MALCOLM ARCHIBALD

Copyright (C) 2022 Malcolm Archibald

Layout design and Copyright (C) 2022 by Next Chapter

Published 2022 by Next Chapter

Edited by Graham (Fading Street Services)

Cover art by CoverMint

This book is a work of fiction. Names, characters, places, and incidents are the product of the author's imagination or are used fictitiously. Any resemblance to actual events, locales, or persons, living or dead, is purely coincidental.

All rights reserved. No part of this book may be reproduced or transmitted in any form or by any means, electronic or mechanical, including photocopying, recording, or by any information storage and retrieval system, without the author's permission.

FOR CATHY

Not of the princes and prelates with periwigged charioteers
Riding triumphantly laurelled to lap the fat of the years
Rather the scorned – the rejected – the men hemmed in with the spears;

The men of the tattered battalion which fights till it dies,
Dazed with the dust of the battle, the din and the cries,
The men with the broken heads and the blood running into their eyes.

A CONSECRATION – JOHN MASEFIELD

PRELUDE

Woods Of Shaykan, Kordofan Province, Sudan, November 1883

*Their dead will be left unburied,
And the stench of rotting bodies will fill the land*
Isiah, 34:3

William Hicks Pasha lifted himself higher in the saddle, wiped the sweat from his face and looked over his men. They had been marching for days, with their guides assuring them they travelled in the correct direction, but he was not sure. Now they were wandering in a dry forest with tree trunks exploding in the heat and men and camels dying with sunstroke by the hour.

"Where are we?" Hicks asked.

Baron Seckendorff, the adjutant, shrugged. "I'm damned if I know, sir. Somewhere in Kordofan."

"I'm sure the Mahdi is around here." Hicks looked around at the wilderness of desiccated trees through which his seven thousand infantry, one thousand cavalry and innumerable camp followers straggled. He had ascended the Nile to El-Dumeim, a hundred miles south of Khartoum, and marched westward across the arid, baking plains towards El Obeid, the Mahdi's headquarters.

The European officers with Hicks looked for inspiration as their army of reluctant Egyptian soldiers and camp followers trudged on hopelessly.

"I calculate we are about thirty miles south of El Obeid," Hicks said. "If the Mahdi is nearby, he'll make himself known soon."

As soon as Hicks had spoken, he heard the faint cry of "Allah! Allah!" from the depths of the forest, and men looked at each other in consternation.

"The Mahdi!" somebody shouted as men jammed cartridges into their rifles.

"Form a square!" Hicks ordered, and his men obeyed, gathering in a confusion of noise. "Build a zareba!"[1] Hicks knew his Egyptian soldiers were fine engineers and would fight better behind the protection of a barricade.

The Ansar, the Mahdi's army, arrived within the hour, advancing through the trees with loud cries and the glitter of sunshine on spears and rifle barrels. "Volley fire by companies!" Hicks ordered and walked around the zareba's perimeter, allowing the Egyptian soldiers, Sudanese mercenaries, European volunteers and Bashi-Bazouks [2] to see him. As well as their Remington rifles, the Egyptians possessed modern Krupp artillery pieces and six Nordenfeldt machine guns. Even so, the soldiers' morale was low, and they were disinclined to fight.

The Mahdi ordered his men forward in wave after wave of screaming attacks. Hicks repelled them with volley fire, with the smoke clouding among the trees and the heat increasing. The Egyptian square held out that first day, despite losing as many men to heat exhaustion and dysentery as to enemy spears and rifles. In the evening, with the forest echoing to the rattle of the machine guns and the acrid stink of gun smoke polluting the dry air, the Mahdi recalled his warriors. The sudden silence was unnerving as the defenders coughed and peered into the trees.

"He's gone," the journalist, Frank Vizitelly, said. "We've beaten him off."

"No." Hicks Pasha shook his head and reloaded his revolver. "The Mahdi's still out there."

Night brought little relief as the tom-toms hammered out around the Egyptian zareba and the Mahdi's men fired at random, hoping to thin out the defenders. At dawn on the second day, the Mahdi's men prayed to Allah and then attacked again, brave, inspired men throwing themselves at the massed musketry. The Egyptians hefted their Remington rifles and fired, knowing there was no retreat and little prospect of surrender.

"Ammunition's running low," Vizitelly said.

"I know," Hicks replied. "We won't last much longer."

Vizitelly nodded, looked around at the smoke drifting through the forest and heard the Mahdi's drums and the chanting of his army. "There are fifty thousand of the enemy," he said.

"I haven't counted them." Hicks wiped the sweat from his face with a powder-stained forearm. He roared encouragement to his men, knowing they had already lost the battle.

"What are your plans, sir?" Vizitelly asked.

"Fight," Hicks said dryly. "We have no other option."

As the smoke cleared, Hicks Pasha saw a group of the enemy watching him. One was a broad-shouldered man of medium height, and even from this distance, Hicks sensed the power of his character.

"That's the Mahdi," Hicks said, lifting his field glasses. "He's smiling!"

The British general and the Sudanese warrior studied each other for a full minute, and then the Mahdi turned away.

Hicks did not lower his field glasses, for the man who had been at the Mahdi's side was nearly equally impressive. Taller than the Mahdi, he wore the unofficial uniform of the Mahdi's army, a jibbeh with coloured patches to show the owner was virtuously poor. His turban was neat on his head, his beard well-trimmed beneath three tribal scars, but it was the sword hilt protruding over his left shoulder that Hicks noticed.

"Who are you, my fine soldierly friend?"

The tall man touched the hilt of his sword in a gesture that could have been a salute or a threat, turned away and followed the Mahdi. The instant he disappeared into the trees, the Mahdi's warriors charged again.

"Volley fire!" Hicks ordered. "Mark your man, and don't waste ammunition."

The Remingtons fired, with most shots wild as nervous men jerked the triggers. At the angle of the square, the Nordenfeldt machine guns stuttered and stammered, scything through the forest, and chopping chips and leaves from the trees. The Mahdi's warriors fell beneath the bullets, dead, wounded, or feigning injury in the hope of rising later and attacking their enemy.

The Mahdi gave an order, and the attackers pulled back.

"He's not pressing home his attacks," Vizitelly said.

"He doesn't have to," Hicks said. "We're dying from the heat and lack of water. All the Mahdi has to do is contain us here, and he'll win." He spoke calmly, a veteran soldier who had already accepted the inevitability of death.

On the third day of the battle, the Egyptians' ammunition ran out. The men knew they were in a desperate situation, with the Mahdi's forces cutting them off from water and home, deep in enemy territory, and without ammunition or hope. Some soldiers sobbed with fear, and others resigned to fighting to the end or decided to surrender and hope for mercy from the Mahdi.

When the Egyptians' firing ceased, there was a momentary silence in the forest as if the world waited for the inevitable slaughter. Somebody shouted, "Allah!" and a thousand, ten thousand voices echoed the cry as the Mahdi sent his warriors forward. The Ansar advanced through the scarred trees to claim their victory.

"Fix bayonets!" Hicks shouted. "Follow me!"

With a sword in his right hand and a pistol in his left, Colonel William Hicks stepped toward the enemy. His European staff officers followed, yelling their defiance as the Mahdi's men closed around them, thrusting with their broad-headed spears. The tall warrior Hicks had noticed earlier stepped forward, and rather than draw his sword, he took a spear from one of his followers, aimed and threw.

The point took Hicks full in the chest, and he staggered, lifted his revolver, and fired his final cartridge. He did not see where the bullet went, but he saw the tall Sudanese walking slowly towards him, drawing his sword.

Hicks plucked at the spear, lifted his sabre, and swung at the tall warrior, who parried without apparent effort, poised his long, straight-bladed sword, and sliced off the British officer's head.

"Good," the tall warrior, Osman Zubeir, said. "Decapitate the Nazarenes. Save the followers of Mohammed who accept the Mahdi and kill the rest." Bending down, he cleaned his sword on Hicks' uniform and slid it back into its scabbard.

CHAPTER ONE

Cairo, Egypt, December 1883

There's trouble in the wind, my boys; there's trouble in the wind.
  Rudyard Kipling

Mary Windrush curtseyed, aware that half the room's occupants were watching her and wishing her shoes were not so tight. She straightened up and faced the Khedive of Egypt, who smiled at her from under his red fez.

"Mrs Colonel Windrush," Mohamed Tewfik Pasha, the Khedive of Egypt and the Sudan, was plainly dressed in contrast to the glorious full-dress uniforms of most men present. He greeted Mary with a courteous bow. "I am delighted you could honour us with your presence."

"The honour is entirely mine, your Highness," Mary said.

"Your husband did great things in Colonel Arabi's late rebellion," the Khedive continued, with his eyes roaming across Mary's dress and returning to her face.

"Thank you, your Highness," Mary replied. "He does his best."

The Khedive gave his pleasant smile. "I hope you enjoy the ball, Mrs Colonel Windrush. If you need anything, please do not hesitate to ask." He snapped his fingers, and a gorgeously attired aide-de-camp hurried up, bowing.

"More champagne for Mrs Windrush," the Khedive ordered, "and for Colonel Windrush."

"At once, your Highness," the servant bowed again and moved to one of the side tables.

"You've made a new friend, Mary," Jack stepped closer to his wife, with a cheroot in his hand and the double row of medals on his scarlet dress uniform gleaming under the crystal chandeliers. Any army officers present would see that Jack's campaigns spanned thirty years.

"You'll notice that the Khedive is very attentive to all the European ladies," Mary said dryly, accepting her champagne from the aide-de-camp with a smile. "You'll also notice that his wife is not present."

"I had noticed." Lieutenant-colonel Jack Windrush of the Royal Malverns drew on his cheroot. "However, I believe that the Khedive is a faithful husband." He gave a tight smile. "I think he is trying to be a gentleman."

They walked across the crowded room, nodding to casual acquaintances and stopping to speak to those they knew well. One of the busy servants directed them to an empty table, and Mary sat with a sigh. "I'd like to kick off these shoes! I don't know who designs lady's shoes, but they insist on making them the tightest and most uncomfortable creations possible."

"It must be a man," Jack told her solemnly.

"Oh, it'll be a man, right enough," Mary agreed. She smiled and lifted her hand to a passing couple. "That's Sir Archibald and Lady Alison."

"I know," Jack said. "I met General Alison during the late campaign." He watched the one-armed general and his wife walk past. "I think he prefers to be on campaign than to prance around in an Egyptian palace."

"As do you, Captain Jack," Mary said. "You're never happy on social occasions, even in such a magnificent setting."

Jack smiled. "The Abdin Palace has style, I grant you, Mary, and the Khedive gives a grand ball, but these events always seem false to me."

"Sit back and allow the servants to care for you," Mary advised. "When you think where we've been and what we've seen, this place is like paradise."

Jack nodded, remembering the disease-ridden forests of Burma and the human sacrifices of Ashantiland, the ambushes and horrors of Afghanistan and the bitter winter in the Crimea. "That is certainly true." When he closed his eyes, he was back in the nightmare of the Indian Mutiny, when trusted friends became vicious enemies overnight, the Mutineers slaughtered women and children and the British retaliated with mass executions.

"Come back, Jack," Mary shook his arm. "I should have known better than to remind you. Look, there's Lord Dufferin. The poor man's wife is sick with a fever. And there's Sir Andrew Colvin; don't his daughters look lovely? I hope he doesn't let them out of his sight with all these unattached men wandering around." Mary diverted Jack with a constant flow of talk, pointing out the great and good of Cairo society. "There are far too few women here, Jack. My dancing card is so full I hardly have time to think. There's the music started again!" She consulted her card. "I have General Hook next dance."

"Be careful with that man," Jack murmured. "Or he'll have you off on some expedition to the back of beyond."

Mary stood up and fluttered her white-gloved fingers at Jack. "I must go, Jack. Mingle, will you? Don't sit there and get all despondent."

"I'll mingle." Jack watched as Mary drifted away. He had only one dance booked with his wife, and until then, he wandered around the brilliantly lit suite of rooms the Khedive had arranged for the ball, then slipped outside. A band played in the square beside the palace, with the music a mixture of European and Egyptian. The flaring light of torches highlighted the faces and clothes of the guests, the sweating Europeans and bland locals who pretended to accept the occupation with good grace. Cigar smoke spiralled upwards, and Jack saw a British woman puffing at a cigarette. The first time he had seen cigarettes had been in the Crimea, and now the craze had spread from the soldiers to the fashionable upper classes.

Jack watched Mary dance with a succession of partners, knowing she enjoyed such social events. He sipped a glass of Glenlivet whisky, smiled as Mary waved at him behind her back, and surreptitiously checked the time. It was two in the morning. *Surely this ball will end soon.*

At last, the call for the final waltz came. Jack reclaimed his wife from a red-faced civilian engineer and guided her around the dance floor, breathing deeply of her perfume as she danced with as much grace as a woman half her age.

"General Hook is watching us," Mary murmured.

"That's a bad sign," Jack said. "We'll keep out of his path and escape before the rest. That way, we'll avoid the crush, and hopefully, the general will forget about us."

"It's been a lovely night," Mary told him. "I wish you could enjoy these events as much as I do."

"I enjoy watching you enjoy yourself," Jack said seriously, responding to her quick smile and brief hug.

As the music died to a halt, Jack led Mary to the front of the palace, where their hired carriage waited. The driver was dozing beside the horse until Jack woke him.

"Shepheard's Hotel, driver!"

"Yes, effendi." The man waited until Jack and Mary were seated, cracked the reins, and the carriage jolted forward.

When Jack glanced over his shoulder, he saw General Hook standing with a cheroot in his hand, watching them.

"General Hook can wait until tomorrow," Mary took hold of Jack's arm. "Leave your duty until then."

Shepheard's Hotel was the oldest established hotel in Cairo and dominated the street known as the Esbekeeyeh, which Mary always likened to a Cairo version of the Champs Elysees in Paris. The Esbekeeyeh stretched from the ornate Place de L'Opera to the more mundane Alexandria Railway Station across the Ismailia Canal.

Mary sang "The Bonny Banks of Loch Lomond" as the carriage rattled across Cairo, la-la-la-ing when she did not remember the words and inviting Jack to join in.

"I think you've had a little too much champagne," Jack said, smiling.

"Nonsense," Mary shook her head. "It's impossible to have too much champagne. How long have we been married for now?"

"How long?" Jack wrinkled his forehead in thought. "Let's see. This is December 1883, and we married in 1859, so that's twenty-four years."

"Twenty-four years, and how often have you seen me drink too much in that time?"

Jack was an experienced enough husband to know when he was venturing into dangerous territory. "Never," he replied, hiding his smile.

"Exactly so," Mary agreed. "Oh, we're here already! I was enjoying the ride."

Shepheard's was a rambling, two-story building with large, airy rooms surrounding a leafy quadrangle. Jack helped his wife out of the carriage, and as he paid the driver, Mary walked through the luxuriant palm trees of the garden and up a flight of steps into the broad, roofed veranda. A doorman opened the principal entrance, and Mary waited for Jack to join her.

"I'm not ready for bed yet," Mary said.

"It's nearly four in the morning," Jack reminded.

"I don't care," Mary said. "I'm not ready for bed yet." She indicated the veranda, floored with marble, and furnished with various lounging and easy chairs. Although Shepheard's hotel was the first choice for the elite, the veranda was also an institution where guests had discussed a hundred business deals, political decisions, and military campaigns.

Mary selected a pair of cane-bottomed chairs at an oval table and stretched out. "Join me, Jack," she ordered imperiously.

Despite the hour, a waiter came from the refreshment bar a few yards from the veranda and smiled when Mary ordered champagne. Jack sighed and asked for coffee.

"Oh, Captain Jack!" Mary scoffed. "Can't you keep up?"

"Not with you," Jack said and settled into the chair. Shepheard's veranda was one of the few places in Cairo permanently free from the clamorous donkey boys, beggars and pedlars that infested the streets. He smiled as Mary sipped at her glass, tasted his coffee, and watched the numberless lights of Cairo spreading around the hotel.

"Ah, here you are, Jack! No, don't get up!" General Hook bowed to Mary and pulled up a chair. "I wondered where you had got to when you left the ball."

"We're winding down after all the excitement, sir," Jack said.

Jack had known General Hook for more than twenty years, although he was unsure how to categorise their relationship. Hook was high up in British Intelligence and acted as a superior and mentor to Jack.

"How is the regiment, Jack?" Hook lifted a hand, and a waiter brought him a brandy and soda.

"In permanent transition," Jack replied. "These short terms of service mean we barely get men trained as soldiers, and they're off again."

"That's a complaint that all regiments have," Hook said. "You're based in Lower Egypt, aren't you?"

"Yes, sir," Jack wondered what Hook wanted. The general was not a man to waste time on social calls. "The regimental headquarters is in the Cairo Citadel, and the rest is scattered in a dozen different small garrisons around the Nile Delta."

Hook nodded. "Most of your men will be acclimatised to the heat by now."

"Yes, sir, except for the latest intake," Jack glanced at Mary, who was beginning to look apprehensive.

Hook sipped at his brandy. "What do you think of the current political situation, Windrush?"

Windrush, not Jack. The preliminary niceties are over, and Hook is moving to the purpose of his visit. When he calls me Colonel, I can begin to worry.

"Not great, sir," Jack said, glad Mary listened quietly without giving the general the benefit of her wisdom. "Ever since the Mahdi's forces defeated Hicks Pasha in Kordofan, some of the populace have been disturbed. I believe the Mahdi's army has increased in size since then."

"It has," Hook said quietly. "What do you think about the state of Sudan?"

The question was not unexpected, but Jack was tired. "I try not to think about it, sir."

"What do you think about Sudan, Colonel?" Hook repeated the question.

The general called me colonel: there's trouble ahead.

"I think the Egyptians have mismanaged Sudan for decades, sir," Jack said. "They've plundered it for what they can get, enslaved the population, weighed them down with taxes, tortured and harassed them until the Sudanese rebelled." He looked up, signalled the waiter, and ordered a whisky.

Hook wrote down what Jack said. "When we defeated Arabi's rebellion last year," he said, "the idea was to ensure free passage through the Suez Canal. We did not want to add Egypt to the empire."

"So I believe, sir," Jack said. He looked up and spoke sharply to the waiter in Arabic. "I asked for whisky, not brandy!"

"Sorry, effendi," the waiter hurried to change Jack's drink.

Hook raised a bushy eyebrow. "You speak Arabic well, Windrush. As I was saying, Great Britain, or at least Gladstone and the Liberal Party, doesn't want to add Egypt to the empire. We're only here to ensure the country is stable, then hand it back to the Egyptians and, by association, the Turks. We are not empire building, whatever the French might think."

Jack sipped at his whisky. "I hope that is correct, sir. In my mind, the Empire is more of a burden than anything else. The bigger it is, the more we have to defend and the more it costs." Jack knew not many people agreed with his views.

"You are a man of original thought, Colonel," Hook said. "Off the record, I tend to agree with Gladstone and you, but there are many who like to see Britain covering the globe in red paint and an ever-expanding Empire."

"I am sure there are, sir," Jack said. "They don't have to police and defend the damned thing."

Hook swirled his brandy around the glass. "However, Gladstone's ideas of a fair and progressive government are alien to many of the current Egyptian ruling class. The present Khedive is an exception. In essence, that leaves Evelyn Baring, our consul general here, as the *de facto* ruler of Egypt."

"Temporarily, I hope, sir," Jack continued. "Britain lacks the military and financial capacity to defend Egypt against external aggression."

"We manage all right in India," Hook probed.

"India is self-financing and produces some of the best soldiers in the world," Jack argued his case. "Egypt produces little, and the fellaheen are not soldier material. I think Hicks Pasha's defeat proves that. Sudan is a huge territory with ill-defined and indefensible borders." Jack paused, wondered what Hook was thinking, shrugged, and continued. "I know we have installed Colonel Valentine Baker to organise an Egyptian gendarmerie, while Major-General Wood is the Sirdar, or commander, with the task of raising and training a new Egyptian army. Even so, I doubt the fellaheen will fight for us."

"Why is that, Colonel?" Hook asked gently.

"They don't want us here," Jack fought off waves of tiredness as he tried to organise his thoughts. "Colonel Arabi led a nationalist rising against Turkish rule and got the British as rulers instead. Why the devil should the Egyptians like us ordering them around in their own country? Particularly as we intend handing them back to the Ottoman Turks."

Hook smiled faintly. "It would be less than diplomatic of me to agree with you, Windrush. The fact is: we are here, and we're trying to clean up the Egyptian administration."

"Yes, sir," Jack glanced at Mary, who had fallen asleep. He took the half-full glass from her hand.

Hook waited until Jack had settled Mary into a more comfortable position. "When Gladstone reluctantly agreed to fight Arabi, he did not intend to occupy Egypt, but it's a *fait accompli,* and now we find ourselves dragged into Egyptian affairs."

Jack nodded. Either the alcohol was wearing off, or he was becoming immune. He held up his glass, and the waiter immediately brought a refill.

"Unfortunately for us," Hook said, "Egyptian affairs include their occupation and colonisation of Sudan. We have inherited a major problem."

"So I believe, sir," Jack said.

"Do you know much about Egypt's history in Sudan?"

"A little."

Hook nodded. "You'll forgive me if I give you a brief history lesson." He smiled, "not that I'll give you a choice."

Jack found the waiter had refilled his glass and removed Mary's empty.

"Egypt began occupying Sudan in 1819 and pressed south. They established a series of military and slaving posts, and by 1870 they reached the equatorial region some eight hundred miles south of Khartoum."

Jack glanced at Mary, who was still asleep on her chair. "That's far south, sir."

"It is," Hook agreed. "Sudan is a huge territory, and the

Egyptians proved to be probably the worst colonisers in the world. They were guilty of every kind of oppression under the sun, extortion, corruption, theft, and slavery. You name it Windrush, and the Egyptians used it. To enforce their will, they had an army of around 40,000 men. An infamous army with poor morale and useless officers backed by Bashi-Bazouks and laced with Sudanese soldiers." He stopped. "Have you encountered the Bashi-Bazouks yet?"

"I've seen the odd individual pretending to act as a policeman, sir," Jack said. "I don't know much about them."

"Let me enlighten you, Windrush," Hook said. "The Bashi-Bazouks are irregular soldiers in the Ottoman Turkish army. One definition of the name is Crazy head or Leaderless, which tells you a lot. They are recruited all over the Turkish Empire and have an unenviable reputation for looting and violence. The Egyptian authorities use them as armed policemen."

"Just what the Sudanese need," Jack said. "Poor buggers."

"Poor buggers indeed," Hook agreed. "The Egyptians controlled their empire through the Bashi-Bazouks, torture and the lash. Slave trading flourished, both from Egypt proper and with Arabs crossing the Red Sea to raid at will."

Jack stirred uncomfortably. "I hope we're not supporting these people, sir."

Hook gave another faint smile. "We'll get to that. Nine years ago, a man named Charles Gordon became the last Khedive's governor of the Equatorial province of the Sudan."

Jack nodded. Gordon was one of the most famous men in Great Britain. A Royal Engineer with experience in the Crimean War, he had made his name fighting against rebels in China and had struggled against the slave trade in Sudan.

"Gordon cleaned the area up so successfully that in 1877 the Khedive made him governor-general of the entire Sudan. He remained for two years, then left."

"Yes, sir." Jack was familiar with Chinese Gordon's story.

"When Gordon left, the Sudan reverted to the chaos it had been before, and then this present outbreak occurred."

Jack shifted in his chair. Hook's voice had developed a new edge, as though he was approaching a significant point in his story.

"You've dealt with jihads before, Windrush," Hook said.

"Yes, sir, on the North West Frontier of India. It's a holy war against the infidels, normally the British. Us."

"That's exactly what it is," Hook agreed, "but the leader of this jihad is different from any Islamic holy man you've ever faced before."

"Why is that, sir?" Jack asked.

Hook finished his brandy and signalled for more. "You'll have gathered by now why the Sudanese hate the Egyptians. You might also know that Islam is amazingly powerful in northern and central Sudan."

"And in parts of Egypt, sir," Jack said.

"Indeed. We became aware of unrest in Sudan in early 1881, but we ignored it. After all, it wasn't our business. We had more important things to worry about in Afghanistan and South Africa. However, we kept an ear to the ground and learned that a new mystic had appeared to lead the rebellion. We didn't much care, for these fellows are forever proclaiming themselves for a few months, then fading away."

Jack stirred restlessly. He had experienced the power of religion and knew the influence it could have.

"However, this fellow did not fade away," Hook said. "His name is Mohammed Ahmed Ibn el-Sayyid Abdullah, and people call him the Mahdi."

"The Mahdi," Jack repeated. Mary sat up, fully awake, although her hair was dishevelled and her dress no longer pristine.

"The Mahdi," Mary said. The Mahdi had occupied columns of newsprint for the previous few months. "His followers believe he is a prophet. He has taken the name of the twelfth Shia Imam, "Al Mahdi," who vanished about a thousand years ago. Some, perhaps most, Shias believe the original Al Mahdi will return to restore justice and truth. They say that Muhammed promised that one of his descendants would appear to bring their faith alive again. They think the Mahdi will arrive before the world ends, a spiritual and temporal leader who will restore the true religion and justice."

Mary stood up, a shimmering figure with the light of dawn behind her. "It's their equivalent of the Second Coming."

"Yes," Hook said. "And Abdullah declared he was that man. To the Sudanese, he is the Mahdi, the Second Coming, and he's just over our border."

Jack stared over the city of Cairo. "Dear Lord, preserve us."

CHAPTER TWO

'Semper aliquid novi Africam adferre [Africa always brings [us] something new]',
   Pliny the Elder

As Hook finished speaking, the muezzins across Cairo proclaimed the azan, the call to prayer, and the beautiful sound floated to them, diffused by distance, enhanced by the subject of their conversation. Throughout Cairo, the faithful halted whatever they were doing and hurried to their local mosque.

Jack stood and looked over the gardens, where a breeze rustled the palm trees. "Tell me about this Mahdi, General Hook."

"My informants can't tell me anything definitive," Hook said as the muezzins continued their ululating call. "He appeared out of nowhere, like a wraith from the desert, at Aba Island, about 150 miles upstream from Khartoum. Some claim he's from a long line of boat builders on the Nile."

"A carpenter," Mary murmured as the muezzins completed their call, and for a moment, the city was quiet. "And a warrior priest."

"Others think his father was a poor religious teacher or perhaps a sheikh."

"Pay your money and take your choice," Jack continued to face out over the garden to the slowly waking city of Cairo.

Hook nodded and continued. "Abdullah had hardly arrived when he set himself up as a religious leader and said he'd rid Sudan of the Egyptians, with their corruptions. He said he'd bring the Sudanese back to the true faith with its austere, pure lifestyle."

"A Cromwell to the Egyptian's Stuart kings," Mary whispered. "Or a Sudanese Covenanter, maybe a Martin Luther from the desert."

Hook allowed Mary to speak before he continued. "Naturally, the Khedive disagreed and sent a couple of hundred men to arrest the self-proclaimed Mahdi. The Mahdi's men waited until the Egyptians landed on Abas Island and attacked as they floundered in the mud. Armed only with sticks and stones, they destroyed the Khedive's professional soldiers."

Jack could imagine the scene as the virtually unarmed Sudanese attacked the white-uniformed Egyptians. He could picture the fear and the blood, and the screaming. "That would please the Khedive."

Hook signalled for another drink. "Rather than wait for the inevitable retaliation, the Mahdi vanished into the Kordofan deserts and called for a jihad. We were too busy fighting Arabi to take notice at the time."

Jack nodded, remembering the skirmishes around Alexandria, the naval bombardment, nighttime march across the desert and the short, fierce battle of Tel-el-Kebir. "We were," he agreed.

"When the Mahdi emerged again, he laid siege to the city of El Obeid," Hook spoke quietly, yet his words were distinct. "His army, the Ansar, camped outside the walls for six months, and when El Obeid fell in January 1883, he massacred the defenders."

Again, Jack pictured the scene; the exhausted, starving

defenders and the tribesmen charging through the town. He could nearly hear the cries of "Allah!" and the pointless begging for mercy as the spears stabbed and slashed.

"When the Ansar finished their slaughter, the vultures feasted, and the blood soaked into the sand," Hook continued, "Abdullah, the self-styled Mahdi, now had hundreds of modern weapons and ammunition, as well as money. He also had an army of devoted followers willing to die for him."

The sun was rising, lighting up the domes and minarets of Cairo, with the pyramids mysterious in the distance. The noise of the modern city swelled to the sky. Jack drew in his breath, imagining the Ansar loose on the streets of Cairo, with the resulting massacre of men, women, and children. Cairo was known as the Paris of the Levant, a civilised city where military bands performed classical music in spacious public gardens. It was a city with gas-lit streets, French-style houses and apartment blocks where elegant women and men sat on iron balconies. Men from across Europe and the Middle East drank coffee in sophisticated cafes, while women wore sweeping dresses to visit the many theatres. Jack could only imagine the chaos if the Mahdi invaded this place with his hordes of desert tribesmen. Scenes from the Indian Mutiny returned to him, the murder, fear, and horror.

"The Mahdi is a dangerous man," he said quietly.

"Probably the most dangerous we've ever faced in Africa," Hook said. "And more formidable, now he has defeated a British-led army and captured all the modern weapons of Hicks' army. The Zulus were excellent fighting men, but King Cetewayo would never have dreamed of attacking Cape Town. The Boers shot us stupid at Majuba, but all they wanted was to be left in peace. The Xhosa massacred settlers in the border districts without any intentions of further conquest. The Ashanti were forest fighters with no knowledge of the outside world. The Mahdi is different."

"How different?" Jack asked.

Hook remained in his seat. "The Mahdi has said that when he's conquered all Sudan, he will capture Egypt and cross the Red Sea for a bloody battle outside Mecca. After that, he'll advance on Jerusalem, where Christ will descend from Heaven to meet him."

"The man is mad," Mary said.

"Maybe," Hook said, passing a cheroot to Jack and lighting one himself. "Once he has combined with Christ, the Mahdi said, Islam will conquer the entire world."

"An African Bonaparte," Jack glanced at Mary. "He won't conquer the world, of course, but he could make things very difficult for us in this quarter of Africa. What do you intend to do about it?"

"Me?" Hook stood up and stepped beside Jack. "I'm only a soldier, Colonel. I obey orders, the same as you and the lowliest recruit in the army. The politicians make the decisions; God help us."

"What have they decided?" Jack drew on his cheroot. He glanced at Mary. *If the Mahdi's forces come into Egypt, you're shipping out, my girl. I'll have you on the first boat to Britain, whatever you say.*

"Gladstone and his men have decided the game's not worth the candle. We're evacuating Sudan and leaving it to the Mahdi."

"Easier said than done, I think," Jack said. "How about the Egyptian garrisons there? Aren't the Egyptian soldiers our responsibility now?"

"Chinese Gordon is returning to Khartoum to arrange the evacuation," Hook said. "But there's fresh trouble breaking out on Sudan's Red Sea littoral. A fellow by the name of Osman Digna has raised the local tribes and is menacing a trio of small garrisons. After Hicks, we can't afford any more disasters, so we're sending Baker Pasha down the coast."

"Chinese Gordon and Valentine Baker," Jack said. "We're using heavy artillery now." *Why is Hook telling me all this?*

Hook smiled. "Osman Digna is threatening the port of

Suakin, Colonel. That's Sudan's main trading outlet and a threat to British shipping in the Red Sea. Baker Pasha is a good soldier, but he leads Egyptian soldiers and Bashi-Bazouks, just as Hicks Pasha did. I want an experienced British soldier in Suakin to observe and tell me what's happening."

"Me?" Jack felt Mary's eyes swivel to him.

"You," Hook confirmed. "Who is your senior major?"

"Baxter," Jack said. "He's a good man, vastly experienced."

"Tell him he's in temporary command of the regiment. I want you to leave with Baker's expedition."

"Yes, sir."

Mary waited until Hook had left before she put a hand on Jack's arm. She did not have to speak.

* * *

"Her Highness paid a shilling for you?" Sergeant Hanley viewed the latest offering for the Royal Malverns with incredulity. "Twelve whole pennies? By all that's Holy, I hope she got ninepence change!" He walked down the line of recruits with his swagger stick under his arm and his moustached face frowning in contempt. "Look at you! I've seen a bag of potatoes with more shape to it! Stand at attention, for God's sake!"

Jack hid his smile. He had witnessed similar scenes a thousand times as veteran NCOs tried to transform raw civilians into soldiers fit to serve the queen. The new men would feel out of place and uncertain. Within a fortnight, they would assume the swagger of old soldiers, and within six months, the regiment would accept them. If they survived the various diseases of the exotic East.

Jack had altered the labelling of the Malverns' companies from a numeral to an alphabetical system. The old Number One Company was now A Company, Number Two was B Company, with the reorganisation continuing through the alphabet. Two companies, A and B, shared the Citadel in Cairo with regimental headquarters and other regiments. Jack strolled across the barrack square, happily at home with the military atmosphere he had known all his life.

Major Baxter had informed him that two new subalterns had arrived with the latest batch of recruits. One was broad-shouldered and confident, looking around as if he had come home. The second appeared more diffident, smooth-faced, and youthful.

That lad looks like he's hardly left school.

"You two!" Jack barked. "Come here!"

The subalterns hurried across to him, sprung to attention and saluted.

"Who are you?" Jack tried to keep the bite from his voice.

"Second Lieutenant Lang, sir," the confident officer said. "We have to report to the adjutant here."

"And you?" Jack asked the smooth-faced youth.

"Second Lieutenant Moffat, sir." The boy looked as if he were going to faint.

"Major Bryant is the adjutant," Jack said. "He'll see you right." He nodded to the barracks. "His office is clearly labelled."

"Yes, sir," Lang said. "Come along, Moffat!"

Jack watched them march away, with Lang in the lead.

Welcome to the Malverns. Sink or swim, my lads.

"Major Baxter!" Jack shouted as he entered the barracks. He saw soldiers stiffen to attention and acknowledged their salutes.

Major Baxter hurried up, adjusting his uniform. "Sir?" In his early forties, Baxter had been with the Malverns since he was eighteen. He stood at attention with his bushy moustache trimmed to perfection and a shaft of sunlight gleaming on the campaign ribbons on his left breast.

"General Hook is sending me to Suakin," Jack told him. "You're in charge of the regiment in my absence."

"Will you be gone long, sir?" Baxter asked.

"That's in God's hands, Baxter, or the Mahdi's."

Baxter nodded. "Take care, sir. I wish the regiment were going with you."

"So do I, Baxter." Jack strode to his quarters, where Donnelly, his soldier-servant, stood at attention.

"I've packed your things, sir," Donnelly said.

"How the devil did you know I was going, Donnelly? I only told Major Baxter five minutes ago."

"One of the Arabs down the bazaar told me last night, sir." Donnelly remained at attention. "These lads know everything before the ink is dry on the paper."

Jack nodded. "I'll need you to come with me, Donnelly."

"I'm already packed, sir. Mrs Colonel Windrush told me to look after you." Donnelly smiled without moving his lips. "She usually does."

Jack grunted. "Who's in charge of this damned regiment? Her or me?"

"You, sir," Donnelly replied without a change of expression. "You're in charge of the regiment, and Mrs Colonel Windrush is in charge of you."

"Thank you for educating me on the chain of command, private," Jack said. "I've offered you promotion twice, Donnelly, and you've turned me down each time. I will offer it again. You'd be an asset to the regiment as an NCO. I can see you advancing rapidly from corporal to sergeant and maybe even to sergeant major."

Donnelly shook his head. "No, thank you, sir. I am quite content where I am."

"As you wish, Donnelly," Jack said. "I'll leave the offer open."

Jack did not need to double-check Donnelly's work. He informed Bryant that he was leaving for an unspecified time and ensured he had the most up-to-date maps, plus two portable water filterers.

Jack glanced out the window when he heard a man singing. Second lieutenant Lang was in full voice.

"We don't want to fight,
But by Jingo, if we do,
We've got the ships,
We've got the men,
And got the money too."

Bryant sighed, lit two cheroots, and passed one to Jack.

"How long do you give that young man before the reality hits him, sir?"

Jack drew on the cheroot. "I like hearing enthusiastic young men, Bryant. It's only sad that we lose so many."

"We lose too many of our best," Bryant agreed with a wry smile. "Lang is full of life and patriotism. I'd hate to tell him that Gilbert McDermott, the fellow that wrote that song, was a brickie's labourer, and the entire West End banned him because of his obscene double entendres."

Jack shook his head. "Not quite the patriotic Briton that Lang might imagine, then."

"Not quite," Bryant said. "McDermott was paid to write that song. The Conservative party and some arms dealers wanted Great Britain to get involved in the war between Russia and Turkey and tried to stir up Russophobia." He shook his head. "It was all about money making and politics."

Lang was strolling around the barrack square, watching Sergeant Hanley drill the men and shaking his head as if in professional disapproval.

"We've fought the Bear before,
And while we're Britons true
The Russians shall not
Have Constantinople."

"Terrible lyrics," Bryant said. "You'd think there was enough trouble in the world without idiot politicians stirring up more. So you're going away again, sir?"

"It seems so," Jack agreed. He looked out the window as Sergeant Hanley continued to drill the sweating recruits.

"You'll have heard that your bundook is your best friend." Hanley held up a rifle to show what a bundook was. "Well, that's a lie spread by uninformed civilians. Your best friends are your boots! Keep them clean and in good repair!"

Jack nodded as Hanley continued.

"Your uniform comes in two sizes," Hanley warmed to his task. "Too big or too small. Make it fit; learn the bugle calls and how to drill, and in time, in ten years or more, you might become a soldier."

Jack remembered Hanley as a private in Afghanistan. Now Hanley was a veteran, skilled in the art of breaking down slouching civilians and rebuilding them as soldiers. He listened to the bawdy banter as a group of men passed the office and heard the barking of Private Wright's dog Nicky, the unofficial regimental mascot.

"We'll look after them for you, sir," Bryant said. "Major Baxter has the Malverns in his blood and bones. He's been in the regiment since he was a teen."

"I leave the Malverns in safe hands," Jack said, smiling.

"Now, you idle layabouts!" Hanley marched from one end of the newcomers to the other and blasted them with iron lungs. "You may think that a soldier's worst enemy comes howling from the desert with spears or hides behind an Afghan rock with a jezzail or maybe a grey-coated Russian." He paused for effect. "You are wrong!"

The recruits stared at him, no doubt wondering what enemy could be worse than a Pashtun warrior or a Cossack. Hanley soon educated them.

"Your worst enemy is your own filthy habits!" Hanley said. "You'll have heard of Delhi belly; well, in Egypt, we have Gyppy tummy, a humorous name for dysentery. I can tell you, lads; there's nothing humorous about it. You probably can't avoid it but keep proper latrine discipline and watch what you eat and drink!"

The recruits stared at him. Some had already experienced the horrors of dysentery and understood. Others had that nightmare still to come. Jack turned away, knowing the Malverns would continue without him. A regiment was organic; the men were its blood and bones, each playing his part but replaceable. He was the commander, yet if he left, another would take his place, and the regiment would continue.

Leaving the Royal Malverns was hard but saying farewell to Mary was much worse.

"Take care of yourself," Mary told him. "No heroics, Captain Jack."

"No heroics," Jack promised. "I'm only in Suakin to observe and report. It's an Egyptian affair; it's nothing to do with us."

"Just you remember that, Jack," Mary said sternly. "It's one thing to court danger when fighting for your country and quite another to be silly when all you're doing is trying to evacuate somebody else's land."

"You take care when I'm gone," Jack said, and, despite the presence of a hundred hard-bitten soldiers, he held her close. *God, how I hate goodbyes!*

"Come back to me, Captain Jack," Mary said softly as all the petty misunderstandings of their marriage faced into inconsequential irrelevance, and only their love remained.

Jack breathed deeply of Mary's perfume and released her. "I must go," he said.

"I know," Mary breathed. "Off you go, Captain Jack, and do your duty." Only Jack could hear the catch in her voice.

CHAPTER THREE

Are all men in disguise except those crying?
　Dannie Abse

The sun hammered onto the riverside at Cairo, with Jack watching a couple of Highlanders ride past, each man precariously balanced on a donkey's back. As their kilts ballooned up behind them, Jack smiled to think what Mary would have said, then looked up as a man strode towards him dressed in the uniform of a senior Egyptian officer.

"So you're coming with me, Windrush?" Valentine Baker, in charge of the Egyptian Gendarmerie, was an experienced soldier. He had fought in the Cape Frontier and Crimean wars and commanded the 10th Hussars for thirteen years. After travelling extensively in Asia, Baker seemed destined for higher command until he sexually assaulted a young woman in a railway carriage. The British Army removed him, and Baker joined the Ottoman Empire, distinguishing himself during Turkey's war with Russia.

"I am," Jack agreed. Despite Baker's impressive fighting record, Jack could not bring himself to like the man.

Tall, with a fierce moustache, Baker wore his fez slightly back on his head and glowered at Jack. "Are you here in a fighting capacity, Windrush? Or are you merely an observer?"

"Officially, I am an observer," Jack said. "Unofficially, I am quite willing to lend a hand where needed."

Baker glanced at Donnelly, who stood at attention ten paces back. "How about your servant?"

"Private Donnelly will accompany me," Jack said.

"You'll be under my command, of course," Baker told him.

Jack felt his anger rise. "No, Baker. I am not in your Gendarmerie. I am in the British Army and not under the control of any mercenary soldier of whatever rank." He saw Baker stiffen and pushed his point. "That goes for Private Donnelly or any other man in my regiment." He waited for a moment. "Now we have that clear, Baker, could you kindly tell me what your mission is? General Hook was rather vague."

Baker looked nonplussed. "You're a cool hand, Windrush."

"I'm a Lieutenant-colonel in the British Army, Baker. What has the Khedive ordered you to do?"

Baker glanced at Donnelly, who stood with the slightly contemptuous look that only an old soldier could adopt while remaining within the bounds of discipline.

"It's all right, Baker," Jack said. "Private Donnelly is professionally deaf, blind and dumb."

Baker grunted doubtfully. "The Khedive has given me supreme military and civil command in all parts of the Sudan that I can reach with my forces."

Jack noted the pride in Baker's voice and wondered if he was correct in stating Baker had no authority over him. *I'll be damned before I have a man like Baker giving me orders.* "Is there an objective to your expedition?"

Baker glanced around, where a company of Egyptian soldiers were shambling towards a boat, with their officers hectoring them. "The Khedive has ordered me to pacify the country between Suakin and Berber and create a line of communications between those towns."

Jack pictured a map of Sudan in his head. "That's a huge chunk of the country to control," he said. "Especially with Osman Digna active in that area." He glanced at the Egyptian soldiers slouching past. "Are your men ready? Hicks Pasha didn't have much luck with his Egyptians."

"Hicks Pasha was a fool," Baker said. "I've trained these men, and they'll fight." He smiled. "I have experience in fighting with Turkish soldiers, remember."

"I remember," Jack said. He watched another company of Egyptian soldiers wander past, some with drooping shoulders and others with dirty rifles. He itched to get among them, but he was here to observe, not command. "Is that all the Khedive expects of you?"

"Oh, no," Baker said. "I have also to relieve a couple of outposts that Osman Digna is besieging."

"I see." Jack produced two cheroots, lit one and passed the other to Baker. "Which are?"

"Sinkat and Tokar," Baker said easily. "Neither is too far from the coast."

"That will be a blessing," Jack said. He had seen the names on the map but knew nothing of the Egyptian outposts.

"A brave fellow called Tewfik Bey is holding Sinkat," Baker said. "From what little I've heard, groups of the enemy gather outside the besieged little town every day and shout curses and threats. They attack repeatedly, but Tewfik's garrison chases them away."

"That's encouraging," Jack said.

"He's a good man." Baker ignored the flies that buzzed around his head. "I've been in touch with Tewfik. His agents told me that many tribesmen believe the Mahdi is the genuine prophet and Osman Digna is his caliph."

"How about the other place, Tokar?" Jack asked.

"A little grim, I heard," Baker said. "The Mahdists have filled up the wells outside the town, and the water in the wells within Tokar is brackish. The defenders are dropping like flies with sickness, and their ammunition is running low."

"Not so good," Jack watched one of the Egyptian soldiers try to run away until an officer wrestled him to the ground. "What are your plans?"

"I'll sail to Suakin first," Baker said, "then down to Trinkitat, a little further down the coast. From there, I'll march inland and relieve Tokar. I've offered a hundred pounds to the first sheikh to enter Sinkat with supplies."

Jack nodded. The British sometimes used bribery to control the tribes on India's North West Frontier.

Baker continued. "I hope this Osman Digna fellow fights, so I can smash him and show the Mahdi that we mean business."

Jack nodded. "I wish you the best of British luck, Baker."

"Once I've defeated Osman Digna," Baker said, "I'll clear the route from Suakin to Berber, then it's up the Nile to Khartoum, evacuate Gordon and the Egyptian garrisons and let the Mahdi have his blasted desert."

"As easy as that," Jack said dryly.

Baker drew on his cigar and allowed the smoke to trickle from his nostrils. "You and I know, Colonel, that it's never easy." He dropped his flippant tone. "But we can't allow the civilians to realise that, can we?"

"No, we certainly can't," Jack agreed. He could see a little more depth to Valentine Baker without any pretence of friendship.

Baker glanced at his men. "I'd better get these reprobates on the move," he said. "I suspect we'll see quite a bit of each other, Windrush."

"I suspect we will, Baker," Jack agreed and watched as Baker hurried off, barking orders.

"All right, Donnelly," Jack said. "Let's find our ship. We're sailing independently."

"It's all arranged, sir," Donnelly said. He marched on as a tall black man in the uniform of an Egyptian sergeant strode towards him. Neither moved for the other, so they collided, with both men muttering insults.

"What the hell are you playing at?" Donnelly snarled and pushed the Egyptian aside.

"I am superior in rank to you," the sergeant replied. "You move for me!"

"And that'll be bloody right, Gyppo!" Donnelly squared up to the taller man with his chin thrust out pugnaciously.

"Enough!" Jack rapped. "Both of you, take one step to the left!"

When the men obeyed, Jack nodded. "Stand at attention!" He looked the sergeant up and down. "You speak English well. Where did you learn?"

"On a ship from the Caribbean to London, sir." The sergeant had an unusual accent that Jack could not place.

"You're not from the Caribbean," Jack said. "I served with a West Indian regiment and know the accent. Where are you from?"

"The western Sudan, sir," the sergeant said, with a glint of humour in his eyes.

"So, how did you get to the Caribbean?"

The humour deepened. "The French shipped me over when I served in the French army in Mexico."

Jack nodded. "That explains the military bearing. What's your name, Sergeant?"

"Deng, Sir, Faiz Deng."

"Carry on, Sergeant Deng."

"Yes, sir!" The sergeant saluted smartly and marched on.

"He was in the right, Donnelly," Jack said quietly. "Next time, you move aside for a soldier of superior rank."

"Even a Gyppo, sir?"

"Would you step aside for a Sikh NCO? Or one of the Guides?"

"Of course, sir. They're proper soldiers, but the Egyptians are just a rabble."

Jack could see Donnelly's point of view. "Treat them as you'd treat a British soldier, Donnelly."

"Yes, sir." Donnelly could say nothing else, but Jack sensed his resentment. It was easy for a British soldier to respect the Guides, Sikhs, or Gurkhas with their proven fighting records, but the Egyptians had fled from every encounter with the Ansar.

"Ensure we have everything, Donnelly. Bring my horses and two for you, spare water canteens, food, and ammunition."

"It's all ready, sir," Donnelly said. "Checked and double-checked."

"Let's get aboard then," Jack said. "We're going to war again."

* * *

The voyage down the Red Sea was hot but uneventful. Jack heard that some of Baker's soldiers had mutinied and had been forced to embark at bayonet point.

"That augers badly for the expedition," he said.

Captain Kelly, one of Baker's European officers, nodded. "We only hope that they rally when they meet the Ansar."

Jack pulled on a cheroot. "Do you think they will?"

Kelly shrugged. "*Inshallah*," he said. "It's the will of Allah. Out here, everything is the will of Allah. One grows fatalistic in this heat."

"Does one?" Jack asked.

The convoy steamed slowly southward, carrying the first part of Baker's small army from Suez to Suakin. The wash from the ship ahead spread in white foam to break against the hull of the next in line, easing the monotony of the voyage. Jack leaned over the taffrail, wondering at this next piece of insanity.

These Egyptian lads have the lowest morale of any soldiers I've ever met. They're defeated even before the fighting starts.

* * *

Jack stepped off the boat and onto the quay at Suakin. The town was in two parts, a more prosperous European section on an offshore island and the native half on the mainland. A 1500-yards long causeway connected the two halves, with the gunboats *Ranger* and *Woodlark* moored on either side, ready to defend the town.

That's both ominous and reassuring. Are we only safe here because the navy protects us?

Used to the climate of Egypt, Jack still gasped as the heat bounced from the white stonework and hung in quivering, dust-laced layers above the ground. Greek, Italian, and Egyptian merchants congregated in the European quarter of the town, each one glancing at the British gunboats as if fearful the Royal Navy would sail away and leave them to the Mahdi's spears.

Augmenting the heat were the flies. Jack had grown used to the flies in Egypt, but in Suakin, they were worse. "Of all the seven plagues, the flies must have been the worst," he said.

"Yes, sir," Captain Kelly agreed, flapping a languid hand around his head in a pointless attempt to dissuade the insects.

Flies settled in hordes on any uncovered food, accompanied bread or meat to the mouth and committed mass suicide in anything liquid Jack tried to drink.

"Why did the Egyptians want to conquer this benighted country?" Kelly asked.

Jack grunted without replying. "You'd better get to your men. Baker's forming them up outside the town."

"He'll call me if he wants me, sir."

Jack raised his eyebrows. "Let's see the army, Kelly."

You'd not get far in the Malverns with that attitude, Captain Kelly.

Jack viewed Baker's force as they lined up outside the encampment at Suakin. "Not the best I've seen," he said.

Kelly adjusted his white uniform and pulled his fez over his forehead. "No," he said. "I've seen better soldiers footing the turf in Tralee."

There were two regiments of Gendarmerie, the quasi-military

force to reinforce the civil police. Each unit numbered seven hundred men, all wearing white uniforms but very few of whom looked enthusiastic. Old veteran soldiers filled the ranks of another all-Egyptian regiment.

"That unit looks capable," Jack pointed to the regiment of veterans. "It's better to have experienced men than young boys."

"That depends on the experience," Kelly said. "These men are experienced at running away and being defeated. Some were at Tel-el-Kebir, others in the armies the Mahdi's warriors destroyed in the Sudan."

"No wonder their morale is low," Jack said. "Constant defeats will depress even the best of regiments." He watched as the European officers ordered their battalions to march and form a defensive square. They attempted to advance in echelon, one unit after another, overreached themselves and ended in a confused tangle with the regiments mixed and men facing different directions.

"They made a mess of that," Kelly said.

"What's worse," Jack pointed out, "they expected to fail. There's no spirit in the men at all. They're listless." He thought of the Sikhs in India, the Malverns and his old 113th Foot. "They don't want to succeed."

"No," the Irishman said. "They don't. I'd rather have these troops as enemies as friends."

"So would the Mahdi," Jack said. He looked beyond the infantry, where some three hundred cavalry were riding in formation to the barked orders of an officer. He watched the blue-coated horsemen, remembering them at Kassassin in 1882, demonstrating before the British lines. They had appeared efficient but quickly withdrew when the British cavalry challenged.

Separating themselves from the Egyptians, two units of regular Turkish soldiers viewed their compatriots with disdain. They marched with the confident swing of old soldiers and obeyed orders with a professional snap.

"Now, these are men," Kelly said. "The Ottomans recruit them from the fighting races of Islam. If we had more of them, the Mahdi could whistle for Sinkat and Tokar. As it is?" He shrugged. "We have to make do with a bunch of reluctant farmers."

Jack nodded, lit a cheroot, and walked away. Behind him, the Egyptian infantry formed up again as the officers screamed their frustration. Jack did not look back, imagining the chaos.

God help you when the Ansar attack.

"Donnelly!" Jack shouted to his waiting servant. "You're with me!"

"Yes, sir." Donnelly kicked in his heels, patted his horse, and joined Jack.

Egyptian sentries manned the entrances to the town, each man looking more scared than the last. One sentry dropped his rifle while attempting to salute, and another's Remington was so dirty that Jack doubted it could fire.

As Jack had expected, given the high standard of Egyptian engineering, Suakin's defences looked formidable. There were five detached forts, each with a large garrison and a modern Krupp gun. Jack noted that the forts were so far apart that attackers could pass between them in relative safety.

We need heliographs here, Jack decided, *and smaller forts connected by a ditch and wall. I hope Baker knows his job.*

The desert outside the forts was bare, bleak, and studded with mimosa and thorn bushes. Flies dominated the air and ants the ground, with the occasional scorpion, stinging tail raised, for variety. The heat increased as Jack pushed Tinker, his horse, further inland until the sweat started from his forehead and soaked his armpits and back.

"This will do, Donnelly," Jack pulled Tinker to a halt and raised his field glasses to scan the interior.

"Yes, sir." Donnelly lifted the Martini-Henry carbine he favoured when accompanying Jack and studied the surrounding terrain. Born and bred in the ranks of the Royal Malverns, he was a vastly experienced soldier, although only in his mid-twenties.

"I can't see any of the Ansar," Jack said.

"Nor can I, sir," Donnelly agreed. He frowned. "Sir! Can you hear something?"

Jack shook his head and then nodded. "Yes, I can, Donnelly. What the devil is it?"

"It's like distant thunder, sir," Donnelly said.

"It's not thunder," Jack said quietly. "It's a drum, or rather, many drums. Tom toms. Maybe we can't see the Ansar, but I'll wager anything they can see us."

CHAPTER FOUR

Friday 8th of February 1884

When Allah made the Sudan, he laughed
    Arab Proverb

Jack surveyed the beach at Trinkitat on the Red Sea coast of Sudan. After a short spell in Suakin, they had accompanied Baker's army southward, ready to march and face Osman Digna.

Gentle waves broke on the sand, with the sky an unbroken blue from horizon to horizon. In England, Jack thought, such a scene would encourage hordes of pleasure seekers, families with children paddling in the sea, bathing huts with shy women cautiously taking to the water and laughter rising over everything. Here in Sudan, the beach only invited slave traders and an invading army.

A host of steamships waited offshore, transports for the infantry, artillery, and cavalry with all their attendant stores. Augmenting the steam vessels were rowing boats, steam launches and Arab dhows and feluccas, all busy ferrying men, horses, camels, and munitions to the shore.

Jack watched Baker's men disembark, took notes, and bit his tongue to prevent himself from giving orders. Donnelly stood a few yards away, dressed in the Indian khaki drill of the Royal Malverns. His face was schooled into the impassivity of a British private soldier, although Jack could guess at the thoughts racing through his mind.

A string of camels stepped from a small boat, complained at the indignity of sea travel, and padded up the soft sand. When they passed a company of Egyptian soldiers in baggy white uniforms, Jack wondered how many of the Egyptians had faced the Malverns at Tel-el-Kebir.

Baker and his European officers were busy shouting orders, giving directions and organising the rapidly growing force on the beach. They seemed confident, and Kelly spared time to lift a cheerful hand to Jack.

"Baker," Jack approached the commander. "There's an area of high ground overlooking the beach." He pointed to a ridge a couple of miles inland. "I'm going to have a look from the top of the heights and see if Osman Digna is waiting to pounce."

"As you wish," Baker said. "I've already sent a couple of pickets out there."

Asking Kelly to ensure his horses were safe, Jack motioned to Donnelly and strode inland.

After only a few yards, Jack found the ground very soft as they entered a shallow depression that soon became an inland lake or an extension of the sea. The lake extended for two miles, with the water thigh-deep and the bottom muddy. In places, the ground seemed treacherous, sucking at his boots like quicksand.

"The men will not like marching through this, sir," Donnelly said.

"Nor will the horses or artillery," Jack said.

If I were Osman Digna, I'd have guns posted on these hills and swoop down as the infantry and artillery struggled through this mire. The Afghans would not miss such an opportunity.

They splashed across the quagmire and stopped on the lower slopes of the hills.

"There's no sign of the enemy, sir," Donnelly said, studying the hills with a soldier's eye.

"Not yet," Jack said, pushing upwards. "Keep your rifle handy, Donnelly. I don't know how these Sudanese fight."

"If they're anything like the Sudanese we met with the Egyptian army, sir," Donnelly said. "They'll be utterly fearless but lacking in guile."

The hills were low and sandy, with the heat hammering down from a brazen sun. Jack slid over the summit and onto the far side, ensuring he was not on the skyline, with Donnelly three yards away.

"So that's the Sudan," Donnelly said.

The land stretched forever, an appalling desert with a scattering of prickly shrubs shimmering in the heat. There was no sound, only an immense silence that weighed down on the two British soldiers. Nothing moved; no wind stirred the surface of the sand.

"Nothing," Donnelly said. "There's nothing here."

"The land of the Mahdi," Jack voiced his thoughts as he studied the terrain through his field glasses. "And some of the most emphatically Muslim peoples in the world. Mohammed himself grew up in conditions like this."

"They've little to thank Allah for in these wastes," Donnelly said. "No wonder they want to conquer the rest of the world."

Jack lifted his field glasses and swept the land from horizon to horizon, finding no trace of life. "I doubt the ordinary tribesman realises there is another world outside their deserts. This harsh landscape is all they know."

Donnelly squatted, holding his rifle in front of him. "We're lucky, sir, coming from where we do."

"We are," Jack agreed, "but we've had to fight for every advantage we have, from the right to vote for most of us to hospitals, education, decent working conditions and an end to slavery." He stood up. "I hope Baker Pasha puts pickets on these hills with a heliograph to communicate with the main force at Trinkitat."

"He said he had, sir," Donnelly reminded.

Jack grunted. He could not see any Egyptians on the slopes.

A sudden wind raised dust devils in the waste, only emphasising the vastness of the land. Jack felt as if he were staring into infinity and wondered how city-bred British soldiers would cope with the endless desert.

Hopefully, they never have to. If Baker is as good as he thinks, he might secure the coast, Gordon will evacuate the interior, and the Mahdi can rule his Sudan in peace.

When Jack returned to the landing site, Baker had his force more organised. The Egyptian soldiers again showed their engineering expertise by creating extensive entrenchments while Turkish cavalry and Bashi-Bazouks mingled with camels and a handful of toiling bluejackets.

"Well, Windrush?" Baker worked tirelessly. "Did you see anything?"

"Not a thing, Baker. Desert and scrubland and damned little else," Jack said.

Baker seemed to be enjoying himself. "Well, I hope we'll see Osman Digna soon. The remainder of the transport will arrive tomorrow, and after that, well, there's no point in hanging about, is there?"

"How many men do you have?" Jack asked.

"Twelve hundred Gendarmerie," Baker replied at once, "around eleven hundred Sudanese, although they're not all fully trained yet, three hundred Turkish infantry and four hundred mixed cavalry."

"About two thousand seven hundred men," Jack quickly estimated.

"Plus two Gatling guns and four artillery pieces," Baker added. "That should give old Digna a scare."

Jack nodded. "I hope so, Baker. Be careful when you head

inland. Donnelly and I had difficulty wading through the marsh behind the landing beach."

"My men are looking for the most practical route," Baker interrupted. "I know how to soldier."

"I never doubted it," Jack said.

When he heard musketry later, Jack walked to the outskirts of the camp to see the Massowah Sudanese Battalion practising their marksmanship. As a British officer gave instructions, the sergeants ran along the ranks translating the officer's words into Arabic.

"Best stand back, sir," Donnelly warned. "These lads don't know what they're doing, and they're holding their rifles like shovels!"

The battalion fired a ragged volley, with some men jerking the trigger as if a display of force would help propel the bullet faster. Not a single shot hit its mark, with every rifle aimed high.

"Oh, dear Lord, save me from amateurs," Donnelly prayed.

"They'll get better," Jack said. *I hope they get better very quickly. Donnelly is right. This lot is just a rabble.* He fought down the desire to interfere. "We'll stand watch and watch tonight, Donnelly. I don't trust this mob to post a decent guard."

"That's not right, sir; you shouldn't have to stand guard."

"Watch and watch," Jack repeated. "And keep your rifle loaded."

* * *

An uproar woke Jack, and he lay still for a moment, unsure where he was. He heard men shouting in a medley of different languages and rose to his feet, scrabbling for his sword and revolver.

"It's all right, sir." Donnelly was kneeling outside the tent with his Martini-Henry held ready. "One of the pickets caught a spy lying on the sand outside the camp."

Jack glanced at the fading stars in the sky. "It's nearly dawn. Let's find out what's happened."

As they walked forward, a group of men appeared, carrying a stretcher on which a semi-conscious Sudanese youth lay.

Sergeant Deng was cleaning blood from his bayonet.

"What happened, Sergeant?"

"This boy was waiting outside the camp, hoping to kill an Egyptian," Deng said. "When I tried to capture him, he attacked my patrol with his spear."

"Did he try to kill you, Sergeant?"

Deng shook his head. "No. He tried to kill one of the men in my patrol."

"An Egyptian?"

"Yes. He wounded one of my Egyptians." Deng shook his head. "He's only a young man, maybe fourteen or fifteen."

Jack knelt beside the wounded prisoner and spoke in Arabic. "You're a brave man, my friend."

The boy looked up. "Let me spear one Egyptian before I die."[1]

A European officer strolled up, glanced at the prisoner, and spoke to Sergeant Deng in French, asking what happened.

"Who are you, sir?" the European asked Jack in English.

"Lieutenant-colonel Windrush of the Royal Malverns, here to observe," Jack said. "And you?"

"Major Gaudin," the man spoke with a French accent. "Ex captain in the *Légion étrangère*, the Foreign Legion."

"You're in an even stranger legion here," Jack said.

Gaudin laughed, with his eyes remaining unchanged. "We're all brothers-in-arms," he said. "We might be enemies because of politics, religion or choice, but we share the same honourable profession of arms."

"I'll tell that to the Ansar when we meet," Jack said.

Baker led his army out from Trinkitat on a dull morning that deteriorated to a rainy forenoon, deepening the quagmire behind the beach. As Jack had predicted, the army struggled across the salt-water marsh, with the horses floundering and the artillerymen dismounting to push their guns through the mud. Water wagons with barrels unloaded from the transports slipped axle deep in the mire as harassed drivers shoved and swore in various languages.

"Shall I give these lads a hand, sir?" Donnelly asked.

"Yes," Jack said. He was unwilling to interfere in Baker's column but signalled to a company of slogging Egyptian infantry. "You men! Help the gunners and the water carts!" When the infantry hesitated, Donnelly encouraged them with fists and boots, showing them what to do and leading by example.

"If you lose the guns, you lose the battle!" Donnelly shouted. "And without water, we'll all die!"

A very tall, debonair man splashed his horse towards Jack. "Are you Windrush?"

"I am," Jack admitted.

"Colonel Fred Burnaby, Royal Horse Guards. You may have heard of me."[2]

"I have," Jack said. Burnaby's adventures made him famous throughout the army.

"I've heard of you as well, Windrush. Your exploits in Afghanistan are well known." Burnaby glanced over the column as it struggled through the morass. "What do you think of this infamous army?"

"I think Baker has his work before him, making them into soldiers."

"Rather agree with you there." Burnaby smoothed a hand over his neat moustache. "I expected Osman Digna to ambush us as we crossed the swamp. Maybe he's not such a good commander as we're led to believe."

"Let's hope not," Jack said.

Baker is leading a force of mercenaries and personalities. I hope he has the character to mould them into a cohesive army.

When his army emerged from the mire, Baker organised

them and set off southwards across the scrubby desert towards the besieged post of Tokar.

"If Osman Digna challenges us, he'll find I'm no Hicks Pasha," Baker said. "I'll smash him, relieve Tokar and be back in Suakin within the week." He shouted to his officers to keep the men in formation. "As if organising a relief expedition was not enough, Windrush, now the Sirdar wants me to find some blasted explorer in Tokar." Baker shook his head. "Civilians have no right to blunder into the middle of a war."

Jack looked around at the empty wasteland of eastern Sudan as Baker sent small, mounted patrols ahead of his main body. Each group left letters in prominent positions, informing Osman Digna his cause was already lost and that if the tribesmen came in, there would be no repercussions.

"You know the Sudanese better than I do," Jack said. "Will they respond to such blandishments?"

Baker adjusted his helmet. "I don't know," he admitted, "but I can only try. I have also sent emissaries to the friendly tribes to relieve Sinkat. With luck, we can save the garrison of both Tokar and Sinkat without firing a shot."

Jack looked over Baker's army. The cavalry looked capable, but the Egyptian infantry marched without any formation, more a confused mob than a disciplined body of soldiers.

"Let's hope you're right, Baker."

"If I'm not, we'll have to fight," Baker said. "Thank goodness we have modern weapons, and Osman Digna's men have mainly spears and swords."

Jack bit off his comment that Hicks' men had rifles and Gatling guns as Baker rode away to try and organise his army.

Kelly was laughing as he harangued his men, with Gaudin kicking at a lagging youngster, swearing in a mixture of French and Arabic.

Jack glanced at Donnelly, who shook his head. "It would never do in the Malverns, sir."

"Nor in the Guides," Jack said.

The column had a short nine-mile march that day and camped in the open. Jack watched as Baker formed a zareba around his camp, a barricade of thorn bushes, boxes, and anything else they could find in the surrounding desert.

"We'll call this Fort Baker," Valentine Baker announced. "It will be our base."

"Watch and watch again tonight, Donnelly," Jack said. "And keep together."

"Yes, sir." Donnelly did not argue as he stared beyond the tangled thorns at the endless desert.

"Where are we?" Gaudin asked.

"We're approaching El Teb," Burnaby replied with a languid smile. "Otherwise known as nowhere, surrounded by nothing."

Jack nodded to Donnelly. "Time for a reconnaissance, Donnelly."

"Yes, sir." Donnelly checked his rifle. "This reminds me of Afghanistan, sir, but hotter."

Jack understood; the geography was unfamiliar, but the sense of menace was similar. "Let's see if the Ansar are around."

Baker had set pickets a few hundred yards outside the zareba, and the Egyptian infantry looked around nervously as Jack and Donnelly passed them.

"Don't shoot us on our way back," Jack tried to sound cheerful.

"No, effendi," a man replied.

Night swooped down, with the ensuing silence pressing down on them. The stars came out surprisingly quickly as Jack and Donnelly found a slight rise and looked around.

"Miles and miles of bugger all, sir," Donnelly said.

Jack swept his field glasses around the desolation. He could sense the presence of something out there.

"Not quite bugger all, Donnelly," Jack said. "People are living in this desolation." He liked the desert. He liked the cleanliness of a world without factories and a controlled environment. *I can understand the appeal of an austere religion out here, whether it's Christianity or Islam.*

"Can you see anything, sir?" Donnelly held his rifle ready, peering from side to side.

"Nothing human," Jack said and focussed his field glasses on a faint glow well on the horizon. "Look over there, Donnelly. What do you see?"

Donnelly took the field glasses. "A fire, sir, or rather fires. Is that the enemy's camp?"

"It might well be," Jack said, reclaiming the field glasses. "I think we'll meet Osman Digna tomorrow."

"God help us, sir," Donnelly muttered. "I wouldn't trust this army to fight a class of schoolboys!"

"Let's get back to camp," Jack said.

The Egyptian sentries were edgy, but when one presented his rifle, Jack growled at him, and the man apologised.

"Keep alert, sentry," Jack said in Arabic.

"You saw campfires?" Baker was still awake, with his tent in the centre of the zareba near the camels and water wagons.

"We did," Jack said. "I'd say you'll have a battle tomorrow."

Baker gave a brief smile. "Let tomorrow take care of itself," he said. "I'm sure my soldiers will give a good account of themselves, and a victorious battle will settle their nerves."

"I hope so, Baker," Jack said, but looking at Baker's army, he doubted it.

CHAPTER FIVE

Even men as strong as wild oxen will die,
The young men alongside the veterans,
The land will be soaked with blood
And the soil enriched with fat.
Isiah 34: 7

The bugles roused the men before dawn, and at half past six, the little army set off to relieve Tokar. Baker had formed his three infantry battalions to march in columns of company and in echelon. The artillery rolled in front and on the flanks, with cavalry vedettes riding a mile around the marching column to give warning of any enemy. Behind the column, hundreds of camels carried the supplies and ammunition.

"That's a decent formation," Jack approved. "I'd have posted a stronger guard for the camels, but I presume Baker knows what he's doing."

Kelly laughed. "We'll fight if we have to and run if we must. It's all in the day's work for a soldier of the Khedive."

The column marched slowly, with the men in front kicking up great clouds of dust that descended on the following ranks. Soldiers coughed and cursed, staggered, and marched on.

"Can you feel it, sir?" Donnelly slid a round into the breech of his Martini. "Something is waiting out there."

"I feel it," Jack agreed. He loosened his revolver in its holster and petted Tinker's ears. "Steady, girl." The Kabul pony plodded on, as dogged and enduring as the people of its homeland.

When the gunfire came from the left front, the cavalry vedettes pulled back, still firing. The shots seemed to echo in the hot air as if they did not belong.

"Here we go, sir," Donnelly said.

"Keep your rifle handy," Jack ordered.

"Yes, sir," Donnelly said. "Sir!" He pointed to a ridge of low hills on the left. As the cavalry withdrew, groups of Arabs appeared on the crest, with banners limp in the still air. Jack levelled his field glasses and studied the enemy.

"They look no different to the Arabs we see every day."

Baker gave rapid orders that saw the Krupps artillery readied, and within a few moments, the guns crashed out. The first shot was well over the target, the second to the left, and the third landed in front. When the dust cleared, the Arabs were gone.

"That scared them off!" Donnelly said.

"For the present," Jack studied the surroundings through his field glasses. The cavalry vedettes remained close to the main body of the column, some within spitting distance of the infantry. The desert stretched to ranges of low hills, with shifting sand, brushwood, and patches of head-high prickly bushes.

"Look over there."

More tribesmen appeared on the low ridges in front, and others on the right, with separate bodies of cavalry and infantry. Jack studied the infantry, large, dark-skinned men with shovel-headed spears or long swords; they wore their hair in a unique style, like a hayrick, and seemed to be dancing on top of the ridges.

"They're coming closer, sir," Donnelly said.

"We're approaching El Teb," Gaudin shouted for no apparent reason. "The enemy is going to surround us."

"Now we'll see how these Egyptian fellows fight," Donnelly murmured.

More Arab cavalry appeared in front, shouting their war cries and waving lances while a profusion of banners waved above their heads.

"Major Giles," Baker snapped. "You'd oblige me by removing these horsemen!"

"Yes, sir!" Major Giles, commanding the Turkish cavalry, saluted and led his men forward, drawing his sword, with the sun reflecting from the polished steel blade.

The cavalry followed with flowing robes and glittering swords, yelling as they rode away from the infantry.

"They look well enough, sir," Donnelly said.

Jack did not reply, reserving his judgement.

"Form a square!" Baker ordered.

Jack saw the fumbling attempts of the Egyptian and Sudanese infantry to change their formation and knew he could not simply observe. He moved to the right flank. "Come on! Move!" Jack leaned from Tinker and shoved the men into position, forming them two deep, pushing the front rank to their knees, and telling the officers what to do.

"Ensure your rifles are loaded!" Jack shouted in Arabic. "Fix your bayonets!" Taking the rifle from a bemused private's hands, he clicked the bayonet in place. "The tighter your formation, the better you'll fight!"

He glanced forward, swore, and lifted his field glasses. Giles' cavalry had advanced in style, with the enemy horse retreating before them. But after half a mile, Osman Digna's cavalry turned to fight, and hundreds of enemy spearmen leapt from the cover of the brushwood to attack the Turkish cavalry's flank. "Ambush, by God!"

"These men are from the Hadendoa tribe," Sergeant Deng had arrived at Jack's side. "They know no fear." He shrugged. "If they die fighting for Allah, they will go straight to Paradise and escape this life of misery and thirst."

Jack watched through his field glasses as the Hadendoa warriors attacked the Turkish cavalry. By all the rules of war, cavalry should defeat infantry in open battle, but nobody had read the rule book to the Hadendoa. The warriors bounded forward, ducking under the swing of the Turkish swords to hamstring the horses, throwing the huge-headed spears at horses and riders, or leaping up to thrust at the horsemen. Rather than match these unconventional warriors, the cavalry began to fragment.

The leading Turkish cavalryman swung at a Hadendoa warrior, missed, and tried to recover. A second Hadendoa thrust a spear into the Turk's side, and the cavalryman's companion turned to flee. Others followed in a sudden panic until Giles' entire cavalry force was soon a terrified mob running from the fuzzy-haired Hadendoa warriors.

Jack swore, checked that the front of the square was solid and realised the left flank and rear had not yet formed up.

"Get these men into formation!" Jack roared, repeating his orders in Arabic as the Egyptian infantry milled about in hopeless confusion and Hadendoa warriors charged towards them. Plunging across the square's interior, Jack pushed men into position. "Stand there! Stand there and prepare to fight!" He ducked as a bullet hummed past him.

"Careful, sir!" Donnelly was at Jack's side, reinforcing his orders with brutal words and muscular arms. "The Dervishes are firing at us!"

Jack realised Osman Digna's men were firing from the front and flanks. He saw an Egyptian soldier stagger, stare stupidly at the spreading red stain on his stomach and collapse. Another leapt from the firing line until Donnelly shoved him back into position.

"Return fire, you bloody idiot!" Donnelly aimed his rifle, fired, ejected the bullet, and pointed to the advancing Hadendoa. "Shoot that way! Load the bloody thing first!"

"Where are the officers?" Jack asked. He looked around. The

rear of the square was a shambles as men jostled with camels, the commissariat tried frantically to enter the square, and some infantrymen tried to flee. "Donnelly! We'd better sort the rear out!"

Sergeant Deng was shouting orders as Kelly took control of a company of Sudanese infantry on the right flank.

"Volley fire, my darlings! On my word! Fire!" Kelly stepped in front of his men. "Follow my lead, you beauties!" Lifting a rifle, he aimed and fired into the scrubby desert. "Now you do it, but don't hit me!"

The cavalry arrived back at that moment. Frantic horsemen galloped onto the front of the square, demanding that the infantry open their ranks and let them in.

Jack was more concerned with the chaos at the rear. "Get these bloody camels inside! You- that company of Egyptians! I don't know your blasted name; incline left and take up position! Form an avenue to let the camels and commissariat into the square!"

Baker was at the front of the square, trying to calm the cavalry when the Hadendoa advanced again. They came from the left flank, where they had crept unseen through the brushwood and scrub and charged out at the unnerved Egyptian infantry.

"Fight them!" Donnelly shouted. "You've got rifles! They've only got spears! Shoot the bastards!"

Gaudin yelled orders in French and Arabic, kicking men into position as rifle shots whined and screamed overhead. A thrown spear thudded into a mule, which reared up, kicking with its front hooves.

The rear of the square was a heaving mass of mules, camels, and horses, with infantrymen struggling to escape as the drivers tried to push inside.

Donnelly was among the Egyptians, loading and firing as the Hadendoas charged with their upraised swords, thick hide shields and broad-headed swords. The Hadendoa were yelling, ignoring their casualties, dodging around the thorn bushes, ducking, weaving but steadily advancing.

"Keep firing!" Donnelly ordered. "Shoot, you useless Gyppo bastards!"

Jack left the rear to join the Sudanese on the left flank, where the Hadendoas were coming within spear range.

"Volley fire!" Jack shouted and unholstered his pistol. "Front rank, fire!" He squeezed the trigger of his revolver as the Hadendoa erupted towards the line. They charged at a run with their spears held ready to stab, leaping the fallen as the defenders' fire hammered into them.

"Keep it up, lads!" Jack roared. He saw Donnelly moving up the line, firing and loading. Donnelly stopped behind a struggling private, cleared the jam in his rifle and moved on, roaring encouragement.

Jack saw Baker standing outside the square, shouting orders, and then the rear of the square collapsed as the camels pushed through the scared Egyptian infantry.

"Stand!" Jack shouted as the commissariat pressed against the back of the left flank. "Rear rank, face about!" He translated the command into Arabic, emptied his revolver into the mass of charging Hadendoa and reloaded, swearing.

Some Sudanese soldiers obeyed, others tried to obey, while about half continued to load and fire at the tribesmen advancing toward them. The Turkish and Egyptian cavalry were not as stoic. Unsettled by their retreat, they panicked anew at the chaos in the rear and the Hadendoa attacking the left.

"What the devil?" Jack shouted as the cavalry rushed to escape the square, knocking down infantrymen and camp followers in their haste. "Get back, you cowardly bastards!"

When the cavalry fled, the Egyptian infantry broke, with a ribbon of men dropping their rifles to run. The European officers shouted at them, pushing men back in line, but the example of the cavalry was infectious. The infantry's firing became wilder, with one shot narrowly missing Baker and another killing an officer named Captain Cavalieri. Jack saw a private lift his rifle, close his eyes and fire, blowing off half his neighbour's head.

"That's not the way, boys!" Kelly shouted, stepping towards the ragged Egyptian line. "Fire at the enemy, not your mates!" He stopped, mouth open as a Hadendoa thrust a spear through his back, with the point emerging at his chest. Kelly crumpled to the ground, and the Hadendoa warrior retrieved his spear and moved on.

The infantry's panic spread. Egyptian soldiers dropped their rifles and ran, in ones and twos, sections and entire companies. Others knelt on the blood-sodden sand, clasped their hands together and begged for mercy. Exultant Hadendoa warriors smashed through the gaps in the square.

"Fight!" Jack roared as Donnelly kicked a begging man in frustration. "Get up and fight, damn you! We outnumber them!"

The Turkish and Egyptian cavalry were gone, with a dozen riderless horses following in their wake. Jack saw one horse throw its rider, who rose and screamed in terror as a Hadendoa warrior loomed over him. Without hesitation, the warrior thrust his long sword into the cavalryman's chest.

Jack shot the Hadendoa, saw the warrior fall backwards with his sword still impaling the cavalryman, and then another rush of Hadendoa arrived. The battle became a massacre. All around Jack, Egyptian infantry were on their knees, begging for mercy and receiving none. The Mahdi's warriors grabbed them by the neck or the hair, thrust a spear through their back, withdrew the blade and expertly cut their throats.

"Sir!" Donnelly turned, shot a mounted Arab and thumbed a cartridge into the breech of his rifle. "We can't stay here, sir! These men are finished!"

Jack saw that Donnelly was correct. The square had collapsed, with those soldiers not trying to surrender already fleeing. He saw Baker slashing about him with his sword and Gaudin firing his revolver at a group of Hadendoa. Ignoring the pistol the warriors charged forward, and one thrust his spear into the Frenchman's chest.

"Come on, sir!" Blood smeared Donnelly's bayonet, his pith helmet was awry, and sweat had furrowed the caked sand and gunpowder on his face. The noise was deafening, with the screams of the Egyptians and triumphant yells of the Mahdi's warriors combining in a cacophony of horror.

"You men!" Jack saw a tight knot of Sudanese soldiers standing back-to-back, with Sergeant Deng in the middle. "You're with us!"

Sergeant Deng stared at Jack, his eyes wide and surprisingly calm.

"Come on!" Jack remembered the carnage of Maiwand and the retreat across Afghanistan, but then he had disciplined British soldiers and sepoys, not broken Egyptians and half-trained Sudanese.

"Load!" Jack shouted and counted his men. Seventeen Sudanese, Deng, Donnelly, and himself. He divided the Sudanese into three groups, using his halting Arab and the sergeant to convey his words. "One group fires, the second fends off the attacks with the bayonet and the third loads!"

The men looked up at him, most with hope in their eyes, some dull and others frantic, ready to run. One man laughed high-pitched, near to hysteria.

"If we stay together, we have a chance to survive," Jack said. "March!" He pressed cartridges into the chambers of his revolver and pushed Tinker forward, keeping a steady pace. He knew if he ran, he would spread further panic.

The Hadendoa surrounded Jack's small group, but few attacked, preferring easier prey. Whenever a body of the Mahdi's warriors looked threatening, Jack ordered one of his sections to fire.

"Aim low, damn you!" Jack snarled when a full volley failed to hit any of the enemy. Snatching the rifle from the nearest man, he adjusted the sights. "You're firing far too high! Donnelly! Check the sights of these men!"

Jack kept his men moving, firing volleys when they could, covering the ground slowly, with the Arabs and Hadendoa killing whenever they saw an opportunity. Corpses marked the Egyptian's retreat, with Baker riding his horse, shouting, trying his best to rally the remains of his shattered army. Jack saw a group of spearmen surround Baker and Colonel Hay, the chief of staff, only for the British officers to spur through.

It was five miles to Fort Baker, and by the time they arrived, Jack had lost four of his men. He ordered the defenders to pull open a section of the zareba to allow the fugitives easier passage, formed his Sudanese into a defensive line and ushered in the survivors who staggered up. There were not many, and some of the Egyptians refused to enter the zareba.

"Where the devil are you going?" Jack shouted after them as they fled, hatless and dishevelled, past his men.

"Trinkitat!" they yelled without stopping.

"The devil you are!" Jack roared. "Stand fast! We can hold the zareba!"

"It's no good, Windrush," Baker said. "They're broken. They're unworthy of the name of soldiers!"

"Dear Lord!" Jack said. "I wish I had the Malverns here or a regiment of Sikhs! A few hundred Sikhs, and we'd show Osman Digna the gateway to Paradise."

"Form a cordon!" Baker ordered. "Stop these cowards running to Trinkitat!"

The attempt was useless. Only a few men stopped at the zareba while the shattered remnants fled past, most having dropped their weapons. One fully equipped Sudanese marched up to Baker, stood at attention, saluted, and asked for orders.

"Join Colonel Windrush," Baker said wearily. "He seems to have his men organised."

After half an hour, Osman Digna's army appeared across the

scrubby desert. They halted five hundred yards from Fort Baker, with their black standards held high.

"I think we should withdraw to Trinkitat, Windrush," Baker said as some of the men within the zareba began to whimper.

"I agree. We're doing no good here," Jack watched Donnelly grab a running Egyptian and drag him back inside the zareba. "Move in formation. My boys will form the rearguard."

The Hadendoas followed at a distance, killing any fugitives.

Jack heard the crack of revolver fire long before they arrived at Trinkitat. "Double, lads! Osman must have beaten us to it!" He led his small party at a run, and when he reached the port, he found chaos. A terrified mob of Egyptian soldiers packed the beach and tried to board the boats, but the Royal Naval officers had drawn their revolvers to maintain some control.

"Bloody rabble." Donnelly spat on the ground in contempt.

"We'll hold the port with what we have," Baker decided.

"What do we have left?" Jack looked at the frightened refugees.

Baker had his remaining officers counting the remnants of his army. "We have seventy men of the Sanheet Sudan regiment from the Abyssinian border, including the men you brought back."

"How many were in the Sanheet regiment?"

"Four hundred," Baker said. "But some might be with that mob there." He nodded to the crowd clamouring to get onto the boats. "We have about thirty Turks, and I don't know how many Europeans have come through."

"I feel sorry for the Egyptian soldiers," Jack said. "They are farmers, fellahin, forced into uniform and sent into an alien land. The officers and officials?" He shook his head. "I've less sympathy for them."

"We did our best with what we had," Baker excused his defeat.

Jack listened as the reports came in. Major Watkins, Lieutenant Carroll and Doctor Leslie of Baker's officers died gallantly, fighting with sword and pistol, when a rush of the enemy cut them off from the main body. Jack had not been with Baker's army long enough to know the dead officers. Captain Pallioka of the Albanian Company, Yussuf Bey, Abdul Rosack, and Captain Bertan were just names rather than the brave, flesh and blood men who had marched out with such hope and attempted to make an army out of unsuitable reluctant conscripts.

Baker pulled his defensive line back to the beach, with the marsh in front and the enemy occupying the hills beyond. As Jack and his handful of Sudanese mounted guard, Osman Digna's men prowled in the swamp and occasionally ventured closer without attacking in force.

"Shoot anybody who comes in range," Jack ordered Donnelly.

"Yes, sir," Donnelly said without lifting his scrutiny of the marshland.

As Jack and a few men patrolled, Baker salvaged what he could from the wreckage of his army, sending men and horses to the waiting ships.

"Where are the Gyppo officers, sir?" Donnelly asked.

Jack shook his head. "Officers in name only, Donnelly. I wonder how the Egyptian infantry would have fought if they were properly trained, disciplined, and commanded."

"I doubt we'll ever know, sir." Donnelly shot at an over-keen Hadendoa warrior. "The Mahdi won that round."

"He did," Jack agreed. "Either we use British troops, or the Mahdists will capture Sinkat and Tokar, and then they can close the Red Sea."

CHAPTER SIX

No one wept for the dead because everyone expected death itself.
    Agnolo di Tura

When he arrived back at Suakin, Jack spoke to Admiral Hewitt, who commanded the Royal Navy in the Red Sea, then strode to the telegraph office and contacted Hook.

February 6th, 1884, at 5.30 PM,

"Egyptian force defeated Tokar. Loss 2000. Baker Pasha and remainder of troops return today from Trinkitat. Only black recruits left here. Egyptians utterly unreliable. Admiral Hewitt intends landing men to take charge of town and allay panic."

"We lost over two thousand men," Baker sounded bewildered. "We outnumbered them, we had better weapons, Krupp artillery and machine guns, and they slaughtered us. What sort of men does the Mahdi possess?"

"Men fighting for their country and religion," Jack said quietly. "And now the Mahdi has even more modern rifles, artillery, and machine guns. I wonder how the garrisons of Tokar and Sinkat are faring." He blew smoke into the air and tried to forget the horrors he had witnessed.

The streets on Suakin Island were of gleaming white coral,

with an occasional sulky Egyptian soldier giving a reluctant salute as Jack and Baker passed. They rode back across the causeway to the mainland, with the Royal Navy gunboats sitting on either side, disciplined sanity in a world of chaos.

The houses on the mainland town were of mud and wood, but the people were lively if agitated at Baker's defeat. The news of Baker's disaster and the ragged return of his army brought consternation. Women crowded the streets, howling, wringing their hands, and throwing dust over their heads.

Jack dismounted and entered the bazaar, mingling with men of a score of races. There were men from Bombay whose language Jack could speak and tall, elegant Bedouins from Arabia, speaking rapid Arabic with accents different from the Egyptian version. There were the ubiquitous Greeks, men of Somali cast, Levantines, and traders that Jack could not identify. The majority were local Sudanese, with their unique hairstyle, frizzled and stiffened with white fat, reminding Jack of some of the footmen he had seen in London but reeking like a candle factory.

Outside Suakin, Baker's camp was like a ghost town, with so many soldiers dead or already shipped back to Egypt. A sand-built entrenchment surrounded the rows of tents, and a few Bashi-Bazouks lounged around, ignoring the shouts of the surviving European officers.

Beyond the entrenchment, a sandy waste stretched to a range of mountains, with their peaks etched sharply against the cobalt-blue sky.

"Osman Digna is just beyond those hills," Jack said. "Or, more likely, he's on them now, watching everything we do."

"That's what I'd surmise." Baker was already recovering from his defeat.

Jack scanned the heights, looking for movement. "We're not quite under siege," he said, "but we might be soon." He glanced over his shoulder. "And with our garrison of rabbits, if Osman Digna attacks, Suakin will fall with hardly a shot fired."

Baker grunted. "We still have the navy."

"Thank God for the navy," Jack murmured.

Baker grunted, lifted his chin, and rode away.

We're in a precarious position here. If Osman Digna realises how weak our defences are, he will send in his Hadendoa, capture Suakin and probably massacre the inhabitants. We're lucky he's besieging Sinkat and Tokar.

Jack called in at the telegraph office. "Was there a reply for me?"

The telegraph operator nodded. "Yes, sir." When he handed over the sheet of paper with the pencil scrawl, Jack scanned it eagerly.

"Telegrams received. Hewitt's action approved. Will he need reinforcements in ships or men? Keep me fully informed."

Hook must think I am a messenger boy.

Begging a lift on a Royal Navy tender, Jack found Admiral Hewitt on the deck of HMS *Woodlark*, speaking with a group of senior officers.

"I remember you from the Egyptian campaign," Hewitt said. "What does General Hook wish to know?"

When Jack explained the situation, Hewitt guided him to the taffrail. "You've seen the present garrison, Windrush. What do you think?"

"I'd be happier with Royal Marines or British or Indian soldiers, sir."

"So would I," Hewitt replied, "and you have my express permission to tell that to General Hook."

For the remainder of that day, Jack relayed intelligence and messages between General Hook, Baker, and Admiral Hewitt. He told Hook that the present garrison was unreliable and British marines and soldiers would be required, adding: "British or Indian troops welcome. Sikhs or Madras artillery."

Hook replied later that day. "HMS *Orontes* awaiting orders at Suez. Have contacted Admiral John Hay at Malta ordering him to send reinforcements if required by Hewitt."

Jack acknowledged and sent another telegram, informing Hook that gangs of reluctant Egyptian soldiers were roaming through the town, with bands of Osman Digna's warriors lurking outside. "Only two defensive forts manned at Suakin and gaps in defences. Ammunition low."

Hook replied. "Hay at Malta sending arms and ammunition to Hewitt at Suakin."

Jack nodded. His telegrams were having an effect, yet morale in Suakin remained low. The European and wealthy Egyptian residents approached Jack every time he left the telegraph office.

"Why didn't the British send their troops?" men asked Jack as if he was personally responsible for the government's actions. "A couple of regiments of British troops could relieve Sinkat and Tokar."

"Maybe so," Jack replied, unwilling to spread optimism that may prove false, "but it's not Britain's war. It's Egypt's, and we don't own the country. We are only trying to help."

"You've got soldiers here!" the Europeans told him. "They're no good lazing about all day on the beaches!"

"What do you think, Colonel Windrush?" Baker asked.

"I don't think we should be here at all," Jack temporised. "Saving the Suez Canal is one thing; occupying the entire country is different. We're carrying a big enough burden trying to civilise half the world without adding the Sudan to our responsibilities."

But we are here, and nobody else is willing or able to help the beleaguered garrisons.

Two days after Baker's men returned to Suakin, Osman Digna's forces captured Sinkat. When the news reached Suakin, the people reacted with horror, once again crowding the streets in a mixture of panic and disbelief.

"We need British protection," shouted a fat merchant. "Where are the British soldiers?"

"That's Abdullah." Fred Burnaby had survived Baker's defeat and joined Jack at Suakin. "He's a slave dealer, and a fortnight ago, he was complaining bitterly about the British stopping his trade."

"Is that right?" Jack eyed the man with contempt. "I've no time for slavers."

"More than half the money in Sudan comes from the slave trade," Burnaby said. "And forget all the protestations of the Egyptian merchants; they're up to their eyeballs in it. Islam does not condemn slavery, and it's been established in this part of Africa for thousands of years."

Jack grunted. He knew European conventions could not apply to countries with vastly different cultures, but the idea of enslaving a man, child or woman was against all his principles. "I met slavery in Ashantiland," he said.

"Well, you'll meet it in Sudan as well, Windrush," Burnaby said.

News from Sinkat gradually filtered into Suakin, brought by travelling merchants and overheard in bazaar gossip.

Jack read the sparse official reports and shook his head. "Donnelly!"

"Sir?" Donnelly arrived at the double. Jack knew he had an old soldier's knack for gathering intelligence from diverse sources and filtering out exaggerations.

"Find out about Sinkat, Donnelly."

Donnelly grinned. "I already have, sir," he said. "When Osman Digna's forces took Sinkat, they massacred most of the population. I heard that only fifty women and a couple of Egyptian secretaries survived, with the Hadendoa killing nearly two hundred women and God alone knows how many men."

"They'll do the same to Tokar, then, and Suakin," Jack said.

"No doubt, sir," Donnelly agreed.

When Jack telegraphed Donnelly's bazaar news to Hook, the reply came within an hour.

"Find out about Tokar. Urgent."

Jack had built up a small network of sources in Suakin, from Donnelly's bazaar gossip to Royal Navy officers who patrolled the Red Sea. Later that day, he replied to Hook that Tokar still held out.

"Why the interest in Tokar?" Fred Burnaby asked.

"Hook wanted to know," Jack told him.

"Valentine Baker was also interested in Tokar." Burnaby looked around the bazaar, with his six-foot-four-inch frame dwarfing everybody else present. "General Hook ordered him to rescue some British trapped inside the town."

"I remember Baker mentioning that," Jack said, drawing on his cheroot. "Maybe that's what it's all about," he said. "Whoever the explorer is, he'll have to take his chance like everybody else."

Burnaby strolled through the bazaar to the edge of the town and peered westward into the limitless waste. "Sudan's a fascinating place, although I can't see what benefit it could bring us."

Jack grunted. "I hope we don't waste any more time here. The best thing we can do is relieve the garrisons and withdraw to Egypt, and as soon as we have that country on a secure financial footing, hand it back to the Khedive."

"Isn't that the official plan?" Burnaby sounded mildly amused.

"I believe so, but since when have politicians been trustworthy?"

Burnaby laughed. "Never," he agreed. "Maybe the Mahdi will help them make up their minds."

Jack thought of his previous telegram to Hook, advising him that all the outposts in Eastern Sudan would fall unless the government sent British troops. Digna's capture of Sinkat only reinforced his words.

"We have garrisons at Kassala, Massawa and Tokar, as well as Suakin," Jack said. "Osman Digna could take any of them if he chose. He might also decide to march across the desert to Berber." He finished his cheroot, lit two more and passed one to Burnaby. "One thing's for sure. He has to do something. It's not the nature of tribal armies to sit quietly. Unless they are active, the warriors will lose interest and disperse."

Burnaby raised languid eyebrows. "You've met them before?"

"Along the Frontier, in Afghanistan and Ashantiland," Jack said. He lifted his head as the sound of distant drums drifted to him. "There's Osman Digna now, reminding us of his presence."

At night, small parties of Hadendoa warriors emerged from the mountains to harass the Egyptian sentries. The Mahdists fired from long-range, slit a throat or two, spread panic and vanished before the sun rose. Jack took Donnelly on night-time patrols of the outposts, trying to encourage the Egyptian defenders and restore some morale.

"You'd be as well with a bunch of Sunday school teachers as these Gyppos!" Donnelly said.

"They've had a hard time," Jack tried to defend the Egyptians while hoping that Hewitt would land his marines soon.

On the 6th of February, Hook contacted Jack. "HMS *Orantes* entered the Canal yesterday with marines, arms, and ammunition. A hundred and forty marines to be transferred to *Carysfort* from *Orantes* for Hewitt."

After consulting with Hewitt, Jack replied, "Hewitt requires five hundred marines, with a hundred Turkish cavalry and five hundred Sudanese to garrison Suakin. Wants to remove all Egyptian soldiers as untrustworthy and a danger to civilians."

Hook replied within the hour. "Inform Hewitt he will be given full powers, military and civilian at Suakin. Lord Hay sending artillery and provisions from Malta. Hewitt to Act accordingly. Hook."

When Jack relayed the message to Hewitt, the admiral slowly smiled. "If I have five hundred marines, two gunboats and a free hand, Osman Digna can whistle for Suakin."

"I've served with the Royal Marines a few times," he said. "Five hundred marines is a formidable force."

"It's about time we showed the Ansar what British troops can do," Hewitt said.

On the 10th of February 1884, HMS *Carysfort,* a Comus class steam-and-sail corvette with powerful armament, landed her Royal Marines at Suakin. *Carysfort* had been built to counter a perceived threat from French light frigates and had been active during the Egyptian campaign of 1882.

Jack was unsure whether his telegrams to Hook had encouraged the landing but joined the crowds that watched the marines march onshore.

Two hundred and twelve marines landed, bronzed, fit and active, with their white sun helmets gleaming and their Martini-Henry rifles held at precisely the correct angle. The sound of their regular footsteps was as reassuring as the blue uniforms, and their presence immediately calmed Suakin.

The populace gathered to watch the marines, some cheering, others unsure what this new incursion meant, yet Jack noted the sense of relief. Adding to the marines were a hundred and twenty seamen, bearded, jaunty men, of great energy.

"Osman Digna can blow smoke up his... nose now, sir," Donnelly said. "His warriors might terrify the Gyppos, but the marines won't care."

Jack nodded. "I hope you're right, Donnelly." *Three hundred marines and bluejackets against unknown thousands of desert warriors flushed with victory. It may not be as clear-cut as Donnelly imagines.*

With the marine's arrival, the nightly incursions of Osman Digna's men ceased.

"Where have they gone?" Burnaby wondered.

"I don't know," Jack admitted. "But they won't be far away." He watched a detachment of Royal Marines march to one of the defensive forts, with sweat streaming from their young, determined faces. Most would be veterans of the earlier operations against Arabi in Egypt and would not flinch from the Hadendoa. Jack grunted, wondering how many would return to Portsmouth to boast of their exploits in this alien land.

Donnelly marched to Jack, slammed to attention, and saluted. "Begging your pardon, sir, but there's a telegram for you."

"Thank you, Donnelly." Jack glanced at the oblong of flimsy paper. The message was in code. "Excuse me, Burnaby. I'll have to decipher this thing."

Burnaby shrugged. "You must do your duty, Windrush."

Jack kept his code book in the inside pocket of his tunic. When he deciphered Hook's latest message, he stepped to the window of the house he had commandeered and stared at the Royal Naval vessels offshore.

"British will relieve Tokar." Hook had said. "Imperative you accompany the expedition."

Why? Jack asked himself. *I am only a regimental colonel and know nothing about the Sudan. Surely the army has a hundred better officers to send.*

"You're in demand, sir," Donnelly said. "Admiral Hewitt has sent a midshipman and a boat to take you to his flagship."

Jack nodded. "You'd better come too, Donnelly. God only knows what will happen next."

"Yes, sir," Donnelly said. "I think we're off to rescue that explorer at Tokar."

"How the devil do you know that?" Jack asked. "Never mind. Come on, Donnelly."

* * *

"You'll have heard we're going to relieve Tokar," Hewitt said as soon as Jack's feet touched the scrubbed deck.

"Yes, sir," Jack said.

"I've telegraphed Bombay for water skins. My lads won't go thirsty on the expedition."

"Very good, sir," Jack agreed. Trust the navy to care for its men.

"How many wagons did Baker manage to bring back?" Hewitt asked.

"None, sir," Jack replied. "We lost them all. We have about two hundred Egyptian cavalry horses but no Gatlings or artillery, camels, or water wagons."

"Two hundred horses. The 10th Hussars can have them. They were returning home from India, but Hook has diverted them here." Hewitt looked at the steam yacht that had carried Jack from the shore. "Come on, Windrush. I'm taking command at Suakin, so no shilly-shallying!"

Hewitt issued orders the moment he arrived in Suakin. He organised patrols of bluejackets and marines, hustled the grumbling Egyptian soldiers off the streets and requisitioned an empty house.

"That one!" Hewitt indicated a large building with windows looking out to sea. He lifted a finger to a shore party of bluejackets. "You lads! I need you." Hewitt opened the door and looked around. "Petty officer! Ensure this place is ship shape for use."

"Aye, aye, sir!" the petty officer, bearded, neat and sturdy, replied.

"Colonel Windrush! I want a full verbal report on the situation here."

"Yes, sir." Jack obliged, with both men standing on the quay and the navy gradually taking over Suakin.

Hewitt nodded. "We'll get the place organised. I want you to take over the outer defences, Colonel. Burnaby is an adventurer, and Baker's a mercenary. I want a solid regimental officer."

Jack nodded, pleased to have something to do. "Yes, sir."

Within two days of Hewitt assuming command, there were no more knots of Egyptian soldiers roaming the streets, and the glowering faces in the bazaar had lightened. The Admiral sat in his orderly cabin every morning, listening to complaints against the army and settling disputes between the townspeople. He issued direct, sensible responses, disciplined any errant soldiers and answered all complaints.

Every day, another segment of Baker's defeated army returned to Egypt, and Suakin became more orderly. Patrolling the outskirts of the town with Donnelly and the marines, Jack extended his operations each day without sighting the enemy.

"I think they've gone, sir," Donnelly said.

"I think they're watching us all the time," Jack said. "They'll be waiting to see what we do next. Osman Digna is a desert fighter who leads desert warriors. He'll fight best in the open spaces. This campaign is just starting, Donnelly."

The campaign is just starting, but why does General Hook want me in the relief of Tokar? What does that man have planned?

CHAPTER SEVEN

I have always observed that when you despise your enemy, he gives you a damned rap over the knuckles.
Lord MacLeod, 73rd Highlanders.

Admiral Hewitt studied the map of Eastern Sudan that spread across the wall behind his desk. He tapped a powerful finger on Tokar.

"Well, Windrush, here we are again. Another town in the middle of nowhere besieged by savages and another man proving his holiness by massacring everybody who disagrees with him."

"Yes, sir," Jack said.

"You've been out there, Windrush, and you've seen the quality of the opposition. How do you rate our chances of relieving Tokar by negotiations or force?"

Jack shook his head. "We'd need many more men than you presently have, Admiral. Your marines are good, none better, and I've nothing but admiration for the bluejackets, but I wouldn't trust the Egyptians in battle, and the Sudanese are untrained."

Hewitt sighed. "It'll be British blood spilt to help a garrison of Egyptian tax gatherers."

"Not just Egyptian tax gatherers, sir," Jack reminded. "There are women there too, and civilians. If the Hadendoa capture the town, there'll be another massacre."

Hewitt nodded. "I have requested more marines and seamen, and *Jumma,* with the 10th Hussars and a battery of Royal Artillery, is due at Suakin any day."

"Yes, sir," Jack said. "We'll need some solid infantry as well."

Hewitt nodded. "How many?"

"I'd say at least three battalions of British infantry and seasoned troops if possible. My Royal Malverns are stationed around the Delta, sir, and we were at Tel-el-Kebir and through the Afghan War."

Hewitt gave a bleak smile. "General Hook informed me you preferred regimental soldiering to intelligence or staff work. You might like to know that Charlie Gordon arrived safely at Berber and is on his way to Khartoum."

"Thank you for the information, sir." Jack did not say Donnelly had found out about Gordon from bazaar gossip.

Hewitt continued. "The Powers that be want me to – and I quote – "try by native messenger at any expense to tell the besieged garrison at Tokar" that we are going to try and relieve them."

"That sounds as if the War Office don't care if the native messenger dies or not," Jack said.

"That's how I read it, too," Hewitt said. "I'm not sure about sending men to their death."

Jack agreed. "I can only suggest you look for volunteers, sir, and promise them a substantial reward if they succeed!"

Hewitt frowned and glanced out the open window. "I'd say the sun is well over the yardarm, Windrush. Wouldn't you?"

"Undoubtedly, sir," Jack agreed as Hewitt produced a decanter and poured two stiff glasses of rum.

"What do you know about this explorer in Tokar, Colonel?"

The rum burned Jack's throat as he swallowed. "Very little, sir. I know Baker had orders to rescue him."

Hewitt tossed back his rum like water, glanced regretfully at the decanter, and put it back in a cupboard. "One only, I'm afraid, Windrush. We need to keep our wits about us here. The Sirdar has asked me to ensure this explorer, Alexander Drummond, is safe."

"I didn't even know the name, sir."

"Nor did I," Hewitt admitted. "That's all, Windrush. You'd better return to your duties."

"Yes, sir," Jack stepped into the baking heat outside. The Royal Naval gunboats still sat beside the causeway, providing security for Suakin.

* * *

Jack continued to patrol outside the defences, but as the reinforcements arrived, the atmosphere in the town altered. He found it very reassuring to hear British voices and see the marines' white sun helmets and dark blue uniforms at the defences.

"I doubt Osman Digna will attack now," Burnaby said. "We'll have to seek him out."

"He won't hide," Jack replied. "He's defeated one British-led expedition already."

Jumma steamed up to the quay and unloaded three hundred and fifty-nine men of the 10th Hussars. Sun-browned by long service in India and Afghanistan, they were stiff after the voyage and grumbling that the War Office had delayed their return home. Jack watched them make the acquaintance of the horses of the Egyptian cavalry as Lieutenant-colonel Wood spoke to General Baker.

Royal Artillerymen disembarked from the same ship without transport or guns. Shortly after, four hundred Royal Irish Fusiliers arrived, joking as soon as they stepped ashore. The accents immediately reminded Jack of the Connaught Rangers at the Redan and the Royal Irish at Tel-el-Kebir.

"*Erin gu Brath*, Ireland forever," he said softly as General Baker's band played Auld Lang Syne. The marines and Hussars lined the wharf to cheer as the Irishmen arrived, with the Fusiliers reciprocating with interest.

"Osman Digna will wonder what all the noise is," Burnaby said.

"Let him wonder," Jack replied. "The Chainy Tenth fought at Ali Masjid in the last Afghan business, and the marines were present throughout Arabi's war. The Ansar won't concern them."

"And the Fusiliers?"

Jack smiled. "They're Irish. Have you ever seen an Irish regiment back away from a fight?"

Burnaby laughed. "Never."

"Nor will the Ansar," Jack said.

* * *

That evening, Jack brought a patrol of Irish Fusiliers outside Suakin's defences to introduce them to the locality. As Jack expected, the Fusiliers mixed their humour with supreme professionalism as soon as they were on operations. They had not long left the security of Suakin's defences when they heard soft padding on the sand.

"That's a camel," Jack said and readied his revolver. "It may be the enemy."

The Irishmen formed a defensive circle without being ordered, staring into the gloom as the padding came closer.

"It's only a stray camel," Private Regan sounded disappointed as the animal loomed into view.

"It must have got lost," Private O'Connor said. "It's got a saddle on it."

"Somebody fell off," Regan put up his rifle. "What do we do, sir?"

"We patrol for another fifteen minutes and then return," Jack ordered.

As Jack led the patrol back, the camel followed, remaining ten yards behind the last man.

"We've got a prisoner," Regan was delighted with their capture. "One of Osman's warriors. I'll call it Osman."

"Osman's too long," O'Connor said. "How about Ozzy."

As the Fusiliers debated what to name their acquisition, Jack wondered what the Fusiliers officers would say when a camel arrived in their camp. British soldiers could make a pet out of anything. He had seen regiments marching with a profusion of dogs, parrots, and monkeys, but a camel was a bit large.

The Egyptians were not as pleased to see the camel, and one officer drew his revolver to shoot the beast.

"You'll leave Ozzy alone," O'Connor readied his rifle. "He's a member of the Irish Fusiliers now!"

Jack stepped forward before the dispute escalated into violence and ordered both sides to put away their weapons. "What's the trouble? Why do you want to kill the camel?"

The Egyptian officer backed away. "Osman Digna sent it here!"

"We found it beyond the outposts," Jack corrected.

"It's cursed. Osman Digna sent it to damage us!"[1]

Jack tried to explain that the camel was only an animal when Private Regan asked what the Egyptian wanted.

"This Egyptian officer believes Osman Digna has cursed the camel," Jack said.

When Jack explained to him what the trouble was, Regan laughed. "Tell the man I'll remove the curse, sir."

"How will you manage that?" Jack asked.

"Just you tell him, sir, and leave it to me," Regan's eyes twinkled as he spoke.

When Jack passed the message on, Regan removed a bottle of

water from inside his jacket and sprinkled some on the camel, repeating a Gaelic prayer.

"There you are, sir. Could you tell the fellow that I've spread Holy Water from St Patrick's Well in Belcoo, County Fermanagh, over our Ozzy," the soldier said. "There's no curse in the world that can break through that."

Jack's explanation puzzled the Egyptian officer, but the Fusiliers had led away their camel before he asked further questions. Jack smiled. Irish regiments always enlivened British encampments, and the Fusiliers seemed no exception.

I'd hate to fight a war without the Irish regiments. The cavalry might think they add class, but the Irish add something else; they lighten even the most desperate situation.

* * *

As the reinforcements arrived at Suakin, each unit diminished the possibility of Osman Digna attacking the town. The British soldiers marched ashore, rifles aslant, with their boots crunching on the causeway and their pith helmets brilliant white or stained a variety of shades of brown. The veterans were tanned as dark as any Arab, while the newly joined men were red-faced, peeling with the sun. When Lieutenant-general Gerald Graham arrived to take over the army, he told Jack that the Royal Malverns would disembark that evening.

"That should please you, Windrush."

Graham had won the Victoria Cross at the Redan during the Crimea War, was wounded at the Taku Forts in China, and fought in the campaign against Arabi.

"Yes, sir," Jack agreed. "It will be good to be back with my regiment."

"I believe Burnaby is also in Suakin," Graham said. "And Valentine Baker."

"That's correct, sir," Jack agreed.

Graham nodded. "With such experienced men in command, I

wonder Baker lost at Teb." He strolled away, tall, moustached, and confident, and Jack prepared a camping ground for the Royal Malverns.

* * *

The Malverns filed off the ships in their Indian khaki, staring about them at the novel scenes, swatting at the flies and wondering what the future held. As the NCOs blasted the men into order, small boats unloaded cargoes of mules, who complained as the seamen ushered them onto land.

Jack watched the mules come ashore. "Major Bryant," he said softly. "Requisition as many mules as you can for the Royals. Beg, steal, or borrow. I don't care how you do it."

"Yes, sir," Bryant said.

"The more transport animals we have, the better pleased I'll be. Sergeant Hanley!" Jack called over the veteran sergeant. "I am going to take as many water-carrying mules as possible. I want a reliable man to look after them."

Hanley nodded. "I know just the fellow, sir. I have a man in mind who would be ideal at looking after mules."

Jack understood. "Is this fellow any good at anything else, Sergeant?"

"No, sir. Her Majesty made a bad bargain when she handed over her shillings for him."

"Everybody is good at something, Sergeant," Jack said quietly. "We just have to find out what."

Hanley nodded. "He's a human mistake called Branley, sir. I'll see if he's any good with the mules. He can't march, shoot, or even dress properly, and we had to wash him."

Jack had experienced such recruits, who usually came from the most revolting slums of London or some industrial town. They had no idea of life, and the army taught them the hard way. A forced wash was performed with hard-bristled brushes when the unfortunate man was stripped, thrown against a wall or in a horse trough and scrubbed raw.

"Branley," Jack repeated the name. "I'll keep an eye on him. If anybody can bring him up to scratch, sergeant, you can."

"Yes, sir. Thank you, sir." Hanley saluted.

"Beg pardon, sir!" Donnelly hurried up. "A telegraph message for you, sir."

"Thank you, Donnelly."

When Jack deciphered the message, he sighed. "Accompany Graham on his relief of Tokar. Rescue explorer Drummond. Imperative."

Why is this Drummond fellow so important that General Hook wastes a telegram on him?

* * *

On the morning of Saturday, the 23rd of February 1884, Admiral Hewitt supervised as the army filed on board the transports.

"Where are we off to now?" Second Lieutenant Lang asked as the Malverns' offices waited at the quayside.

"Trinkitat," Major Baxter told him. "You're off to meet the Hadendoa."

"Hadendoa!" Lang laughed. "A parcel of naked savages against a royal regiment. I'd prefer a more reputable enemy."

"They're reputable enough," Jack growled. "Never disrespect a brave enemy, Lang. The Mahdi's forces have defeated well-armed British-led armies more than once."

"Yes, sir," Lang said.

With his vivid memories of General Baker's abortive expedition, Jack watched the British regiments with trepidation. Although many were veterans of Afghanistan and the Egyptian campaign, they had never met the Hadendoa in their native desert.

"Come on, Royal Malverns!"

"Will Osman Digna fight, sir?" Major Baxter asked.

Jack nodded. "I believe so. According to our spies, Digna has dug in his army at El Teb, close to where he defeated Baker Pasha."

"You were there, sir," Lang said. "How did the rebels fight?"

"I'm not sure they are rebels," Jack said. "I'd doubt the legality of the Egyptian position in Sudan. I rather think the Sudanese want to remove any foreigner from their land."

"Sudan for the Sudanese?" Lang asked with a short laugh.

"I'm not even sure the Ansar recognise Sudan as a country," Jack said. "The Mahdi and Islam seem to be the only things that unite them. That and a dislike of Egyptians and Turks." He paused for a moment. "Maybe a dislike of us as well."

"Osman surely can't expect to defeat a British army," Second-lieutenant Moffat said.

"Why not?" Jack asked. "He defeated Baker, an experienced British commander, who had an army half as large again as his, equipped with modern weapons, artillery and Gatling guns."

Moffat looked away. "I see, sir."

"Our job is to ensure the Malverns are at the peak of their efficiency," Jack said. "I've seen the Hadendoa, and they're as brave as the Afghans. Indeed, I've never seen braver men. However, their marksmanship is poor, thank God. Baker's men had all the advantages of numbers and more modern weapons, yet Osman Digna won."

"Why, sir?" Moffat asked the question he knew was expected of him.

"The Egyptians panicked, and fear and lack of discipline cause panic," Jack told him. "We've drilled our men to obey orders." He looked out to the desert beyond Suakin. "In a few days, we'll meet the Hadendoa and see how good we are."

"We defeated the Egyptians at Tel-el-Kebir, sir," Lang reminded. "Most of our lads were at that battle."

Jack knew that most senior officers would not deign to argue with subalterns, but he believed that such discussions formed part of his officers' military training. "The Mahdi's men also defeated the Egyptians three or four times and armed only with spears and swords."

Major Baxter listened, drew on his cigar, and said nothing as, far in the distance, the tom-toms began to throb.

"General Baker evacuated Trinkitat fast enough," Lang said. "*Insalutato hospite* – without saluting one's host, as they say." He grinned. "We took French leave, running like the French at Waterloo."

"The French would say *filer a l'anglaise,* to take English leave," Jack said, lighting a cheroot. "We all tend to ascribe dishonourable actions to other cultures while we do the same thing." He looked up. "That's the men on board, gentlemen, and now it's our turn."

"All set for a cruise down the Red Sea," Lang said. "Bring your buckets and spades, what?"

"And your rifles and bayonets," Moffat added quietly.

CHAPTER EIGHT

Its horror and its beauty are divine
    Shelley

The ships left Suakin one by one, leaving a small garrison of mostly Sudanese troops to guard the port. As the Royal Malverns crowded the deck, Jack toured the men, asking questions, and gauging their temper.

"We're off to war, lads. Keep your bayonets bright and your ammunition pouches filled."

"We will, sir," Private Brotheridge wore the campaign medals of Afghanistan and Egypt. He gave a gap-toothed grin. "We're the Malverns!"

Somebody began to sing the old Royal Malvern's song, and others joined in, with the noise rising from the ship. Jack had known the words since his cradle and sang with the men, not caring it was not an officer's place. This regiment was his; these were his men, and they would fight or die together.

"Always victorious,
Glorious and more glorious,
We followed Marlborough through battle and war,
We're the Royal Malverns, the heroes of Malplaquet,
We carry victory wherever we go."

The sound carried across the calm Red Sea to the neighbouring ships, and other regiments responded with catcalls and jeers, as expected in the British Army. Fifty yards away, the men of the 42nd foot, the kilted Black Watch, sang an obscene parody of the Malvern's song.

Private Brotheridge struggled to the rail, lifted two fingers, and shouted across.

"Men of the Black Watch, do not weep
It was not us that stole your sheep,
From over the hills and land of whisky
There came the cry: we're not that frisky!"

The Malverns cheered as some highlanders threw sharpened coins at them until the NCOs roared them back into order. The two ships parted, and Jack nodded to Major Baxter.

"There's no doubting the men's morale, although we might be fighting the Black Watch as well as the Hadendoa when we land."

"There's not much to pick between them," Baxter said. "Except the Hadendoa warriors are probably more civilised and easier to understand."

Jack watched as Private Branley walked past with one bootlace undone and his shoulders hunched. He opened his mouth to reprimand the man until Deblin, the Regimental Sergeant Major, blasted him from the opposite side of the ship.

We might be fighting the Hadendoa, but we also have internal disputes. Beneath the veneer, I doubt we're much different.

***

The British expeditionary force landed at Trinkitat and immediately took over the old defensive position. "Follow me, Malverns!" Jack said.

Osman Digna will know what we're doing. If I were him, I'd attack at once before we get organised.

Jack led the Malverns into the zareba between the beach and the morass, posted strong pickets and covered the landing. The sun reflected from the salt marsh, with the cries of birds harsh and the still water somehow sinister. Jack positioned his men and ensured the NCOs and junior officers checked the men's rifles and each man had a full water bottle.

"Sand will get into the firing mechanism and the barrel. Keep them clean!"

Then he waited.

"Come on, you useless old grump!" Private Branley persuaded his mules to enter the zareba. "Honestly, sir," he said to Captain Sarsens. "These animals have a mind of their own. Clara there, she'll take any load you give her but won't climb even the smallest incline. Jasmin likes to kick with her left leg without any warning. She hates me. Emilia is a grafter, though, and there's nothing she won't tackle."

"Keep trying," Sarsens said with a smile. "You're the best man for the job."

"Thank you, sir." Branley threw a clumsy salute.

Jack remembered Sarsens as a young fire-raising ensign and a friend of his nephew, Crimea Windrush. Crimea had died in Afghanistan, and now Sarsens was a captain and one of Jack's most dependable officers.

The regimental cooks were sweating over a fire, each man with a fierce moustache and his hair with a broad central parting. Jack spared time for a word, ordered Sergeant Anderson and his bearded pioneers to strengthen the zareba and looked for the regimental surgeon.

"How many sick?" Jack asked.

"Only seven," Dr Park replied. "Heat stroke. I'll need some camels to carry the lads that drop out on the march and the inevitable wounded. And, Colonel, we'll need more water carts."

Jack nodded, with his mind busy with all the administrative details of running a regiment.

"And more orderlies, sir," Dr Park continued. "I dismissed the last two because they were clumsy and callous."

"I'll send you some good men," Jack promised. *The RSM will know who best to send.* He shouted for the RSM and watched his company officers form the men for the march. *Here we go, Royal Malverns; it's a long way from Hereford to Tokar.*

* * *

Major-General Gerald Graham had 4,200 men, with famous regiments such as the Black Watch, the Gordon Highlanders, and the King's Royal Rifle Corps. The Royal Irish Fusiliers were there, joking as always, and the First Battalion of the York and Lancaster, fresh from a peaceful posting in India and Aden. The 10th Hussars provided cavalry cover, although some were still making friends with the horses they requisitioned from the Egyptians. With this being a seaborne expedition, the Royal Marines made up a solid chunk of blue, and a section of seamen operated the Gatling guns. Eight seven-pounders gave Graham's little army some formidable firepower.

"It's hot." Captain Jamieson wiped the sweat from his face. "I think it's even hotter here than at Suakin."

"We're further south," Jack told him laconically. "Closer to the equator." He lifted his field glasses and examined the low hills beyond the marsh. "Osman Digna is watching."

The flags hung limp on the heights. Most were black, and even using field glasses, Jack could not see details, although he could describe them without looking. Each flag would have an inscription from the Koran, and each marked the position of a tribal chief.

"How many men does Osman Digna have?" Captain Jamieson asked. A decent enough soldier, Jamieson lacked imagination, and Jack doubted whether he would progress beyond his present rank.

"I don't know," Jack said as he scanned the heights. Some flags were clearer as the chiefs led their men down the facing slopes. "I'd say many more than he needed to defeat Baker's Egyptians. Maybe ten thousand."

"Twice our numbers," Jamieson said.

"At least," Jack agreed.

The tom-toms began their rhythmic throbbing that seemed to come from the land itself as if Africa resented these intruders on its ancient desert.

"Warn the men to watch for warriors crossing the marsh," Jack said. "They might come over en-masse or in ones and twos. I don't want the men to fire until they feel threatened, but if they fire, shoot low."

"Yes, sir," Jamieson passed on Jack's instructions.

"Windrush!" Major-general Sir Redvers Buller had fought beside Jack in Ashantiland and Egypt. Now senior in rank, he was known as a bold officer who had won his Victoria Cross in Zululand.

Jack pulled Tinker aside as Buller splashed through the morass to his side.

"Have you heard the news from Suakin, Windrush?"

"Not since we left, sir. I've been rather busy with the regiment."

Buller grinned. "Regimental soldiering, eh? Details about rations one day and blood and corpses the next. As soon as we left Suakin, the Sudanese soldiers mutinied. Admiral Hewitt ordered them to pile their arms, and they refused and ran into the bazaar. Hewitt said some threatened to join the rebels, but he plans to send the whole damned lot to Cairo."

Jack took a deep breath. "That will leave Hewitt in a quandary."

"It does," Buller agreed calmly. General Graham was hoping for more Royal Marines, but he'll need to retain them at Suakin, or we'll also lose that base."

Jack nodded. "If the Mahdists capture Suakin, the Red Sea will be a dangerous place for British shipping."

Buller nodded. "There's worse news, Windrush. Osman has captured Tokar."

Jack felt a jolt. *Hook expects me to rescue that explorer, Drummond.* "Have you heard anything about the inhabitants, sir?"

"I don't know yet," Buller said. "We know the garrison surrendered, but there are no details yet."

"Are we still marching in, sir?"

Buller nodded. "We are. Our spies report that Osman Digna has dug in at Teb, where General Baker had his unfortunate encounter, and if we withdraw now, the world will think we shirked a fight." He glanced over the beach where soldiers and seamen carried up stores; camels loped up with disdainful looks, and gunners struggled with horses, guns, and wagons.

"The French and Italian papers will have a field day if we withdraw without fighting," Jack agreed.

"We'll march in, smash Osman Digna, bury the British dead at El Teb and see what happens," Buller said.

Jack pulled on his cheroot. "Yes, sir. If you hear more about Tokar, please let me know."

"I will." Buller narrowed his eyes. "Why the concern, Windrush?"

If Hook has not told Buller, nor should I. "I heard there was at least one British subject in the town, sir."

Buller grunted. "More fool him, then. You'll have heard about Hewitt's dealings with Osman Digna?"

"I have not," Jack admitted.

"You regimental lads miss all the gossip." Buller grinned and updated Jack with the news. "Admiral Hewitt informed Digna that a British force would march to relieve Tokar but would not seek a battle and would avoid useless bloodshed if Digna did not oppose it."

"I've never known a war where we tell the enemy what we're doing," Jack said.

"We're not at war with the Sudanese," Buller said. "We're only evacuating the Egyptians."

"We'd best tell Digna that," Jack told him.

Buller smoothed his moustache. "When he got the admiral's message, Digna, the one-time slave trader, and now victorious warrior, said, "I regret the inevitable bloodshed," and added that anybody who accepted the Mahdi would probably not suffer.

"I feel constrained to take Tokar," Osman Digna told Hewitt, "and will be obliged to compel the British to leave Suakin."

"That's very candid," Jack said.

Buller smiled. "If the Mahdi's warriors leave us in peace, we won't attack them." He looked over the men struggling across the mire. "Even General Graham is unsure what we're meant to do, and he's wired Cairo for further instructions."

Jack thought of the old days in India, when General Havelock marched his small, underequipped army to the relief of Lucknow, defeating much larger enemy armies en route.

What happened to the old spirit? This telegraph has altered army commanders' freedom to think for themselves. Rather than make decisions that reflect the military situation, they are at the whim of politicians hundreds, even thousands of miles away.

"Osman will oppose us, Windrush," Buller said. "We might defeat him in open battle and destroy his encampment or burn his crops, but we don't have the means to recapture Tokar. It's a walled town, and we only have seven-pounder mountain guns."

Jack sought some optimism. "Osman's warriors have never fought British soldiers, sir. They might surrender Tokar to us."

Buller shook his head. "That's unlikely, Windrush. There's also the possibility that Osman Digna might move his entire force to Suakin and burn the place to the ground while we're fooling around down here."

Jack was unused to such pessimism from a British officer. "The Navy and the Royal Marines are there, Buller. I'd say that Suakin is in safe hands."

Buller allowed himself a smile. "There is another possibility, Windrush. If Osman Digna marches on Suakin, we might meet him in the open. He would have to fight a fair battle then."

"If we keep our discipline and keep him at arm's length, British musketry will defeat him."

"I am sure you're correct, Windrush."

Jack returned to the Malverns, wondering at Buller's pessimism. *It must be the heat.*

As they prepared to march on Osman Digna's position at El Teb, rumours spread around the army. Jack listened, discarding those he thought least likely. Only the stolid Major Baxter seemed immune. Baxter said the Mahdi had written to the Christian King Johannes of Abyssinia, demanding his adherence. Johannes had rejected the offer with some contempt and warned the Mahdi from attempting to attack his kingdom.

"I can believe that," Jack said.

More rumours claimed reinforcements had arrived at Suakin, with regular infantry and more Royal Marines.

Baxter rode beside Jack, his red face concerned, "Did you hear that when a Sudanese regiment refused to obey orders, their Turkish officers demanded to be relieved of their positions?"

"That should not be a hardship," Jack said. "They were no good when Baker led them."

"If we don't have Egyptian or Turkish officers," Baxter said, "Who will lead the Egyptian army?"

Jack pondered for a moment. "That's an excellent question, Baxter. I wish I knew the answer."

I can only see one answer. We will have to lead the Egyptian army. Great Britain blundered into this country to protect the Suez Canal and British financial investment in Egypt, and it looks as if we'll be here for some time.

* * *

"Gentlemen!" General Graham had called the senior officers together. "I have at last received instructions from the War Office. I have full discretionary power regarding our next move." He waited for a moment. "We march tomorrow afternoon. We will bivouac at Fort Baker tomorrow night and then move to engage Osman Digna if he stands to face us."

With his regiment as ready as possible, every man with his ammunition pouches full and an extra water canteen, Jack left Baxter in charge of the Royals and crossed the mire on a reconnaissance mission.

"I'll come with you, sir," Donnelly said.

"I didn't give you permission to come along," Jack snarled.

"No, sir, you didn't have to," Donnelly said. "It's my job as your soldier servant to look after you."

Jack sighed. "Whose horse is that?"

"I don't know, sir. It looked lost, so I requisitioned it." Donnelly tried to look innocent, but he knew every dodge in the book and others that nobody had ever written.

"All right, keep a watch behind us. We don't want the Hadendoa to cut us off."

"Yes, sir."

They dismounted, waded through the mire, and remounted on the far side.

"Sir." Donnelly pointed to the ground, where recent evidence of horses and camels littered the sand.

"Osman's men, I'd guess," Jack said. "Is your rifle loaded?"

"Yes, sir," Donnelly said.

They moved on slowly, following the trail Baker's retreating army had left, with the skeletons of horses, camels, and men a macabre reminder of how dangerous the Hadendoa were.

"Some of these corpses lack a head," Donnelly said.

"I noticed," Jack said. "I'd guess that the Hadendoa removed the heads of the officers, or maybe just the Europeans."

As they threaded through the low hills, they saw men watching them, some on camelback and others on foot.

"How many?" Jack scanned the enemy with his field glasses. "I'd estimate forty or fifty on camels."

Donnelly took the field glasses. "I'd guess fifty on camels, sir, but I couldn't estimate the foot soldiers. They move around too much, and with the heat haze and the dust, I'm not sure at all."

"We'll push on a bit," Jack said. "We might get a better vantage point."

"They might try and get behind us," Donnelly warned.

"I imagine they will, but our horses are faster than camels or a running warrior."

They moved on, swivelling in their saddles to watch the enemy. Once past the hills, the ground was the well-remembered hard sand, interspersed with scrubby thorn plants.

"Sir," Donnelly said softly. "They're behind us."

"Keep an eye on them, Donnelly. If they get too close, we'll withdraw." Jack moved on. As they came closer to Baker's battle site of Teb, he saw men moving about, and the flash as the sun reflected from steel.

They've dug entrenchments there and mounted artillery. That will be the Krupps guns Osman Digna captured from Baker.

He focused his field glasses, seeing the different colours of recently turned sand, a profusion of banners and the movement of hundreds of men.

"Sir," Donnelly reported calmly. "A company of Hadendoa is leaving the heights. I reckon we have about twenty minutes before they cut us off."

"Thank you, Donnelly. Time to return to Trinkitat. We've seen all we needed to see." Jack turned Tinker and began the journey back. He saw a mass of the enemy moving quickly down the slope quarter of a mile in front, with camel riders and a score of running infantry.

When the Hadendoa warriors began to increase speed, Jack did the same until the horses trotted over the sand, raising a cloud of dust.

The warriors outpaced the camel riders and raced down the hill with spears upraised in their right hands and heavy ox-hide shields in their left. "Spur, Donnelly," Jack said.

"I am, sir!" Donnelly replied. Holding his Martini-Henry one-handed, he tried a snapshot at the mass of the enemy as Jack unholstered his revolver. "I'm glad I kept the carbine I carried as a mounted infantryman in Afghanistan, sir!"

"Remind me to order some more when we get back to Suakin," Jack fired, knowing the chances of hitting anybody at extreme range were minimal.

"Yes, sir!"

"Now put down your bundook and spur!" Jack ordered.

With the Hadendoa warriors chasing them, and a thrown spear whizzing past, Jack and Donnelly reached the marsh. They pushed the horses as far as they could, dismounted and waded into the thigh-deep water. Another spear hissed past, plunging into the water ten yards away with the haft quivering.

"They've halted at the edge, sir," Donnelly reported.

A section of khaki-clad soldiers plunged into the water from the opposite bank and waded towards them. "We've got you covered, sir!" Captain Sarsens said. "Give them a volley, lads!"

The Malverns fired at once, with the sound echoing to the high sky above. The Hadendoa waited for a moment and then loped casually away.

"Thank you, Sarsens," Jack said as he and Donnelly returned to the safer side of the marsh. "I think Osman Digna will contest our march to Tokar."

I hope that damned explorer is safe, whoever he is.

CHAPTER NINE

E's all 'ot sand and ginger when alive
An' 'e's generally shamming when 'e's dead
'E's the on'y thing that doesn't give a damn
For a Regiment o' British Infantree!
Rudyard Kipling

General Graham looked solemn when Jack stepped into his tent. "The Mahdi has captured Tokar," he said.

Jack felt something slide in his stomach. "Oh, dear God! When?"

"I don't know yet," Graham said. "When I find out more, I'll pass the intelligence on."

"What do you intend to do, sir?"

"March," Graham said. "We came here to march to Tokar, and my God, we'll march to Tokar." He sat on his camp chair. "Although God only knows what we'll find there." He mustered a smile. "In the meantime, we carry on as usual. What news do you have for me?"

Jack cleared his mind of Tokar to give his report. "Osman Digna's dug in at El Teb, sir," Jack reported. "I am unsure about the enemy's numbers, but I'd guess at around ten thousand."

"Did you see any artillery?"

"Yes, sir. They've got Krupps guns behind earthworks."

Graham nodded. "That's around what I expected, Windrush. I'll make my arrangements to match." He forced a smile. "We'll get to Tokar, Windrush, Osman Digna or no Osman Digna."

The following morning Graham left a small garrison to hold the zareba and advanced with his British infantry, a clutch of seamen for the Gatling guns, and the artillery's seven-pounders.

"Here we go," Lang half drew his sword, tested the edge, and slid it back inside the scabbard. "I can't wait to get at them."

Moffat gave a twisted smile and said nothing.

"Tenth Hussars!" Graham ordered, "Take two hundred men forward and look for the enemy. Osman Digna might try and ambush us on the road, as he did with Baker."

Jack watched the cavalry ford the morass, with some horsemen swearing as they sunk to their girths in the muddy water.

"Watch the heights," Jack advised. "If Digna has any sense, he'll have his artillery there and hammer us when we cross the swamp." He kept the Malverns in formation, with each company marching together and skirmishers out in case of ambush.

With the example of Baker before him, Graham had sent out pickets to guard the far side of the marsh while Jack had marked the safest routes, so the entire army crossed in a couple of nerve-racking hours. Jack heard the Irish Fusiliers before he saw them, with three men guarding their new mascot and Ozzy appearing to accept its privileged position as a right.

"Osman was foolish not fighting us at the morass," Major Baxter said.

"I agree, Baxter," Jack clenched his teeth around a cheroot. "He'll make his stand at El Teb."

"If he defeats us," Baxter said, "he'll take his whole force and run right over Suakin, which means the Mahdi will control the entire Red Sea coast."

"We'll try to ensure that does not happen," Jack said.

"There are only about fourteen hundred troops at Suakin." Baxter was in a talkative mood. "About four hundred and fifty at the outer redoubt, and the rest spread far too thin."

"Forget Suakin," Jack said. "Our duty is here."

"There's no point to this expedition," Bryce sounded depressed, "if Tokar has already fallen."

"If we don't march, the Mahdi will claim he pushed us out," Jack said. "And we don't know what's happened in Tokar until we get there."

As the British column crawled towards El Teb, General Graham sent Major Harvey, a Black Watch veteran, and a survivor of Baker's defeat, with a note for Osman Digna. Never a man to hold back when there was danger, Lieutenant-colonel Burnaby trotted out to join Harvey.

"What's the to-do, sir?" Lang asked.

"Harvey is taking a letter to the enemy," Jack explained. "He'll place it somewhere prominent so that somebody will carry it to Osman Digna." Jack followed the two officers with his field glasses. They rode two miles ahead of the column, ascended a slight rise and thrust a white flag into the ground with the letter attached.

Lang frowned. "What does the letter say, sir?"

"It asks Osman Digna to allow us peaceful passage to Tokar."

Lang rattled the hilt of his sword as if impatient to be fighting. "Will he, sir?"

"It's unlikely," Jack said, "but we don't want a war in Sudan. We're trying to withdraw the Egyptian garrisons, not conquer the damned place."

"If they still exist," Lang said. "I'd say that the Dervishes have massacred them all."

"We march on the assumption that they're still alive," Jack told him.

The Dervish; that must be what our men call the enemy.

Lang looked away. "Yes, sir."

The enemy opened fire on Hervey and Burnaby, with the bullets raising spurts of dust all around them, but both men returned without any injury. Burnaby was laughing as if he enjoyed the momentary excitement.

"The Hadendoa have taken the flag," Jack reported. "We'll know Digna's reply tomorrow."

Graham formed an encampment that night, ready for an advance in the early morning. "Make a zareba," he ordered as the darkness swooped upon them, and the tom-toms began their monotonous beat.

As always before an action, Jack found it hard to sleep. He dozed when he could and patrolled the Malverns' double pickets. "Keep alert, lads!"

"We will, sir," Private Kerswell promised. A veteran of Afghanistan and the Egyptian campaign, he stared out at the dark, ignoring the Hadendoa's occasional sniping. "These Dervish lads are no better sharpshooters than the Gyppos, sir. They couldn't hit a bull's arse with a banjo."

Jack smiled. He had heard the same expression in campaigns from Burma to Ashantiland. "We're lucky they're not Pashtuns."

"Yes, sir," Kerswell agreed. He did not flinch as a bullet whined past. "See, sir? That one was miles too high."

Around midnight, Jack made a final circuit of the pickets and retired to his tent. He barely noticed the Hadendoa's sporadic firing, but the sound of rain hammering from the canvas woke him an hour before dawn.

"That's a good omen, sir, good old British rain!" Donnelly greeted him with a mug of hot coffee and a hunk of bread and cheese. "It's only goat's cheese, sir; not great, but the best I could find."

Jack checked his revolver was loaded, ensured his sword was loose in its scabbard and toured the morning pickets before waking the cooks to ensure his Malverns had a decent breakfast.

Reveille sounded, with the sweet call of the bugle alerting the soldiers to the breaking of another day. Jack watched Major Harvey trot out of the camp to see if Osman Digna had replied to the letter. Harvey returned through a spatter of musketry, dodging a rush of mounted Arabs. "No reply, sir!" he reported.

"That means Digna doesn't want a truce," Redvers Buller said calmly.

"It appears so," Jack agreed.

"Then hell mend him," a stocky major of the Gordon Highlanders said, stamping his feet. "We'll see if he's so damned cocky when my lads get at him."

Jack glanced over at the Gordons. A pipe corporal was blowing up his bag, with his cheeks frighteningly distended, two young soldiers were playing with a dog, and a sergeant was reprimanding an old soldier. The others were checking their rifles, playing cards or filling water bottles. They did not look particularly warlike when compared to the Hadendoa.

"Check the men's water bottles and ammunition pouches," Jack told his men. "I know I don't need to remind most of you, but these Hadendoa are as fast and aggressive as anybody I've ever seen. I don't want anybody to lack cartridges or collapse through lack of water." He looked upward at the teeming rain and grinned. "Although that doesn't seem likely at present."

"We'll show them, sir!" Lang shouted, and some of the younger men cheered. The veterans, Jack noted, remained silent.

At eight o'clock, with the regiments formed up, Graham gave the order to advance. Jack hid his anxiety about the Malverns, put on a confident air and looked over the column. Graham had about three thousand infantry, cavalry, and mounted infantry, plus one hundred and fifteen seamen of the Naval Brigade. He also had two hundred of the vital artillerymen and engineers.

"It's a small force," Buller said, "when you consider Osman Digna defeated a larger army with only half their numbers."

Jack watched the Black Watch swagger past, kilts swinging and boots lifting a fine film of sand. He remembered them at Tel-el-Kebir and Ashantiland and, a lifetime before that, storming the Alma heights in Crimea. "We may be a small force, Buller, but we're filled with quality."

Graham had left an unfortunate Colonel Ogilvie with a hundred and fifty men to hold Trinkitat and another three hundred in the more exposed Fort Baker. The remainder advanced in a hollow square, wary of a sudden attack. The Gordon Highlanders formed the front face, with the Irish Fusiliers on the right. The Rifles, another regiment for whom Jack had fond memories, formed up inside the Gordons and Fusiliers. The 65th York and Lancaster made up the left face, with the Royal Marines inside them. The Black Watch marched in line at the rear of the square beside the Royal Malverns.

Jack noted his junior officers and NCOs watching the men, with the veterans keeping the recruits calm.

"Look to your front, boys, and trust your mates," RSM Deblin said. "We're the Malverns, the best regiment in the world!"

As the square was only two hundred and fifty yards broad by a hundred and fifty deep, the transport animals, hospital supplies, spare ammunition and Ozzy, the Irish Fusiliers camel, were tightly squeezed inside. The eight seven-pounder mountain guns rolled in the centre of the square, much to the gunners' disgust. The Naval Brigade and their six machine guns rattled beside the Gordons, with the seamen making lewd comments about the Gordons' kilts. The Highlanders replied with threats of dire revenge as soon as they "sorted oot they fuzzy-heided bastards."

"You're next, tarry-backs," the Gordons promised, with shaking of fists and oaths in Buchan Doric.

Jack let Tinker pick his route as he lifted his field glasses to survey the surrounding countryside. He knew it well now, from his reconnaissances and Baker's expedition, and he watched the cavalry that rode in advance of the column and on both flanks. Graham had ordered them to act as scouts in case Digna hid his Hadendoa among the scrub as he had with Baker's column.

Graham had ordered the scouting cavalry to withdraw to the square if they made contact with the enemy. Meanwhile, the main body of the 10th Hussars rode a quarter of a mile behind the infantry. Graham had ordered them not to fight until the infantry had broken the Hadendoa and then to pursue the retreating enemy.

Jack considered that General Graham's dispositions had given his force a fighting chance of victory. He was not so sure about the order that the infantry was only to fire in volleys, with the first when the enemy was three hundred yards distant.

"We have Martinis now, not the old Brown Bess muskets. I think we should fire the moment they come in range," Jack said. "I've seen the speed they move, and the more we kill before they get close, the better."

Baxter nodded. "Let's hope that they never get too close."

"Amen to that," Jack agreed, remembering the Hadendoa's lethal skill with their spears.

The British set off into the desert, with the men grumbling happily and the sun already uncomfortably warm. After only a couple of hundred yards, Graham ordered a halt. The officers dressed the lines, made a few minor alterations, and the column marched again, with the scouts scouring the scrub. Baker sat on his horse beside Graham, guiding him as they passed the route of his defeated army.

Jack listened to the comments of the Malverns as they saw the skeletons of men and animals.

"The Dervish did some bloody work here," Brotheridge commented.

"They did." Doncaster put a hand to his throat. "Let's hope they don't do any more."

Jack rode close to the younger soldiers, some of whom looked shaken. "We'll be taking our revenge soon, lads!" he said cheerfully. "If the Hadendoa come, aim low and listen to the word of command!"

Kerswell looked up. "We will, sir." He patted the lock of his rifle. "They haven't met old Marty yet!"

The square marched for two hours with the heat steadily increasing and the scrub silent on each side except for the hum of insects. As they approached the site of Baker's defeat, the skeletons lay in hundreds, some still kneeling with their hands raised for mercy.

"Look at these beggars," a teenage soldier said. "Most of them are lying on their faces, and would you look at the wounds?"

The spears had gouged into the desiccated flesh, broken ribs and even the spine in their passage. The British soldiers had to step over the remains, muttering in horror or voicing their anger. Second Lieutenant Moffat stopped to vomit beside the line of march.

"Head up, Moffat," Jack said. "It's not a pretty sight, but their suffering is over now. Take a swig of water and march on!"

"Yes, sir," the boy said unhappily, wiping his mouth.

Sergeant Hanley viewed the scene. "Their dead will be left unburied,

And the stench of rotting bodies will fill the land," he murmured. "That's from Isiah, 34:3."

"This is no time to quote the Bible," Deblin said. "This is a time to ensure your rifle is loaded and your bayonet is sharp!"

A few hundred yards past Baker's battlefield, the forward scouts returned.

"The enemy is ahead, sir," they reported to Graham. "They're on a small hill, with banners displayed and a couple of cannon."

"They're covering the wells of El Teb," Baker told Graham.

Jack focussed his field glasses ahead. Osman Digna had added more earthworks and rifle pits to the fortifications he had noted two days earlier.

"Close ranks," Jack ordered. "Fix bayonets! Sarsens, take half A Company to the left rear and watch for the enemy. If you see them, don't engage unless you've no choice. Retire to the square."

"Yes, sir!" Sarsens said and called on his men.

Jack watched them trot off, with Sarsens in the lead. It was customary in war to send the best and brightest to the most dangerous spot, which meant that these bloody, wasteful wars at the back end of the world cost Britain some of its finest young officers.

Is it worth the constant dribble of good men to act as the world's policeman and occupy a desert? Is it worth fighting for a town that may be full of corpses?

When the enemy fired their Krupps artillery, the first shots were far too high. The shell bursts prettily against the blue sky, with the smoke drifting and some younger soldiers watching nervously.

"Face your front, lads!" the sergeants advised. "That's what soldiers do. Ignore the shine."

In the front of the square, the Gordons marched solidly on, kicking up dust clouds, green kilts rustling and rifles against their shoulders. A few Arabs rose from behind thorn bushes and ran as the British advanced. One fired his Remington rifle, with the shot whistling overhead.

"The Gordons are coming for you!" one man shouted. "Bydand, you bastards!"

Graham spoke to a bugler, and the call to halt sounded. The square stopped, with the dust slowly settling and men looking at each other. In every direction except the enemy-occupied ridge, the scrubby, thorn-bush-covered desert stretched towards a limitless horizon.

"Loch Long, and it far away," an officer of the Black Watch muttered and raised his voice. "We're not in Perth now, lads. Make sure your rifles are loaded!"

The enemy's artillery fired again, with the shots screaming overhead to burst between the square and the following cavalry.

"Steady, lads," Jack toured the Malverns, exchanging a word

with his officers, acknowledging the men he had served with in Afghanistan and on the field of Tel-el-Kebir. "Remember to listen for the word of command and aim low. Don't mind their yelling; trust your mates, and you'll be fine!"

Brotheridge hawked and spat on the ground. "Well, Kersey, if we die today, we don't have to die tomorrow."

Kerswell grunted. "If we're dead, we don't have to listen to that bastard Deblin's grating voice."

"I heard that, Kerswell!" RSM Deblin snarled, walking past.

Osman Digna's artillery fired again, with the shells exploding closer to the square, lifting fountains of sand and small stones. Acrid smoke drifted over the marching soldiers.

"Missed!" one of the Gordons shouted, and others whistled and jeered.

Jack rode to the front of the square and scanned the enemy positions through his field glasses. The ridge ran northeast to southwest, with a profusion of flags above an old graveyard on a hillock at the north-eastern extremity. The Krupps guns rested behind an earthwork on the facing slope of the southwestern peak, while a low rise in the middle held enemy riflemen.

Jack saw the guns fire again, with the jet of flame and smoke visible a second before the sound reached him.

"Over there!" Captain Holmes of the Royal Artillery shouted and brought his seven-pounders into action. The sharp crack of the British artillery heartened the infantrymen.

"That's the stuff to give them!" Private Kerswell shouted.

"That's the give to stuff them!" Brotheridge amended and laughed at his play of words.

"Don't you mind these rough men," Wheelie Wright said to Nicky, the regimental dog, as Branley kept his mules calm.

When the enemy artillerymen altered their aim, the shells crept closer. Private Morgan fell back, swearing, as a shell splinter tore across his chest. Dr Park leapt to his side, and Jack walked Tinker behind his Malverns, openly sharing the danger.

"They've got the general!" Lang shouted excitedly.

For a moment, Jack thought that enemy fire had hit General Graham, but it was Baker who reeled in his saddle, holding his face. A shell had exploded above him, with a sliver of shrapnel slicing the skin under his eye. As the artillery duel continued, Baker recovered, holding a handkerchief to the wound, and forced himself upright in the saddle. After a few moments, an aide-de-camp helped him off his horse.

"Come to the surgeon, sir!"

After a few moments' protest, Baker allowed the aide-de-camp to lead him away. He returned shortly afterwards with his face bandaged.

"Say what you like about General Baker," Bryant said, "he's got guts."

"If he hadn't," Jack said, "he would not have survived as a British officer." *That was true. Stupidity, pig-headed idiocy, and arrogance were permitted as long as an officer showed courage.*

The Royal Artillery soon proved their superiority over the entrenched enemy guns, with shrapnel exploding immediately above the Krupps' emplacements. After a few rounds, the Ansar's artillery stopped firing, and Jack saw a crowd of men drag their guns to a different position.

"Round one to the Royal Artillery," Jack said.

"Saint Barbara will be proud of them," Lang murmured.[1]

With the enemy artillery temporarily silenced, General Baker ordered the square to advance again. They marched to the right of Osman Digna's entrenchments, with the enemy firing rifles at long range and with little effect. When the British passed the ridge, Graham inclined the square to the left, so they were now behind Osman Digna's position. A thousand yards from the entrenchments, Graham ordered a slow advance toward the enemy. The Black Watch and the Malverns were now the leading regiments, and a Black Watch piper struck up a martial air.

"God," Private Brotheridge grumbled. "As if heat, dust, gunfire and flies were not enough, now the Jocks are strangling a pig!"

"You'll be glad of the Jocks when the fighting starts," Sergeant Hanley replied. "Load!"

Brotheridge muttered something incomprehensible and slid a cartridge into the breech of his rifle.

"We're directly in the firing line, men," Jack warned. "Be ready for the enemy to charge at us."

"We're ready, sir," Sarsens said as the senior officers passed Jack's words to the subalterns, who told the NCOs.

Osman Digna's remaining guns opened up again, causing several casualties. Jack saw Lieutenant Royds, one of the seamen from HMS *Carysfort*, crumple as a shell burst beside him.

A sailor should not die in the desert, far from the sea.

Sitting snug behind entrenchments and rifle pits, the enemy riflemen opened a heavy fire on the advancing square. Jack saw Private Barthorp stagger as a bullet hit him high in the chest. His back marker stopped to look after him until a sergeant barked to get back in line.

"Leave him for the doolie bearers, Mathews!"

"Close ranks!" Jack ordered. "Hold your fire until I give the word!" He saw another man fall to writhe on the ground, screaming and holding his belly. The square thrust on, with some men white under their covering of dust and others looking grim. The Black Watch's piper stepped in front of the regiment, marching with a swagger as he encouraged the men to war. Now none of the Malverns complained about the wild music from the Scottish hills.

The enemy's firing suddenly stopped, and all Jack could hear was the bagpipes, the throb of tom-toms and the monotonous crunch of boots on the desert sand.

"Get ready, lads!" Jack shouted.

The Hadendoa and Arabs hoisted their flags, yelled fiercely, and charged with the same courage and ferocity that had broken Baker's square on nearly the same ground. Waving spears and swords and covering their heads with small shields, they ran onto the front and flanks of the square. The Black Watch, the

York and Lancaster, the Malverns and the Naval Brigade faced the brunt of the attack.

While Jack had expected a mass charge by thousands, the Hadendoa advanced in groups, some of twenty to thirty and others of only a handful, with the occasional lone warrior hurling himself against the British ranks. Each man held a spear or a long-bladed sword and advanced with incredible courage. Some sheltered behind their tough rhinoceros-hide shields as they threw themselves at the British square, yelling, with their distinctive hairstyles bobbing.

"Company commanders!" Jack said. "Fire when you think it best!" He wished to be at the forefront, making the decisions, but the captains and lieutenants knew their men. The first volleys crashed out, with the grey-white smoke jetting forward with the red tongues of the muzzle flares.

The Hadendoa charged into the volleys without a single man hesitating as they ran to their deaths. They knew a death fighting the Nasrani – the Nazarenes or Christians - was a ticket to Paradise, where all sensual delights waited. The British soldiers obliged, firing low, working the Martini Henry's ejection lever, thumbing in a fresh cartridge, and firing again.

"Come on, you bastards," Brotheridge invited. "The Malverns are waiting for you!"

"Come and meet Marty!" Kerswell yelled.

The volleys crackled all around the square, felling the attackers long before they reached the waiting bayonets. Within a few moments, the Hadendoa learned that their opponents were a different breed from the reluctant fellaheen that filled the Egyptian ranks. These were British soldiers recruited from England's city slums and sodden fields, the glens and industrial towns of Scotland and Ireland's limestone wastes and rolling countryside. These men had two thousand years of warrior blood in their veins, backed by regimental pride and the acid tongues of veteran sergeants. They also knew how to use their Martini-Henrys and the chattering machine guns.

"Fire!" Sarsens ordered, and another volley crashed out.

"Fire!" Jamieson snapped, and the smoke and fire blazed across the parched scrubland.

"Fire!" Lieutenant Jarvis shouted, aiming his revolver at the charging Hadendoa.

The Black Watch piper stepped forward, facing the enemy as his music wailed to the sky. In the distance, on the far side of the square, the pipers of the Gordon Highlanders likewise encouraged their riflemen.

On the York and Lancaster's flank, the Hadendoa pressed harder, lying low when the volleys came, then bounding up and charging with the spears. The infantry met them bayonet to bayonet, men from the hard mill towns and bleak moors of Yorkshire and Lancashire clashing with the courageous warriors of the desert.

Again and again, the Hadendoa continued their near-suicidal charges, throwing spears and brandishing swords as they rushed through the scrub towards the levelled rifles and lines of bayonets.

Jack remained behind his men, firing his revolver when the Hadendoa approached, allowing his junior officers to make the decisions for their companies and watching the course of the battle. After half an hour, the tribesmen's attacks faltered, and they fell back, with the British still firing volleys at them.

"Cease fire, Malverns," Jack ordered, and the trumpeter's call reinforced his words. The musketry died away, with the gun smoke drifting slowly across the battlefield and the men staring out over the carnage they had created. All around the square, dead and wounded Hadendoa lay still or writhed with the agony of their wounds.

When somebody began to cheer, Jack snarled at him to keep quiet. "That was only the first round," he said. "Reload!" Sending a subaltern for the water wagon, he ensured each man's canteen was full, replenished their ammunition pouches and ensured the surgeon treated the wounded.

"They'll come again," Jack said.

A few hundred yards away, the enemy waited in their entrenchments, with their flags limp under a brassy sky. Their tom-toms began again, the sound of Africa surrounding the waiting, sweating British soldiers.

Above the square, a score of vultures circled, waiting patiently for food.

CHAPTER TEN

So 'ere's to you, Fuzzy-Wuzzy, at your 'ome in the Soudan
You're a pore benighted 'eathen but a first-class fightin' man.
Rudyard Kipling

Jack checked his watch, swore when he realised he had neglected to wind it, and looked up when Sarsens shouted a warning.

"Here they come again!"

The Hadendoa had gathered their courage and returned to the attack, not in dozens and scores, but thousands. They emerged from behind the ridge and, after the British repelled their initial rush with musketry, came a second time. Rather than expose themselves to the massed rifles, the Hadendoa ran from cover to cover, hiding behind the thorn bushes and in the folds of dead ground. The seamen fired their Gardner guns, with the multiple barrels throwing a curtain of bullets that scythed into men and bushes, killing dozens of brave warriors. Every time the Hadendoa tried to close, the machine guns and volleys of musketry laid them flat until they withdrew.

"They must be the bravest men in the world," Lang was gasping, white faced under his tan.

Jack agreed as he looked over the men lying on the hot sand. Already vultures were at work, tearing at the dead and dying with cruel beaks.

With the Hadendoa attacks beaten back, Graham ordered the bugler to sound the advance, and the British moved against the enemy. Now, the Black Watch were the leading regiment, with the Royal Malverns in support. Jack saw the tall, elegant figure of Colonel Burnaby among the Black Watch, holding a double-barrelled shotgun and moving as casually as though he were going on a pheasant shoot in his native Bedfordshire. Burnaby stood head and shoulders above the infantrymen as they advanced against the enemy rifle pits and entrenchments.

"With me, Malverns!" Jack stepped in front of his regiment. He held his sword in his right hand and his pistol in his left, saw a group of bearded bluejackets jogging beside the Malverns and pushed on.

The enemy sheltered behind their earthworks, bobbed up to fire and dodged back down again. Fortunately, they mostly fired high, but Jack heard shouts behind him, wondered who had been hit and strode on.

The first earthwork was shallow, with half a dozen defenders. Jack fired his pistol as he approached, saw the blaze of musketry, felt something tug at his sleeve and threw himself over the chest-high parapet. The next few seconds were a chaos of wild-eyed, lunging men, some with spears and others with swords or bayonets. He saw Brotheridge thrust his bayonet into a warrior's stomach, knock the man down with a shrewd swing of his rifle butt and plant a studded boot on his chest to extract the blade.

"That's you done for, Fuzzy!" Brotheridge growled.

A Hadendoa warrior swung his sword at Jack, who ducked and fired simultaneously. The bullet thudded into the man's right thigh, splintering the femur. The warrior spun, still trying to slash at Jack, and Donnelly fired. The heavy Martini bullet smashed into the warrior's head, spraying fragments of bone and a thin film of blood and brains over the back of the trench.

Jack nodded to Donnelly, who was reloading as Brotheridge vaulted out of the trench to seek further victims. Kerswell followed, fired at a running warrior, and stopped to thumb a cartridge into his rifle. A bullet whined overhead to thump into the sand a few yards away.

While Jack had been busy, the Malverns and Black Watch had surged past, fighting to clear a succession of rifle pits and earthworks. The piper had slung his pipes around his back and was advancing with a rifle and bayonet. Jack saw Burnaby riding forward, firing his shotgun into a trench.

"Major Baxter"

"Here, sir!" Baxter was panting with a revolver in his right hand.

"C Company is drifting to the right. Get them back in line!"

"I will, sir."

Jack saw an Arab rise from a trench, aim at Colonel Burnaby and fire. The shot hit Burnaby's horse, which collapsed, throwing the colonel onto the ground. Burnaby rose, shook his head, lifted his shotgun, and strode on.

Captain Wilson of HMS *Hecla* encouraged the Naval Brigade and the marines, shouting nautical oaths and waving his cutlass. He surged forward when half a dozen Hadendoa warriors rose from a rifle pit and charged at the marines, surrounding one man, and stabbing with their spears.

"No, you don't, you devils," Wilson roared. He thrust his sword deep into the chest of the nearest warrior and swore when the blade broke. Three Arabs attacked him, so Wilson used the broken sword as a knuckle duster, knocking two men down, but the third slashed at his head, slicing through his helmet, and cutting deep into the scalp. A red-headed marine finished off the surviving Arab and helped Wilson back to the medical team, where Surgeon-General Macdowell, an Irish veteran of many campaigns, dressed the wound.

Jack saw Wilson a few moments later, with his head

bandaged and wielding a long Hadendoa sword to replace his broken cutlass.

"This is a fine weapon, Windrush," Wilson said, grinning. "I might issue some to the hands!"

Jack moved on, trying to ignore the innocent-seeming puffs of sand where bullets ploughed around his feet. "What the devil is that ahead?"

The building looked incongruous amidst the desert vegetation, standing tall and square behind a copse of jagged thorn bushes.

"It looks like an old mill, sir," Major Bryant said. "I heard the Egyptians tried to harvest sugar cane here."

"Halt C Company," Jack said and lifted his field glasses. The defenders had loopholed the mill's walls and dug rifle pits in front. A rusted but huge and solid boiler stood behind the mill.

"Will I signal for the mountain guns, sir?" Bryant asked.

Jack made a quick decision. "No. They're too light to blast the walls, and I doubt we have the time to wait for them. Out here in the open, we're vulnerable to a Hadendoa counterattack, and Osman Digna will know that."

Before Jack finished speaking, the Black Watch cheered and charged forward with the seamen at their side.

Sarsens lifted his sword. "Come on, lads! Don't let the Jocks and the tarry-arses steal our glory!"

Glory? Where's the glory in getting killed fighting for a disused sugar mill in the middle of a desert?

Jack took a deep breath of the stifling air and charged as the Malverns lapped around him. Jack saw the rifle barrels protruding from the loopholes and men firing from the trenches in front of the mill. For a moment, he was no longer the man in command but a young officer racing to make his name.

"With me, Malverns!"

The mixed force of highlanders, seamen and Royal Malverns crashed over the trenches, firing at nearly point-blank range, and stabbing with long bayonets. Few of the defenders fled; most fought and died where they were. The seamen scrambled up the mill wall, grabbing hold of the protruding rifles and firing their pistols through the loopholes.

"Avast, you Arab devils! We've got your measure!"

Some of the Black Watch followed, with one man scrambling up the wall and his back marker handing him his rifle.

"Hey, Jock!" a grinning petty officer shouted. "You forgot your petticoats!"

"Aye, get tae Freuchie, ye tarry-backed bastard!" [1] The Highlander added a mixture of obscenities and profanity that impressed Jack, although he had lived with soldiers' foul language all his life.

Barnaby grunted, spun around, and fell as a shot hit him in the arm. "I'm all right!" he roared from the ground. "Push them back!"

After a few desperate moments, the British captured the mill and pushed on. The Gordon Highlanders passed over a shallow depression behind the ridge, bypassed a row of wells and advanced onto the village of El Teb. It was not much of a place, a group of mud and reed huts clustered on a small hill, but important amid the landscape of aridity. Osman Digna tried to make a stand here, and the Gordons had to resort to their bayonets and close-quarter musketry to clear the Arabs and Hadendoa.

"Bydand!" the kilted warriors yelled their regimental motto. "The Gordons are here!"

With the British infantry crashing over their defences, Osman Digna's army was in full retreat towards Tokar; Graham unleashed the cavalry. Jack had been too busy to hear the order that sent Colonel Barrow's 10th and 19th Hussars around Osman Digna's flank. As they moved forward with the squadrons in regular order, bridles jingling and horses' hooves thudding on the sand, the horsemen came to an area of small hills and dunes.

The Hadendoa waited there, and as the cavalry passed, they attacked. Some warriors rammed their broad-headed spears into horses or riders, and others threw them with incredible accuracy from fifty yards. A few lay on their backs and hamstrung the horses as they passed, with the riders finding it nearly impossible to reach the prone warriors with their swords.

Jack saw a body of thirty bareback Arab cavalry gallop against the Hussars and crash into them. The Hussars reacted immediately, gasping with effort as they slashed and thrust at the Arabs with their swords. Of the thirty Arabs, only three came through the Hussars' ranks unscathed but immediately turned around and charged back into the British cavalry.

A stalwart Hadendoa warrior poised and threw a spear that pierced Colonel Barrow's left arm and embedded itself in his stomach. As Barrow slumped in the saddle, the leaderless line of hussars continued in a straight line until General Stuart raced from the British lines to take command and wheel them around.

The cavalry action continued for two hours, with the horsemen repeatedly charging over the Arab and Hadendoa positions. At one point, the 19th Hussars wheeled around to see a mass of Arabs on camelback. The hussars charged and split the camel riders to find an even larger squadron of enemy horsemen behind the camels.

As the hussars burst through the camels, the Arab cavalry raised their two-edged swords and launched themselves forward. In the cut-and-thrust of cavalry combat, the 19th proved their mastery of the Arabs, but when they defeated the enemy horsemen, hundreds of Hadendoa infantry attacked them with spears. Major Slade of the 10th Hussars died there, with Lieutenant Probyn of the Bengal Cavalry and Lieutenant Freeman of the 19th Hussars.

The fight between the British cavalry and Hadendoa warriors was desperate, but Osman Digna's army eventually retreated, leaving General Graham commanding the field.

"See to the casualties, Dr Park," Jack ordered. He had lost two dead and six wounded out of a total British loss of thirty killed and a hundred and forty-two wounded.

"That's not a bad casualty list," Bryant said.

"Unless you happen to be one of the casualties," Jack said. "But we've proved the Ansar are not unbeatable. We faced one of the Mahdi's best commanders on his own soil and defeated him in defence and offence." He looked over his men, the battered soldiers in sweat-stained khaki who had faced and defeated the Hadendoa. Men with teeth like tombstones in an ancient cemetery, men dragged up in sour-smelling slums, men of small stature, born without hope and frequently without love, had faced and overcome the fiercest warriors of Sudan. "Our men did well, Bryant."

"They did, sir," Bryant agreed.

Buller had more details when he met Jack that evening. "We counted nine hundred Arab dead in Osman Digna's defensive position and another thousand where they attacked the square." He lit a cheroot with his large, capable hands. "There will be others, and we don't know how many enemy wounded will die." He grinned. "You could say we gave him a bloody nose."

"We did," Jack agreed. When he closed his eyes, he could see the Hadendoa charging, spears poised and long swords ready to kill, the screaming black faces under the thrusting hair. "They were brave men, fighting for what they believed."

"They were the enemy." Buller sounded surprised at Jack's point of view.

"They were," Jack agreed.

"Did you hear what the prisoners said?" Buller asked.

"I didn't know we took any prisoners," Jack admitted.

Buller smiled. "That's one of the disadvantages of being a regimental officer, Windrush. You are too intent on regimental details. You should try for a staff appointment."

"I'm happy with my Malverns. What did the prisoners say?"

"They didn't know they were fighting British soldiers until they saw our faces in battle. The chiefs kept that fact from them." Buller blew smoke into the air. "The prisoners said they didn't want to fight us. Their quarrel was with the Turks and Egyptians, the people who had oppressed them for years."

"I can agree with that," Jack said. "They've no quarrel with us, and we've none with them. Why the devil are we fighting each other?"

"We're doing our duty, Windrush." Buller's eyes narrowed. "We're doing our duty." He lowered his voice. "If I were you, Windrush, I would not voice your thoughts. It's unbecoming for a British officer." He walked away.

Jack grunted. He knew that Buller's advice was sound. An officer's first duty was to obey orders, and his second was to look after his men. If he questioned higher command, he imperilled discipline, which set a dangerous precedent. Now all they had to do was march to Tokar, withdraw any surviving Egyptians, and find this blasted explorer.

Private Brotheridge was discussing the late battle, holding up a Hadendoa sword he had liberated from the field. "These fuzzy-haired boys are the descendants of Saladin's Saracens, you see," he said. "Their ancestors captured the swords from the Crusaders. That's why they've got straight blades. They're nothing like the curvy Eastern swords we saw in Afghan."

"The Khyber knives weren't curvy," Kerswell said. "They were straight, like a butcher's cleaver."

Kerswell's facts did not faze Brotheridge. "The Paythans got them from Alexander the Great's army," he explained. "Everybody knows that."

Jack moved on. He saw Private Wright feeding his dog and a section returning from burial detail, weary and covered in dirt. More men were playing cards, already forgetting the recent scenes of slaughter.

You'll remember at nighttime, lads when you're alone with your thoughts.

Somebody else was singing a song Jack did not know while Sergeant Hanley was blasting a squad of defaulters. The cooks were cursing as they toiled over great fires in the desert heat, the adjutant fretted over administrative problems, and a veteran private sipped happily at his canteen that certainly did not contain water. Men cleaned their rifles and talked over the late battle, sergeants organised working parties, and the chaplain consoled the downcast.

All is as it should be in my regiment, Jack said. He had to remind himself that he had achieved his lifetime's ambition. He was Lieutenant-colonel of the Royal Malverns, his family regiment.

All should be right with the world. All we have to do now is rescue the survivors at Tokar and find this damned explorer.

CHAPTER ELEVEN

Men are generally more law-abiding than women. Women have the feeling that since they didn't make the rules, the rules have nothing to do with them.
Diane Johnson

General Graham left three companies of Gordon Highlanders at El Teb with orders to identify and bury the bodies of the European officers who had died in Baker's defeat. The remainder of the column marched towards Tokar, with the cavalry scouting and the men wary of a Hadendoa attack. After their experiences with the Hadendoa warriors, many hussars carried the long spears captured from the enemy to better fight men lying on the ground.

"Maybe the Mahdists have murdered everybody in Tokar," Baxter said.

"We'll soon see," Jack stared ahead, wondering if Osman Digna planned to stop the column before it reached Tokar. He remembered the horrors of the Mutiny and dreaded what he might find in the captured town.

At three in the afternoon, a column of dust heralded the return of the scouting cavalry.

"No sign of the enemy, sir," an eager lieutenant reported to Graham. "We rode to within a mile of Tokar without any problems."

Let's hope that this Drummond fellow is unharmed, or General Hook won't be pleased.

After two major battles, the eventual relief of Tokar was an anti-climax. Jack saw a solitary Arab horseman on the horizon as Graham's column marched towards the town without a shot fired.

"Where are Digna's men?" Baxter asked.

"Not here." Jack raised his voice. "Donnelly! You're with me!"

"Very good, sir!" Donnelly mounted his requisitioned horse and followed Jack to the head of the column.

"Watch for a British explorer," Jack said and trotted through the open gate.

Jack was not relieved there were no piles of dead bodies in Tokar. *Thank God for small mercies.*

The town was a small cluster of sun-dried brick buildings amid a sandy plain. As usual in Sudan, the houses were flat-roofed and low, neglected and dirty, with ramshackle huts of reeds and matting on the outskirts. A minaret thrust to the unforgiving sun, and women peered at Jack from behind barred windows until the men realised who the newcomers were and emerged into the street.

Christ would recognise villages like this.

"You're safe," Jack shouted in English and Arabic. "There's a British column behind us!"

However squalid the town, the people seemed pleased when Graham's force arrived. They gathered around the column, cheering, with the women ululating and the men waving. One tall Arab sat on a grey horse with a scarf across the lower half of his face and his eyes watching everything Jack did.

"I thought they didn't like Nazarenes here?" Moffat said.

"That's only when it suits them or when the men with

swords are listening." Service in Afghanistan and Egypt had turned Sarsens into a cynical young soldier.

Jack was not impressed with Tokar's fort. It was about three hundred yards by two hundred, with low mud walls surrounding a collection of small houses.

"A single decent rush could take this place," Buller said. "I doubt Osman Digna had to exert himself to besiege this garrison. All he had to do was camp nearby, and the Egyptians would give up."

"I am not sure what happened," Jack said.

Buller grunted. "You're too involved with your regiment, Windrush. The commander of the garrison and the Civil Governor were hand-in-hand with the Mahdists. Digna didn't have to mount a formal siege of Tokar because he knew he controlled the town in all but name. The governor surrendered the town and handed the inhabitants to the Mahdi."

"How about the garrison soldiers?" Jack asked. "And I heard there was a British explorer here, too."

Seventy of the Egyptian garrison had remained, with the others joining Osman Digna's men and agreeing to serve the Mahdi. Buller knew nothing about Drummond's whereabouts.

One man nearly hugged Sergeant Hanley as he led a section of Malverns into the fort. He spoke rapidly in Arabic until Hanley pushed him away with an expression of disgust. "What's this fellow gabbling about?"

Jack stepped over, pulled the Egyptian soldier aside, and asked him to repeat his words.

"You speak Arabic?" The Egyptian was nearly in tears.

"Some," Jack said.

"The Mahdi's men were going to kill us all," the man said. "After your General Graham defeated them, the Hadendoa wanted revenge."

"Were they going to kill all the garrison?" Jack asked.

"Everybody in Tokar," the man said.

"I'm glad we came, then," Jack said. "I'm looking for a

European; a traveller called Alexander Drummond. Have you seen him?"

"There are no Europeans in Tokar," the man replied. "Osman Digna would have killed them."

Jack nodded, thanked the man, and hid his disappointment.

The garrison soldiers looked gaunt and hungry, yet Jack's veterans soon uncovered sacks of grain hidden within the town.

"I don't understand this," Private Wright said, sipping at his water bottle. "There was food in the village, but the garrison was starving."

"Maybe they're not all thieving bastards like you, Wright," Brotheridge told him.

Wright considered for a moment. "Maybe that's right," he said. "I'd have been over these walls and into the village like a knife. I'd not starve, I'm telling you, boy!"

Brotheridge stamped his boot on the ground. "I can believe that. Now stop hogging the rum and pass it around. You're like a Scotchman with a penny on collection day, not giving anything away."

Jack moved on. So Wright was drinking rum. *I wonder what he swapped with the navy for that.*

Within a few moments, Jack saw a petty officer of the Naval Brigade with one of the long Hadendoa swords strapped to his waist.

My men swapped a captured sword for a bottle of navy rum. That's a good deal for both parties.

"Windrush!" Graham said. "You speak Arabic. I intend to evacuate everybody from Tokar who wish to leave. Find out who wants to come."

"Yes, sir." Jack knew that a British army officer was expected to obey every order, however unusual. Without fluent Arabic speakers in his regiment, he called on the NCOs with a version of British Army Arabic.

"You lads are experts in making yourself understood by all kinds of recruits and reluctant soldiers."

The NCOs nodded; some laughed.

"Now, I need you to make yourselves understood by these Arab people. I want them to gather outside the fort, where I can talk to them."

The sergeants grinned, stamped their feet, and got to work. As a young ensign, many years before, Jack had learned that the NCOs were the backbone of any regiment. Nothing that had happened in the intervening years had changed his mind.

"Come on, you Arab fellows! Let's be having you! Jildi now!"

Either the sergeant's natural authority or the tone of their voices convinced the population of Tokar to leave their homes. They gathered in front of the fort in a confused mass as Jack waited for them, standing on the wall.

He explained the situation and offered them all safe passage to Suakin. "You can only bring what you can carry, but you'll be safe from the Mahdi's warriors."

The populace listened with more attention than Jack had expected, then broke into a yammer of comments and questions. A sergeant roared for quiet in Herefordshire-Arabic, and a sudden silence fell, except for one child who began to cry. The roaring sergeant quickly picked up the child.

"Go home," Jack had to strain his Arabic to reach the crowd. "Let me know tomorrow." He waited for a second, and the sergeants took the hint.

"Parade dismissed!" the RSM roared, and the sergeants ushered the civilians back to their homes.

The tall Arab Jack had noted earlier rode up to the sentinels at the Malvern's camp.

"What are you after, Abdul?" Kerswell presented his rifle.

"Colonel Windrush," the Arab said.

"No, I'm Private Kerswell," Kerswell told him affably. "The colonel won't be disturbed by the likes of you. Now trot along back to your harem or whatever you call it and leave us alone."

"Take me to Colonel Windrush," the Arab demanded.

"I already told you, Abdul, Colonel Windrush won't be bothered by stray Arabs. Bugger off!"

"What's the trouble, Kerswell?" Jack asked.

"This Arab fellow wants to see you, sir." Kerswell snapped to attention. "I already told him to bugger off. Do you want me to boot his arse?"

"No, thank you, Kerswell." Jack nodded to the Arab. "Come with me." He led the Arab to his tent. "I presume you are not who you seem to be."

With the heat bouncing from the canvas walls, the Arab removed his *keffiyeh*, the traditional head covering. "I am Alexandrina Drummond," she said. "I believe you have been searching for me."

"You're a woman?" Jack could not disguise his surprise. "You're the explorer?"

"I am," Drummond said.

"No wonder General Hook wanted me to rescue you," Jack said. "God knows what Osman Digna would do if he captured a British woman."

"You may tell General Hook that I have no intention of being captured and will continue to travel," Drummond told him.

Jack had no experience with explorers. If anything, he had expected a bearded British man, a Speke, Grant, Livingston, or Burton, who was grateful to be rescued. Instead, he had a sun-browned woman in her early thirties with a deep voice, short-cropped hair and determined air. "You can tell him that yourself," Jack said, "the minute you meet him in Cairo. I have orders to take you back safely, and that's what I will do."

Drummond replaced her keffiyeh. "How do you intend to do that, Colonel Windrush?"

"Hopefully, you will cooperate," Jack said softly. "If not, I'll tie you to the back of a camel and put an armed guard on you."

"You'd do that to a British woman?" Drummond sounded more amused than afraid.

"If the occasion demands," Jack told her.

"You know," Drummond eyed him through musing eyes, "I rather believe you would."

"The choice is yours, madam," Jack said.

"Do you know who I am?" Drummond asked.

"No, Madam," Jack said. "I do not. Do you realise the Ansar control much of Sudan and Osman Digna's Hadendoa have already defeated a British-led army in this area? If you remain here, God only knows how much danger you are in."

Drummond nodded slowly. "I will not add to your difficulties, Colonel Windrush. I will allow you to take me to General Hook."

"That's very kind of you, Madam," Jack said. "Do I need to put you under an armed escort?"

"You do not, sir," Drummond replied. "Although I will inform General Hook that you suggested such an expediency."

"You can inform General Hook anything you damn well like," Jack responded to the implied threat. "I'll find a tent for you and assign you a servant and a guard to ensure your safety."

"I do carry a pistol," Drummond produced a revolver from within her robes, "and I have a knife."

"Shall I tell your guard you're a woman?" Jack asked.

"That depends on the guard," Drummond said.

Jack grunted and stepped outside his tent. "You!" He pointed to a passing private. "Wright! Find me Second Lieutenant Moffat and ask him to come to my tent."

"Yes, sir!" Wright slammed to attention, saluted, and marched away, with Nicky the dog running at his heels.

Moffat looked nervous as he reported for duty.

"I have a job for you, Moffat," Jack told him.

"Yes, sir?" Moffat's eyes slid across to Drummond.

"I want you to look after this lady," Jack chose his words. "Her name is Alexandrina Drummond, and only the three of us know she is not a man."

"Yes, sir," Moffat said.

"Corporal Borway is trustworthy, Moffat; take him into your confidence, find Miss Drummond a tent and ensure she is safe."

"Yes, sir," Moffat looked ready to faint.

"She is in your hands, Moffat," Jack said. "Dismiss. And Miss Drummond, I expect you to follow Lieutenant Moffat's orders."

"I'm sure we'll get along famously," Drummond said. "Come along, Lieutenant."

* * *

As the infantry settled in around Tokar, a cavalry patrol found a thousand Remington rifles and large quantities of ammunition in the nearby village of Dubbah. They destroyed the rifles and ammunition and recovered the artillery and Gatlings.

"That must be the munitions Digna gained from Baker's column," Baxter said. "Better in our hands than theirs."

Jack agreed. "The Hadendoa are dangerous enough with their spears."

Although Graham had defeated them, the Hadendoa still had spirit. On more than one occasion, corpses came back to life to maim or kill unwary sentries around Tokar and the old battlefield.

"Don't take chances," Jack warned his men. "If you have any doubt, thrust your bayonet into them. Don't think of mercy, for I'll guarantee they'll have none for you."

"You're very cold-blooded," Drummond had listened to Jack's words.

"I value my men's lives," Jack replied. "If the enemy fight honourably, then so shall I. If they resort to underhanded devices, I will do the same."

Drummond gave an ironic bow. "I wonder how the British public would view such actions."

"War is never like people imagine," Jack replied. "It is sordid, brutal, and ugly. The only thing that alleviates the horror of war is comradeship and bravery." He stamped away, not envying Moffat his job of looking after Drummond.

Just over a thousand people, men, women, and children, agreed to leave Tokar, with the remainder willing to chance Osman Digna's wrath rather than relocate to an uncertain future. Of the thousand, over a hundred had been criminals the Egyptian authorities sent to Sudan as punishment, and others were Egyptian soldiers desperate to return home. The residue were merchants, with sixty male villagers and over three hundred women and children.

"Where's Osman Digna?" Buller wandered over to Jack. "The cavalry can't find hair nor hide of him. It's like he's put his army into his pocket and vanished."

"He'll be around," Jack said. "He'll be watching us. Now we've relieved Tokar and rescued what remained of the garrison, I don't think there's much else for us to do here."

The sooner I get Alexandrina Drummond on a ship, the better. It's over fifty miles to Trinkitat, and Osman Digna could attack any time.

With the Mahdist threat lifted, General Graham decreased his forces at Tokar. He sent the Naval Brigade, Royal Marines, and 10th Hussars back to Trinkitat, leaving the Irish Fusiliers, the Yorks and Lancs, Royal Artillery, and Mounted Infantry with the 19th Hussars camped outside Tokar. The Black Watch remained at El Teb while the Rifles garrisoned Fort Baker and Trinkitat. One hundred and thirty of the sick and wounded boarded *Jumma* for the voyage to the hospital at Suez.

The heliograph winked across the desert from Trinkitat to Tokar, and a sweating messenger brought a message to Jack. After he read it, he ordered Baxter to parade the men. As they gathered, Buller walked toward him, adjusting his pith helmet.

"Ah, Windrush, here you are. What do you think of the current situation? And don't tell me we shouldn't be here."

"We're spread in penny packets around eastern Sudan," Jack was concerned that the army at Tokar had diminished. "If I were

Osman Digna, I'd concentrate my forces and flatten one of our camps to regain some morale."

"Digna doesn't think like us," Major Baxter pointed out. "Maybe we've caused him too many casualties to risk another battle."

Buller lit a cheroot. "My spies believe that Digna will continue the fight. We know he still has about three and a half thousand men within ten miles of Tokar and a further five thousand south of Suakin."

"He still vastly outnumbers us, then," Jack said.

Jack surveyed his regiment, drawn up in ranks before him, the men mostly all sun-browned with only a few still red-raw and peeling.

"He does," Buller said. "And he may wish to get his hands on your special guest."

Jack cursed. He should have known that there were no secrets in the British Army.

"Everybody is aware of your woman, Windrush," Buller said. "Who is she?"

"A friend of General Hook's," Jack told him as Baxter tactfully stepped out of hearing. "Some woman who likes to travel."

Buller frowned. "Drummond?"

"That's her," Jack said.

"I thought Alexander Drummond was a man." Buller shook his head and glanced at the Malverns, standing patiently in the glaring heat. "I'll leave you to your regiment, Windrush."

Jack waited until Buller rode away before addressing the Malverns. "I have a message for the regiment from the Queen," Jack said. "Her Majesty sent a telegraph to General Stephenson in Cairo, and he passed it on to us. I'll read it in full:

"Please convey congratulations and my deep sense of his service and of those under him to Sir Gerald Graham, as well my sorrow for the loss of the officers and men and my anxiety for the wounded."

When the men looked confused, Jack explained the contents.

"Her Majesty is congratulating us," he said. "Remember, we defeated an army of men who have vanquished larger armies of Egyptians armed with modern weapons. The Ansar – the Dervishes, as you know them - thought they were unbeatable, and we proved they were not."

The men looked at one another until RSM Deblin raised his powerful voice.

"Let's have three cheers for her Majesty, lads! Hip, hip!"

"Hooray!" The first cheer was half-hearted, so Deblin shook his head.

"Try that again and put some effort into it, or I'll have you all doubling around Tokar in full kit! Hip, hip!"

"Hooray!" The second and third cheers were louder, and Jack dismissed the men.

"That didn't go too well, sir," Baxter commented.

"These men didn't join up out of loyalty to the queen," Jack said. He looked up when Buller returned, smiling.

"We're moving out! General Graham's decided that the expeditionary force has achieved its object. We've defeated Osman Digna in open battle and relieved Tokar, and he's ordered us back to Suakin."

Thank the Lord for small mercies.

The Malverns struck camp within an hour and joined the column returning to Trinkitat. Only half a battalion of the Rifles and the mounted infantry remained at Fort Baker to ensure Osman Digna's warriors did not swoop on the stores.

"We're escorting the civilians," Jack told the Malverns. "Along with Colonel Ardagh of the intelligence service." He ensured Drummond remained separate, with Moffat as her permanent escort but Corporal Borway and Private Wright nearby.

"If she gives you any trouble," Jack said. "Report to me immediately."

"I will, sir," Moffat said.

Some of the Tokar civilians had changed their minds about

leaving, while others were waiting before the Malverns arrived. The transported criminals and Egyptian soldiers were most eager to return, jabbering in their enthusiasm to leave Tokar.

"Watch for stragglers," Jack warned as the untidy column set off. He had requisitioned, borrowed, and stolen as much transport as possible, with the elderly and young civilians mounted on donkeys, mules, and camels. The old soldiers and the quartermaster NCO had been most useful in gathering animals.

"Bloody Moses couldn't have done better," Brotheridge groused. "But he was leaving Egypt, not travelling there."

"He had more sense than us, then," Kerswell said. "Heat, dust, thirst, desert eye-strain, sand fly fever and bloody savages."

"And that's just in Cairo with the Jocks," Brotheridge added.

"Who are the Jocks?" Drummond perched easily on the back of a camel, listening to the conversation.

"Any Scottish regiment," Moffat explained. "Private Brotheridge doesn't like the Scots."

"Doesn't he know we're on the same side?" Drummond sounded amused.

"I'm not sure what Brotheridge knows," Moffat said.

Drummond smiled and looked away. "No, perhaps not."

By the time they reached Trinkitat, the officers and NCOs were exasperated. Escorting undisciplined civilians tried the patience of even the quietest man. Jack tried to ignore the sight of hard-bitten private soldiers with reputations for drunken violence carrying children and corporals with twenty years' service holding up staggering women.

"Come on, Missus," Wright encouraged a limping, heavily veiled woman. "We're nearly there! Only a mile or so to go."

Branley, looking more disreputable than ever, had perched an elderly man on one mule and a heavily pregnant woman on another and was leading them across the morass.

"You just sit still, and we'll get you across," Branley said, swore and plunged his hand into the water to reclaim a boot the mud had claimed. "It's not deep!"

"Get these people onto the beach!" Jack roared. "Captain Jamieson! Put that child back with its mother and organise the water carriers! Lieutenant Jarvis, escort these men across!" He splashed Tinker across to Drummond. "Are you all right, Madam?"

"Perfectly, thank you. Lieutenant Moffat is a consummate escort."

Jack grunted and rode away, rounding up the strays, ensuring the surgeon attended to the sick and lame, and checking the rearguard in case the Hadendoa returned.

"No sign of them, sir," Sarsens said. "I've posted pickets a quarter of a mile in the rear to give us advance warning."

"Well done, Sarsens. I'll leave the rearguard in your hands."

The beach was busy, with men rushing about loading troops, refugees, and stores into open boats for passage to the ships moored offshore. Piles of ammunition, tents, fodder, and spare parts for the guns waited on the beach, with frantic NCOs giving orders and trying to create organisation out of chaos.

"If the Hadendoa attack now, they'll not find much resistance, sir," Lang said.

Jack pointed to the warships offshore. "These lads would love a chance to show what they can do. Have you heard about the bombardment of Alexandria in '82? Now imagine that firepower unleashed on an army without fortifications."

As always, the Royal Naval seamen were busiest, each sailor working as hard as any two soldiers, carrying, loading, and encouraging with unique nautical phrases. As hard as they worked, the piles of stores on the beach did not seem to lessen as camels and mules arrived in a constant stream from Fort Baker.

"We'll need fourteen transports," Graham said. "We have ten here." he indicated the ships lying offshore. "I've asked for another four from Suakin. How are your refugees, Windrush?"

"All present and correct, sir," Jack reported. "A few found the journey rough, but my lads helped them."

Graham gave a rare smile. "Perfect combination, British soldiers and children. How about the explorer?"

"Quite serene, sir. Second Lieutenant Moffat acted as chaperone, guard, and adviser."

The Black Watch and 10th Hussars were the first regiments to leave the shore, with the others following. The seamen helped the refugees on board with typical efficient, good humour.

"On you come, my lady. Watch your starboard leg now. Lively there, my lad! The tide won't wait for you!"

Jack pulled Moffat aside. "How was Miss Drummond?"

"Not a whisper of trouble, sir," Moffat had matured over the past weeks. "Honestly, sir, she's very charming and has some fascinating anecdotes."

Jack accompanied Drummond onto *Osborne,* a small transport, where a long-nosed civilian took her under his wing.

"I'll take over now, Colonel Windrush."

Jack looked the man up and down. "And you are?"

"Sir Anthony Cockburn," the man spoke as if he expected Jack to know the name. "General Hook sent me."

"If Mr Drummond agrees," Jack said.

"I know this gentleman," Drummond reassured him. "Thank you, Colonel Windrush."

"It was a pleasure," Jack replied. He watched Cockburn escort Drummond onto the ship, sighed with relief and turned away.

"Thank God for the Navy," Jack said, thankful to hand over responsibility.

That's one problem less.

CHAPTER TWELVE

Men went to Catreth with the dawn, their high courage shortened their lives.
The Gododdin.

"They'll be safe here," Jack said cheerfully as the refugees landed in Suakin. He watched a steam launch nose alongside *Osborne* and a smart naval lieutenant escort Cockburn and Drummond to the flagship.

"Maybe not," Buller said. "Osman Digna wants revenge after his defeat, and he's massing his men a few miles inland. We may have taken the refugees out of the frying pan and into the Hadendoa fire." He nodded to the steam launch. "And as for that woman? I don't know what all the fuss is about."

"Nor do I," Jack mused. "I'm glad to see the back of her, though."

"The Mahdi's influence is spreading beyond Sudan," Buller said. "The Bedouins around Jeddah are rising against the Turks, and there are placards in Damascus encouraging people to drive the Turks out of Syria."

"If the Turks maltreat their people like the Egyptians do, maybe that's not a bad thing," Jack watched the first of Tokar's civilians file into Suakin. They looked lost, frightened, and confused.

"There's more to it than that," Buller said. "Turkey is Russia's longstanding enemy, and on the basis that the enemy of my enemy is my friend, we are, therefore, Turkey's bedfellow. If the Bedouin rebellion weakens Turkey, Russia may become emboldened and attack her, which could lead to the fall of Constantinople."

Lang's jingle ran through Jack's mind:

"We've fought the Bear before,
And while we're Britons true
The Russians shall not
Have Constantinople."

He shook away the nonsense words. "We certainly don't want to hand Russia a Mediterranean port to threaten the Suez Canal and our trade route to India."

"A Russian fleet in the Mediterranean could upset the balance of power. They're too cosy with the French as it is," Buller said.

Jack grunted, watching Drummond and Cockburn leave the steam launch. Admiral Hewitt and General Hook welcomed both onto the flagship. "Who the devil is that woman?" He shrugged. "No matter. What's been happening here when we were away?

"I've only heard rumours and speculation," Buller said. "Osman Digna is said to be camped only seventeen miles from Suakin, and there's another fellow named Osman Zubeir hanging around further south. Zubeir was involved in defeating Hicks Pasha."

Jack shook his head. "I don't know that name at all."

"Zubeir is said to be gathering an army to threaten Berber, and there's another Dervish fellow causing trouble in the Assouan area. Even around Cairo, the Bedouin tribesmen talk about a great British defeat. I presume they have heard a garbled account of Baker's disaster."

"The sooner we're out of Sudan, the better," Jack said. "This whole adventure is a waste of blood and money. Keep the Suez Canal secure, hand the rest of Egypt back to the Turks, or even better, the Egyptians, and let the Mahdi have Sudan."

Buller threw Jack a sidelong look and changed the subject. "General Graham is popular after his victory. When he returned to Suakin on board *Sphinx*, the crew of HMS *Euryalus* manned the yards and cheered him to the echo."

Jack nodded. "We seem to need a hero." He wondered what old Colin Campbell or Havelock would have thought of such a reaction. Campbell would have grunted and looked away, and Henry Havelock died before people could appreciate his series of victories. "I must leave you, Buller. My lads are guarding the town tonight."

Buller nodded. "No rest for the wicked, eh? You should find yourself a staff appointment, Windrush. More appreciation and less footling about looking at returns for boots and pith helmets."

"Thank you for your advice, Buller," Jack said and strolled to the Malverns.

Brilliant stars punctured the sky, with a half-moon throwing weird light across the desert. Jack rode around the pickets, speaking to the officers and men, gauging their morale, and scanning the land outside. He reconstituted the Malvern's mounted infantry and organised mobile patrols between the forts.

"All well, Lang?"

"Yes, sir," Lang reported.

Jack checked his watch. "Should Moffat not be here?"

"Something must have held him up, sir," Lang reported.

Jack frowned as Moffat ran from the town, adjusting his uniform.

"Where have you been, Moffat?" Jack checked his watch. "You're three minutes behind your time."

"Yes, sir," Moffat panted. "Sorry, sir."

"If Lang had not been conscientious and remained after his time, there would not have been an officer at this post," Jack did not hide his displeasure. "Osman Digna might have attacked and taken the town."

"Yes, sir," Moffat said.

"Consider yourself reprimanded, Moffat, and you're duty officer all week."

"Yes, sir," Moffat said again.

Jack rode on. *It's unlike Moffat to be lax in his duty. I hope the lad's all right.* He heard the drumbeat of hooves ahead and signalled to his escort. "Ready your rifles, men!"

"It's a British officer, sir," Donnelly said.

General Graham pulled ahead of his aides-de-camp and signalled for Jack to join him.

"Don't get too settled in Suakin, Windrush," Graham said. "We've not finished with Digna yet."

"What's happening, sir?"

"We taught him a lesson, but I want to ensure Suakin is safe before I leave. Britain can't afford to have a huge garrison here while we evacuate the rest of Sudan, and the best security we can have is to thrash Osman Digna and his Hadendoa."

Jack understood the logic. "I see, sir."

"We'll reorganise in Suakin, Windrush. Admiral Hewitt is about to sail to Abyssinia. He'll hand some of southern Sudan to King John to lessen the Mahdi's influence over the tribes on the border."

Jack nodded, wondering if the tribesmen on the Sudanese-Abyssinian frontier would suffer if arrogant rulers exchanged their lands.

"Keep your Malverns up to scratch, Windrush," Graham ended the conversation. "They did well at El Teb, and I'll take them with me when we smash Osman Digna."

"Thank you, sir," Jack said. "The Royal Malverns will be ready."

* * *

"Windrush!" Buller met Jack as he returned from visiting the outposts the following morning. "You won't have heard yet."

"Heard what?" Jack asked.

"That woman, Drummond, absconded last night!" Buller was usually a phlegmatic man, but now he pulled at his moustache in agitation.

"Ran where?"

"Out of Suakin," Buller said. "She slipped away from her quarters during the night."

"She didn't get past my lads!"

"No," Buller said. "She lifted a couple of camels and scampered along the coast. Hook is blazing mad with Cockburn, who was meant to keep an eye on her."

"Alexandrina Drummond struck me as a very capable woman," Jack said. "If she set her mind to something, I am sure she would succeed." He stepped away. He had brought Alexandrina Drummond from Tokar to Suakin and handed her over to Cockburn. She was a grown woman, well able to make her own decisions.

Or did she have help? Drummond and Moffat had become friendly, and Moffat was late on duty. Jack shook his head. He had dealt with Moffat and was adding two and two to come up with five. *Forget Drummond, Jack. You have a regiment to prepare for another campaign.*

* * *

On the night of the 11th of March 1884, Graham's column camped about ten miles from Osman Digna's camp at the Wells of Tamai. The British immediately created a zareba, cutting thorn bushes and laying them with the trunks inward and the thorny vegetation facing outside.

"We might be fighting tomorrow," Jack told his officers. "Tell your men to get whatever sleep they can and wake them early. I want every man to have a decent breakfast."

The officers nodded and returned to their duties. Jack lit a cheroot and toured the defences, listening to the murmur of the soldiers, gauging their mood by the banter, and speaking to NCOs and men.

"How's Nicky, Wheelie?"

Pleased that the colonel knew his nickname, Private Wright ruffled his dog's fur. "He's doing fine, sir, thank you."

"Glad to hear it. I'm going to promote Nicky to corporal soon, Wheelie, and he'll be giving you orders."

Wright grinned. "He'd make an excellent NCO, sir!"

Jack moved on, acknowledged Branley's clumsy salute with a raised hand, and approached RSM Deblin.

"How are the men, RSM?"

Deblin pondered for a moment. "They're ready to fight, sir."

"That's why we're here, RSM," Jack said softly.

The men slept with their rifles at their sides. Above them, a bright moon and brilliant stars punctured the sky, with the desert outside empty and silent, until around one in the morning, when an unseen rifleman fired into the camp.

"Stand to!" The bugles sounded, and men scrambled to their positions, peering over the thorn barrier into the dark, muttering curses and brushing the sleep from their eyes. Jack unholstered his revolver and waited for the rush of Hadendoa tribesmen. Nothing happened. Graham sent out a cavalry patrol, who advanced cautiously, circled the zareba and returned, having seen nobody.

"Get back to sleep, men," Jack ordered. He paced inside the zareba until Donnelly and Major Bryant ushered him back to bed.

"We'll need you to be sharp tomorrow, sir," Donnelly said.

Jack slept fitfully, dreamed of the Mutiny, and stared up, bleary-eyed, when Donnelly woke him with a mug of strong coffee.

"Reveille will sound in ten minutes, sir."

"Do you ever sleep, Donnelly?"

"Like a baby, sir. Will that be all?" Donnelly stepped back and stood at attention.

"Yes, thank you, Donnelly."

The trill of the bugle woke the camp, and Jack watched the men stir, some to immediately check their rifles, others to stagger to the latrine pits or lie for a few moments, gathering their thoughts. Branley spoke to his mules with his bootlaces trailing and tunic unfastened.

As the men breakfasted, a force of cavalry and mounted infantry rode into the zareba, and Graham ordered the mounted infantry back on patrol and consulted his intelligence officer, Colonel Ardagh. Irish-born, Ardagh was also an engineer, a thin-faced, much-experienced man that Jack respected.

As Jack ensured his men had full water bottles and weeded out the reluctant sick, the mounted infantry returned.

"Osman Digna's out in force, sir, about six miles distant!"

A thrill of anticipation ran through the camp. Graham worked out the order of march and set off from the zareba. The sun seemed hotter than usual that day, and Jack was glad he had requisitioned extra water for his men. He ordered Moffat to take charge of the water-carrying mules.

"Sir?"

"The lads need water, Moffat," Jack said.

Halting frequently to prevent sunstroke, the column trudged across the unrelenting plain, seeking the enemy and finding only the empty desert until a haze of dust announced the return of the cavalry scouts.

Jack checked his watch. "Five in the evening," he said. "It will be dark in an hour." He waited for the scouts' news to filter down.

"Digna's forces are two miles ahead, sir," a panting mounted infantryman reported. "They're advancing towards us!"

General Graham marched the column to the crest of a slight ridge. "This will do," he said. "We have a clear field of fire in front when the Hadendoa attack."

"Sergeant Anderson!" Jack ordered, "Get your pioneers to cut down thorn bushes and make a barrier in front of the regiment!"

He watched as the pioneers hurried to obey. With every battalion commander giving similar orders, the pioneers, together with the engineers, hacked at the prickly mimosa bushes that covered the ground. "Captain Sarsens!" Jack said. "Take A Company and give the pioneers a hand!"

The British regiments stood in formation, looking outwards, each man holding his rifle, waiting for the rushing enemy. Every moment they gained was vital, with a completed zareba a formidable obstacle for even the Hadendoa.

"Check your ammunition, men," Jack strolled along the double rank of the Malverns, trying to appear calm. "Make sure there is no dust in the locks and your bayonets slide out easily."

The light was fading, with the sun nearly touching the western horizon. Graham ordered the cavalry and mounted infantry to the previous night's zareba to escort a supply convoy.

"Now there's a tempting target for the Arabs," Baxter said. "Graham should have sorted that two hours ago."

As the darkness deepened, the glow of the enemy's campfires lit up the horizon.

"The Mahdists are not coming tonight, then," Baxter said.

"The longer they delay, the stronger our zareba," Jack said. "I want double pickets tonight in case the Hadendoa attack in the dark."

At eight in the evening, Graham ordered a ration of grog, and men queued, mugs at the ready.

"That's the way to end the night," Brotheridge said.

"Rum, rum, give me rum," Kerswell chanted. "Rum, rum, give me rum."

Two miles distant, Osman Digna's campfires sent their flickering light to the distant sky. At about nine that night, the Ansar occupied a ridge a thousand yards distant from the British and began long-range sniping. When the bullets whined over the zareba, Graham summoned Major Holley of the Royal Artillery.

"Show them the error of their ways, Major Holley," Graham ordered, and two of the mountain guns replied with shrapnel. The first shots were wide, but the next burst directly over the enemy positions.

The sniping stopped when Captain Rolfe and his seamen aimed a Gardner gun at the ridge and opened accurate fire. In its place came the beating of tom-toms and an occasional high yell.

During the brief artillery duel, the cavalry escorted the supply convoy to safety inside the zareba. Two hundred and forty-five camels carried two days' water supply, over four thousand rations, reserve ammunition and forage for the twelve hundred horses.

"Now Osman Digna can attack and welcome," Sarsens said. "We've sufficient spare ammunition to shoot all his men three times over."

"Windrush," General Graham said. "I believe you served on the North West Frontier."

"Yes, sir."

"You'll know how to dodge and hide then. Accompany Captain Rolfe on a scouting mission. I want to know what the Dervishes are doing."

"Yes, sir." *Dervishes again.*

Rolfe was a bearded and eager man in his thirties. "On we go then, Colonel," he said. "Let's see what's happening over the hill."

Giving Donnelly stern orders to remain behind, Jack slid outside the dubious security of the zareba with Rolfe at his side. With the sun down, the night was cold, but stars and a bright moon provided plenty of light. Jack showed Rolfe how to move quietly, and they drifted from mimosa bush to mimosa bush, watching for moving shadows that could signify one of the Hadendoa creeping up on them.

They crossed the open ground to the ridge without incident, and Jack signalled a halt in case the Hadendoa were watching them approach. After a few moments, he led them on again, climbing up the thorny slope, careful of dry twigs and sliding from shadow to shadow. Jack stopped again when voices came to him, but when he realised they came from the far side of the ridge, he continued.

The first body lay crumpled in a slight depression, with slivers of shrapnel embedded in the head and upper body. Jack ensured the man was dead and moved on. He did not need to check the second body, for a British shell had taken off an arm and half the skull. Grey-pink brain matter had oozed onto the sand.

Rolfe nodded grimly. "Good shooting," he said.

All around them, machine gun bullets had ripped into the thorn bushes or embedded themselves in the sand.

"Shall we return?" Rolfe asked.

"Not yet," Jack said. "If we crest the ridge, we can see who's making that hellish din."

Rolfe accentuated his grin, so his white teeth were visible. "Come on then, Colonel."

They climbed carefully until the sound of somebody snoring alerted them to the presence of a sentry. Jack fought his temptation to cut the man's throat. One warrior more or less would not affect the outcome of a battle. *Anyway, I'm a soldier, not a murderer.*

Leaving the snoring sentry, they reached the crest of the ridge and looked over. In the gleam of Digna's campfires, they saw men dancing while the murmur of conversation drifted to them.

If I had a couple of squadrons of the Guides, or Sikh cavalry, I'd send them to raid that camp. I wonder if Graham could send the Hussars.

"Have we seen enough, Colonel?"

"We have," Jack said. "We'll report to General Graham."

They returned at speed, avoiding the sentries, and nearly running back to the British zareba.

Graham listened to Jack's report with grim satisfaction. "I've sent the hussars back to last night's zareba, Windrush. It would be too risky to send them without infantry and artillery support."

"As you say, sir." *Oh, for an hour of Havelock or Roberts and a regiment of Sikh irregular cavalry.*

By the time Jack returned, the Malverns' had settled for the night, with double pickets posted and each man sleeping beside his rifle.

"We'll be fighting tomorrow," Jack said.

"Yes, sir," Baxter agreed.

"You'd better get some sleep."

"You too, sir," Baxter said.

Jack had no sooner closed his eyes than one of the pickets shouted a challenge. He pushed himself upright, decided that the duty officer could take charge and dropped back to sleep. He was dimly aware of the distant crack of a rifle, turned over and returned to sleep.

"You slept well, sir." Donnelly was as immaculate as conditions allowed when he woke Jack with a mug of coffee. "You missed all the excitement."

"What happened?" Jack sipped at his coffee.

"The Dervishes have been firing at us throughout the night," Donnelly said. "They killed one poor fellow, Private Sheldon, of the York and Lancaster. Shot him as he slept so the poor fellow woke up dead. There were a few men wounded as well, a couple of camel drivers, four lads, and an officer."

Jack noted Donnelly's order of priority. "I heard a few bangs," he admitted.

Donnelly seemed disposed to talk as the bugler sounded reveille. "General Graham was a bit miffed, sir, and he got the

Naval Brigade to get their Gardner machine guns ready to retaliate."

"I didn't hear that," Jack admitted.

"They didn't fire," Donnelly said. "The seamen estimated the range between fourteen hundred and fifteen hundred yards by the interval between the muzzle flash and the sound. They were all set to retaliate." He shrugged. "But the general decided if we fired without effect, it would look bad, so we didn't reply at all."

Jack nodded. On the Northwest Frontier, it was a point of honour not to shoot back at snipers.

At seven, the cavalry returned with jingling spurs and bridles. The infantry watched them, and some openly wondered where they had been during the night.

"Are you scared of the dark?" Brotherstone taunted, and Kerswell and Doncaster joined in the jeers. The horsemen had hardly arrived before Brigadier-general Stewart sent the mounted infantry out of the zareba.

"Find the enemy," Stewart ordered.

"Windrush!" Graham strode through the Malverns' ranks, noticing everything without comment. "Where were the enemy camped last night?"

"Over the other side of that ridge, sir."

"Could you find it?"

"Yes, sir," Jack said.

"This is Asif." Graham beckoned forward a nervous-looking Arab. "Osman Digna's men took him prisoner. He told me the army was in a *khor,* a dry watercourse. Would you agree with that?"

Jack nodded. "I saw men dancing by a fire, sir. The fire may well have been within a watercourse." He pondered for a moment. "If so, the enemy could defend the sides."

Graham nodded. "Thank you, Colonel. I will act accordingly." He called together the staff officer and battalion commanders and split his army into two brigades.

"Gentlemen," Graham said. "We will advance in direct

echelon of brigade squares, with Davis's Second Brigade leading. The regiments will march in open column of companies, with thirty yards between the columns. The Naval Brigade will operate their guns within each square, and the Royal Artillery's nine-pounder battery and the transport animals will march in the rear of the right front of Second Brigade's square."

Here we go again.

CHAPTER THIRTEEN

Oh God, if there be a God, save my soul, if I have a soul.
Prayer of a private soldier before the battle of Blenheim, 1704

Graham planned to advance to the left of the ravine where Osman Digna was based, occupy some high ground, and weaken the enemy's position with artillery fire before sending in the infantry. The Royal Malverns were in Buller's First Brigade, marching a thousand yards behind Davis's Second Brigade.

"We won't see much fighting back here," Kerswell grumbled.

Brotheridge stumbled over a loose stone. "Good. Let the other brigade do the work. We done our bit last time."

Jack noted the speakers and said nothing. He watched the surrounding countryside as they passed the ridge but saw no sign of the enemy.

General Davis's Second Brigade marched forward at half past eight, with Buller's First Brigade moving slightly slower, increasing the gap between the two formations. Beside the Malverns, the Royal Irish displayed their customary good humour, and the Rifle Brigade marched smartly, with their green uniform matching the kilts of the Gordon Highlanders.

The terrain was rough, harsh desert with mimosa bushes,

crossed by dry watercourses and deep nullahs or valleys, with boulders and detached rocks that broke up the formation.

"There's your friends, Brothers," Kerswell pointed upwards, where half-a-dozen vultures circled.

"These buggers know there's going to be dead bodies," Brotheridge said. "I hate them!"

Jack agreed. He did not like to see vultures feasting on dead or dying men.

In front of the infantry, two cavalry squadrons moved in open order, probing for the enemy. After half an hour of steady marching, a sudden irregular popping of musketry showed the horsemen had made contact with the enemy. Jack raised his field glasses and saw the cavalry had dismounted to fire their carbines at groups of rapidly advancing Hadendoa warriors. When the enemy closed, the cavalry mounted again and withdrew to the shelter of the leading infantry square.

After another fifteen minutes, with the Malverns moving on the right flank of the First Brigade, Jack saw movement around Davis's brigade.

"The Second Brigade's made contact with the enemy!"

A large force of Hadendoa emerged from a hidden ravine and charged the front of the leading square. Lifting his field glasses, Jack watched the course of the encounter.

The warriors ran towards the front of the square, where the Black Watch replied with volley fire. Jack heard the regular cracking of the rifles and saw the gun smoke rising above the mass. The charge faltered, and the Black Watch cheered and counter-attacked with the bayonet.

"Who gave that order?" Jack asked as the kilted Highlanders smashed into the wavering Hadendoa's ranks. Not expecting to be attacked, the Hadendoa resisted for a few moments, then fled, with the Black Watch chasing them to the lip of the ravine, stabbing with the bayonet, loading, firing, and loading again. In pursuing the enemy, the Black Watch advanced beyond the square, leaving the Yorks and Lancasters behind.

The Royal Artillery's four-gun battery stood outside Davis's square, with the gunners toiling in the heat as they fired grapeshot at the enemy. The rising dust and smoke hid the details from Jack until he saw another mass of Hadendoa rise from behind rocks a few hundred yards from the right flank and rear of the square. They charged the right-hand corner, where more of the York and Lancaster regiment stood. The Yorks and Lancs fired a volley, and then the Hadendoa emerged from the bank of gun smoke and smashed into them.

Jack swore as the Hadendoa fell to the ground, rolled, and crawled beneath the bayonets and the muzzle of the Gardner machine gun.

Major Holley's gunners continued to fire their seven-pounders, with each discharge of grapeshot felling dozens of the enemy.

Either because of poor visibility from the dust and smoke, a breakdown of command or the inexperience of the Yorks and Lancs, the right flank of the square collapsed. A horde of Hadendoa rushed inside, hacking with their swords, and thrusting with their spears as the British infantry fell back on the supporting Royal Marines.

"Dear God!" Jack said. "Buller! The Hadendoa have broken the square!"

"What?" Buller lifted his binoculars and studied the leading square. "We can't have that! Increase the pace, gentlemen!"

The square's interior was a mass of fighting, cursing, struggling men. The Hadendoa warriors caught the bayonets with their shields and stabbed with their spears as the British lunged, parried, swung with rifle butts, and kicked with their heavy, steel-studded boots.

Outside Davis's square, the Hadendoa surrounded the machine guns, slashing and stabbing with spears and swords. Unwilling to flee, the sailors disabled the guns and fell, fighting with cutlasses and fists, game to the end.

"Dear God! They've broken the square!" The news spread around Buller's brigade.

"Come on, lads!" Brotheridge roared. "Get the lead out, you idle bastards!"

Unaware of the disaster in their rear, the Black Watch continued to advance towards the ravine until an officer shouted an order, and they fell back to the square. As the front rank fought a renewed Mahdi attack, the second line of the Black Watch faced about. The men fought back-to-back, bayonets and rifle butts, boots, and fists against the long, double-edged Hadendoa swords and the probing, viciously sharp spears.

One section of Osman Digna's army saw Buller's brigade advancing and peeled off to attack. The sun glinted from the shovel-headed spears and long straight swords as the Hadendoa shouted their war cry.

"They're coming at us now!" Jack warned. "Royal Malverns! Stand by!"

"A Company! Load!" Sarsens roared. "Present!"

"Stand fast, the Malverns!" Baxter said, unholstering his pistol. He checked the chambers, pulled his horse closer to the men and waited.

The Hadendoa charged in a mass of screaming faces, with spears and swords raised and shields held in front.

"Wait until they're at five hundred yards!" Jack was aware of the chaos of Davis's brigade, where the British soldiers struggled to expel the attackers. "Aim low!"

The Hadendoa were five hundred and fifty yards away, five hundred and twenty, with the sun glinting off these deadly spears and swords. Jack thought of the piled-up skeletons where Baker's men had fallen. He saw a mass of screaming faces and smelt the grease from their hair, mixed with gun smoke and fear.

"Fire!"

Jack heard his words repeated all along the right side of Buller's square and then on the rear as the enemy lapped around. The volleys crashed out, jetting smoke around the square and knocking down scores of the Hadendoa. Despite their casualties, the Hadendoa pressed forward, with the warriors diving behind mimosa bushes and rocks or lying in the folds of ground to escape the British bullets.

A thrown spear thudded into the ground a few feet in front of Jack as he walked Tinker behind the Malverns' double line. He saw smoke rising from the British line of march and guessed Osman Digna had launched a simultaneous attack on the zarebas.

"Pick your targets!" Jack shouted. "Aim low and fire on the officer's command!" He saw Sarsens stepping in front of his men to be visible. "Sarsens! Get back behind your company! Somebody might shoot you by mistake!"

A bullet whizzed past Jack's head, and another smacked into the hospital wagon in the centre of the square, raising a shower of wood splinters.

"Here they come again!" Sergeant Hanley shouted. "Ready, boys!"

The Hadendoa emerged from behind their cover and charged again, reckless of the bullets that cut them down.

"They don't care about our fire!" Bromley had left his mules to join the firing line.

"They welcome it," Kerswell replied. "If they die fighting the infidels, they go straight to Paradise."

"Do they?" Brotheridge worked the underlever of his Martini, ejected the spent cartridge, thumbed in a bullet, and waited for the order to fire. "I can help them! Come on, you fuzzy-wuzzy bastards!"

"Aim!" Jack shouted. The Hadendoa were closer now. Each rush covered about thirty yards and left scores of bodies on the ground. The large calibre centre-fire Boxer bullets were man stoppers, blowing off arms and heads or leaving massive injuries in frail human bodies. However, the Martini-Henry, despite its power and accuracy, had faults. It possessed a tremendous recoil that quickly bruised the shoulders of inexperienced soldiers, and could overheat, which was not ideal when fighting in a scorching desert. The Hadendoa charged again, yelling as they bounded toward the thin British line.

"Fire!"

Another volley crashed out. More tribesmen fell. The soldiers reloaded, peering through the choking smoke, swearing, sweating, and fighting their fear. Jack heard trumpets shrill and saw squadron after squadron of cavalry trot past to relieve some pressure on Davis's leading square.

"Sergeant Hanley!" A desperate soldier struggled with his rifle. The thin brass cartridge had jammed in the breech as the private worked the ejector lever.

Hanley stepped across, yanked out the offending cartridge with a clasp knife and handed the rifle back. "Keep calm, son; you're a soldier, not a schoolgirl."

"They've gone!" An excited aide-de-camp waved his pith helmet to Buller. "The Dervishes have gone, sir!"

"Advance in formation!" Buller ordered. "Watch your flanks!"

Buller's brigade moved slowly forward, stepping over the dead and dying Hadendoa and drew close to Davis's beleaguered second brigade.

"Jesus, they're in trouble," Baxter said.

"Volley fire on the enemy!" Buller ordered. "Make sure you don't hit our men!"

Swathes of the Hadendoa altered their attack from Davis's brigade and surged towards Buller's square. One mass headed directly for the Malverns, with the sun glinting from wickedly sharp spearheads and sword blades.

"Fire when they reach three hundred yards," Jack ordered. He focussed his field glasses on the broken square and saw the British soldiers gradually pushing out the Hadendoa. The Black Watch and the York and Lancasters fought side by side, with men falling to spear and sword but still thrusting and stabbing with the bayonets.

Two officers of the Black Watch were in the forefront, each man busy with his broadsword. Jack saw one plunge his sword right up to the hilt in a spear-waving warrior, withdraw it and face another. Colonel Green of the same regiment had blood running down his face from a wound in his ear but did not flinch when a thrown spear scraped against his holster. Around the officers, kilted highlanders fought bayonet-to-spear with Hadendoa warriors. They thrust their bayonets into naked stomachs, parried desperately and gradually pushed the enemy away.

Even through the crashing thunder of the volleys and yells of the Hadendoa, Jack realised there was a commotion behind Buller's square. He swivelled in his saddle and saw a small water convoy approaching from the zareba. A single Arab warrior ran at the convoy until Sergeant Deng stepped from the convoy and shot the Arab dead.

Well done, Deng. We need water as much as ammunition out here.

Buller, as unemotional as a lump of granite, marched his brigade to the right of Davis's. On the left, the cavalry dismounted and opened fire with their carbines. In their khaki drill frocks, blue pantaloons and puttees, the 10th Hussars proved themselves capable foot soldiers, firing and withdrawing, stinging the Hadendoa mass. Buller grunted when a bullet perforated his horse's ear, switched mounts, and continued.

Jack rode inside the Malverns' line, encouraging the men by his presence, giving sharp orders when needed and occasionally dismounting to free a jammed cartridge.

"Fire!" Captain Sarsens shouted, and A Company fired, with the heavy bullets smashing into the Hadendoa.

"Fire!" Jamieson roared, and C Company fired.

"Fire!" A shout rose from Davis's brigade, and one entire flank fired, catching the enemy in a vicious crossfire.

"Fire!"

The Malverns, Royal Irish Fusiliers, Gordons and Rifles fired their deadly controlled volleys.

"We're winning, sir!" somebody shouted, and Jack watched as the Scottish, Irish, and English soldiers expelled the last of the enemy from Davis's square. They moved forward and recaptured the Gatling guns, with the seamen lying where they had fallen. Jack noticed that one sailor still gripped the hilt of his broken cutlass and wondered at the parsimonious government that sent brave men to war with inferior weapons.

Some arms manufacturer made his profit by using cheap steel, and that poor lad paid with his life. I hope the company director chokes on his bank balance.

A handful Jack's men raised a cheer as the two squares came closer, with the ground carpeted with dead and wounded tribesmen. One warrior lay prone until the Malverns were three feet away, then rose and lunged with his spear.

"No, you don't, you shamming bastard!" Brotheridge snarled and thrust his bayonet into the man's stomach. "I know your dirty tricks!"

The Hadendoa began to pull back, slowly and with no sign of panic, with the British still firing, still causing casualties. The terrible chatter of the machine guns joined the regular hammer of musketry.

After the Hadendoa overran the navy's disabled machine guns, they pushed a Gatling into the ravine and set fire to the ammunition limber. A British working party recovered the weapon, but the flames were too advanced on the limber, so the ammunition crackled for the next half hour, with bullets hissing overhead.

"Enough," Jack said, sickened by the slaughter. "Cease fire."

The musketry across both brigades gradually ceased, and men stared at each other. Some were smiling, others shaking; one or two wept. One man began to sing, but nobody joined in. Wheelie Wright sunk to his knees beside Nicky while Branley left the firing line to tend to his mules.

"Casualty report," Jack called. He realised the firing from the zareba had also stopped and hoped the tiny garrison had repulsed the attack.

General Graham ordered the Second Brigade to follow the enemy to the lip of the ravine, with the First Brigade in support.

Jack glimpsed the carnage inside Davis's square, with dead and wounded British soldiers mingled with enemy corpses and men holding bent and broken bayonets.

One man stood over his mate, swearing, and shaking his head. "Pete had his bayonet," he said. "He done all he was taught and rammed it home, but the bugger caught it on his shield and the bayonet bent. Poor Pete hadn't got a chance! His bayonet folded, and the dervish bugger killed him. It bent, I tell you!" His voice rose in near-hysteria until a long-faced corporal put an arm around his shoulders.

Other men stood with twisted bayonets, and Jack wondered anew which arms manufacturer had profited by supplying poor-quality weapons to the British troops. "Anything for more profit," he said. "I'd love to get some of these creatures in the front line for a day. They don't care about men's lives, only about the size of their bank balance. Pure, utter vermin."

"It is easier for a camel to go through the eye of a needle than for a rich man to enter the Kingdom of God," Sergeant Hanley echoed Jack's thoughts. "Matthew nineteen, verse twenty-four."

A runner rode his sweating, dusty horse from Davis's brigade. "I have a message for Colonel Buller from General Graham!"

Buller rode forward. "Written or verbal?"

"Verbal, sir," the runner said. "The general asks you to follow up the enemy and capture and destroy his camp at the village of Tamai."

Buller nodded. "Please tell the general that the First Brigade will comply."

The runner saluted and rode away.

"Keep in the square formation," Buller said, "and advance."

The Gordon Highlanders were on the right, the Irish Fusiliers on the left, with the Malverns in support. The Rifles made up the rear, with Major Gough's seven and nine-pounders of the Royal Artillery in the centre.

"Our primary objective is that second ridge." Buller pointed to a ragged ledge of rock about eight hundred yards away, hazy in the heat and drifting smoke. He lifted his hand and kicked his horse into motion.

"Come on, Malverns!" Jack shouted.

Buller's brigade followed the retreating enemy to the ravine and slid and slithered down the side, still in formation. They advanced over red granite, baked by the heat that burned the men's feet through their boots and reflected upwards. The crunch of iron-shod boots echoed in the ravine.

"Keep together, Malverns!" Jack shouted. "B Company, you're pressing too far ahead!" he addressed the line. "Captain Jamieson, your supporting line is too close; the men need more space to fire."

The retreating enemy gathered on the second ridge, with the sun reflecting from spear points and sword blades. A few Hadendoa tried to fight back with small groups of desperate warriors charging, but the British musketry swept them away, and Buller pushed the brigade on. They reformed on the opposite side of the ravine, with a vista of rocky ridges and heat-hazed rock before them.

"It's like looking into Hell," Sergeant Hanley whispered.

"We're going to capture Osman Digna's camp!" Buller announced and pointed ahead.

As the brigade advanced, the enemy melted away. Some fired, but when the British replied with company-strength volleys, they trotted away towards the higher ground.

Still moving as a square, Buller's brigade marched over the rugged ground, firing volleys to dispel threatening groups of the Hadendoa. They moved on, stumbling, swearing, sweating, and pushing the enemy before them. When the brigade ascended the next ridge, they saw Osman Digna's tented camp beside the village of Tamai, one hundred and eighty feet below.

"Over there, sir!" An aide-de-camp pointed to a mixed force of infantry and cavalry gathering on the left flank.

"Shell those fellows!" Buller ordered. Within a few moments, the Royal Artillery dispersed the enemy with half a dozen shells, and Buller ordered his brigade onward.

"Come on, Malverns!" Jack led his men towards the camp, where British shellfire had destroyed half a dozen huts and shrapnel had ripped into the canvas tents. A few score Hadendoa remained to fight, firing wildly, or running forward with raised spears.

"Skirmishers!" Jack shouted. "Clear these men away!"

The Malverns' skirmishers advanced, kneeling, firing, and reloading as the main body followed in a solid clump of khaki. The British swept the defenders aside and moved on with the Malverns in the van.

"Sir!" Sarsens shouted. "There's another village here!"

"Extended order! B Company, cover the right flank! C Company, cover the left. Skirmishers a hundred yards in front!"

As the British advanced, the enemy fired a few shots, threw half a dozen spears from long range, and melted away. The Malverns found three villages of mud huts and round tents, with the local people staring at the British soldiers in mixed fear and wonder.

"Check the houses!" Jack ordered.

Sergeant Hanley pushed inside the first house, rifle at the ready and two men at his back. He emerged a moment later, holding a Koran and a small bag of money. "We found these, sir!"

Jack looked inside the bag to find it full of silver Marie Theresa dollars, the common currency of northeast Africa. "Put the Koran back inside the house," Jack ordered. "We'll take any money we find."

Jack reasoned that as ordinary villagers would not have

money, it would belong to Osman Digna's forces. The Koran should remain in case the villages used their holy book.

Sacks of grain leaned against each house, and as the British skirmishers advanced, the Hadendoa warriors fled. The intermittent spatter of musketry died away.

"Sir!" A corporal ran from a hut with a green and black standard in his hand. "I've found Osman Digna's standard!"

"We've captured the villages and the standard," Jack said, "but not Osman Digna." When he checked his watch, it was 11.40 AM.

Baxter rode beside Jack. "Osman Digna put up quite a fight."

"He did," Jack said, lighting a cheroot. "And in a few years, nobody will remember the name of this victory. They'll only recall that the Hadendoa broke a British square. Not even the Zulus managed that."

"Burn the camp," Graham ordered. He sent Davis's brigade to occupy the wells. "Fill the water bottles and water the horses, then let the men rest."

As the British cared for their wounded, Jack learned that they had lost six officers and one hundred and five men, with a further eight officers and one hundred and three other ranks wounded.

The dead lay in piles, with heads, arms and legs lying where shrapnel or spears had sliced them off. Flies descended on the bodies like black fur, and already the vultures were busy feasting on the corpses.

The British gave a rough count of the enemy casualties, finding some two thousand bodies and others with no hope of survival.

"Watch for men feigning death," Sarsens advised. "They can rise and stab you in the back."

Veterans now, the British soldiers were not merciful, plunging bayonets into any warrior who seemed a threat.

While Davis's Second brigade occupied the rising ground

and the wells, Buller's First Brigade scoured the huts for weapons and ammunition.

"Torch the villages," Graham ordered. "Show the Mahdi what it means to stand against British troops."

As flames and smoke rose to smudge the clear air, refugees from the villages watched. The British salvaged any weapons and ammunition they could use and destroyed what remained, so the crackle and pop of exploding cartridges proclaimed their withdrawal.

"And so we say farewell to the village of Tamai," Lang murmured. "*Venit vidit victa*, we came, we saw, and we conquered."

"We came, we killed, and we left," Moffat said.

Jack stood at the head of the ridge, blinking away the smoke and staring at the desolation.

I hope it was worth all the deaths.

CHAPTER FOURTEEN

After the battle, may their souls get welcome in the land of Heaven, the dwelling-place of plenty.
Attributed to Aneirin, c600

When he saw the casualties, General Graham sent for ambulance wagons and mule cacolets - litters mounted on the animal's side.

"Carry these poor fellows to our first zareba," Graham ordered. "Mounted infantry, patrol the heights and watch for the Dervishes."

"What now, sir?" Bryant asked Jack as he presented his casualty report.

Jack drew on his cigar. "Back to Suakin, I think," he said. "And after that, it's in the Lord's hands. Or the generals."

The British victory must have tempered the Hadendoa's warlike spirit, for the night passed without incident, although the sentries reported voices and wailing from the battlefield.

"Maybe the Hadendoa women are looking for their dead," Jack hazarded. "Keep alert."

With Osman Digna's army defeated in two battles and his village destroyed, Graham withdrew his force to Suakin. He sent back the cavalry first, except for a single squadron to act as scouts. Two companies of the Black Watch, together with two hundred seamen, guarded the convoy of sick and wounded, with the ambulance and mule cacolets plodding between the double file of soldiers.

Within a few days, the entire force was back at Suakin, the desert wind blew away their footsteps, and only the mourning women remained as a memory the British had ever visited.

Jack called his officers together in their camp outside the town. "Well, gentlemen, we have now faced and fought the enemy in two actions, and we know their strengths and weaknesses. They are brave in the attack and press home. Their marksmanship is not so good, and, like the Egyptians, they fire high."

The officers nodded in agreement, and Baxter added, "We also know they pepper our lines with musketry before they charge and harass our camps with rifle fire at night."

"They are experts at using cover," Jack continued. "They take advantage of every bush, rock and piece of dead ground, and they are fast and deadly at close quarters." He waited for a moment. "We may meet them again, gentlemen, so everybody think of countermeasures."

"I thought we were abandoning Sudan, sir," Bryant said.

"I hope we are," Jack said and looked up as a lieutenant rode up with his face as scarlet as his tunic.

"Colonel Windrush, sir?" The lieutenant saluted.

"That's me," Windrush agreed.

"General Hook sends his compliments, sir, and could you join him at his quarters at your earliest convenience."

"Thank you, Lieutenant. Please tell the general that I will be there forthwith." Jack watched the man ride away.

Trouble. When General Hook is involved, there is always trouble.

"Major Baxter, please take command of the regiment in my absence."

"Yes, sir," Baxter replied formally.

* * *

General Hook had claimed one of the best houses in Suakin, next to the coast to catch any ocean breezes and with easy access to the Royal Navy vessels moored offshore. Maps of Egypt and Sudan covered one wall of the front room, while another held a peg from which his sword belt and holster hung.

"Ah, Windrush!" Hook greeted Jack with a cheerful nod, offered him a cheroot and waved him to a seat.

"Well, Jack, you've met the enemy now. What do you think of them?"

He used my Christian name, so he's trying to be disarmingly friendly.

"They're fast, brave, aggressive and dangerous," Jack replied. "They rely on close-quarter fighting, and their marksmanship and gunnery are poor."

"Do you think we have their measure?" Hook leaned back in his seat and smiled. With an open door behind him and a panorama of blue sea and sky, Jack thought he looked like a man on a Thomas Cook's holiday to Egypt rather than a senior British soldier.

"If we keep our discipline, sir, I do."

Hook nodded again. "I believe there was a debacle in our last encounter. The enemy broke Davis's square."

"I was in the First Brigade, sir, so I didn't see what happened."

"That's a pity; I've had conflicting reports," Hook said. "I'll see what Gerald Graham has to say."

Jack waited. He knew Hook had not invited him to discuss the recent battle. He drew on his cheroot.

"You rescued Alexandrina Drummond from Tokar," Hook changed the subject.

"Yes, sir, although I am not sure she wished to be rescued."

Hook blew out a thin ribbon of blue smoke. "I heard you threatened to put an armed guard on her."

"I did, sir. I wanted to keep her safe."

Jack did not expect Hook's smile. "Her Ladyship was quite amused. She told me you were the first British gentleman to treat her in such a cavalier fashion."

"It was necessary, sir," Jack said. "Is she a genuine Lady?"

"She is a grandniece of the queen," Hook said softly. "And as wild as the heather in her native Perthshire."

Jack shrugged. "I didn't know that, sir."

"Would it have made any difference if you had?" Hook raised his eyebrows.

Jack pondered for a moment. "No, sir."

"That's why I choose you for these missions, Jack. You do what has to be done. You'll have heard that Her Ladyship slipped away again."

"I heard that, sir."

Hook nodded. "I put Cockburn to watch her. Evidently, he did not use an armed guard."

Jack nodded. "From what I saw of Miss Drummond, sir, she seems capable of looking after herself."

"Yes, unfortunately," Hook sighed. "Now, onto other matters. Do you know the plans for withdrawing from Khartoum?" Hook said.

"I know we sent General Gordon there to bring away the garrison," Jack said.

"There are two routes by which Gordon can take his garrison out of Khartoum," Hook said. "He can put them in boats and sail down the Nile, which is the longest journey and made dangerous by a series of cataracts. Or he can sail as far as Berber, where the Egyptians have a garrison, and strike overland to Suakin."

Jack waited. "Yes, sir."

"General Graham's two victories have hopefully lessened the danger from Osman Digna and the Hadendoa, which should make the overland route easier. That is the route General Stephenson and the War Office prefer."

"I see, sir," Jack wondered what part he would play in the next campaign.

"It's about two hundred and fifty miles from Suakin to Berber," Hook said carefully, "and mostly on a well-established caravan route."

"So I believe, sir," Jack said.

Hook rose, stepped to the large-scale map of Sudan, and traced the route with his finger, stopping halfway. "This is El Kutuk, a village and watering spot, Windrush, and the Khedive has a garrison here."

Jack stepped to the map. "I see, sir."

"As long as we hold El Kutuk, the route from Berber to Suakin is possible, and General Gordon can get the garrison out. If we lose El Kutuk, then Gordon will have to negotiate the cataracts of the Nile; six dangerous rapids with fast water and maybe hostile tribes on either bank."

Jack studied the map again. "El Kutuk must be a hundred miles from Berber," he said.

"One hundred and twenty miles," Hook said. "And an Egyptian garrison holds both." He paused. "Would you trust an Egyptian garrison with such an important post after witnessing their performance so far?"

Jack guessed what Hook was going to say next. "They have no reason to fight, sir. They don't want to be in Sudan; their officers mistreat them, and I doubt the Egyptian government ever pays them."

"I agree with all of that, Colonel." Hook leaned back, smiling. "General Stephenson and I discussed the situation at some length, and we decided that El Kutuk is too important to leave in Egyptian hands. We plan to evacuate it, but not until Gordon has withdrawn the garrison from Khartoum."

"I understand, sir."

"We want a reliable, experienced British officer to take over the garrison and ensure the place holds out. When Gordon arrives, the garrison will feed and water him and his refugees, then join him on the last stage to Suakin, where the Navy will carry everybody to Cairo."

Jack guessed who that experienced British officer would be. "I'd like some British soldiers with me, sir."

"You are taking the Royal Malverns, Colonel, with two seven-pounder mountain guns, a string of camels and mules, and a Royal Navy Gatling and its team."

"Yes, sir." Jack was already working out the logistics. "I'll need at least fifteen water carts, sir, for the march."

"Your men are not marching, Windrush," Hook smiled. "They're travelling on camelback. I've already sent instructors to teach them the basics, and they'll learn the rest en route."

Jack tried to hide his surprise. "Has that ever been done before, sir?"

"I don't know, Jack, but out of Africa always comes something new."

"Yes, sir. Do I have telegraph communication at El Kutuk?"

"You have a line to Berber," Hook said, "and Berber has a line to Khartoum and Cairo, so you are not cut off. You'll be in daily contact with the outside world."

"Thank you, sir. How large is the current garrison?"

"You have two Egyptian regiments, Windrush, with about sixteen hundred men, and your Malverns." Hook opened the top drawer of his desk. "Oh, and you have this as well," he handed over a sealed envelope.

Jack broke the seal and opened the envelope. Inside was a stiff piece of parchment which he read with disbelief.

"Sir?"

"You are now Brigadier Jack Windrush," Hook said. "I'd advise you to start for El Kutuk immediately while Osman Digna is reeling from his defeat and his army is scattered." Hook smiled. "Why did you think we authorised this campaign against the Hadendoa?"

"Thank you, sir. Who will command the Malverns?"

"Your senior major is in temporary command until I can arrange for his promotion to Lieutenant Colonel."

"Major Baxter deserves no less," Jack said. "Do you have any information about the morale of the Egyptian garrison?"

Hook shook his head. "The present garrison commander told us that all was well."

Jack nodded. "When was that, sir?"

"We haven't heard from him for ten days," Hook admitted.

"That's a little discouraging. Perhaps the Mahdists have already captured the town."

Hook shook his head. "If they had, the Mahdi, or my spies, would have let us know."

"When was the garrison last paid?" Jack asked.

Hook shook his head again. "I'm not sure. The Khedive is a little reticent about such things."

"The Khedive?" Jack raised his eyebrows in surprise. "Is General Wood not in charge of the army?"

"The Khedive has retained some power."

Jack frowned. "Indeed. When we captured Tamai, we found a decent amount of the Mahdi's treasure in Marie Teresa dollars. I've handed it to the quartermaster general, sir, but I think it's only fitting we pay the Egyptian garrison with the Mahdi's money."

"I'll look into it," Hook said with a smile. "In the meantime, Brigadier, I suggest you prepare your column."

"Yes, sir," Jack saluted.

I am a Brigadier. What the devil will Marie say to that?

CHAPTER FIFTEEN

But I'm riding now an animal
A Marine never rode before,
Rigged up in spurs and pantaloons,
As one of the Camel Corps.
Sergeant Eagle, RM 1884.

The Malverns stared at the camels as if they had never seen such an animal before.

"What's happening, sir?" Captain Jamieson asked.

"We're all going to learn to ride a camel," Jack told him. "It's a new skill that will come in very handy."

Jamieson shook his head. "Not in Hereford, sir. We don't go in much for camel riding in Hereford."

"You can be the first," Jack said solemnly. "Others may follow."

Jack watched as grinning natives began the lesson by mounting the camels themselves. Sergeant Deng took over the instructions.

"You see? It is easy!"

The Malverns disagreed as they struggled onto the animals, with very few managing to remain mounted for more than a few moments. Sensing their riders' discomfort, the camels proved obdurate, hissing and spitting.

"The camel," said Sergeant Hanley, picking himself up from the sand, "is the most awkward and ill-conditioned beast you can tackle!"

"You can tackle him, Sergeant," Moffat encouraged as an Egyptian instructor made this camel kneel. "Don't tell me you'll allow a camel to defeat a sergeant of the Royal Malverns!" He patted the neck of his mount, spoke a few words to the Egyptian instructor and climbed onto the camel's back.

"You see, Sergeant," Moffat dismounted and explained. "You hold onto the saddle with one hand and lean back, which counteracts the camel's movements."

Jack stepped closer, watching, and listening as Moffat continued.

"Lean forward slowly as the camel gets onto its front legs. Don't rush or panic the animal. It's a sensitive soul. When it has found its footing with its back legs, the camel will move to the front, so you lean forward as it pushes itself upright. That way, you end with your back straight, like a soldier."

Sergeant Hanlon nodded and tried straddling the camel as if riding a horse.

"Not like that, Sergeant," Moffat said gently. "Cross your legs or at least one of them. That way, your weight is better distributed, and there's less pressure on your tailbone."

Sergeant Hanlon crossed his legs, and Jack saw that all the privates within hearing were also listening and copying Moffat's instructions.

"A camel doesn't move like a horse," Moffat said. "It's irregular, so allow your body to swing with the camel's gait. And ensure your kit is tied on. Your animal has a mind of its own, so let it pick the best route. Don't try to force it."

Jack nodded as Moffat took control, walking down the Malverns' line, adjusting the men's stance, and correcting with gentle words.

"Relax, lads. The camel senses your tension and may panic. Relax and enjoy the ride." Moffat grinned, "It's a damned sight easier than marching!"

When some men laughed, Jack knew Moffat had made his mark.

"You'll find it uncomfortable at first," Moffat continued. "Your backside will suffer, and your tailbone will ache, but that will ease in time. When you dismount, the camel will sit on the ground, and all you have to do is swing your legs over the hump."

"Well done, Moffat," Jack said. "How do you know so much?"

Moffat coloured as he realised he was the centre of attention. "I watched the Arabs, sir."

"Congratulations," Jack told him. "You are now in charge of camel instruction for the regiment. I heard you speak some Arabic, too."

"Yes, sir," Moffat's face was beetroot under its tan. "I thought it best when I knew the Malverns were in Egypt."

Jack nodded. "Carry on, Moffat."

After a day of struggling with the camels, Jack called the regiment together.

"As you may have guessed, we're going on a journey. It will be hot, hard, and troublesome, and the British army has done the like only twice before."

Jack waited until the men's initial murmur died and told them what was happening.

"In 1882, General Wolseley marched a British army from Ismailia to Tel-el-Kebir. We were part of that army, and we made history."

The Malverns looked at each other with renewed pride, as Jack had intended.

"Over eighty years ago, General David Baird led another British army across the desert to face the French. We will emulate and surpass both feats, and we will succeed because we are the

Royal Malverns!"

It was a short speech but effective, for the men cheered, with some throwing their pith helmets into the air. Jack allowed the display of indiscipline to continue for a few moments, then raised his hand.

"Enough, lads. We only have a few days to learn how to ride a camel, so listen to the instructions, be kind to the camels and try not to fall off."

Some of the men laughed at that.

"That's all, Malverns. Get to it. Senior officers, report to me."

The majors and senior captains clustered around Jack as the men concentrated on their camels.

"You may have realised the army has promoted me to Brigadier," Jack said. "Major Baxter, you are in temporary command of the regiment."

"Yes, sir," Baxter said. "Congratulations, sir."

"Thank you," Jack said. "We are embarking on a march of over a hundred miles," Jack told them. "It's a well-known caravan route, but we don't have the experience of the Arabs in these conditions."

The officers nodded solemnly, waiting for Jack to enlighten them.

"When David Baird led his men from the Red Sea to the Upper Nile, he asked the local Arabs for their advice and discovered that their concept of distance did not equate with our ideas. What he did was send advance parties ahead to reconnoitre the route and establish stores of food and water. We will do the same."

"Is that wise, sir, with Osman Digna's warriors around?" Bryant asked.

"We hope General Graham's victories had subdued the Hadendoa, at least temporarily," Jack said. "We'll send out strong parties, well-armed, and bury the stores," Jack said.

"Will we leave a guard, sir? The local tribes are not friendly." Bryant asked.

"The guard will be vulnerable to attack," Jack said. "After our twin victories over Osman Digna, killing a small party of British soldiers may be more tempting than stealing a store of food and water."

The officers nodded, agreeing with Jack's words.

"We'll use musacks – skin water bags - slung over the backs of camels as we use in India. Casks are no good in the heat. They'll warp when they're emptied and then leak. I've asked the Egyptian authorities for advice and a map with watering holes and wells."

The officers listened, giving advice or suggestions.

"We could increase the mounted infantry, sir," Baxter said. "Most of the old Afghan hands are still in the ranks."

Jack agreed. "We'll do that, Major. Who do you suggest should lead them?"

"Captain Sarsens," Baxter said immediately.

Jack agreed. "Find us some horses, Bryant. Baxter, reform the MI."

"Yes, sir."

As the men gradually came to terms with the camels, Bryant requisitioned thirty horses for the mounted infantry. Jack sent Sarsens and twenty old Afghan veterans from A Company with the first load of supplies.

"Start before dawn," Jack ordered. "March ten miles and deposit the water. Mark the spot on the map and return."

Sarsens grinned. "Yes, sir!"

"No heroics, Sarsens. Avoid trouble. Your job is to create a supply dump, not engage with the enemy."

"I won't let you down, sir," Sarsens said.

"Take Moffat with you," Jack said. "He seems to have an affinity with Egypt and camels."

"He's only a griff, sir," [1] Sarsens said.

"So were you, once," Jack reminded.

Jack watched the twenty men ride off the following morning. It was hard to send brave young men into danger, but that was the price and responsibility of command. Sarsens rode at the head, with Moffat, slim and very young, at his side.

"May God go with you," Jack said softly. He worked out the route on a map. From Suakin, he would take the regiment to the small towns of Handub, Otao, and Tambuk, and then it was a desert crossing to El Kutuk, with no more stops for water. Jack marked the distances in his head and wondered into what he was leading the Malverns.

* * *

"There are two types of camels," Sergeant Deng delighted in his new position of lecturer to the British troops. "The caravans use baggage camels, which move at the speed of a walking man."

About three miles an hour.

"These camels can travel no more than six hours daily, as they require time to browse."

Jack did a quick calculation. Six hours at three miles an hour was a maximum of eighteen miles a day. With a hundred and twenty miles to travel, he would be seven days on the journey, providing there were no hold-ups.

"There are also the thoroughbred camels or racing camels as I call them." Deng might have expected appreciation or praise, but his audience stared at him, stony-faced.

"Racing camels can travel long distances at seven miles an hour. They are grain fed, so they don't require grazing time."

Jack interrupted. "What kind of camels do we have?"

Sergeant Deng glanced at the Malverns' stock of camels and pulled a face. "Baggage camels," he said. "Little better than cattle."

Jack had expected nothing else. "We will work with what we have," he said.

Jack's last trip on a camel had been in Afghanistan when he had travelled in a panier. Now he stood at the side of a proud-looking beast, who looked down at him with utter disdain.

"You must get on her, sir," Deng said. "You cannot ride her by standing at the side."

Jack obeyed the instructions. He held on with grim determination as Sergeant Deng led the camel in a slow, dignified walk. Jack swayed back and forward, feeling like he would fall any minute.

"Tie yourself in," Deng suggested.

With a sash around his waist and another supporting his armpits, Jack found himself more secure on his mount.

"Now we'll trot," Deng said and climbed on his camel.

Jack hid his trepidation as the camel increased its speed. He looked across at Deng and realised he was no longer jolting. The camel's motion at a trot was smoother than when it walked.

"This is better," Jack called over.

Sergeant Deng smiled and nodded.

We'll be trotting across the desert, Jack told himself. *The quicker we arrive at El Kutuk, the better.*

Jack was ready when Sarsens and Moffat returned from placing the first supply drop. He counted the men anxiously, relieved that nobody was missing. "Any problems, Sarsens?"

"No, sir," Sarsens dismounted with a flourish, with his men following. "Straight down and straight back without a hitch and not a sign of the enemy."

Jack nodded. "Well done. How was Moffat?"

Sarsens lowered his voice. "I think he's half-Arab, sir. He rode through the desert as though he'd been there all his life."

"Tomorrow, I want you to go further," Jack said. "I want another supply dump twenty miles out."

"Yes, sir," Sarsens agreed.

"Now send Moffat to me."

Moffat looked apprehensive when he came to attention. "You sent for me, sir?"

"How was the desert, Moffat?"

Moffat grinned. "I loved it out there, sir. I loved the starkness and the austerity of the wasteland."

Jack understood at once for he appreciated the deep silence and beauty of the wilderness. "It looks like we could be here for some time, Moffat, so you'll get more experience."

"Yes, sir."

"Look after your men, now. As we're rotating them, you'll need volunteers for tomorrow's journey."

"I'll find them, sir."

"I'm sure you will. Carry on, Moffat."

"Yes, sir." Moffat was too flustered to salute as he strode away.

Jack watched Moffat and lit a cheroot. Wherever the army sent him in future, he was leaving the Royal Malverns in good hands. Major Baxter was an efficient, steady regimental officer and Bryant was one of the finest administrators he had ever met. Captain Jamieson was unimaginative but reliable, while Sarsens was thrusting and enthusiastic. Among the subalterns, Jarvis was slow and steady, Lang was bright, and Moffat was beginning to find his feet.

Jack drew on his cheroot. The Royal Malverns had a fine cadre of officers. Now he had to lead them into the heart of the desert.

CHAPTER SIXTEEN

This terrible vacuum on earth's surface
  Harry Williams

Two hours before dawn, Jack led his command out of Suakin. He had purchased a light racing camel for an eye-watering amount of money and looked over his shoulder as the column followed. His Malverns were not yet adept at camel riding and looked uncomfortable perched on their ungainly mounts. Behind them came the baggage animals, the small naval brigade, and the mountain guns, with the mounted infantry acting as scouts and flank guards.

The Malverns wore their Indian khaki tunics, brown riding breeches with puttees, and brand-new pith helmets and pugarees. Both helmets and pugarees had been white when the war office sent them to Suakin, but Jack thought them too distinctive and an inviting target. He ordered the men to dye them brown, despite the indignation of the RSM and Major Bryant, who preferred pristine order above everything.

"It might save the men's lives," Jack said.

"Yes, sir," Bryant agreed sadly, while RSM Deblin obeyed the order immediately, although his violent salute revealed his disagreement.

The men had used mud and boiled bark stripped from trees to dye their equipment, resulting in a hundred different shades. Jack smiled at Deblin's face.

"It's all the better this way, RSM," Jack said. "We're not going on parade."

"Maybe not, sir," RSM replied, "maybe not." He turned away. "I like my men to look like soldiers, not blasted tramps. We may as well be Frenchmen!"

Jack resisted the temptation to laugh. "I do see your point, RSM, and I promise that once we're back in Britain or another quiet posting, you can hammer the regiment back into shape."

Deblin smiled. "Thank you, sir. I'll make them proper soldiers again."

As well as the usual ammunition pouches and the spare ammunition the mules and camels carried, Jack had the quartermaster find bandoliers for the men.

"We don't know when we'll get more ammunition," he explained. "The men will curse them and me, but a few more bullets might save their lives."

Branley and two other men had volunteered to walk and care for the mules.

"The mules need me, sir," Branley said. "I understand them."

"I'm sure you do, Branley," Jack agreed.

Jack reinstated Sarsens in command of A Company and ordered Moffat to take over the mounted infantry.

"It's a lot of responsibility for a subaltern," Jack told him. "Can you handle it?"

"I think so, sir," Moffat replied.

"I need better than that," Jack said softly. "Can you handle the mounted infantry?"

Moffat raised his head. "Yes, sir."

"I thought so. Now go and prove it."

"Yes, sir," Moffat stepped away and turned round to face Jack. "Thank you, sir. I won't let you down."

In the middle of the column, with a guard of six men under the quartermaster and RSM Deblin, Jack had a mule carrying the treasure chest. Inside the chest was the pay for the men, plus back pay in Maria Theresa dollars for the Egyptian garrison. The treasure chest gave Jack sleepless nights, for he knew how much of a temptation it represented. Although the British army no longer contained the same collection of desperadoes it had in the previous century, many men came from terribly poor backgrounds. The thought of so much money close at hand might force them into theft. Jack checked on the treasure chest three times a day.

"Keep a steady pace," Jack ordered his officers, "and look after the men. I don't want anybody falling out."

"I've set a rearguard with spare camels, sir," Baxter said. "They will scoop up any stragglers."

"Good thinking, Baxter," Jack approved.

Moffat's mounted infantry led them on the first day as the camels stretched their necks into the furnace-hot air of the desert. Jack remained in front, glancing back to ensure his men remained balanced on their still-unfamiliar mounts. However ungainly the camels appeared, their legs moved steadily, and their thick, padded feet landed on the sand with a soft thump. Within minutes, the camels kicked up a curtain of dust that descended on the men further back, causing them to cough, cover their mouths and noses and narrow their eyes.

The men joked, some because of the novelty of their situation and others to conceal their nervousness. As they struck deeper into the desert, with the solitude of the wasteland stretching all around, the humorous remarks died away. They had all marched with General Graham and most with Wolseley, but this column was smaller, there was no naval support, and they knew they were heading into the deep desert.

"The lads are not happy," Baxter said.

"Give them a couple of days," Jack told him. "They'll soon relax into the rhythm of the march."

The first ten miles were slow as Jack allowed the men time to accustom themselves to this new mode of transport. He stopped for an hour at the first supply dump, watered men and camels, and pushed on to the next.

I estimated we'd travel fifteen to eighteen miles a day, but I want twenty the first day.

Water and heat were the main privations. The veterans were used to the extreme climates of Afghanistan and Egypt, but lack of water would always be a worry. Jack had calculated two pints a day for each man was the bare minimum they would need and ensured he had spare capacity on the camels. However careful he was, the skin bags always leaked and lost some of the precious fluid.

As Jack had anticipated, men complained about the bandoliers, with the unfamiliar weight pressing on sweat-softened flesh. He ignored their moans, for ammunition was second only to water as a necessity in this campaign.

When they reached the second supply dump, the men were tired after the unusual exertions but happy to have survived the first day and surprised at their new-found skill. Sarsens had chosen a good spot for the dump, between the towns of Handub and Otao, with a slight elevation giving a good field of fire should the enemy attack.

Only the shouts of officers and NCOs prevented the men from fighting for water, and Jack stepped in front of the store.

"One two-pint waterskin per man," he said. "The RSM will supervise the allocation." He waited until the men had taken their water, with some casting jealous glances at their neighbours to ensure they did not receive more than the official allocation.

"Now you're all refreshed," Jack said, "I want a zareba. Sergeant Anderson and the pioneers will cut the mimosa bushes! B Company, give them a hand. C and D Companies drag the bushes into position. A Company water the camels. Royal

Artillery set up the guns pointing south and east, and Royal Navy set the Gatling to the west."

Now accustomed to creating zarebas and aware of the threat of the Hadendoa warriors, the Malverns worked with a will. Within half an hour, a prickly bush barrier stretched around the camp, with the camels grazing outside under a guard. Branley fussed over his mules, talking to each animal individually.

"That's the first twenty miles completed," Jack said. "Only another hundred to go." He stepped to the highest point of the ridge and swept the horizon with his field glasses.

"No sign of life," he said. "Nothing except scrubland and desert."

"Miles and miles of bugger all," Baxter agreed.

Yet this wasteland is home to the Hadendoa. They understand and possibly even love the desert.

After an uneventful night, Jack ordered reveille long before dawn and had them heading west in the dark to make the most of the cool morning. He rationed water and recommended that the men suck at date stones to retain some moisture in their mouths.

"Off you go, Moffat," Jack ordered the mounted infantry ahead. "Keep in touch with us."

"I will, sir!" Moffat mounted and headed into the desert with his men at his back.

"Right, lads," Jack shouted, "We know what we're doing now!"

Most of the men were saddle sore and weary but soon settled into the rhythmic swing of the march. One man started to sing, and others joined in.

"A gay fusilier was marching down through Rochester,
Bound for the war in the Low Country
And he cried as he tramped through the dear streets of Rochester,
Who'll be a soldier for Marlbro with me?

And he cried as he tramped through the dear streets of
 Rochester,
Who'll be a sojer for Marlbro with me?"

The song died away in the endless monotony of the landscape, and all Jack heard was the soft thump of the camel's hooves on the hard sand and the jingle-crunch of the wagons.

Two camels fell that second day, and one man slid from his mount and lay still on the sand, gasping with sunstroke.

"Doolie bearers! See to that man!"

Dr Park hurried to the stricken man, and the column marched on, a relentless khaki snake across the desert.

Above them, waiting for fresh meat from men or beasts, the vultures circled, ugly scavengers that the men hated only slightly less than the flies and scorpions.

"No washing or shaving," Jack ordered. "We'll be the scruffy Malverns, but nobody in my regiment will die of sunstroke or thirst."

They reached the third and last supply dump between the villages of Otago and Tambuk at noon, and Jack pushed them a further five miles before the heat grew too unbearable to march.

"Forty miles completed," Jack said as the men hacked down thorn and sage bushes for a zareba. "We're a third of the way there already."

"Eighty desert miles to go until we see water," Lang sat hunch-shouldered on a rock, staring at the sand.

"Eighty more miles of desert!" Moffat sounded pleased.

Jack listened to the murmur of the men's conversation and the soft padding of the camels as they walked around the zareba and soldiers patting their mounts to restore their circulation after the march.

As darkness fell, men lit campfires and herded the camels inside the zareba. Jack stepped outside the thorn barrier and stood under the brilliant night sky. He walked away until the sounds of the camp receded and allowed the intense silence to envelop him.

Mary would like this. It's like the dawn of creation, with God viewing the world before he added life.

Something disturbed the silence. Jack listened for a while, unable to identify what it was, and then he heard the tom-toms, faint, distant but unmistakable.

The enemy is still out there, so the sooner we reach El Kutuk, the better.

Jack drove them hard for the remainder of the journey, not knowing what lay ahead or who might be waiting beyond the wavering horizon. On the fourth day, a sudden wind rose from the south, bringing a curtain of sand so high that it blocked the sun.

"Do we carry on, sir?" Moffat brought back his scouting riders.

"No!" Jack cursed. "Men will straggle and get lost." He raised his voice, shouting above the rising shriek of the wind. "Major Baxter! Bring everybody together!" Men were already ducking their heads against the barrage of stinging sand and covering the camel's eyes. "Bring the camels into a circle facing inward! NCOs and officers, check your men!"

The storm hit the Malverns moments later, with the blasting sand stinging faces and hands, forcing men to duck and turn away.

"Keep together!" Jack found he had an irrational fear of having his men buried alive. He patrolled inside the circle as long as possible and then crouched down with the others. The storm increased in volume, and the sand piled high against the camels' haunches. Sand got into eyes, noses, and mouths, entered every gap and crevice in the men's clothing and boots and irritated their scalps.

"Do you still like the desert?" Jack shouted in Moffat's ear.

"Maybe not this part!" Moffat replied, with his eyes narrowed.

When the storm passed over, men shook themselves clear of the sand and dug out the baggage animals.

"Roll call!" Jack called, with his throat hoarse with dust. "Every man check on his neighbour."

Sergeant Deng looked solemn. "This is a bad place," he said.

Jack surveyed their surroundings. The storm had covered all the bushes and rocks with an inch of sand and altered the contours of the area. He hoped his compass bearings would suffice to get them to El Kutuk.

"Why is it a bad place, Sergeant?"

"The sandstorm," Deng said. "The djinn who inhabits this place must have sent it. He doesn't like Nazarenes in its land."

"We'll move away, then," Jack said. "I thought you were a Moslem."

"I am a Moslem," Sergeant Deng agreed.

"Then surely you don't believe in djinns," Jack said.

"Of course not!" Deng said indignantly. "But they're still there, whether I believe or not."

"Clean your rifles," Jack walked around the Malverns. "Ensure the barrels and locks are clear of sand and cover both!" He wanted to check each man but knew that would subvert the authority of the junior officers and NCOs.

I have to learn to delegate.

Jack was not alone in hearing the tom-toms that night, and he doubled the sentries and ordered the men to keep the fires and the noise down. He knew that the average British soldier liked to talk around the campfire, but sound travelled in the dark. Above the doleful beating of the drums, he heard the screams of the tribesmen.

"Is that the Dervishes?" Baxter asked quietly.

"I don't know," Jack said. "I heard them last night as well, just like that, faintly in the distance."

"It might be something innocent," Baxter said. "A tribal wedding or some other celebration."

"It might be," Jack said, "but I'll be happier when we're securely behind walls."

"We beat them in the open before." Baxter fingered his revolver.

Jack nodded. "And we'll do it again if we have to." The following morning, he sent out Moffat's mounted infantry on extended patrols and pushed on, with the men tired but now used to the swaying camels.

Jack circled the column, ensuring nobody dropped out. Wright had Nicky beside him on the saddle, staring into the vastness without expression. Branley alternatively walked or rode one of his mules, talking to them constantly, while RSM Deblin rode to attention, not deigning to relax merely because he was on camelback.

Sarsens had adapted better than most and seemed born to ride a camel. He sat as gracefully as any Bedouin, with his beautiful white camel padding over the sand and his pith helmet tilted to protect his head.

Sergeant Deng was equally adept. As well as his regulation issue Martini-Henry, he carried a spear and a rhinoceros hide shield, plus a couple of ancient double-barrelled flintlock pistols at the side of his saddle.

"You're prepared for anything, Sergeant," Jack said.

Deng grinned. "Always best to be ready, sir."

"Sir!" A mounted infantryman appeared, sweat having created dark rivulets in his sank-caked face.

Jack recognised Doncaster under the sand. "Report, Doncaster."

"Lieutenant Moffat's compliments, sir, and there's dust ahead. Something is coming this way."

CHAPTER SEVENTEEN

He who has a thousand friends has not a friend to spare,
And he who has one enemy will meet him everywhere.
Ali Ibn-Abi-Talib, c 602-661

Jack nodded. "How much dust? A patrol? A company? An army?"

Doncaster considered. "Maybe a company, sir."

"Very good. My regards to Lieutenant Moffat and tell him to keep an eye on it and report any further developments to me."

When Doncaster trotted off, Jack ordered the leading company to move into extended order.

"C Company, take the left flank! D Company, the right!"

The column moved on with the atmosphere tenser, men more intent on watching the surrounding landscape, some seeing movement where was none, or enemies in the play of the residual wind through thorn bushes. More vultures joined the dozen that had followed them since they left Suakin.

An hour later, Doncaster galloped back to Jack. "Lieutenant Moffat says there are about thirty camels and maybe fifty men on foot!"

"Hostile?" Jack asked.

"I don't know yet, sir."

"I'll come," Jack said and pushed his camel forward.

Moffat had positioned his mounted infantry in a line with twenty feet between each man. Moffat was two hundred yards ahead on a small ridge, peering forward through his field glasses. "Over there, sir."

As usual in the desert, Jack had to focus through a screen of dust. He saw an untidy double column edging towards him, with Arabs mounted on camels and a slow trudge of people on foot. "It's an Arab caravan," Jack decided, "not the Mahdi's warriors."

The caravan passed the mounted infantry and then the main column, with the Arabs staring at the unusual sight of British soldiers on camels. The Malverns muttered uncomfortably when they realised the people on foot were yoked together.

"They're slaves!" Bryant said.

Baxter reached for his revolver. "Should we not free the poor buggers, sir?"

Jack agonised over his decision. If he freed these slaves, he could not leave them to die of thirst in the desert. He would have to take them with him into a possible battleground, where they might be killed or enslaved the minute the British left.

"No," Jack said, hating himself.

The two columns passed; the Arabs, who had been in the area for centuries, practising their trade of exploiting human beings, and the British, aliens and unsure in this desert environment. Jack watched the caravan move on, checked his compass, and pressed on, sick at heart.

The drums started an hour later, a monotonous throb that came from beyond the horizon, always present and all the more threatening for being unseen. Jack brought back his mounted infantry, changed their horses, and sent them out again.

"Widen your scope," Jack ordered. "Report to me the moment you see anybody."

"Yes, sir!" Moffat said. He was tired but still smiling.

That lad has found his forte in the desert.

When they halted for the night, the drums were still beating, and the men needed no urging to create the zareba.

"C Company, help the pioneers!" Baxter shouted.

"The lads are already outside, sir!" Jamieson replied.

With Donnelly hovering at his side, Jack snatched an hour's rest and then patrolled the zareba, ordering slight alterations where he thought he saw a weakness.

"Lieutenant Rawlinson," Jack said to the artillery officer, "would your guns not be better over there?" He pointed to a depression on the left.

"No, sir," Rawlinson defended his choice of position. "The ground rises in front, and from here, we can rake that ridge from the flank."

Jack nodded. "You're correct, Rawlinson." He moved on, glad he had an artillery officer who knew what he was doing and could stand up to a senior officer.

The drums continued all night and then abruptly stopped.

The sudden silence woke Jack as effectively as any outbreak of noise.

"What's happening?" He emerged from his tent.

"Nothing, sir," Lieutenant Jarvis, the duty officer, said. "It's all gone quiet; there's no movement."

Jack walked around the zareba, talking to the sentries and peering into the night as the stars faded above.

"Bugler! Sound the reveille!"

The trumpet call woke the men, and Jack ensured they had breakfast and had the column moving half an hour earlier than usual. He rotated the mounted infantry to allow fresh men to gain experience and strengthened the flank guards.

"March in a regimental square, with the baggage animals and artillery in the centre," Jack ordered. "The Ansar is out there."

The moment the Malverns began to move, the drums started again.

"They're watching us," Baxter said.

Jack nodded. "They are," he said. "They must wonder what we're doing."

As the dawn broke, Jack saw a group of men standing on a ridge to the left. "I see a dozen warriors."

Baxter grunted and lifted his field glasses. "Yes, sir, and they want us to see them."

The warriors stood on the skyline, each holding a rifle, sword, or spear.

Lieutenant Rawlinson strode to Jack. "Should I fire at them, sir? I can place a couple of rounds of shrapnel above their heads."

Jack shook his head. "Not yet, Rawlinson. They're no threat to us. Signal to Moffat to keep close."

Corporal Borway placed the heliograph on a slight ridge and flashed the order; moments later, the mounted infantry rode into sight.

The column marched on, with the men watching the warriors on the ridge, expecting a rush of howling Hadendoa at any moment.

"Sir!" Doncaster trotted back. "Lieutenant Moffat's respects, sir, and we've sighted three more groups of warriors ahead."

"Did they attack you?"

"No, sir. They only stood on the top of ridges and sand hills, letting us see them."

Jack nodded. "They're trying to unsettle the men."

"They're unsettling me," Baxter growled said. "We're marching deeper and deeper into their territory every moment."

Jack thought of Hicks Pasha and the fate of Baker's column. "If they attack, we'll fight them off. Until then, we continue."

The number of warriors increased by the hour. They gathered on ridges and massed among the thorn bushes, watching the British march past. Jack observed them through his field glasses, noting the black flags that hung limp in the still air and the utter silence of the watchers.

"These lads are well disciplined," Jack said. "And they're all wearing the same clothes, like a uniform." Each man had a jibbeh with square, coloured patches to signify their virtuous poverty. "Somebody has trained them well."

"Maybe the Mahdi himself," Baxter said.

"Maybe," Jack agreed. "I'd like to meet that man. I've met a few of his ilk in Afghanistan and along the Frontier. I wonder if the Mahdi is any different."

"He's said to be a direct descendant of Muhammed," Bryant told them. "And to be the expected one."

"So I've heard," Jack glanced over his regiment. They were moving on, heads swivelling to watch the watchers, some men fiddling nervously with their rifles. "I also heard that some of his followers carry charms to repel rifle bullets, and I don't believe that, either." Jack nodded. "Signal the mounted infantry and tell them to keep closer to the column. I don't want the Mahdi's men to cut them off."

"These men are Baggara," Bryant said. "We must be out of the Hadendoa's territory now. "These fellows wear turbans. The Baggara are herdsmen who live mainly on the milk and meat of their beasts. They keep horses and slaves."

"Thank you, Bryant," Jack said. "All information is useful. Here's Moffat coming."

"Sir!" Lieutenant Moffat retained his smile despite the Baggaras' proximity. "El Kutuk is in sight sir. I saw the town ahead."

Jack wondered if he should leave the column to view his new command but decided it was best to remain with the Malverns. If the enemy attacked when he was gone, he'd have failed in his primary duty to look after his men.

"Thank you, Moffat," Jack said. "I'm glad we've come the right way."

"The enemy is moving, sir!" Moffat warned.

The warriors rolled down the ridges on both sides of the column, with the black banners above them. In the background, the drums continued their monotonous beat.

"Close the ranks," Jack ordered. "Ensure the rifles are loaded and clean and prepare to defend the square." He refused to be panicked by tribesmen who might not even be hostile, but on the other hand, he would not be caught off-guard.

The Baggara tribesmen formed two large groups a mile ahead of the column, with a quarter-mile gap in between.

"They may be planning to attack each flank," Baxter said.

"That may be so," Jack agreed. He lifted his voice. "Infantry, dismount and retain your formation! Royal Navy, move to the rear right of the square! Bugler recall the mounted infantry! Artillery, guard the rear left and front right of the square!"

The warriors did not interfere as the Malverns marched forward with the camels and baggage on the inside.

"They're not moving," Baxter reported, "but there's another group coming towards us."

Jack could taste the tension as he lifted his field glasses. A small group of a dozen men rode slowly towards the square with three flags carried high. One was the green flag of the Mahdi, and the other two were black, with writing that Jack knew would be inscriptions from the Koran. At two hundred yards, the small group halted.

"They want to talk," Jack said. "I'll meet them."

Donnelly stepped forward, "You can't go alone, sir. I'll accompany you."

Baxter lifted a hand. "Moffat, take six of your mounted infantry as escorts."

"Yes, sir!"

Jack parted the square and rode forward with Donnelly a length behind. Moffat and his mounted infantry were a solid clump of dusty khaki that made up the rear.

Jack frowned as he rode closer to the waiting warriors. *I know that man.*

The leading tribesman pressed his horse forward and stopped, with Jack ten yards away. Very tall, he had three tribal scars on his face, and the cross hilt of a sword protruded from behind his left shoulder.

He was the Sudanese sergeant that caused us so much trouble during the Egyptian war. He killed two of my best men.

"I am Osman Zubeir," the tall man said. "Leader of the Mahdi's armies in the west."

"I am Brigadier Jack Windrush, commanding the Royal Malverns and commandant of El Kutuk," Jack said.

"El Kutuk is our town," Zubeir spoke in a deep voice. "The Mahdi will take it and expel all who do not acknowledge him."

"We have defeated the Osman Digna's forces in two battles," Jack said. "If you attack us, we will defeat you as well."

Zubeir lifted his hand in a gesture that encompassed all the gathered tribesmen. "The Mahdi's forces have defeated many Egyptian armies and British commanders."

"I'd advise you to withdraw, Osman Zubeir," Jack said. "In the past, you have been successful against Egyptians, but your men cannot defeat British soldiers. To avoid further bloodshed, you should retreat."

When Zubeir pushed his horse a step closer, Jack sensed his mounted infantry escort preparing to fight. He waved them back.

"Go now, Osman Zubeir," Jack said. "You have brave men behind you. We do not wish to interfere in your Sudan. We wish only a peaceful journey to El Kutuk and back to Suakin."

"Go with God," Zubeir said, "and may Allah guide you to the truth."

"That is also my wish for you," Jack replied.

Zubeir turned his horse at once and cantered away, with his escort closing around him.

"That was interesting." Donnelly had his carbine across the crupper of his horse, with the muzzle pointing at Zubeir.

"Now we've seen the face of the enemy," Jack said, "and we know how dangerous he is."

Retaining the square formation, Jack ordered the Malverns to march, with each man alert for a sudden attack. Zubeir's forces had melted away, with not a single warrior visible on the heights. Even the drumming had ended, so the British moved in an uneasy silence only broken by the pad of the camels' feet and the occasional soldier's mutter.

"Where have they gone?" Lang asked.

Sarsens replied shortly. "They've gone into the desert where they belong."

Jack glanced at his map, checked his compass, and grunted. "We should be at El Kutuk just after dark." He shook his head. "We'll camp a mile away and enter the town in the morning."

"Why is that, sir?"

"We want to make an impression," Jack explained. "By nightfall, we'll be tired, dusty, and haggard. If we arrive in the morning, we'll have slept and eaten. We'll look like soldiers, not ragged travellers."

I'm not scurrying into shelter the day we met Osman Zubeir. If he comes, we'll face him in the open.

CHAPTER EIGHTEEN

God has permitted trafficking, and forbidden usury
   Sura 2, Koran

After another night undisturbed by the tom-toms, Jack pushed ahead with Moffat, Donnelly and two mounted infantrymen for an escort. He rode to the crest of a ridge and focussed his field glasses on his new charge. At first sight, El Kutuk was not impressive, being a straggling village at the foot of a ruinous mud-brick fort.

"I can't see a flag flying," Jack said.

"Neither can I, sir," Moffat agreed.

Jack grunted. He remembered Lord Roberts' fury after his march from Kabul to Kandahar to find no Union flag flying above the garrison. "We'll have to do something about that, Moffat."

As they rode closer, Jack saw that El Kutuk stood in the centre of a plain, with only a few long pools of water and some wells giving the village a reason for existence. The walls were ruinous in places, and the gate sagged on a single hinge, guarded by a single lounging sentry.

"This place couldn't stop an assault by a bunch of children,"

Baxter said.

"We have a lot of work in front of us," Jack said. "Especially with Osman Zubeir in the vicinity. I'm surprised he hasn't captured the village already."

Jack ordered the men to dismount a mile from the village. "Spruce yourselves up, lads. I want you as bright and shiny as if Queen Victoria herself was going to review us. We will march in by companies and show El Kutuk that the Royal Malverns have arrived!"

Ordering Moffat to take a section of the mounted infantry ahead to announce his coming, Jack gave the Malverns an hour to get ready and then mounted Gonda and rode forward. He knew first impressions were important when taking over a garrison and was determined to make his mark quickly.

As Jack approached El Kutuk. He saw somebody had dragged the main gate open, and an Egyptian sentry stood at approximate attention at either side. They watched the British through dull eyes without attempting to challenge or salute.

"God save us from amateur soldiers," Baxter breathed.

Jack led his men through the gate and onto a long main street of single-storey, flat-roofed houses. The garrison had turned out to line the route, with red fezzes worn at a hundred different angles and white uniforms dirty and torn.

Jack heard the tramp of marching feet alter as the Malverns entered the village. He acknowledged the salutes of Egyptian officers and NCOs and pushed on to the fort, where he saw a group of senior officers waiting for him.

Behind the Egyptian soldiers, the village women ululated, the sound shrill as they welcomed the new commandant and his British soldiers. Cynically, Jack wondered if they would be as welcoming if Osman Zubeir rode in and decided they would.

Of course, they would. All these people want is to be left alone to live their lives, and if cheering in the streets makes their lives easier, why the devil shouldn't they?

Dismounting, Jack introduced himself to the shambling

collection of Egyptian officers and added he needed accommodation for his men and animals.

"I am Brigadier Jack Windrush, the Khedive's new commandant of the village and fort of El Kutuk," Jack announced in English and Arabic.

A stout officer with a shabby uniform festooned with medal ribbons stepped forward. "Welcome, Windrush Pasha. "I am Colonel Mahmoud Wahiba, commanding the composite 18th and 25th Battalions of the Khedive's Army in Sudan."

"Colonel Wahiba," Jack returned the colonel's salute.

"These gentlemen are Bimbashi Ahmed Mabruk and Bimbashi Suleiman Khalif." Colonel Wahiba introduced the two officers at his side. Both were large men with luxuriant moustaches. Jack knew that a Bimbashi was the Ottoman equivalent of a major.

"I believed the Khedive had two Egyptian battalions here," Jack spoke without dismounting.

"Yes, effendi," Wahiba said.

"Call me sir," Jack ordered. "Or Brigadier."

"Yes, sir," Wahiba said.

"In that case, there should be two colonels and two groups of senior officers," Jack snapped.

"Colonel Gamal deserted two months ago," Wahiba admitted, "taking the senior officers of the 25th with him."

"Good God," Baxter whispered.

Jack dismounted. "You did not desert, Colonel Wahiba."

"No, sir," Wahiba agreed. "We will have a banquet to celebrate your arrival and then a display for you."

"Thank you," Jack said. "Once we settle in the men and animals."

As Jack had expected, the barrack rooms in the fort were filthy. "Get these cleaned up," he ordered. "I'm not having my men live in a place not fit for pigs."

Bryant saluted. "I'll see to it, sir."

"Use the Egyptians," Jack said. "They made the mess, and

they can damned well clean it up!" He felt his temper rising at the state of the barracks. "Find a safe place for the treasure chest, Baxter, and keep it under armed guard at all times. The RSM can arrange the guards."

"Yes, sir."

"I want clean water and fresh food for the men and animals. There will be a bazaar or a souk in El Kutuk, but I don't want the men wandering alone until we see how safe the village is."

It was fortunate that the fort had its own well, so there was sufficient water, and within ten minutes, the NCOs had Malverns and Egyptians running around with makeshift brooms and pails of water. Busy men removed the cobwebs and sundry crawling insects, while others eradicated layers of dirt and coated the walls with whitewash.

"Where did we find the whitewash?" Jack asked.

The RSM grinned. "The quartermaster sergeant sniffed it out by some genius known only to quartermasters."

"That's better, RSM," Jack said after three hours of scrubbing, washing, brushing, and swearing.

"It'll do for the first night, sir," the RSM agreed. "I'll keep the lads at it. The defaulters will have something to keep them occupied, and you know how much they like that."

Jack smiled. "I am sure you know how to keep them busy, Major."

The RSM looked slightly nervous as he spoke again. "Begging your pardon, sir, but I don't think the barracks are clean enough for the lads to live in yet. I'd prefer them to camp in the desert behind a zareba than in the filth."

Jack agreed. "Yes, RSM. We can fight the Ansar's spears easier than we fight disease."

"That's right, sir." The RSM seemed relieved that Jack agreed.

"Consult with the surgeon, RSM."

"I will, sir!" Devlin's salute was of genuine respect.

The men needed no instructions in creating a zareba, and

Jack left the details to the junior officers while he attended the celebration Colonel Wahiba had arranged.

"You look grand, sir," Donnelly said as Jack struggled into his best uniform with the array of medal ribbons that revealed his service from Burma to Egypt and half a dozen campaigns in between.

"I don't like official receptions," Jack growled as Donnelly brushed his shoulders.

"I know, sir," Donnelly said. "But you're the guest of honour. The Gyppos are nervous about meeting you, and they'll bend over backwards to make you welcome."

"I don't want to be made welcome," Jack said. "I want an efficient force to guard this damned place."

"Yes, sir." Donnelly adopted a diplomatic silence as he ensured his officer looked his best.

Baxter waited for Jack outside the tent with his uniform spruce.

"Damned waste of time," Jack said.

"Maybe not, sir," Baxter said. "It will allow us to get to know these Egyptian fellows, and then we can improve their efficiency without animosity."

"Animosity?" Jack growled. "I don't care if I hurt their feelings when Osman Zubeir is lurking around with God-alone-knows how many men."

"Of course, sir," Baxter said smoothly.

Jack thought for a moment. "You're correct, of course, Baxter, damn you."

"Thank you, sir. Shall we go and allow our hosts to entertain us?"

Wahiba greeted Jack with smiles and ushered him into an airy, if dirty, chamber with tall arched windows that overlooked the central courtyard and parade ground.

"This room is the largest in the fort," Wahiba's eyes were anxious.

"It's a splendid room," Baxter said diplomatically in halting Arabic.

Sputtering lined the walls, and every Egyptian officer present wore a spotless uniform complete with arrays of medal ribbons.

Jack thought that Wahiba must have drained the bazaar of half its contents, for a variety of dishes filled the single round table. As well as rice-stuffed vegetables, there were hummus and falafel, shawarma, and kushari. Silent servants waited behind the table, and the Egyptian officers demonstrated the various foodstuffs to Jack and Baxter.

After the meal, Wahiba sat back in his chair and smiled at Jack. "I chose this next display for Windrush Pasha."

"Thank you," Jack replied.

Jack caught Baxter's bemused expression and smiled. Both men were wondering what Colonel Wahiba had planned.

"I am sure you appreciate our dancers," Wahiba said and clapped his hands.

The dancers were all female, Sudanese and very supple. Jack watched them with little interest, for his mind was busy thinking about the defence of the village and fort, how to evacuate and whether Chinese Gordon would withdraw via El Kutuk. Jack realised that Major Baxter and the Egyptians were staring at the dancers, who had stripped nearly naked. They wore only a profusion of bangles and a hand-width of leather around their hips.

"Don't get too interested," Jack whispered to Baxter. "They're probably somebody's slaves and diseased to the eyebrows."

Baxter nodded, transfixed. "They're still worth watching, sir."

As the dancers gyrated before the officers, an unseen hand drummed on a tom-tom while the bangles clicked in time to the movements of the women's hips and torso. Leaving Baxter to drool over the show, Jack slid away from the building to check on his men.

"Are they getting settled in all right, RSM?"

"Right as rain, sir," Deblin responded.

"I want pickets out tonight, RSM," Jack said. "Captain Jamieson is duty officer, and he'll talk to you about the details."

"Very good, sir. I've created a provisional list."

Of course, you have RSM, and Captain Jamieson will accept it without a second glance, knowing it's perfect.

Jack glanced behind him, where Donnelly had appeared, rifle in hand.

"Come with me, RSM; I want to inspect the fort and the village."

"Very good, sir!" The RSM joined Jack on a tour of the fort. Jack guessed it had been built some centuries ago by some long-forgotten sheikh to defend the water supply for an ancient caravan route. The walls were irregular, twelve feet to twenty feet high, with a walkway behind the battlements and a square tower at the northern corner. Many of the merlons – the vertical sections of the battlement - were crumbling, thus exposing the embrasures to enemy musketry.

"I'll have the pioneers work on this," Jack said.

"Very good, sir," The RSM made notes in a small black book.

"Do we have a Union Flag, RSM?"

"No, sir, only the regimental colours and an Egyptian flag."

Jack nodded. "I'm not displaying the Colours to be faded by the sun here, so hoist the Egyptian flag. It's not our flag, but it will show Osman Zubeir that we're here as long as we choose to be."

"I'll arrange that, sir."

"I want a ditch and rampart around the entire village," Jack said, "not just around the fort. The ditch to be at least eight feet deep."

"Very good, sir," the RSM knew precisely how much labour that simple order would entail, but he would see the garrison completed it efficiently and quickly. "Sergeant Anderson will see to that."

"The Egyptians are good engineers, RSM; after all, they built the pyramids. Use them."

"I will, sir."

Jack saw a gleam in Deblin's eyes and knew he itched to put El Kutuk to rights. He noticed the Royal Artillerymen busily cleaning their guns and resolved to speak to Lieutenant Rawlinson immediately after he had completed his rounds with the RSM.

"I want men posted in the tower, RSM."

"I have four men there, sir," Deblin snapped.

"And mobile pickets on the fort's walls."

"Twenty men, sir, in pairs, one to observe and one to report."

"And on the village walls."

"Forty men, sir, with three on the gate," Deblin spoke in a series of staccato sentences without wasting a word.

Jack smiled. The British army might do without its officers, but the entire edifice would collapse if the NCOs departed. "You've done marvels, Major. You may return to your duties."

The RSM saluted. "Thank you, sir!"

Jack peered through an embrasure at the village, barely visible in the fast-fading light. He saw a broad street with a network of side alleys, with close-packed, flat-roofed mud houses, some with courtyards away from the streets. The most prosperous buildings had gardens with date palms or the occasional lemon or orange tree. Men on foot or astride donkeys walked the streets with the rare heavily veiled woman.

It's all my responsibility now, Jack told himself. *I have to care for this village and get ready to receive General Gordon and the garrison of Khartoum when he evacuates.*

Leaving the fort, Jack acknowledged the salutes of the sentries and entered the village. He knew it was not advised for a senior British soldier to enter an Arab village alone, in case the Mahdi had supporters among the population, but he would only get to know the place by walking. An official visit, with an entourage and meeting only officials, was worse than useless.

The single main street had quietened in the few moments since Jack left the fort, with the side streets narrow and dirty, as he had expected. He heard the occasional voice from within the houses, a mother talking to her children, the deeper tones of a man, and a donkey's bray. The bazaar space in the centre was quiet, with a slight breeze rustling over the dusty ground. A stand of palm trees would offer shade in the heat of the day.

The mosque stood alone within a space of dust, slightly ramshackle, with the minaret the tallest edifice in El Kutuk. A small herd of goats wandered past with a ragged youth in charge.

"*As-salaam alaykum,*" Jack said. "Peace be upon you."

The youth looked startled and replied, "*alsalam ealaykum 'aydan,* peace be upon you, too," before running away, driving his goats before him.

All is as it should be, and all is as expected.

When Jack returned, the Malverns' sentries challenged him and stiffened into attention when he announced his identity.

"Beg pardon, sir. I didn't expect to see you here."

"No reason to beg my pardon, Graham. You did your duty."

"Thank you, sir."

The Egyptian sentries huddled behind the battlements and barely looked up when Jack passed. Their NCO gave a reluctant salute, as sloppy as any first-day recruit.

We'll teach you to act like soldiers, Jack promised silently. He did not see any Egyptian officers on his rounds.

* * *

"Colonel Wahiba!" Jack opened the colonel's door as the Malvern's bugler sounded reveille.

Wahiba struggled up in bed, with the woman at his side rolling away. "Windrush Pasha!"

"Is the lady your wife?" Jack asked.

"No," Wahiba said.

"Then get rid of her," Jack waited until the woman scrambled away, half-dressed. "When were your men last paid, Colonel?"

Wahiba looked confused. "Months ago," he confessed.

"Do you have a pay chest here?"

"No, sir."

Jack was not surprised. "Who is your adjutant? Who keeps the regimental records, Colonel?"

"Bimbashi Mabruk," Wahiba seemed pleased to pass responsibility to a junior officer.

"Send him to my tent with the records of wage arrears," Jack ordered. "I want him there in thirty minutes, washed, shaved and dressed, and your regiment on parade in the courtyard in two hours." He withdrew before Wahiba could protest.

* * *

The Egyptian soldiers slouched in ranks, with their white uniforms crumpled and stained, fezzes and dirty Remington rifles at different angles.

Jack stood in front of the Egyptians with Bimbashi Mabruk at his side.

"I am Brigadier Windrush," Jack began. "You may know me as Windrush Pasha." He saw very little interest in the dull, beaten eyes. "If you speak to me, you will call me sir."

The men did not respond. Jack called for a table to be placed in front of the men. He was aware that half the off-duty Malverns lined the walls, watching the scene unfold.

"Colonel Wahiba informed me that you are due back pay," Jack continued. "The Khedive and the Sirdar have supplied me with a treasure chest to ensure your wages are up to date."

As Jack said the words, Private Branley brought forward a mule with the treasure chest on its back. Two men carried the chest to the table, and Jack ceremoniously unfastened the padlock and pushed back the lid.

"Bimbashi Mabruk will call out your names. When you hear

your name, double to the table, salute, and Bimbashi Mabruk will hand over your wages in Marie Theresa dollars."

As Jack intended, paying the men raised their morale. By the end of the pay parade, the Egyptian soldiers were smiling, and some slipped away to the bazaar.

"Good," Jack said as he dismissed the Egyptians, and Bryant joined him. "That's the first step."

"Slaves, sir," Bryant reminded. "How shall we deal with the slaves?"

"Are there many?" Jack asked, with his first reaction to free every slave in the village.

"Yes, sir," the adjutant said. "Hundreds, I think. If we free them, what will they do? And where will they live?" He lowered his voice. "About a quarter of the population are slaves, sir. It's not illegal here, for Islam does not condemn slavery."

Jack considered his position. The British Army decreed that British soldiers should not interfere with the indigenous religions except in the case of human sacrifice or blatant cruelty. The British tried to suppress slavery and slaughter, such as the practice of Thugee in India, but otherwise turned a Nelsonian eye to local religious beliefs. In Jack's eyes, missionaries were incredibly brave and well-meaning people who often caused more trouble than they cured. Yet Mary, his wife, had gone to a missionary's school, and she turned out all right.

"Slavery is wrong," Jack realised his attention had drifted. "It's degrading and cruel."

"Yes, sir," the adjutant agreed. "But if we freed all the slaves overnight, we'd have a large number of unemployed people with no way of earning their living and nowhere to stay. These slaves are cooks, gardeners, housemaids, soldiers even. They'd have no option except to steal to live, and the villagers would suffer."

Jack swore. He knew Bryant was correct, even though he hoped he was wrong. "What the devil do we do? We don't own the Sudan, so we can't lay down our laws here." He thought for a moment. "I want you to investigate the situation, Bryant. If the slaves are content as they are, we will not disrupt them. If we find them ill-treated, we will free them."

"What shall we do with the freed slaves, sir?"

"If they can't find work, we'll enrol them into the village militia."

"Very good, sir." Bryant hesitated. "Is there a village militia, sir?"

"We'll form one," Jack decided. "I don't expect Osman Zubeir to remain quiet for long, and if he attacks, we'll need every man who can pull a trigger."

"Very good, sir!" Bryant saluted.

Jack knew he had added another problem to the adjutant's already heavy burden, but if anybody could cope, Bryant could. He sighed and prepared to check RSM Deblin's progress with the defences.

CHAPTER NINETEEN

The side that stays within its fortifications is beaten.
    Napoleon Bonaparte

From the fort's tower, the desert stretched into the distance in all directions, lit only by the glimmer of stars. The rigours and responsibilities of the march had occupied Jack's full attention, but now he realised how isolated he was from the world. Only a single telegraph line connected him to Berber and from thence to Cairo. Apart from that, there was sand and scrub, with possibly an occasional Arab caravan.

Jack stared into the wilderness.

Osman Zubeir was out there, a man who had helped defeat Hicks Pasha, a soldier trained in the Egyptian army and a personal expert fighting man. Somewhere out there may even be the Mahdi, supposedly the descendant of the Prophet and undoubtedly a man worshipped by tens of thousands of Sudanese.

The sooner Gordon Pasha evacuates Khartoum, the better. We're in a precarious position in El Kutuk.

Jack had moved into a large, airy suite of rooms in the fort, with windows overlooking the courtyard and furniture that would be luxurious if anybody had ever cleaned it.

I have a great deal to do to put this place in order.

* * *

The bugle call for reveille woke Jack, and he lay for a minute, unsure where he was. Something was wrong.

Where's Donnelly? He rose, already bad-tempered that the morning had broken his routine.

"Donnelly!"

He heard scurrying footsteps, and Donnelly appeared, unshaven and with his belt hanging loose. He proffered a mug of coffee.

"Sorry, sir!"

Jack glared at him, decided Donnelly's appearance was unimportant and drank the coffee. He had not enjoyed Egyptian coffee when he arrived in the country but had grown accustomed to the taste.

"Anything to report, Donnelly?"

"No, sir. It was a quiet night."

Jack grunted and nodded. The coffee was already working its magic, waking him up and improving his mood. "I didn't hear the muezzin calling the faithful to prayer."

"No, sir," Donnelly agreed. "Nor did I. Perhaps there is no mosque in this place."

"There is," Jack told him. "Who's the duty officer today? Lang, isn't it? My compliments to Lieutenant Lang and ask him if he heard the muezzin this morning."

"Yes, sir," Donnelly uncharacteristically hesitated. "Shall I get your breakfast first, sir?"

"No," Jack growled, proving that even coffee was insufficient to banish his foul mood completely. "Take my message first, damn it!"

"Yes, sir!" Donnelly vanished, and Jack pulled on his

uniform. He walked to the arched window to view the courtyard.

The RSM had been busy, with a parade of defaulters already marching in full kit, but the actions of a squad of Egyptian soldiers caused Jack's frown to deepen further.

What the devil is happening down there?

Jack took another gulp of his coffee and strode from the room and down the stairs to the courtyard. The Egyptians had placed an ugly wood and metal framework on the ground. As two soldiers pulled a scared civilian towards the contraption, a burly sergeant wielded a *kourbash,* a wicked rhinoceros-hide whip.

"What's all this?" Jack roared and repeated the question in Arabic. "What's happening here?"

Jack did not need to ask. Ignoring him, the two soldiers threw their prisoner on the ground and tied him to the structure, so he lay on his back with the soles of his feet facing upwards.

It's a bastinado, by God!

"Enough of that!" Jack snarled. He realised the RSM and all the men in the courtyard, British and Egyptian, were watching with some interest. Reaching out, he grabbed the *kourbash* from the Egyptian sergeant's brawny hand. "Release that man!"

"He's broken the law!" the sergeant protested, surprised that the fort governor should pay attention to such a trivial matter.

"Set him free," Jack lowered his tone to a vicious hiss.

The Egyptian sergeant opened his mouth, changed his mind, and ordered the prisoner free.

"What had he done?" Jack watched the prisoner nearly run from the courtyard.

"He disrespected an Egyptian," the sergeant explained his actions.

"Get out," Jack felt his temper worsening by the minute. "All of you." He viewed the contraption in the middle of the courtyard. "Leave the whip behind."

The sergeant dropped the *kourbash* and withdrew with his men at his back.

"RSM!"

"Sir!"

"Get rid of these damned things," Jack said. "Break them up, burn them; I don't care what you do."

"Yes, sir," RSM said.

"Lieutenant Lang!" Jack shouted for the duty officer. "You're with me!" The Egyptian officers scattered as Jack began a tour of the fort. He found the Egyptian soldiers' quarters squalid, their food inadequate, sanitary arrangements virtually non-existent, and the armoury filled with poorly maintained weapons.

"We have a lot to do," Jack said.

"Yes, sir," Lang agreed tactfully.

"What's in here?" Jack pushed at a locked door on the ground floor.

"I don't know, sir."

"Well, find out," Jack said. He raised his voice to a shout. "RSM!"

"Sir!" Deblin arrived at the double.

"Find me a key for this door!"

"Very good, sir!"

A shaking Egyptian officer arrived three minutes later with a bunch of keys.

"What's down there?" Jack asked.

"The prisoners, sir," the Egyptian said.

"What prisoners? Some of the Mahdi's men?"

"No, sir. No Mahdi's men." The officer stepped back.

"Open the door!" Jack ordered.

When the officer opened the door, the resulting stink made Jack gag.

"Step aside," he said to the Egyptian. "Lang, take the keys."

The door opened onto a flight of stairs that led into blackness. The RSM produced a lantern, and Jack ventured down, with the stench growing more formidable by the minute.

"This place is positively medieval," Lang said.

The lantern light bounced from rough-hewn rock, with the

marks of pickaxes still visible, although Jack guessed the work was centuries old.

The stairs ended at a low-roofed chamber, from which two heavy doors opened. Both were locked, and Lang had to fumble with his bunch of keys to open the first door.

"Light!" Jack snapped, and Lang held the lantern high.

"Oh, dear Lord in heaven!"

The lantern light passed over a score of people, men, women and two children, chained against the wall of a stone-hewn chamber without light or sanitation.

"What's this?" Jack gagged at the stink. "Fetch me one of the Egyptian officers."

The RSM brought the nervous Egyptian, who trembled as Jack pointed to the prisoners. "What have these people done?"

"They are criminals, sir," the officer said.

"What crimes have they committed?"

The officer spread his hands. "Many, sir."

Jack spoke to the nearest prisoner, a middle-aged man. "Why are you here?"

The man blinked in the unfamiliar lantern light, wondering why this strange European was asking him questions. "I owe a shopkeeper money."

"How much?"

The man mentioned a paltry sum.

"How long is your sentence?"

"No sentence, effendi. The Egyptians put me in here."

"Was there a trial?"

"No, effendi."

"Lift the lantern, Lang," Jack said and raised his voice. "Has anybody here had a trial?"

The light flickered over scared faces. Nobody had been tried.

"Find out if anybody is guilty of rape or murder," Jack said. "Free the rest. Whatever they've done, spending time in here is punishment enough."

"Yes, sir," Deblin said.

The second door led to a similar chamber that was empty of everything except rats and insects.

"Find somewhere more humane to put any prisoners that remain," Jack said, "and use these rooms as ammunition stores. I haven't found the garrison's ammunition yet!"

Some prisoners wept as Corporal Cooper led a working party that struck off their chains. Few of the prisoners could stand without assistance.

"They're stinking!" Corporal Cooper said.

"They are," Jack agreed. "Take them into the empty chamber, women first and then the men. Bring buckets of water, soap, and clean clothes."

"Yes, sir," Cooper said. "Kerswell, escort the ladies. Brotheridge, find buckets, brushes, and soap."

As Brotheridge hurried away, Kerswell opened the door into the second chamber. He found a lantern, quickly removed the rats and as many insects as possible and invited the women inside.

"In you come, my beauties! Jildi now! And no fighting for position!"

With the women relatively clean and decent, Jack helped them up the stairs and into the courtyard. Some had been in the dark so long they could not face the light, and Jack watched them support each other. He ordered Sergeant Deng to pass a message for any relatives to come to the fort, reassured them they would be safe and wondered what sort of regime the Egyptians had imposed on this little village.

"I'm not surprised the Sudanese join the Mahdi," Jack said. "Any occupying power that mistreats the people it controls deserves to be hated."

The men acted the same way, with one man cowering from every soldier who came close.

"You, there," Jack addressed him as kindly as possible. "You've no reason to fear now. How long have you been locked up?"

Screwing up his eyes against the unaccustomed light, the man could not answer.

"Five years," another prisoner said. He was about thirty, with a ragged beard and impressively steady eyes. "He's been in the dark for five years."

"Do you know this man?" Jack asked.

"I was his fellow prisoner," The man smiled. "We have learned to know each other."

"Can you take care of him?"

"By Allah's will."

Jack nodded. "You seem to be a capable fellow. What's life been like under the Egyptians?"

"Mendacity, peculation and corruption," the man replied. "A repression of everything that matters."

Jack grunted. "That has ended now."

"Will you restore the Imam to his position?" The man eyed Jack levelly.

"I noticed there was no muezzin," Jack said. "I know how important religion is here, so yes, I'll restore the Imam if I can find him."

"I am the Imam," the man said.

"Then may God go with you," Jack said. "Beware of the false prophet."

"The Mahdi?" The Imam gave a gentle smile. "We have not met."

"He is spreading his power over Sudan," Jack told him.

"We have not met," the Imam repeated. "I cannot decide who or what he is until we meet."

Jack nodded. "That decision is yours alone, sir."

Leaving Lang and the RSM to organise the rehabilitation of the prisoners, Jack returned to his military duties. He ordered another parade of the Egyptian garrison and inspected them as they stood in the courtyard. Although being paid had raised their morale, the soldiers were round-shouldered and untidy, with ill-fitting uniforms and dirty rifles.

"Like first-day recruits," Sergeant Hanley said.

"Well, sergeant, you're experienced in turning gutter dwellers and yokels into soldiers. Now is your opportunity with fellahin."

Hanley stamped his boots and grunted. "Leave them to me, sir."

Jack faced the waiting ranks. "You men were recruited as soldiers," Jack told them. "Yet you have acted here as bandits, robbing and mistreating the local people. That time has now ended. We will train you to be soldiers until you think like soldiers, act like soldiers, and become soldiers." He paused to see the reaction to his words.

There was none. The Egyptians appeared as lethargic as before, shuffling under the growing heat.

"The Mahdi's forces are not far away," Jack said. "Osman Zubeir is to the east with a strong army, and the false prophet is somewhere to the south of us. The only way we can survive is to be better, stronger, and tougher than they are."

The Egyptians continued to look and act like fellahin who belonged in the fields. Jack nodded. "You'll improve," he promised them.

Having laid the groundwork, Jack left the details to the junior officers and NCOs, who had a sufficient grasp of Arabic to convey their message through sheer lung power. Jack assembled the Egyptian officers and told them what he required from them.

"I don't know how many of you have military training, and I don't care. As of today, you will learn from the Royal Malverns. You'll treat your men and the local population with respect. That's all. Dismissed."

Jack drove the garrison hard the next few days, always expecting Zubeir's forces to appear on the arid plain outside. While the junior officers and NCOs drilled the Egyptian other ranks, Jack sent the Malverns' majors to train the Egyptian officers in what he expected of them.

"RSM," Jack said. "Who are the best shots in the regiment?"

"Corporal Cooper and Privates MacLeod, Scott and Graham, sir," Deblin replied immediately.

"I want a small cadre of sharpshooters," Jack said. "Those four will do, with Cooper in charge."

"Yes, sir!" Deblin said.

"Train them with the Martini and the Remington and give them extra musketry drill. Not firing by volleys, but precise, accurate firing, particularly at long range."

"Very good, sir," Deblin said.

* * *

After a few days within the confines of the fort, Jack understood some of the Egyptian garrison's lethargy. The heat was so intense it killed the appetite, and Jack had to force himself to any movement. At times he found himself in a near-trance-like state where nothing mattered.

He heard the muezzin's call every morning and knew the Imam was organising the mosque as he was organising the garrison.

"How are our Egyptians shaping up?" Jack asked the RSM.

"Not well, sir," Deblin replied. "I've never known such a lazy bunch of scoundrels, but we'll get there, sir."

While the officers and NCOs licked the Egyptians into shape, Jack toured the village to get to know the people he was supposed to defend.

El Kutuk contrasted with Suakin as the people kept to their old traditions of dress, not influenced by outsiders. The women wore simple robes of dark blue calico, with white muslin veils that left only the eyes exposed. They also wore strings of beads around their necks, waists, and wrists, so they rattled as they walked. The wealthier merchants' wives preferred agate necklaces with gold earrings and nose rings.

The houses were of sun-burnt brick, plastered with a mixture of manure and sand. When Abu Bol, a minor merchant, invited

Jack inside his home, he found a single large room with a single window high in the wall. There were no chairs, only a few stools and the *angareb*, a bed frame with strips of hide in the place of springs, topped by a palm leaf mat. Pitchers of water stood in the coolest corner, with the rim of a gourd as a drinking vessel.

The man's wife was kneeling, working in a hut behind the house, grinding maize into fine flour with a simple mill of two stones.

"You will eat with us," Abu Bol said.

The meal was simple, *assida* or maize porridge with a vegetable sauce with highly seasoned powdered meat. The *assida* was served in a wooden dish and eaten with the fingers.

"Now, Windrush Pasha," Abu Bol said. "What can we do for you?"

"I want to form a militia," Jack told him. "Our enemies surround El Kutuk, and the more defenders we have, the better."

Abu Bol spread his hands. "We are not fighting men," he said. "And if we lift a hand against the Ansar, the Mahdi will kill us all."

"I understand that," Jack said. "But unless you agree to everything the false prophet says, he will kill you anyway."

"Sometimes it is better to bow to fate than to fight the inevitable," Abu Bol replied.

Jack realised the time was not right to form a militia. *Why should these people fight for a regime that had abused them for decades?*

"Perhaps you are right, Mr Bol," Jack said. "Thank you for your hospitality." As he left the village, he heard the bugle call the alarm and hurried to the fort.

"What's the to-do?"

"Dust, sir! Somebody's approaching from the east!"

Jack nodded. *That could be Osman Zubeir.*

CHAPTER TWENTY

No matter how long you train someone to be brave, you never know if they are or not until something real happens.
   Veronica Roth

"Moffat!" Jack shouted. "Take out a dozen mounted infantry and see what's happening!" He glanced at the walls, where the sentinels were at their posts, peering into the desert. "Sound the stand-to!"

The bugle call rang out. "Colonel Wahiba! Get your men onto the walls!"

The dust crept closer, hazing the horizon as Moffat led out his mounted men, trotting eastwards. After a few hundred yards, Moffat sent out scouts on either flank.

"Good man, Moffat; you're learning."

The mounted infantry returned within half an hour. "False alarm, sir," Moffat reported. "It's a caravan bound for Berber!"

"Stand down!" Jack ordered, watching the Egyptians. About half were at their posts, which was better than he had expected.

The caravan arrived an hour later in a chaos of horsemen, camels, and men leading donkeys, with others, footsore and weary, trudging across the sand. The horsemen galloped to the gate, firing rifles in the air, and yelling as they showed off their horsemanship.

Most headed for the wells, with a few riding to the bazaar, and one lone camel rider halting in El Kutuk's main street as if undecided about what to do.

"That bloke's on Ozzy!" Private Branley was on duty at the fort's gate. "Halloa! You!" He lifted his hand. "Arab!"

"Enough of that, Branley!" Sergeant Toner reprimanded. "Keep a quiet tongue in your head!"

"Yes, Sergeant," Branley said indignantly. "But that Arab fellow's riding Ozzy, the Irish Fusilier's camel!"

"What's that you say, Branley?" Jack stepped to the gate.

"It's Ozzy, sir, the Irish Fusiliers' camel," Branley said. "I'd know him anywhere."

Jack strode from the fort to the camel rider, who remained standing in the main street. "*As-aalaam alaikum*," he began.

"And peace be upon you, too, Colonel Windrush," Alexandrina Drummond replied calmly. "I didn't expect to see you here."

Jack hid his surprise. "Nor I you, Miss Drummond. One of my men recognised your camel."

Drummond dismounted. "He was running loose outside the British camp in Suakin."

"People are worried about you," Jack said.

"They needn't worry," Drummond replied. "I'm safer here than you are."

"What are your plans now?" Jack wondered at the extra responsibility a relative of the queen could cause.

Drummond smiled. "Throw myself on the hospitality of the pasha of El Kutuk, rest for a few days and head west toward Berber. I want to find the oasis of Zerzura if it exists."

"I am the pasha," Jack said. "And I am afraid the Mahdi's forces are too close to allow you to explore anywhere."

Drummond smiled. "I'm a civilian, Colonel. You have no authority over me."

Jack knew she was correct. "We'll discuss that later," he

temporised. "In the meantime, I'll find you a room in the fort and appoint a guard."

Lang is the ideal man for that job. I suspect Moffat helped Drummond escape from Suakin.

"Thank you, Colonel Windrush," Drummond said. "Lead on!"

* * *

After a week in El Kutuk, the telegraph messages from Berber stopped. Jack ordered the operator to keep trying his machine.

"I will, sir," the operator said. He looked up. "I've been trying all morning, sir. Maybe the line is broken."

Five days later, with no news from Berber, a ragged Arab appeared at the fort's main gate.

"Sir!" Jarvis, the duty officer, threw a smart salute. "There's a native person wishing to speak to you. Shall I send him on his way?"

Jack looked up from his operational plan. "No, Jarvis, bring him in."

The Arab looked like he had been travelling for days, covered in dust and with his clothes in rags. Jack poured him a glass of water.

The man finished the glass in one draught.

"Now, my friend," Jack poured him another glass. "What do you want to see me about?" He was aware of Donnelly standing by the door with his rifle in his hand.

"I have a message for you, effendi," the man said and sat down, much to Donnelly's anger.

"Stand to attention in front of the Brigadier!" Donnelly stepped forward.

"Leave him, Donnelly. He knows what he's doing," Jack said.

"He might pull a knife, sir."

"If he does, you have my permission to shoot him."

"Yes, sir." Donnelly levelled his rifle hopefully.

Rather than producing a knife, the Arab pulled off his sandal, sending a shower of sand onto the floor.

"You dirty bugger," Donnelly said.

"Do you have a knife, effendi?" the Arab asked.

When Jack handed over the dagger he used as a paperknife, Donnelly drew in his breath. Ignoring the threatening rifle, the Arab sliced at his shoe, removing the sole to reveal another layer of leather beneath. A single sheet of thin paper lay between the two soles. The Arab placed the dagger on the desk and handed the paper to Jack.

Jack glanced at the Arabic script and shook his head. "I can't read Arabic. Can you?"

The messenger shook his head.

"Find me Sergeant Deng," Jack ordered and waited until the sergeant arrived.

"Read that, sergeant, and keep the information to yourself."

Deng nodded. "It's from the commandant at Berber to the previous garrison commander here," he said. "The Mahdi's warriors have cut the telegraph and are besieging the town."

"Thank you," Jack said and returned his attention to the messenger. "What's your name, my friend?"

"Abdullah, effendi."

"Well, Abdullah, you're a brave man. Go to the cookhouse and find something to eat and whatever else you need. Sergeant Deng here will ensure you are safe." Jack slid five silver Maria Theresa dollars across the desk. "Thank you."

With the telegraph to Berber cut, we have no communication with the outside world. We're on our own, and the only town the Ansar have ever failed to capture is Suakin. Berber will fall.

While his officers and NCOs trained the Egyptians, Jack had most of the garrison improving El Kutuk's defences. He supervised the pioneers and working parties as they extended the villages' ditch and rampart to wrap around all three wells.

"Any attacking force will need water," Jack explained. "If we can deny them water, we can withstand a long siege. That section of wall will be their target, so we must ensure it is strong."

"We'll need to allow access for caravans and other travellers, sir," Sergeant Anderson said.

"Create a wide gate in the wall about fifty yards from the wells," Jack said. "Defend it with redoubts."

"Yes, sir," Anderson agreed. "We've created a glacis on the defenders' side of the ditch, sir. That's an open space with no cover for the attackers."

"A short-range killing area," Jack had a working knowledge of siege technology, picked up at Lucknow and other forts in India.

"Yes, sir," Anderson agreed.

I'll station the Gatling gun at one of the Wellgate redoubts. The Ansar will concentrate their attack there.

Beyond the glacis was the ditch, eight feet deep, with a U-shaped bottom lined with sharp stakes. Anderson had repaired the battlemented parapets and the defender's walkway.

"You've done a good job," Jack said.

"I just gave the orders, sir," Anderson said. "The lads and the Egyptians did the work." He hesitated for a moment. "The Egyptians are the best workers I've ever seen, sir. They seem to grasp what's needed faster than our boys and toil like Trojans in the heat."

Sergeant Anderson was a one-time railway navigator with vast experience working in harsh conditions with unforgiving men. "They may not be the best soldiers in the world, sir, but they're unbeatable at engineering."

Jack nodded. "That's maybe a good thing, Anderson. Soldiers tend to destroy buildings while engineers create them. They are more useful than we are."

"Maybe so." Anderson rubbed a hand over his bearded chin. "I hadn't looked at it that way."

Every day Osman Zubeir held off his attack granted Jack time to strengthen El Kutuk's defences and train the Egyptians.

Jack had the bugler blowing reveille an hour before dawn to use every minute of the day, pushing his men hard, installing discipline into the Egyptians, increasing the skills of his sharpshooters, and learning about the local terrain.

When Jack worried about ammunition, Colonel Wahiba showed him the Egyptians' store in a house in the village.

"We have ammunition and weapons for two battalions," Wahiba explained. "When most officers of the other regiment deserted, hundreds of men followed. Now we have only a battalion and a half, with weapons and ammunition for two regiments."

Jack quietly exulted. "Thank you, Colonel," he said. "Bring all the ammunition into the fort and store them in the old dungeons."

Every morning, Jack sent patrols out into the countryside, gradually extending their range until they knew every square yard of territory in a ten-mile radius. "I want a map," he said. "I want to know every wadi, every sand hill and every rock you pass."

Moffat proved most adept at patrol work, volunteering so often that Jack sometimes had to turn him down.

"I need to give other men experience," Jack said. "Otherwise, they would be no good when we leave El Kutuk."

"Yes, sir," Moffat looked crestfallen. "Of course, sir."

"You like the desert, don't you, Moffat?"

"I do, sir. I like the vastness, and I like the Arabs, too." Moffat sounded eager. "I spoke to the Imam yesterday afternoon as well."

"Why was that, Moffat?"

"I wanted to learn the basics of their religion, sir," Moffat said. "I thought that the more I know, the better I'll understand the people."

"Good thinking, Moffat," Jack approved.

Other problems arose. Jack's appointment of Lieutenant Lang to look after Alexandrina Drummond had been a disaster. Lang was too autocratic and traditional to cope with the unconventional Drummond.

"She's utterly impossible, sir," Lang reported. "She won't obey any of my orders."

"Will she not?" Jack tried to sound surprised. The idea of the strong-willed Alexandrina Drummond obeying a youngster such as Lang amused him. "I'll relieve you of that duty, Lang. Maybe Moffat will be better suited."

"Moffat?" Lang laughed. "He can hardly give his men an order, let alone that woman."

"All the same, I'll try him," Jack said.

Moffat agreed with something like shock. "I don't know anything about women, sir!"

"Very few men do," Jack told him. "But you have the sense to admit it." He glanced around the fort. "Miss Drummond is discussing camels and mules with Private Branley. Go and introduce yourself."

"Yes, sir," Moffat said miserably.

Jack watched him walk stiffly across to the animals, where the scarecrow figure of Bramley and the aristocratic Drummond were already engaged in an animated conversation.

Now, there's an ill-assorted trio.

Jack sighed when Jamieson marched purposefully toward him. *Here's another distraction.*

Jamieson saluted and stood to attention. "We have a problem with some of the Egyptians, sir."

Jack was not surprised. There was always some trouble with the Egyptians. "What's happened this time, Jamieson?"

"They've heard all sorts of rumours about the Mahdi, sir, and they believe that their bullets will turn to water if they fire at the Mahdi's holy warriors."

"Do they, indeed?" Jack asked. "Have you told them otherwise?"

"Yes, sir, and I had the men tell them of our experiences fighting at El Teb and Tamai."

"All right," Jack said. "I doubt there's anything we say that can dissuade them of their folly until they see the reality for themselves."

"That will mean our Egyptians facing the Ansar," Jamieson said. "I doubt they're ready for that yet."

"It's your duty to get them ready," Jack reminded. "Thank you for the information, Jamieson, and now continue with the training."

"Yes, sir!"

Jack watched Jamieson march away. *I'll speak to Colonel Wahiba about his soldiers' superstitions. Maybe he can help.*

With the ditch and defensive completed, Jack moved on to the next stage of his preparations.

"Sergeant Anderson!"

"Sir!" Anderson came to attention.

"Take your pioneers and remove most thorny scrub outside the walls. The less cover we leave the enemy, the more chance we have of killing them when they come," Jack said. "And I am convinced they will come."

"We can remove it all, sir," Anderson offered.

"No." Jack shook his head. "I want you to leave half a dozen clumps a hundred and fifty yards from the wall."

"As you wish, sir." Anderson nodded, trying to hide his confusion.

"The thorn bushes you leave will lure the Ansar into a killing zone," Jack said. "I want a half barrel of explosive buried just under the ground at these bushes, with the top half filled with case shot, scrap metal and pebbles."

Anderson's face cleared. "I understand, sir."

Jack explained further. "We'll use the explosive as a mine. We'll leave a fuse of gunpowder and light it when the enemy takes cover there."

"I see, sir!" Anderson said. "Leave it to us!"

"I'll make sure you have sufficient men," Jack promised. "Bring the bushes you cut down inside the walls; I may have a use for them."

Every day, Jack sent out parties to extend the bare ground outside the village, mixing the Malverns with the Egyptians so both units grew accustomed to working together. Simultaneously, he continued training the Egyptians, taking it upon himself to lecture the officers in man management and tactics. Some were woefully inadequate, some had only joined the army for the loot, but a few matured and grew under Jack's training.

"And still, Osman Zubeir holds back," Baxter said.

"Thank God," Jack replied.

With the scrub cleared to a radius of five hundred yards, Jack set out range markers at fifty-yard intervals.

"I remember the Egyptian musketry at Tel-el-Kebir and with Baker's column. In both cases, they fired too high. If we give our Egyptians the range and plenty of practice, they should have more confidence in themselves."

"Yes, sir." Deblin sounded doubtful.

"Now," Jack said. "We have dozens of thorn bushes cluttering up the place. I want the trunks and the most stout branches formed into stakes and planted in the ditch and on any area of dead ground. If the Dervishes throw themselves down, they should get a nasty surprise."

"Yes, sir."

"Keep branches with long thorns, especially these wickedly hooked *wait-a-bit* thorns and these two-inch-long horrors. I want them placed on the ground with the thorny side up. The Dervish warriors run barefoot, and I don't care how tough they are; anybody standing on a two-inch-long thorn will know all about it!"

"I'll see to it, sir!" Deblin said. "The defaulters will love that job."

Jack nodded. "I'm sure they will, Major."

We're making progress, Jack told himself. *If Zubeir grants us another ten days or even a week, we might be ready for him.*

When he had a few free moments, Jack toured the fort's

battlements and looked out into the surrounding desert. Every day, his defences grew stronger, and his Egyptian soldiers were slightly better trained. He knew that somewhere out there, the Mahdi and his warriors were busy. If they captured Berber, they were only a hundred and thirty miles away, no distance for men born and raised in the desert.

To the south, the Mahdi would be locked in a contest with Chinese Gordon. If Gordon decided to evacuate, he could arrive at El Kutuk any time, and with the telegraph cut, Jack knew he would get no warning. If Gordon came with the refugees from Khartoum, all his defensive preparations would be for nothing. On the other hand, if Osman Zubeir or the Mahdi arrived, El Kutuk would need every man and rifle Jack could muster. He had to prepare for either eventuality.

Jack became aware of another officer staring into the abyss.

"How are you bearing up, Lang? Now you're free from Miss Drummond?"

"This is a terrible place," Lang said. "It's horribly cold at night and broiling hot all day." He adjusted his pith helmet.

"Would you rather be in England?" Jack asked with deceptive gentleness. "Poodle faking in Hyde Park?"

"Is the regiment due to be posted home soon?" Lang could not keep the despair from his voice. "The desert drains the energy from a man." He looked over at the village, where a dozen men sat in the shade of palm trees, endlessly smoking and talking while a scattering of goats wandered in their eternal search for food.

"Consider this, Lang," Jack said. "Egypt and Sudan are not part of the Empire and hopefully never will be, but we are British soldiers, and the War Office posts us wherever it sees fit."

Lang wiped beads of sweat from his forehead and said nothing.

"If we were in London or elsewhere in the United Kingdom, discipline in the regiment would be far tighter, in uniform and everything else. Service in these remote posts allows more flexibility from the rigid regimes and protocol of regimental life in Britain or Indian cantonments."

"Yes, sir," Lang said reluctantly.

"Out here," Jack said, "You can develop your ideas and interests and exercise authority in a manner impossible back home. You are a subaltern, still green behind the ears, but next week, perhaps tomorrow, maybe even today, you might find yourself in charge of a company well outside the authority of a senior officer."

Lang looked nervous at the idea.

You were so buoyant when you arrived, Lang, and I don't think you're afraid of responsibility. The desert scares you.

Jack pushed his point, indicating the surrounding wasteland. "You could be in an area where conditions are harsh, even dangerous, with primitive communications and a remote chain of command. Your superiors could be sick, injured, or dead, and you have to show initiative, or you and your men will die."

Lang bit his lower lip.

This lad's idea of soldiering is all glamorous uniforms and admiring ladies. He might not fit into the Royal Malverns.

"That's what defending the empire is all about, Lang. Out here on the frontiers, you can throw away the rule book and act according to local conditions."

"Yes, sir," Lang said.

Jack decided he had lectured enough. "Time you got started. Take Sergeant Hanley and ten men of the Malverns, plus ten Egyptians and sweep north. Patrol in a circuit of a mile from the fort and report what you find." Jack saw Lang start. "Take Sergeant Hanley's advice, Lang. He's an old hand at this game."

"Yes, sir!" Lang said.

"Move!" Jack put an edge to his voice, and Lang nearly ran.

These isolated posts can play tricks on a man's mind. The French call it cafard, and the best thing for Lang is to work.

* * *

"How are they now, RSM?"

"Their drill is improving, sir." Deblin viewed the Egyptian soldiers. "I've used men from the Malverns as markers to show them what to do, and kicked them up the backside, beg pardon, sir, the bottom, every time they're slovenly or slow."

"Are they ready for a patrol yet? I've ordered Lang to take out some Egyptians."

The RSM grimaced. "I'd say they're not, sir. I wouldn't trust them if the Dervish lads attack."

"We'll soon see," Jack said. Everything depended on General Gordon's decision. If he evacuated Khartoum soon, the garrison of El Kutuk might still leave without firing a shot.

"Yes, sir," The RSM sounded doubtful.

"I want you to keep up the drilling, RSM, and spend more time on the firing range."

"Yes, sir. We were fortunate Colonel Wahiba showed us the Egyptian's ammunition store. I wish we had more ammunition for the Martinis and seven-pounders, though."

Jack knew the RSM must be worried if he admitted his fears. "We carried a decent supply with us, RSM." *All the extra rounds in the bandoliers will come in handy.*

"Yes, sir, of course, sir."

Lang looked apprehensive as he left the fort with his mixed bunch of Malverns and Egyptians. Sergeant Hanley was expressionless, and Jack noted he had selected ten old soldiers from the Malverns. The Egyptians looked terrified, with at least one praying before he set out.

Tempted to accompany the patrol, Jack compromised by climbing to the top of the tower and watching through his field glasses.

Lang led them from the gate beside the wells, the Well Gate as the soldiers termed it, and over the drawbridge an innovative Egyptian soldier had devised for the ditch. Once on the far side, some of the Egyptians looked nervously over their shoulder until Sergeant Hanley barked at them in pure Gloucestershire, and they moved on.

Jack remained still. He did not want Lang to see him watching.

Lang's patrol threaded through the killing zone of the mined bushes and sharpened stakes and headed left, around El Kutuk's perimeter. Even from a distance, Jack could see the Egyptians nervousness irritated the Malverns.

I intended the Egyptians to learn from the veterans' experience. I hope their fear does not affect the Malverns.

Lang moved quickly, barely looking around as he sought to complete the circuit in as short a time as possible.

Slow down, man! Show the men you're not scared, even if you are!

Lang did not stop to survey the ground but moved at a fast walk until Hanley had a word with him. After that, the patrol moved slower, twenty-two soldiers in the vastness of the desert, men who did not belong. Jack watched them with sinking disappointment, for he had hoped Lang would do better. The patrol returned to the village at speed, with some of the Egyptian running ahead despite Sergeant Hanley's roars. Jack shook his head.

These men have much to learn yet, and so has Lang. We are not ready.

CHAPTER TWENTY-ONE

Ladies, whose bright eyes,
Rain influence, and judge the prize
John Milton

"Purchase as many camels and mules as possible, Quartermaster," Jack spoke from behind his desk. "We'll need all the transport we can muster when Gordon arrives with his refugees."

"I'll do what I can, sir," the Quartermaster promised.

Jack leaned back in his chair and lit a cheroot. *I'll have to be careful with the cheroots,* he thought. *I brought a limited supply, and I doubt the bazaar sells any.* He looked at the piles of paper on his desk. The higher the ranks he climbed, the more his job seemed less soldiering and more administrator. Jack looked up as somebody tapped on his door.

"Come in!"

"Your excellency." Colonel Wahiba looked slightly apprehensive.

"Yes, Colonel, but I am no excellency. Sir will do."

"Yes, sir." Wahiba glanced around the room. "You have been working hard since you arrived."

"We live in precarious times, Colonel," Jack said.

"I think you should take some time to relax. I have prepared a Turkish bath for you."

Jack stopped himself from bellowing at Wahiba, recognising that the colonel was offering an olive branch. He considered for a moment, aware that he itched from the desert sand that found its way everywhere and probably stunk from dried sweat.

"That was a kind thought, Colonel." The prospect of a bath was suddenly appealing.

"This way, sir." Colonel Wahiba ushered Jack into a small room on an upper floor. There was a scattering of chairs and a few objects on a circular table.

"A Turkish bath," Wahiba said.

Jack sighed as his enthusiasm waned. For a moment, he had contemplated wallowing in a bath of deep water, while the Turkish bath consisted of a wooden bowl containing dough and a cup full of sweet oil.

"What do I do?" Jack asked.

Wahiba smiled. "You rub the dough into your body to clean off the dust and sweat, then smooth on the scented oil."

"Thank you," Jack hid his disappointment, aware that Wahiba was trying his best.

"Shall I find you a helper?" Wahiba smiled. "A young woman to apply the dough and oil?"

"No, thank you," Jack said. "I'll manage." He ushered Wahiba out of the room, sighed, wished he had refused and decided to proceed.

Jack found the operation surprisingly refreshing and had dipped his fingers into the oil when the door opened, and Miss Drummond stepped into the room.

"What the devil!" Jack stepped behind the table to cover himself. "Please get out."

"Oh, Brigadier Windrush. I've seen a man before." Drummond sat on a chair and smiled across at him. "Don't stop on my account."

"What do you want, Miss Drummond?" Jack asked without moving.

"Only to talk to you," Drummond said. "It's difficult finding the time when you're either working in your office or with your men." She smiled. "I hope you realise they worship you."

"Hardly that," Jack reached for his clothes. "Please turn your back and allow me to dress."

Drummond's smile broadened. "A shy brigadier! My, my." When she swivelled in her chair, Jack hauled on his uniform.

"What did you want, Miss Drummond?"

"I want to be useful." Drummond eyed Jack. "I have certain skills and knowledge about Sudan and the desert that most of your men lack, and I want to pass it on."

"Are you offering to give a lecture, Miss Drummond?" Jack felt more comfortable in uniform.

"That would be a start," Drummond said. "I could also accompany some of your patrols into the desert."

"I won't allow that," Jack told her.

"I know more about travelling in the desert than your men do." Drummond retained her smile.

"Even so," Jack realised Drummond was serious. "I won't put a woman in danger."

"I put myself in danger," Drummond countered.

"No," Jack said. "Now, please leave. I have work to do."

"Yes, Brigadier." Drummond rose from her seat. "You have a fascinating collection of scars, Jack. You'll have to tell me about them sometime." She left the room, still smiling.

That woman is trouble, Jack thought. *Her attitude reminds me of Mary.*

"Are you all right, sir?" Donnelly met Jack as he returned to his office. "I noticed Miss Drummond was outside the room. She's a peach, isn't she?" He smiled.

"Attend to your duty, Donnelly!" Jack growled.

She is a peach. Tall, graceful, with a serene expression in her eyes and a determined chin. That woman could unsettle the men if I allow her.

Swearing, Jack pulled a sheet of paper towards him and began a letter to Mary. He knew he could not send it, but the act of writing helped bring her closer.

Damn you, Alexandrina Drummond. Why did you have to arrive in El Kutuk?

* * *

Jack gathered the officers and senior NCOs of both regiments in a room overlooking the courtyard. Moths and other insects flickered around the lamps, and the night-time sounds of the village were audible beyond the window.

"Gentlemen," Jack said, relying on Sergeant Deng to translate his words into Arabic rather than repeating everything himself. "Lieutenant Moffat's latest patrols have discovered evidence of enemy activity. It seems that the Ansar is coming closer. I have not heard from General Gordon, so I don't know if he has evacuated yet. Given these two circumstances, I think it safe to say Osman Zubeir may soon besiege us."

He waited for his words to sink in.

"There are two methods to endure a siege," Jack said. "We can sit passively and react to the enemy's assaults or be active and carry the fight to them."

Sarsens nodded his approval, with mixed reactions from the others.

"I favour the latter method," Jack said. "Keep the enemy on the hop; make him worry about us, rather than us worrying about him. Now, most of you Malverns served in Afghanistan and fought against Arabi. You've seen some irregular fighting already."

He waited for Deng to translate to the Egyptians. Bimbashi Mabruk shifted uneasily in his chair, and Jack remembered he had fought for Arabi in the operations around Ramleh and

Kafr-ed-Dauar. He might have unhappy memories of the Malverns."

Jack continued. "I will give some advice, which you will pass on to the men under your command. Some of it you'll know already, some you might have forgotten."

Jack had gathered a collection of paper and pens or pencils, which Donnelly handed out to every man who lacked them. For the next half hour, he passed on his experience of irregular warfare, some drawn with broad brush strokes, others aimed at individual soldiers.

"Osman Zubeir's men will seek to intimidate us," Jack said. "They will use their tom-toms to unnerve us at night and keep us awake with long-range shots. We can counter that by marking where their riflemen are and either blasting them with artillery, sending out raiding parties or using the sharpshooters that RSM Deblin has trained."

The Malverns' officers did not note what they already knew, while the junior Egyptian officers scribbled furiously as Deng translated Jack's words. Most of the senior Egyptians spoke English and needed no translator.

"We will control the ground around El Kutuk with offensive patrolling," Jack said. "By day and night. The Mahdists will outnumber us, but we're better than them." He could see the doubt in the Egyptian faces as they remembered the defeats the Mahdists had inflicted on them.

"I want thinking soldiers," Jack said. "Not unthinking sheep who blindly obey orders." He knew his words were contrary to most officers' beliefs that other ranks were only fit to be led while officers had a virtual monopoly of intelligence. Yet Jack knew officers who had to be guided through the most elementary manoeuvre and rankers who understood soldiering as competently as any entitled gentleman.

"I am well aware that a soldier's first duty is to obey, and that is as true out here as it is when parading in front of Queen Victoria. I also know that men without thought won't last in the sort of campaign we'll be waging here." Jack waited a few moments to ensure his words sank in. "That's all, gentlemen. Dismissed."

Over the next few days, Jack reinforced his theories with practical demonstrations. As most of the Malverns' officers had experience in Afghanistan, they already knew some techniques; Jack concentrated on the Egyptians. As he had expected, he found that they blossomed when their officers paid them regularly, treated them better and provided fair discipline.

"Your men have the potential to become decent soldiers," Jack said to Colonel Wahiba.

"Thank you, sir," Wahiba said.

When he was confident that both his regiments had mastered shooting at stationary targets, Jack introduced moving targets. First, he created a man-sized canvas screen and had a soldier-artist paint the image of a running warrior with a spear.

"That's your target," he said, mounted the screen on rollers and asked for volunteers to ride a horse and draw the screen across the desert. As he expected, Second Lieutenant Moffat was first in line.

"Let's hope none of your men has a grudge," Jack said.

Moffat grinned. "Yes, sir."

Jack remembered the diffident young subaltern who had arrived in Cairo and wondered at the change the desert had made.

The initial attempt was a failure.

Jack ordered the men to fire by platoons. While some of the Malverns' shots perforated the screen, the Egyptians came closer to Moffat than the target.

"Never mind," Jack said. "We'll have more training."

"I could help, Brigadier," Drummond offered.

"That won't be necessary," Jack said.

The NCOs spent the remainder of the morning teaching both regiments how to traverse and aim at a moving target, then tried again, with marginally better results. The attempts gathered quite a crowd of civilian onlookers, although Jack was unsure whether they understood the rationale and wondered if some thought Moffat was the target.

"Training the troops and simultaneously providing free entertainment?" Drummond again strode to Jack's side. She stood close, with her hip nearly touching his. "Your talents are endless, Brigadier."

Jack grunted. "We don't know when Osman Zubeir will attack," he said. "We only know that he will."

Drummond laughed. "You're such a serious man, Brigadier," she said and walked away as Donnelly watched.

By mid-afternoon, the shooting had improved, but Jack was far from happy with the standard of marksmanship.

"Keep them at it!" he ordered and changed the rider. "Moffat! You've spent sufficient time playing on that horse. Attend to your duty!" When Moffat dismounted, Jack lowered his voice. "You did well; now look after Miss Drummond."

"Yes, sir," Moffat said.

In the evening, Jack called another meeting of the officers.

"When we march, we're tied to supply columns and mules," Jack said. "That slows us down and restricts our freedom of movement. In the old Scottish border wars, the Scots carried bags of oatmeal and travelled for days eating only cold-water porridge. I want our men to be equally mobile."

Predictably, it was Moffat who looked enthusiastic at the idea. "We don't have oatmeal here, sir, but the bazaar sells dura flour and salt, and I've heard that some of the Dervish warriors live on ground-down date pips."

"Where did you hear that?" Jack asked and guessed the answer when Moffat coloured.

"It was a lady, sir," Moffat said.

Jack nodded. "Be careful, Moffat. Don't tell her too much." It was natural that a young, healthy man should find a woman, but anybody could be supplying information to both sides in a volatile place like Sudan.

"I'll have the quartermaster buy dura flour and salt from the bazaar," Jack softened his earlier rebuke with humour. "I don't think our lads can survive on ground-down date pips."

Jack joined a couple of patrols, imparting some of his experience to the officers and men. "No smoking on patrol, lads. The smell of tobacco can drift a long distance and alert the enemy to our presence. It can also lead to coughing, and sound also travels far in the desert."

He showed them how to find dead ground and keep their rifles clean, navigate by the stars and walk silently. "Lift your feet at every step and avoid kicking loose stones or stepping on dry twigs. Try to walk in a single file so any enemy that comes across your tracks can't calculate your numbers. And talk in whispers. A human voice can carry a thousand yards, a whisper only about ten."

Jack trained the men with mock fights and taught them to march one way in daylight and move in the opposite direction at night.

"Keep the enemy on the back foot. Take and seize the initiative. The way to defeat the enemy is to be tougher and better than they are."

Without knowing how much time he had to train them, Jack pushed his men hard, ignoring the subdued curses from the Malverns and the sulking from the Egyptians.

"The Ansar will outnumber us," Jack reminded everybody. "So we'll hit hard and fast until they won't know where we're coming from next! By moving quickly from one position to the next, we'll give the impression of having larger numbers."

Both regiments listened and learned as Jack hammered home his mantra.

"Remember, mobility and speed of thought. Maintain the momentum of surprise!"

Jack ordered his patrols to probe east and north, searching for Osman Zubeir's forces. They saw traces of men, horses, and camels without sighting a living soul. And all day and night, Jack had men on watch in the tower, looking to the west and south in case Gordon should arrive. And each day, he was disappointed as the horizon remained clear, and no messenger arrived from Khartoum, Cairo or Suakin.

"Have they forgotten about us?" Baxter asked as the days stretched into weeks and then months. They stood on the tower, scanning the surrounding desert through their field glasses.

"No," Jack shook his head. "They know we're here, and they know we're the Malverns. We can take whatever the Mahdi throws at us and return it with interest."

I wish I believed that.

"Moffat," Jack said, "I've limited your patrols to fifteen miles, but now I want you to extend them. Take a strong patrol and head twenty miles west and south. Find the lie of the land and watch for the enemy."

Moffat looked pleased, as Jack expected. "Now, sir?"

"Leave before dawn tomorrow."

"Yes, sir."

Moffat shaded his eyes from the sun and peered to the west, where the desert stretched in every direction, featureless, harsh, and unforgiving.

"How are you finding El Kutuk?" Jack asked.

"I like it here, sir, and I like the desert," Moffat said. "I like the starkness, and I rather admire the Baggara."

"There's a lot to admire in them," Jack agreed. He grimaced as Drummond joined them.

"Nobody can conquer the desert," Moffat stared into the distance, with Drummond listening, her face composed. "We can only live with it, accept the harshness and adapt to what it presents."

Jack allowed Moffat to speak as Drummond edged uncomfortably close.

"Somewhere out there, Cambyses marched with fifty thousand Persians in 525 BC. A sudden sandstorm swallowed the lot; they vanished and were never seen again."

"Don't forget the lost oasis of Zerzura, Douglas," Drummond

said. "I've looked for it and found nothing. The old legends claim it is home to a race of beautiful black giants, with sweet water and huge flocks of songbirds."[1]

Moffat looked at Drummond. "I don't know that one, Alex," he admitted.

Douglas? Alex? These two are on first-name terms.

"Wouldn't you like to find them?" Drummond said. "Wouldn't you like to be the first to find the oasis or locate where Cambyses vanished?"

"Oh, I would," Moffat said. "I'd like to follow the travels of Ibn Battuta as well."

"Yes." Drummond's face lit up as she stood beside Moffat. "Western histories ignore him, although he was the greatest traveller of his age."

"Arguably, Ibn Battuta was even greater than Marco Polo!" Moffat said. "I've never met anybody who's heard of him before!"[2]

"Have you read his journal?"

"Only fragments."

"I have the full text in Persian." Drummond's eyes were glowing. "Can you read Persian, Douglas?"

Moffat shook his head. "No, I'm teaching myself Arabic, though. I'll try Persian next."

"I'll teach you," Drummond volunteered. "Persian is the most beautiful language in the world."

Jack cleared his throat. "I'd be obliged if you two could continue your discussion elsewhere. I have work to do."

"Yes, sir," Moffat replied while Drummond smiled.

"Come, Douglas. The Brigadier is busy."

Jack did not smile until Drummond had ushered Moffat from the tower.

That night the tom-toms began.

CHAPTER TWENTY-TWO

Thought shall be the harder, heart the keener,
Courage the greater as our might lessens
The Battle of Maldon (translated by R. K. Gordon, 1926.)

Lang was duty officer and saluted when Jack performed his pre-dawn inspection of the defences. "*Hannibal ad portas,*" Lang said. "Hannibal is at the gates."

"I heard the drums," Jack confirmed.

Colonel Wahiba emerged from his quarters, looking drawn as he adjusted his fez. "The Mahdi has arrived," he said.

"The Mahdi or Osman Zubeir," Jack agreed.

"They'll outnumber us about ten to one," Lang said, "but at least we'll be fighting rather than sitting still."

Jack nodded. "Have you heard of General Grant, Lang?"

"The American fellow, sir? Yes, I have."

"On the first occasion Grant commanded an army, his superior officer sent him against a Confederate force. When Grant saw his opposition, he thought it prudent to withdraw to a safer position. However, before Grant moved, he realised the Confederate army was already withdrawing. The lesson Grant learned, and you should learn, Lang, is that on a battlefield, as in most other places, when you are afraid of your opponent, he is also afraid of you. Put on a bold front, and they will often back down."

"Yes, sir," Lang said. "Do you think Zubeir will back down?"

Jack shook his head. "No, he won't, but I think he'll have more respect for British arms than he pretends. It's up to us to increase that regard to fear."

"Yes, sir," Lang said.

Colonel Wahiba nodded. "We'll teach him that the Egyptians can also fight!"

"I am sure of that, Colonel," Jack heard footsteps behind him.

"There's a couple of fellows to see you, sir," Sergeant Toner reported. "The Imam and a man from the village."

Jack glanced at the sky. "They're early. It's not even dawn yet."

"Yes, sir," Toner agreed.

"Show them into my office, Sergeant."

Abu Bol and the Imam stood opposite Jack's desk. "Windrush Pasha," Abu Bol said. "The Imam has told me about the false prophet who claims descent from Mohammed."

"The Imam is a wise man," Jack said.

"I have spoken to some of the villagers," Abu Bol said. "We want to create a militia to defend El Kutuk."

"You are also a wise man, Abu Bol," Jack said as one of his burdens eased. If the villagers were on his side, he had more chance of success. "I'll appoint a good man to train your men."

"Thank you, Effendi," Abu Bol said.

"No, Abu Bol, I should thank you for your trust." Standing up, Jack held out his hand. "I'll send an officer and an NCO this morning."

Captain Jamieson has experience in the North West Frontier, and Sergeant Hanley is an intelligent man. I'll send Bimbashi Mabruk to translate unless the villagers resent an Egyptian. The Ansar's tom-toms may have done some good.

* * *

"Increase the patrols, Moffat," Jack ordered as the subalterns stood before him. "I want fifty men in each, mixed regiments, and go further out each time."

"Yes, sir," Moffat never complained when sent into the desert.

"*Audaces fortuna iuvat,*" Lang commented. "Fortune favours the brave."

"It does," Jack agreed. "And your fortune is to join Captain Jamieson in training the El Kutuk militia. You look the part of a British officer. Gather volunteers and show them the basics of drill and musketry."

"Me, sir?" Lang said.

"You, sir."

As pasha of the fort and village, Jack acted as a judge to the civilian population. He held an open court every morning in the fort, listened to complaints and made decisions that affected the people's lives. One day he could decide on a property dispute, and the next, a case of theft or family. When the disagreements involved religion or Islamic law, Jack called on the Imam for help.

"I thought Islam had Sharia law," Jack said as the Imam decided on a matrimonial case. "Cutting off hands and noses."

"That's the extremists," the Imam gave his soft smile. "I am sure you Nazarenes have extremists too, who call for an eye for an eye."

"I am sure we do," Jack agreed.

The tom-toms sounded the following night, and then the campfires appeared. The lookouts on the tower reported the glow just beyond the horizon, and Jack ran up the stairs with his field glasses.

"To the north," Corporal Walters said as the flicker reflected above his line of sight. Jack traversed the field glasses, seeing the orange glow continue in a wide circle, increasing even as he looked.

"They're all around us, sir," Walters said calmly.

"They are," Jack agreed. He could feel the thumping of his heart as the ring of fire spread around the horizon.

Gordon will have to fight his way through, and we'll have to help him.

"What do we do, sir?" Sarsens had run up to the top of the tower.

"We continue as before," Jack said. "We are only assuming these campfires are hostile. Perhaps they are not." He forced a grin. "Moffat's been out all day, so you and I will recce in the early morning."

"Yes, sir," Sarsens did not hide his satisfaction.

Jack led out a strong patrol an hour before dawn. He took Sarsens and half the mounted infantry, added a dozen Egyptians, threaded through the defences, and headed for a small ridge a mile and a half from the village.

"Sir," Sarsens pointed to a tangle of footprints in the sand.

Jack dismounted and viewed the evidence. "Mostly barefooted men," he said. "I'd say well over a hundred, with about half a dozen on horseback."

"The horsemen would be the leaders, sir," Sarsens said helpfully.

"They would," Jack agreed. "They must have been watching us during the night. Let's see where they came from." He remounted, and they followed the trail, with the horses' hooves padding on the sand and the dawn light a silver gleam to the east.

Jack sent out three riders on each flank. "Keep your rifles handy, lads." He missed this close association with the men. Commanding an entire garrison was fascinating, but higher ranks tended to view the men as numbers rather than individuals.

The trail led in an undeviating line to the north, with the hoof prints surrounded by footprints for three miles.

"Wait!" Jack held up his right hand. The patrol halted, horses tossing their heads in the already oppressive heat and men sweating, swatting at circling flies. A corporal removed his pith helmet, wiped his forehead, and replaced the hat. A vulture flew above in its perennial quest for food.

The trail continued into the distance, arrow straight into the perpetual waste. "I think we've gone far enough," Jack said. "The horses will be tiring in this heat, and we know how fast these Dervishes can run."

"Do you think they might cut us off, sir?"

"I don't want to give them the opportunity," Jack indicated the surrounding scrubland with its profusion of thorn bushes and scattering of rocks. "There are a thousand places where they can hide."

"I can ride ahead, sir," Sarsens volunteered eagerly.

Jack shook his head. The best men were the boldest and the most willing to court danger.

"No, Sarsens, thank you. We've come far enough. Call in the scouts." He glanced at the surrounding desolation baking in the heat. "Sound the recall."

Sarsens signalled to the trumpeter, and the shrill call sounded across the desert.

"The Mahdists will hear that, sir," Sarsens said.

"No doubt," Jack agreed, "but they're probably watching us anyway. I am sure they'll be aware of everything we're doing."

Jack headed back to El Kutuk, with the dust rising around them and the steady thud of the horses' hooves reassuring.

"We're being followed, sir," Sarsens said.

Jack looked over his shoulder. A score of men ran a few hundred yards behind the patrol, carrying circular shields and long spears. They kept a steady rhythm, neither falling back nor coming closer.

"Keep moving," Jack ordered. "Don't increase the pace.

Smith and Doncaster, you're the rearguard. Ride ten yards behind the column and let me know if these fellows come any nearer but don't engage them until I give the order."

The two privates fell back. Both were steady men and wore the Afghanistan and Egyptian medal ribbons.

Jack remained in front of the patrol, looking right and left. He saw a faint smear of dust lifting to the left and was not surprised to see another group of warriors jinking in and out of the thorn bushes.

"Over there, Sarsens," Jack said quietly. "They'll be on the right as well."

"I can't see any, sir," Sarsens said.

"See that haze?" Jack nodded to the right. "Just beyond that sagging mimosa bush?"

"I see it, sir."

"Keep your eye on it," Jack advised. "I'd wager there are warriors beneath it."

Three minutes later, Sarsens grunted. "You're right, sir. I see them now."

Doncaster trotted up. "Sir, there's more Dervishes behind us now. I never saw them arrive, but I'd say there's double the number."

"Thank you, Doncaster," Jack said. "Sarsens, keep the men moving at a steady pace." He spurred to a small knoll on the left and swept his field glasses across the horizon. Doncaster was correct; the number of warriors behind them had increased, with others arriving on both flanks.

How far to the village? Two miles and the enemy is creeping closer.

"Increase the speed, Sarsens," Jack said when he re-joined the column. "Just a little; we don't want to give the impression that we're running away."

The patrol moved faster, with the enemy edging slightly closer. Now Jack could clearly see the men on the flanks. Fifty warriors trotted on each side, jinking past the bushes and rocks and each carrying a spear and shield.

Jack looked ahead, where the fort's tower and the mosque's minaret showed prominently above El Kutuk's walls. The patrol had only half a mile to go, an easy gallop to the shelter of the guns. He grinned in sudden recklessness.

"Halt!"

The patrol halted with the dust drifting slowly across the desert and the men staring at him in wonderment. "Take a drink of water, lads; moisten your throats."

The men did as Jack ordered.

"Now sing. Let the Ansar know who we are." Jack led the way with the first verse of the Malverns' marching song,

"A gay fusilier was marching down through Rochester,
Bound for the war in the Low Country
And he cried as he tramped through the dear streets of
 Rochester,
Who'll be a soldier for Marlbro with me?
And he cried as he tramped through the dear streets of
 Rochester,
Who'll be a sojer for Marlbro with me?"

The Malverns joined in, with the Egyptians trying their best and the song getting louder as the men gained confidence. Doncaster shouted, "Why Rochester? Why not Hereford?" and substituted their home barracks town with the Kent town.

"That's the way, boys!" Jack shouted and circled the patrol. The Ansar had stopped in a horseshoe formation, holding their spears without approaching any closer to Jack's men.

Somebody has them under tight discipline.

"Move on," Jack said. "Walk!"

When the patrol moved, the enemy followed, keeping their distance, threatening the British with their presence yet without attacking.

"Keep singing!" Jack ordered. He knew that in future, men would tell tales of the day Fighting Jack ordered his men to sing in the face of the enemy. He did not care about enhancing his reputation; he only wished to make it obvious the Ansar had not chased his men back to El Kutuk.

The enemy began to shout in a constant chorus of "Allah Akbar" that Jack remembered well from Afghanistan and the Frontier. They increased their speed, inching closer to the British patrol.

"Keep your nerve, men!" Jack shouted. "Sarsens, lead the patrol into the village." Pulling Tinker aside, Jack stood as the patrol walked past, noting each man's attitude. Some looked understandably nervous, but none were close to panic. One or two were truculent, as if they wished to stand and fight.

"Doncaster and Smith," Jack said. "Take my compliments to Lt Sarsens and tell him I am bringing up the rear."

"Yes, sir." Neither man argued at being relieved from the rearguard and trotted to the head of the column.

Jack took his position behind the patrol, turned his horse, and lifted his field glasses. The enemy was only three hundred yards away, moving as smoothly as they had an hour previously. He ignored the infantry and looked for a leader.

A moment after Jack halted, the warriors also stopped. They stood in perfect silence as the dust settled around them and the sun glinted from the tips of their spears.

That's better. Let the Ansar wait until my men are safe.

Jack lowered his field glasses and glanced over his shoulder, where his patrol threaded through the killing area towards the Well Gate. He waited until the head of the column was at the gate before turning his horse and walking away.

Immediately Jack moved, the enemy followed, increasing their speed to a trot as the sides of the horseshoe began to close in.

Jack dug in his heels, watching as the warriors on his right came so close, he could make out their features. They were running now, taking great bounds over the ground as their intentions became evident.

They're trying to cut me off!

As the tail of the patrol disappeared through the gate, Moffat and Donnelly emerged on horseback. They galloped to Jack without hesitation, with Donnelly holding his rifle.

"Don't fire!" Jack shouted, hoping his words could carry the distance.

If we fire first, the Mahdi or Osman Zubeir will say we began hostilities. If they fire first, we are justified in defending ourselves. It's all part of Zubeir's attack on our nerves.

Moffat and Donnelly kicked up dust as they galloped forward, and Jack wondered who would reach him first, the Ansar or Donnelly. He refused to spur but advanced at a sedate pace as suited a senior officer.

Donnelly shouted, "Come on, sir! The Dervishes are close!"

"They won't fire, Donnelly," Jack said. "Ride at my side."

Moffat shouted a moment later. "You must hurry, sir!"

"Is that an order, Lieutenant?" Jack asked, smiling.

"No, sir, of course not!" Moffat looked confused.

He's still a very young man.

"Then ride at my side." Jack saw the Well Gate reopen, and Sarsens reappear with the mounted infantry, their hooves hammering on the wooden drawbridge. "Hold your fire!" Jack roared.

The naval party at the defending redoubt crouched behind their Gatling, waiting for Jack's order.

The two sides of the horseshoe were within fifteen yards of each other when Jack eased through the gate with Moffat and Donnelly beside him.

"Now," Jack ordered, "get back inside and close the damned gate!"

When the last of the mounted infantry dashed inside, a mixed party of Malverns and Egyptians hauled in the drawbridge and pushed the gate shut. Three men lifted a hefty beam and fitted it into the slots to barricade the door.

Jack heard a thud, and the gate shuddered. Private Wright, on guard on the wall, shouted, "Permission to fire, Sergeant?"

"Not until an officer gives the word!" Sergeant Trafford snarled.

"What's happened out there?" Jack asked.

"One of them threw a spear at the gate, sir."

"I'm coming up," Jack said and mounted the half-dozen steps to the redoubt. Most of the warriors had already withdrawn, leaving only three within fifty yards of the gate. All three wore the usual patched robes of the Mahdi's warriors, but the central man was a head taller than his companions.

"Osman Zubeir," Jack said softly.

"General Windrush," Zubeir shouted, "We claim El Kutuk for the Mahdi and the true religion."

"Your false prophet has no claim here," Jack replied. "Your men have failed against British bullets at El Teb and Tamai. Do you want to lose more of them?"

"We could have killed you at any time today," Zubeir shouted. "We refrained because the Prophet and the Mahdi are merciful. I will give you until sunrise tomorrow to open your gates. Everybody who submits to the Mahdi and accepts the true path will be spared."

"And the rest of us?" Jack asked.

Zubeir drew a finger across his throat.

Jack lifted a hand in acknowledgement. "I have a counter-proposal, Osman Zubeir. Take your warriors and depart, and we will leave you in peace. If you attempt to capture El Kutuk, we will destroy you." Jack turned away with no more to say.

"We can kill him now, sir," Lieutenant Hamilton offered, aiming the Gatling.

"No, Hamilton," Jack told him. "We must force them to be the aggressors. We'll give them every chance to withdraw peacefully."

"Aye, aye, sir," Hamilton said.

Jack felt the tension as he marched to the fort. "Well, now we know where we stand. I want a proclamation sent out to everybody in the village informing them of Osman Zubeir's offer. Tell them that anybody who wishes to leave is free to go, with my blessing, and they can carry all their household possessions with them."

"We might have an exodus, sir," Baxter said.

Jack nodded. "I know. We have limited food in the village, so the more people leave, the longer our supplies will last."

As long as Gordon does not arrive with a horde of refugees, we should manage to hold out for a few weeks. Maybe even a couple of months, but after that? I do not know.

CHAPTER TWENTY-THREE

And fight in the way of God with those who fight with you, but aggress not: God loves not the aggressors.
    Sura 2: Koran

Two hundred people fled the village, crowding through the Well Gate into an uncertain future, with the remaining population wondering if they should also leave. The following morning, as the sun rose in glorious dawn, Jack ordered two strong mounted patrols to leave the village.

"Sarsens, head south and east, Moffat, north and west. See if Zubeir is close by," Jack ordered. "Take half a dozen Egyptians with you, and don't engage the enemy unless it's essential."

"Yes, sir."

Jack mounted the tower with his field glasses to watch the progress of the patrols. *I dislike sending young men into danger while I remain in safety.*

From his vantage point, Jack saw the patrols pass over the killing area and head left and right. He scanned the desert further out. The land baked under the sun, with distances deceptive and rocks wavering in the heat. Jack saw nothing living, only the unending plain, scattered with thorn bushes, rocks and dust blowing in the wind.

Except there wasn't any wind. Jack focussed his field glasses on the rising dust and waited. He saw the banner first, and then he saw the white-clad horsemen. Lastly, Jack saw the Baggara infantry, running with spears upraised, the tireless, patch-robed warriors of the Mahdi following their black banners.

"Bugler," Jack shouted. "Come up here!"

The Malverns' bugler trotted up the stairs. "Sir?"

"Stand by," Jack said. "I might need you."

"Yes, sir," the bugler said and sprang to attention.

"Stand easy, man," Jack said testily. "You're not on parade!"

He watched the dust, calculating how many men it concealed. Should he call in the patrols or allow them to continue? Should he run from every Mahdi shadow? No.

"Sound the alarm, Bugler," Jack said softly and raised his voice. "Major Baxter! I want One and Two Sections of A Company, Bimbashi Khalif and fifteen Egyptian infantrymen, with as many mounted infantry as you can saddle."

"Yes, sir."

"Immediately, Major. And have Gonda saddled and ready."

The dust cloud was closer now, and Jack could estimate the enemy's numbers as around a hundred foot soldiers and twelve cavalrymen. The banners were visible above the haze, two black and one green.

Major Baxter had gathered the force Jack requested. The men stood at ease in the fort's courtyard, waiting for orders. Jack mounted Gonda and nodded to Donnelly, who rode behind him.

"There's a Mahdist force approaching the village," he said. "We're going to confront it." He said no more, kicked in his heels and walked his horse out of the fort and through the Well Gate.

Now we'll see if the training worked and if the Egyptians can fight. If so, we can hold this place; if not, I hope we have sufficient Malverns to give a good account of ourselves.

Once over the drawbridge, Jack headed straight for the

approaching Mahdists. The leader must have seen his dust, for he spread out his men to outflank the British force. The banners protruded above the riders, proclaiming the might of the Mahdi, and challenging the intruders in his territory.

"Right, lads," Jack kept his voice calm. "Form a square, mounted men in the centre." For the first time in his career, he had deliberately sought a battle. One of his reasons was to divert the enemy's attention from the patrols he had sent out. Another was to provoke the Mahdists into firing first, and the third was to prove to his Egyptians that they could fight, and their bullets would not turn to water.

The Mahdists were five hundred yards away and approaching fast. Jack looked over his men, noting that the Malverns stood stoically. They had seen it all before and knew what to expect. The Egyptians were nervous, glancing over their shoulders, fiddling with their rifles, and muttering to one another.

Jack did not see who fired the shot but heard the bullet scream overhead. Another shot followed, equally high.

Thank you, Mahdists. Now I can retaliate with a clear conscience.

Jack pushed Ganda in front of the square. "You can see these Mahdists are terrible shots," he said casually. "Do you still believe the Mahdi can make your bullets turn to water?" he asked. When the Egyptians either grinned nervously or chose not to answer, Jack chose a private at random and borrowed his rifle. It was a Remington, a make with which he was less familiar, but he had confidence in his marksmanship.

Dismounting, Jack took a deep breath, hoped the owner had maintained the weapon properly and aimed for one of the rapidly advancing infantrymen.

Keeping both eyes open, Jack aimed low, allowed for windage, and squeezed the trigger. He saw his target stagger back, recover and crumple.

I just killed a man as an example to my soldiers. Was that good leadership? Or was it murder?

"There," Jack returned to the square and handed the rifle back to its owner. "Load that, please." He raised his voice to ensure all the Egyptians heard. "Your bullets are lethal, gentlemen. As you have witnessed, they kill the Mahdi's warriors."

Although some Egyptians looked reassured, others looked terrified. Jack forced a laugh. "Come on, lads! We've got rifles, and they have spears! Aim!" he cracked out the last word in his parade ground voice, and British and Egyptian soldiers jumped to action.

"Spears, yes," somebody grunted, "spears with heads like masons' trowels."

"Volley fire!" Jack snapped. "On my word!"

The Mahdi's warriors had circled the square and slowed down. They now advanced in short rushes, taking advantage of every piece of cover.

"Fix bayonets!" Jack heard the sinister metallic click as the British and Egyptians slotted their bayonets in place. Sunlight glinted from the eighteen-inch-long sword bayonets. "Aim!"

Jack paced behind the left flank, where the Egyptians stood. Bimbashi Khalif looked at him wide-eyed.

"That's the way, Bimbashi," Jack said. "You and your men will prove your worth today." He watched Zubeir's warriors approach. "Set your sights to three hundred yards," he said and walked the length of the square, checking a man here and there. "Present!" The rifles slammed into shoulders as men automatically reacted to hours of drill.

"Aim!" The rifles shifted slightly as men aimed.

Fire!"

The volley was ragged, but all the men stood. A few of the enemy fell.

"Load!" Jack stood behind the most nervous of the Egyptians.

"Present! Aim!" Jack tapped the nearest private on the shoulder. "Lower your rifle a little. That's the way; you're doing well, lads! Fire!"

The next volley was slightly better. Three more of the enemy fell, but the remainder kept coming, spears raised, and ox-hide shields ready to fend off the Egyptian bayonets.

"Load!" Jack shouted. "Present!"

Bimbashi Khalif pushed a man back into line, unholstered his revolver and extended his arm.

"Well done, Khalif!" Jack encouraged.

The enemy warriors emerged from cover and charged, yelling. "Fire!" Jack shouted. Because the warriors surrounded the entire square, they lacked depth in any one place. Jack unfastened his holster and pulled out his revolver. "Meet them!"

When one of the Egyptian soldiers dropped his Remington, Jack lifted it, grabbed the man, and thrust the weapon back in his hands. "Fight them!" he snarled, "or I'll shoot you here and now!"

Faced with the threat of Jack's revolver an inch from his face, the private turned around. The Mahdi's warriors were so close that Jack could smell them. He aimed his revolver at the nearest, squeezed the trigger and saw the man's head jerk back. An Egyptian private yelled and lunged at a warrior with his bayonet. The Mahdist parried with his shield until a second Egyptian fired, with the heavy bullet knocking the warrior off his feet.

Behind him, Jack heard the regular volleys of the Malverns, with an occasional comment from the men.

"That's done for you, you ugly beggar!"

"You'll not be sticking that spear into me, Fuzzy!"

"Watch your flank, Joe! There's another one coming!"

Jack snarled an order, and the rear of the square parted to allow the seven mounted infantry to trot out, yelling and firing their carbines.

"Come on, my Egyptian soldiers!" Jack roared. "See them off!"

Gunsmoke already shrouded the square, hanging heavy in the still air, and Jack became aware of another force on his left.

He heard the regular crash of a volley and knew that Sarsens had ridden to the sound of battle.

"We've caught them between two fires," he shouted. "Be careful we don't shoot our own men!"

With the arrival of Sarsens, the Mahdists began to melt away, and when Moffat came in from the right, their withdrawal became a full-scale retreat. After the mounted infantry harried the enemy for half a mile across the desert, Jack ordered the bugler to sound the recall.

"Back to El Kutuk," Jack said. "We've achieved our objective."

My Egyptians know their bullets kill, and they fought off a Mahdist charge. That's progress.

* * *

The sound of the heavy timber Well Gate closing was like the thud of a dungeon door. Jack viewed his Egyptians, laughing and talking, marching like soldiers after their small victory.

Even a little success bolsters morale. These lads will boast to their comrades, who will want to share in the next triumph.

"Now what, sir?" Sarsens was smiling.

"Now, we continue patrolling," Jack replied. "Zubeir hopes to besiege us, but I want to keep him jumping. We know the surroundings better than he does and have better men and weapons."

Sarsens nodded to the jubilant Egyptians. "You never gave up on the Egyptians, did you, sir?"

"No," Jack said. "When I joined my first regiment, the 113th Foot, they had an even worse reputation than the Egyptians. People called them the Baby Butchers, and higher command gave them the dirtiest jobs and didn't trust them to fight."

"The 113th?" Sarsens repeated. "That's our second battalion?"

"It is, and as fine a fighting regiment as any in the army," Jack said. "They used to get the worst officers, the broken down, the hopeless, the old, sick, lame, and infirm. If the 113th could find their soul, so could the Egyptians. It's about spirit and morale, training and decent leadership. Given that, there's nothing wrong with the Egyptian soldiers."

"Yes, sir," Sarsens said.

Rather than rest on their laurels of a single defensive victory, Jack ordered another patrol that afternoon.

"I only want information," he said to Moffat. "Nothing else. No fighting. Take some Egyptians with you and try to find Zubeir's camp."

Moffat rode out gladly with a combined British and Egyptian force. Jack watched them leave with mixed emotions.

Danger is part of the soldier's bargain, he told himself. *Moffat would not have it any other way.*

"Major Baxter!"

"Sir!"

"I want standing pickets outside the village. One section strength, with mobile pickets between them, and at least two long patrols daily. No fixed time or strength, so the enemy doesn't know what we're doing next."

Baxter nodded. "I'll arrange it, sir."

"Liaise with Colonel Wahiba and include some Egyptians."

"Yes, sir."

"The Malverns will guard the north and western walls, including the fort, and the Egyptians the south and west, with the village militia on the least vulnerable parts."

"Very good, sir."

When Jack was not on the tower, he walked the walls, checking the defences. He allocated each company a dedicated section of the walls and paid particular attention to Abu Bol's militia.

"Continue with their training," Jack ordered. "I want them to know how to load, aim and fire, but don't waste ammunition."

We have limited ammunition and food, which will be a problem if Zubeir decides on a prolonged siege.

Moffat's patrol returned after three hours, with the men tired and dusty. "Not a sign of the Dervishes, sir," Moffat reported. "It's as if the desert has swallowed them up."

"Oh, they'll be there," Jack said. "Zubeir knows what he's doing. One little skirmish won't frighten him off."

Jack pulled in the pickets half an hour before night and listened as the tom-toms began their threatening beat. He had expected no less and toured the barracks after the bugler sounded retreat. He always felt a little melancholic when the beautiful notes drifted across the fort, the quarter guard presented arms and an NCO in full dress lowered the flag.

Jack felt satisfied to see the men were in high spirits after the day's success, laughing and joking. He did not interfere. He knew that soldiers liked a commander who could amuse them with his eccentricities, but he was not inclined to play the clown. Rather than wearing a white fighting coat like General Gough or facing the enemy in a top hat like Sir Thomas Picton at Waterloo, Jack preferred to look after his men's welfare and give them a decent chance of success and survival.

He looked at the desert sky and wondered if Mary was viewing the same stars.

I'll see you sometime, Mary, just as soon as Gordon evacuates Khartoum, and we leave the Sudan.

Except for the drumming of tom-toms, the night was quiet. Jack grabbed sleep between his patrols and was on the tower when the sun broke the horizon. He watched Baxter send out the pickets as the notes of reveille faded, with the men doubling to their positions, rifles held ready.

That's the way, boys.

Jack ensured the Khedive's flag was hoisted from the tower and added a makeshift Union flag. "I know we're not in British territory, but if my Malverns are to fight and die, we'll do it under the Union flag, by God!"

"Yes, sir," Baxter agreed. "We're still British soldiers, even if this isn't our territory."

When Jack toured the walls, he realised the men shared his views.

"There goes Fighting Jack," Private Brotheridge said. "He'll do things his way and bugger the politicians."

"It's good to see the old flag again," Kerswell stuffed something into the bowl of his pipe. "Have you tried this muck, Brothers? I bought it in the bazaar. They called it tobacco, but I think it's horseshit and dried grass."

Brotheridge shook his head. "Maybe old Jack will give you a cheroot. He smokes seven a day, every day."

Jack ignored the words but grunted. Perhaps he did have eccentricities of which he was unaware. Trust British soldiers to know more about him than he knew himself.

That day passed with no sign of the Mahdists. The pickets endured their hours in the sun and returned, and the patrol saw nothing except the glaring heat of the desert.

"Maybe Zubeir has decided to leave us alone, sir," Lang suggested.

"Maybe," Jack said. "But I doubt it."

There were no drums that night, nor the next, as Jack sent his patrols further afield and had the pioneers deepen the defensive ditch. As the days passed, Jack fretted and wondered what Zubeir had planned. He watched Sergeant Hanley training the militia, attended his daily court, dispensed what he hoped was fair justice and toured the village.

"We're doing all right so far, sir," Lang said.

"So far," Jack agreed and withdrew to his sleeping quarters. He had learned to ignore the occasional sounds of female giggles around the barracks and the furtive light footsteps after dark. He heard Donnelly's soldier-Arabic request to keep quiet and smiled. Soldiers needed women, and some women preferred a man in uniform. He missed his wife and understood.

"You look like a cat with a bucketful of cream," Jack said as Donnelly stood before him on the fifth morning after the skirmish.

"Yes, sir."

"Your women keeping you happy, Donnelly?" Jack asked and enjoyed Donnelly's moment of confusion.

"Yes, sir," Donnelly said at last and drew back his shoulders even further, preparing to endure Jack's displeasure.

"Be careful, Donnelly. Don't let your guard drop."

"I won't, sir," Donnelly said.

* * *

Moffat and Sarsen's daily patrols ventured deeper into the desert, with the men becoming more familiar with the terrain each time. They rode like seasoned warriors, with Moffat and some men adopting an Arab keffiyeh headdress. Jack said nothing. He did not care what they wore as long as they could fight.

On the tenth night after the skirmish, the Mahdists struck.

The sudden noise woke Jack, and he started from bed, shoving aside the mosquito netting, and reaching for his sword belt and pistol.

"Bugler! Sound the alarm! Duty officer! Report!" Jack ran from his quarters, buckling the sword belt around his waist.

"We're under attack, sir!" Lieutenant Jarvis reported.

"Which wall? How many?"

"I don't know, sir,"

"Well, find out! You're the duty officer, damn it!" Jack ran to the top of the tower, shouting orders. "Sound the stand-to! Light the torches! Lieutenant Hamilton! Stand by at the Gatling! Lieutenant Rawlinson! Star shells!"

Jack listened to the bugler's frantic call, saw the lights begin to flare along the wall and heard the irregular crackle of musketry. The Malverns were scrambling to their positions along the fort's walls.

"Move, lads!" RSM Deblin's voice rose high. "Don't fire until an officer gives the order!"

The torches gave some clarity to the scene. Outside the walls, a mass of warriors advanced across the killing zone. Some were writhing on the ground, victims of the pointed stakes, others carried long ladders, and some fired their rifles at the defenders who lined the walls.

"Volley fire!" Jack ordered. He knew that excited or frightened men might fire without aiming while having an NCO or officer give clear orders could calm down men used to disciplined commands. "Aim low, lads and use the range markers!"

As the first volley crashed out, Jack saw a section of Egyptians under their officer on the wall around the village. Despite the sudden shock, they looked steady. They raised their rifles and fired, with the muzzle flashes bright in the night. A row of red fezzes guarded El Kutuk while Abu Bol's militia scrambled to their posts.

Jack nodded as the first star shell burst, illuminating the ground beyond the killing zone.

"Fire!" A volley crashed out from the Malverns' ranks.

"*Nar*! Fire!" Colonel Wahiba roared, and the Egyptians fired in a volley as regular as any British regiment.

The star shell's light faded, leaving intense darkness. "Fire!" Rawlinson ordered, and another star shell exploded, showing a black mass of infantry in the distance, with a group of horsemen in the middle.

"Corporal Cooper!" Jack shouted. "Can you reach the horsemen?"

"We'll try, sir!" Cooper shouted, and then the navy joined in.

"Shoot, boys!" Lieutenant Hamilton ordered, and the Gatling began its mechanical chatter, sweeping across the bare ground outside the Well Gate.

Jack nodded as the Mahdists' fury ebbed away. He saw a group of warriors with a scaling ladder approach until a withering volley from the Egyptians felled every man.

"That's my children!" Wahiba exulted.

This attack failed. I'll need to organise something to give us a more advanced warning.

The noise of the assault had roused the village, but the militia reported no incidents in their section.

"They didn't come our way, sir," Abu Bol said.

The Mahdists attack melted away, and Jack ordered the bugler to sound the cease-fire.

"We beat them!" Lang yelled.

"That was only a probe," Jack warned. "Osman Zubeir was testing our defences."

"We showed him, didn't we, sir?"

"We did," Jack agreed.

Now Zubeir knows where we've positioned our Gatling and how long we take to man the walls. Zubeir gained information at the cost of his men's lives.

"Sarsens! Take half of A Company at dawn and see what's happening."

"Sir!"

Sarsens returned after a forty-minute patrol and reported thirty dead warriors around the fort.

"I thought there might be more," Sarsens sounded disappointed.

"They could have carried away some of their casualties," Jack told him.

That morning, Jack had trip wires stretched across the killing ground, with pieces of metal, glass bottles and anything that could make a noise attached to the cable. "I want an advanced warning when the Ansar come again."

With the pioneers deepening the defensive ditch and adding more pointed stakes, Jack called for volunteers for a long-distance patrol.

"I'll go, sir," Sarsens said.

"Not this time," Jack told him. "Moffat, take the mounted infantry and search for Osman Zubeir's camp. I want to know how many men he has."

Once again, I'm sending out my best and bravest. Bonaparte called the Peninsular War his Spanish Ulcer, and I think the same about these campaigns on the Empire's fringes. We bleed our young officers and experienced men year after year.

Jack checked the pickets outside El Kutuk's walls and waited for Moffat's return. When he saw a thread of dust rising to the north, Jack focused his field glasses.

"Too much dust for Moffat's men." Baxter sounded worried.

"That could be the Ansar," Wahiba said. "I'll get my regiment ready."

"Not yet," Jack said. "We'll wear the men out if we have them running around whenever we see dust. The forward pickets will keep us informed."

A lone rider detached from the dust and galloped towards El Kutuk.

"One of ours," Jack focused on the man. "Private Donaldson. Lang, see what message he is carrying."

Lang galloped out, with the sound of his horse's hooves echoing on the drawbridge. Jack watched as he met Private Donaldson, and both men returned together.

"Have C Company ready, Baxter," Jack murmured.

"I already have," Baxter replied. "I've put a company on mobile reserve, rotating the men daily."

Lang ran up the stairs to Jack. "It's all right, sir," he said. "Lieutenant Moffat has captured some cattle."

"Beef on the hoof," Jack said. "Send Moffat to me when he's sorted himself out. I'll be in my office."

* * *

Moffat tapped on Jack's door and ushered in a slender Arab. "This fellow wants to speak to you, sir."

"Abdullah!" Jack recognised the spy. "I'm glad to see you're safe. I'll speak to Lieutenant Moffat first and then come to you."

"Yes, effendi," Abdullah said.

"We found Osman Zubeir's camps, sir," Moffat reported. "He has two, at least. I'd estimate ten thousand men."

Jack nodded. "We can cope with ten thousand. You found some livestock, I see."

Moffat grinned. "We came across a herd a couple of miles from Zubeir's camp and decided they'd be better in El Kutuk."

"Well done, Moffat. Was there any resistance?"

"A little, sir."

Jack wondered how much Moffat left unsaid. "Write me a report, Lieutenant. Where did you find this fellow?"

"He found us, sir. When he ran to join us, Private Armstrong nearly shot him."

"I can imagine. Thank you, Moffat."

When Moffat saluted and left, Jack asked Abdullah to sit. "Do you have news for me, Abdullah?"

The spy nodded. "Only three things, effendi. The Mahdi has given Osman Zubeir the title of *Kaid il Sirrya il Masria*."

"Has he now?" Jack said. "The Commander-in-Chief of the army of Egypt. That's an imposing title."

"Yes, effendi," Abdullah said. "The Mahdi wants him to annihilate your garrison to block Gordon's retreat to Suakin and then invade Egypt."

Jack nodded. "Thank you."

"Osman Zubeir knows your strength, with one British and one Egyptian regiment and a few mounted infantry."

Jack nodded. "The villagers who joined him would have told him all about us. Is there anything else, Abdullah?"

"Yes, effendi," Abdullah said. "Abd-el-Rahman, Wad-el-Najumi is on his way to join Osman Zubeir with another army."

CHAPTER TWENTY-FOUR

Battle on bloody battle, panic on horrifying panic, and around Tal Moelfre, a thousand war-cries.
  Gwalchmei, 1157

"They're not probing this time." Baxter peered over the defences from the top of the tower. "Osman Zubeir has mustered his full force."

"He has reinforcements," Jack replied. "One of General Hook's spies informed me that Abd-el-Rahman, Wad-el-Najumi was on his way."

Baxter looked blank. "Who is he, sir?"

"Najumi is the man who defeated Hicks and commands the siege of Khartoum," Jack said. "Perhaps the best of the Mahdi's generals."

Baxter grunted. "He's never met the Royal Malverns yet."

"You're right," Jack agreed. "And the only Egyptians he's fought were ill-trained and lacked spirit. We've trained our Egyptians to be fighting men, and they now have successes under their belts. They'll give Wad-el-Najumi a surprise."

Wahiba had arrived in time to hear the end of the conversation. "My boys will show him how Egyptians fight!"

Jack's patrols reported renewed activity among the Ansar, with Moffat adding that another army had joined Zubeir's, bringing another herd of cattle for food.

"That would be Wad-el-Najumi," Jack said.

"It could be, sir," Moffat said. "I didn't get the commander's name."

From the patrols' reports and observations, Jack estimated the Ansar to muster around twelve thousand warriors, with a host of camp followers. Of the warriors, about six hundred had Remington rifles taken from the Egyptians they had killed in battle. The remainder carried spears or long, double-edged swords.

"Zubeir and Najumi will use the same tactics then," Jack said. "They'll snipe at night and try direct assaults to get hand-to-hand."

Jack had learned about the various tribes and peoples. The Hadendoa were around Suakin, while Osman Zubeir commanded Arabs of the Jaalin and Baggara tribes.

"Where are the Jaalin from, sir?" Moffat, always eager to learn, asked as they paced along the fort's northern wall.

"They're from the lands between Berber and Khartoum," Jack said, "and Najumi's Baggara tribe is from the Kordofan deserts southwest of Khartoum."

"That's a long way from here," Moffat observed thoughtfully. "I'd have thought the Baggara would be investing General Gordon in Khartoum."

"Abdullah told me the Mahdi wants to ensure Gordon doesn't have an escape route," Jack said. *Or maybe Khartoum has already fallen, and nobody can get the news to us in this isolated spot.*

"What's Wad-el-Najumi like, sir?"

Jack lit two cheroots and passed one over to Moffat. He thought of the dwindling supply in his room and sighed. Cheroots weren't necessary, but he was damned if he would leave any for the Ansar if they captured the village.

"Wad-el-Najumi?" Jack paused to light his cheroot. "I've

found out a little about him, mainly through bazaar gossip," *thank you, Donnelly.* "And the rest, Drummond told me. I believe his name means the astrologer's son. He rose from a poor background in the Jaalin tribe, partly because he was religious and partly through his skill at war. When Najumi and Osman Zubeir defeated Hicks Pasha, Najumi's prestige rose further, despite his humble birth."

Moffat drew on his cheroot and coughed. "Sorry, sir. I don't smoke, as a rule."

"Don't smoke just to impress me, Moffat. If you don't take my cheroots, there are all the more for me!"

"Yes, sir," Moffat coloured, reminding Jack how young he was.

"Wad-el-Najumi eats, drinks and lives like the poorest of his warriors," Jack exhaled a plume of blue smoke. "And, from what I've heard, he believes everything the Mahdi says."

"Everything, sir?"

"So I've heard. Najumi believes that the Mahdi will conquer the world."

Moffat drew on his cigar and coughed again.

"For God's sake, man, throw the damned thing away if you're not a smoker!"

"Yes, sir, thank you, sir," Moffat tossed the cigar over the battlements to land in the ditch outside. "I'll say one thing for Wad-el-Najumi, sir; he makes it difficult to see his men. I'm only guessing at his numbers."

Jack nodded. "He is a wily and brave man. He'll be a redoubtable opponent."

"What do you know of Osman Zubeir, sir?"

"We met him in Egypt, Moffat before you joined the regiment and when he was a sergeant in Arabi's army. I think he was gathering information about the Egyptian forces, and maybe ours, too." Jack considered for a moment. "I didn't take much notice of him, thinking him less important than the officer he seemed to shadow, but ultimately, I realised he was the more dangerous of the two. He killed two of our best men."

"If he captures El Kutuk, sir, he'll make it very hard for Gordon to escape to Suakin. We're the only water for a hundred miles."

"That's probably the idea." Jack lifted his field glasses and swept the horizon, seeing the sun reflecting from thousands of spear points. "Here comes the Ansar now. From what we know of Najumi, he plunders the country of everything he can, cattle, goats, and women. Anybody who refuses is mutilated or killed, and he's forced the Berabra people to act as his labourers."

"Slaves?" Moffat asked.

"Slaves," Jack confirmed.

The Ansar was moving towards them, raising the usual curtain of dust and with the insistent throbbing of tom-toms already vibrating through the air.

"They have about twelve thousand men," Jack said. "We have the Malverns, with five hundred and ten fit men, fifty mounted infantry, twenty Royal Artillerymen and half a dozen seamen with a Gatling gun. Add to that two Egyptian regiments with a nominal strength of thirteen hundred but an actual strength of five hundred and eighty. We also have the village militia, fifty-two men, only partially trained."

"The odds are against us," Moffat said.

Jack smiled. "Our Egyptians are from Aswan northward to Cairo," Jack said. "Rather than from the delta. They are more at home here in the desert." He finished his cheroot and threw the stub over the wall.

"Let's hope Zubeir lacks artillery," Moffat said.

"Let's hope so," Jack agreed. "Sound the alert and send the men to their stations. Have the cook prepare food and ensure there is extra drinking water and ammunition to hand."

"Yes, sir," Moffat said.

"Lieutenant Rawlinson!" Jack raised his voice slightly. "Fire a couple of rounds at extreme range. Aim for the centre of the enemy line. I want to see if they respond."

"Very good, sir!" Rawlinson replied.

Jack had placed the guns inside a small earthwork overlooking the wall. He watched the artillerymen scurry around, with Lieutenant Rawlinson estimating the range, and then, five minutes later, both seven-pounders fired. The bark seemed to echo for a long time, and Jack saw the white puff of explosions, seemingly so harmless and innocent, above the advancing Ansar.

The sound of the explosions reached the village a few seconds later. Jack focussed his field glasses on the target, seeing the flags and banners above the line as the attacking army halted.

"Give them another," Jack ordered and watched as the shells screamed away with the same result. A moment later, he saw six bright flashes from the enemy, and their shots landed short, throwing up fountains of dust and stones twenty yards outside the walls.

"They have artillery," Jack said.

"Krupps, I'd say," Rawlinson replied calmly. "They'll outrange us. Shall I target their guns, sir?"

"Yes, Rawlinson," Jack said. "If you wish to move your guns, feel free to use as many infantrymen as you need."

"Thank you, sir," Rawlinson said absently and gave orders that saw the guns' elevations drop by half an inch. A moment later, both his seven-pounders fired. Jack thought he saw a faint black line as the shells screamed toward the enemy, and then came the resulting explosions. Seconds later, the Ansar's artillery fired.

"All six guns," Jack reported as the shells again landed short, and the salvo spread over a wide area.

"I heard, sir," Rawlinson agreed as he made minute adjustments to his left gun. "Fire when you're ready."

The seven-pounders fired again, with the right-hand gun

slightly faster than the left. As soon as the shells left the barrels, the artillerymen worked frantically to reload. Jack left them alone, aware his presence did not help.

"Colonel Wahiba!" Jack bellowed and waited for Wahiba to join him, then mounted the tower for a better overall view. He looked down the village, a straggle of houses and palm groves half a mile in length and two hundred yards in breadth. "Post a section of your men in that house at the south end of the village. Loophole the walls if you think it best, and place men on the roof."

Jack had already built a small parapet on the roofs of houses he thought may be useful. He had mixed feelings about firing through loopholes, which restricted the defenders' vision and ability to move, while a man on the roof had a superior field of fire and a better view of the enemy.

"Yes, sir," Colonel Wahiba acknowledged.

"You and I are professionals," Jack said, "with professional soldiers. I depend on your men to defend the walls and look after the village militia. They are more enthusiastic than skilful, but we have to work with amateurs occasionally."

Colonel Wahiba smiled, and Jack guessed that his flattery had worked. He had found that praise was often more effective than abuse.

Jack had planned the ditch and walls to include the wells and as much fertile ground as possible without compromising defence. Now he wondered if he had made the wall too long for his small force to defend.

The artillery duel had continued, with the enemy's shells exploding around the village wall or the fort. A shell landed square on the fort's wall, throwing up a fountain of dirt and mud, and Jack heard somebody swear.

"Is anybody hurt?" Jack shouted.

"No, sir," Sergeant Anderson replied, "but these damned Dervishes are giving us more work to do!"

"You'll cope, Sergeant!" Jack replied. He focused his binoculars on the attackers. He saw their artillery behind a bank of smoke and counted five muzzle flares as they fired.

"Only five enemy guns left, Lieutenant Rawlinson! You've accounted for one of them!"

"Five more to go," Rawlinson said, and his guns fired again.

Jack ran his gaze along the walls, checking the men, who waited in their positions, rifles in hand. He grunted as he saw Alexandrina Drummond join them, holding a Remington rifle.

"Moffat!"

"Yes, sir?" Moffat ran up the steps to the top of the tower.

"I ordered you to look after Miss Drummond. Take her somewhere safe! If she refuses, use a couple of your more muscular horsemen to carry her away."

"Yes, sir." Moffat saluted and fled.

How would the queen react if her niece died under my command?

Jack watched as a group of flags congregated on a slight rise a mile to the north. A few moments later, the Ansar generals sent a strong detachment to the east of the village as though they intended to attack the Egyptians' positions. Jack saw the flags creep closer as the enemy leadership rode forward.

"Corporal Cooper" Jack shouted. "When the Dervishes come in range, aim at the men with the banners."

"Yes, sir!" Cooper's sharpshooters found suitable positions, set their sights to the maximum range, and waited.

The next Ansar salvo crashed out, with three shells screaming over the wall of the fort to explode in the courtyard and the other two well wide. A man yelled and collapsed, holding his face.

"Doolie bearers!" Captain Jamieson roared. "Look after that man!"

"Their gunners are getting better," Rawlinson said as he watched his perspiring men load again. "We've only got fifty common shells left, sir, and twenty-four shrapnel."

Jack nodded. "Make them count, Rawlinson. Keep half in reserve."

"Will do, sir."

With a limited supply of artillery ammunition, Jack would have to rely on his infantry to hold the village. He flinched as a shell exploded at the foot of the tower, sending a fountain of dirt and stones as high as the parapet.

Maybe the enemy has similar supply problems. Remember Grant.

Cooper's section fired in an irregular crackle. Although the sharpshooters regarded themselves superior to the average soldier, Jack did not care what they thought, provided they hit their mark. He heard Private Graham grunt with satisfaction. "Got you!"

"I got him!" MacLeod complained. "He was mine!"

"We must have both fired at the same man."

Corporal Cooper kicked Graham on the leg. "Stop chinning and get firing! You're like a bunch of bloody schoolkids!"

Jack saw one enemy horseman lying on the ground and another flopping loose in the saddle. He doubted they had ever experienced accurate long-range rifle fire before.

"They're altering direction, sir!" Baxter reported.

The main Ansar force advanced towards the north side of El Kutuk, with the breakaway company moving quickly to the eastern wall. The leadership group increased their speed, holding the banners high. Jack watched his sharpshooters fire again, eject the used cartridges and reload. They were firing faster as the enemy came closer, and another horseman tumbled, dropping his standard. Three of the infantry also lay on the ground, one prone and two kicking in agony.

"They're out of sight, sir!" Cooper reported as the angle of the walls hid the enemy from view.

"Follow them round," Jack ordered. "Target the horsemen."

If we kill Najumi or Zubeir, we'll have dealt the Ansar a massive blow.

The sharpshooters obeyed, running from the fort onto the outer walls of the village to continue sniping.

Jack heard a crash as a Mahdi shell smashed into the wall

near the Well Gate, and then another landed a moment later, throwing pieces of mud high into the air.

Lieutenant Hamilton swore. "They're after us, boys!"

The seamen responded with a salvo of obscene oaths and mocking laughter. "Another three hundred yards, and we'll pepper them!"

"They've got our range now, sir!" Rawlinson reported. "Give them two rounds of shrapnel, boys!"

The seven-pounders cracked out again, throwing their shells above the enemy guns to kill the gunners. Greasy smoke hovered around the gun emplacement, growing thicker with every shot fired.

"Keep at it, Rawlinson," Jack ordered, shifting his attention to the more immediate danger in the village. He heard the crash of volleys as he mounted the wall and saw Colonel Wahiba organising the defence. The Egyptians lined the battlements, red fezzes bobbing as they aimed and fired, with NCOs barking orders and occasionally adjusting a man's aim.

The Ansar had entered the killing area with only three horsemen still mounted and the sharpshooters aiming, firing, and reloading with unhurried professionalism.

Two more horsemen fell, with another banner fluttering to the ground. Jack nodded in satisfaction.

Cooper's sharpshooters are proving their worth.

The Ansar kept together, moving in a column across the cleared ground and heading for one section of the wall. Each Egyptian volley chopped down half a dozen warriors, and others fell as they trod on the hidden spikes, but the mass continued.

"They're getting closer!" an Egyptian private shouted, glancing over his shoulder.

"Colonel Wahiba! Thin the men on the south wall," Jack said. "Strengthen your defence on the east!"

The warriors were only two hundred yards away, their faces clear as they broke into a run.

"Sharpshooters! Get these blasted riders."

Colonel Wahiba had called up every second man from the south wall and positioned them at the threatened point. He had them firing alternative volleys, so the east wall was a constant blaze of musketry.

Well done, Wahiba! We'll make a Royal Malvern of you before we're finished!

As the Mahdists reached the ditch, Cooper's sharpshooters toppled the last horseman, with a black standard falling into the ditch.

Have we killed their leaders? Jack scanned the attackers, quietly cursing the dust and gun smoke that hazed the desert. He swore as he saw another group of banners at the rear of the Ansar.

They've fooled me! Zubeir knew I would target men with standards, so he sent a diversionary group.

The Mahdists hesitated as they reached the ditch with its lethal stakes. One man threw his spear at the defenders, with the long, deadly weapon seeming to hang in the air for a long second before it hissed down to thud into the parapet. The shaft vibrated for a few seconds.

"Lieutenant Smith!" Jack roared. "Now's your time!"

As Jack spoke, the Gatling opened up. The mechanical chatter added to the crackle of musketry and the shrill yells of the Ansar. The Gatling traversed left and right, with the sheets of bullets felling men like a scythe on a field of wheat.

"*Nar!*" Wahiba ordered.

The Egyptians fired a volley, with the heavy bullets smashing into the Mahdists. Men fell backwards, with some shots cutting through one warrior to hit the man behind. Jack saw a man's arm spin away from his body and a film of blood rise from the mass. The Egyptians loaded, some yelling, one or two stepping back.

"*Nar!*" Wahiba shouted as Bimbashi Mabruk grabbed a young soldier and pushed him back to the wall.

Another volley crashed out, with Jack firing his revolver. He had no recollection of taking it from his holster.

With nearly a third of their men dead or wounded, the Mahdists hesitated. Some threw their spears. One man tried to jump the ditch, only to fall and lie, screaming as the pointed stakes beneath impaled him.

The Egyptians were shouting now, loading and firing without waiting for orders. Sensibly, Wahiba did not interfere. The Ansar fell back slowly, then turned and ran, losing more men to the pointed stakes as the Egyptians fired at them.

"Cease fire!" Jack shouted. "Don't waste ammunition!" He allowed them a few moments to celebrate.

God knows they've had little enough to cheer about recently.

"Colonel Wahiba, send the men back to their correct positions. Zubeir may attack the southern wall soon."

"Yes, sir!"

Jack realised that the Gatling and artillery fire had also stopped. Gunsmoke drifted across the village, and he heard the moans and screams of the wounded Mahdists.

I should try to help these men, but they'll likely only stab the helpers.

"Send out a flag of truce!" Jack ordered. "Tell Zubeir and Najumi to attend to their wounded." That was the best he could do without endangering his own men.

The Egyptians did well today, but I fell for Zubeir's trickery. My sharpshooters wasted time and bullets. That won't happen again.

CHAPTER TWENTY-FIVE

So let them fight in the way of God who sells the present life for the world to come; and whosoever fights in the way of God and is slain, or conquers, we shall bring him a mighty wage.
Sura: 4: Koran

Bryant looked strained, with new lines on his face. "Three men wounded, sir, including one of the gunners. No dead."

"Thank you, Bryant," Jack returned the salute. He asked Wahiba the same question. The enemy had killed one Egyptian and wounded two others, with no casualties in the militia.

"Baxter, send Anderson's pioneers to repair the wall," Jack said, "and warn them to be careful in case the dead warriors return to life. They have a habit of doing that."

"Yes, sir." Baxter saluted and withdrew.

"We beat off Zubeir's first assault," Bryant said.

"We did," Jack agreed. "How many of his guns did we disable?"

"I don't know, sir."

Jack nodded and strode to the artillery post where Lieutenant Rawlinson was blackened with powder smoke and shaking with reaction.

"We silenced two, sir," Rawlinson said. "But we're already running short of ammunition. We'll have to conserve our shells."

"Do what you think necessary, Rawlinson."

Jack always felt depressed and sick after an action. He knew that the images would return at night, that human arm spinning in the air, the spear vibrating as it thudded into the parapet and the shell exploding on the wall.

"Effendi!" An Egyptian NCO saluted, his uniform powder-stained but his face animated and the rifle in his hand newly cleaned. "One of the false prophet's men has deserted. We have him prisoner. Shall I shoot him?"

"Certainly not!" Jack snapped. "Bring him to me."

Young and smooth-faced, the warrior looked eager to please as he smiled at everybody.

"Why did you desert?" Jack asked at once.

"I don't want to follow a false prophet," the youth said. "The false prophet's men murdered my father and raped my wife before killing her."

That story sounded plausible.

"Tell me about the Zubeir's army," Jack did not expect an ordinary warrior to know much, but every scrap of intelligence might help. The more he knew about the enemy, the more he could counter his attacks and exploit his weaknesses.

"It is huge," the prisoner said. "As many men as the sands in the desert."

Jack realised the man could probably not count and had no conception of figures.

"Sir," Lieutenant Rawlinson saluted. "Does he know anything about the Krupp artillery?"

Jack nodded. "Tell me about Zubeir's big guns," he said. "How many does he have?"

The warrior nodded eagerly, held up one hand, and then folded a finger away.

"Four," Jack said. "He has four guns left. Is that correct?" He held up four fingers.

The man nodded again.

"Where are they? How much ammunition does he have?" Lieutenant Rawlinson seemed oblivious to his junior rank when he burst in to find out about Zubeir's artillery.

"Shall I do the questioning, Lieutenant?" Jack rebuked mildly.

"Yes, sir. Sorry, sir."

Jack understood Rawlinson's anxiety. He had put up a good show against superior numbers, but the outcome was inevitable when the enemy had heavier guns and more ammunition.

"Where does Zubeir have his guns?" Jack asked, and the deserter broke into a torrent of Arabic too rapid for Jack to understand.

"Send for Colonel Wahiba," Jack ordered. "He can take over here."

When Wahiba arrived, the deserter cowered away until Jack spoke again.

"You're in no danger, my friend."

Jack had wondered if Wahiba would hector the prisoner, but he used a surprisingly gentle tone and related the answers to Jack.

"He says that Wad-el-Najumi brought the artillery, sir, and not Zubeir. He has hidden them in a gulley near the centre of his position with a strong guard."

"Is he in range of our artillery?" Rawlinson asked again and stepped back when Jack frowned. "Sorry, sir."

Wahiba asked more questions. "Najumi's guns are out of range," he said. "The gunners had to drag them forward to reach us."

The idea kindled in Jack's mind. "Ask him if he could lead us there."

"He can," Wahiba confirmed a moment later.

"Then that's what he will do."

* * *

Jack did not know if it was displaced pride, a reluctance to send a man on a dangerous mission while he remained in safety, or a refusal to accept his advancing years. Whatever it was, Jack insisted on leading the raiding expedition.

"Sir!" Major Baxter protested. "You're too important to go!"

"Nonsense," Jack scoffed. "We're all equally important, and I have more experience in this type of endeavour than most."

"Most of the regiment served in Afghanistan and on the Frontier," Baxter reminded. "I could lead the men."

About to blast the major into silence, Jack realised he was trying to help. "Take control of El Kutuk in my absence, Major. If I fall, remember our purpose is to hold the place as a base for General Gordon if he chooses this route to Suakin."

"Yes, sir," Major Baxter could say no more.

Jack had a lean force of fifty men, mainly from the Malverns, with Rawlinson of the artillery, Bimbashi Mabruk and ten Egyptians.

"Our objective is to destroy the guns," Jack instructed the striking force. "We can't drag them back. Our secondary objective is to blow up the ammunition. A gun with no shells is only useless metal." He saw Rawlinson blanch at his words.

"Captain Jamieson is following a quarter of a mile behind with a covering force, and Moffat has the mounted infantry ready to come to our aid."

The British cautiously opened the Well Gate an hour after dark, extended the bridge and walked over as quietly as possible. The night felt hostile as if the stars were glaring at the small force that moved silently and purposefully across the desert sand.

"You two," Jack chose Brotheridge and Kerswell, "scout ahead, not too far. Keep together and report back immediately if you see anything."

The silence pressed down on them, not oppressive, but seeming to magnify each sound they made, so the scuff of a boot on sand or a subdued curse could carry like a bugle call to Zubeir's waiting ears.

The scouts returned. "I heard something, sir," Kerswell whispered. "I dunno what it was. Metal hitting a rock, I think."

Should we abandon the enterprise on a sound that might have originated a mile away? Or continue into a possible ambush.

"Stay here," Jack said. "I'm going ahead."

"Sir!" Sarsens protested.

"Look after the men, Captain," Jack ordered.

He walked for ten steps, then dropped to a crawl. The sand felt gritty under his hands, and he had a sudden fear of snakes or scorpions but moved on, unsure for what he was searching.

I'm searching for anything out of place, he told himself.

Some animal called through the night, and Jack paused, staring ahead. He thought he saw movement. Was that a man? Or an animal? Or only his imagination? Jack moved on, keeping low, watching for anything that might make a noise.

The shout came from behind him, a sudden cry of "Allah!" followed by a single shot. Jack swore and ducked as scores of rifles opened up in a ragged fusillade ahead. Bullets whined and hissed overhead, death unseen in the dark. Jack hugged the sand, feeling his heartbeat increase.

"Sir!" Donnelly arrived at his side. "It's an ambush, sir!"

"I gathered that!" Jack replied.

"That deserter, sir, he shouted to warn the Dervishes that we were there, and they opened fire."

Jack flinched as a bullet burrowed through the sand an inch from his left hand. As if in slow motion, he saw the sand rise, hover, and then fall, covering the bullet.

Sometime in the future, a scrap metal merchant will make a fortune digging up the lead and steel from these old battlefields.

"Where's the deserter now?"

"Dead, sir. Brotheridge shot him when he tried to run off."

"Let's get back to the men," Jack said.

They crawled backwards, trying to dig holes in the sand

whenever bullets came too close. Donnelly swore when something whistled past his pith helmet. "Here we are, sir!"

"Sir!" Sarsens lay on the side of a sand hill and greeted Jack with a twisted grin. "We can retaliate now!"

Jack realised his men had been withholding their fire for fear of hitting him.

"Retaliate away, Sarsens," he said.

"Independent firing!" Sarsens barked. "Aim at the muzzle flares!"

Lying on the sand, the Malverns returned fire, with the Egyptians following their lead.

"How many casualties?" Jack asked.

"One dead, sir, and two wounded, one seriously. Thank God these Dervish lads are not the best shots."

"Move back by sections," Jack said. "We're not here to indulge in a firefight."

The raiders withdrew in good order, firing and withdrawing until Moffat's mounted infantry trotted past to engage the enemy and Jamieson's supporting company provided cover.

"Sound the retire," Jack ordered the bugler. "We lost that round."

The men withdrew in good order, with Moffat last, firing a final round before he clattered over the drawbridge.

"Zubeir tricked me again," Jack said. "If the supposed deserter had not shouted too soon, the ambush would have been more effective."

I lost a good man today and may lose another in my abortive operation.

Baxter nodded. "You made arrangements to counter an ambush, sir, or nobody would have got back. I'd think Zubeir is more disappointed than we are."

"I hope you're right, Baxter," Jack said.

* * *

After the excitement of the night, the following day dawned quietly.

"Moffat, take the mounted infantry on patrol," Jack said. "I want to know where Zubeir's guns are, but I don't want him to realise our interest."

"Very good, sir," Moffat understood at once. "I'll take the lads near last night's ambush and study the position from one of the ridges. I know just the place."

"Where? Show me on the map."

Moffat indicated a rocky hill that rose about two hundred feet above the surrounding plain.

"That looks right," Jack approved. "I'll arrange a diversion on the south in case things get sticky."

"Thank you, sir." Moffat strode away, calling for his men.

"That lad's developing into a useful officer," Jack said.

Major Baxter nodded. "I agree, sir. I can foresee a bright future for him unless he gets himself killed."

Jack nodded. "General Wolseley advocates that young officers attempt just that. I want you to take a company strength patrol to the south, Baxter. Mixed Malverns and Egyptians. Make a noise, draw the Mahdists to you and withdraw. Allow Najumi and Zubeir to push you back."

"Yes, sir," Baxter said. "I'll keep them occupied."

Once again, Jack found himself in a position where he was sending men into danger, but he knew Baxter was a competent, cautious officer who would not take unnecessary risks. He watched Moffat ride north, and then Major Baxter led his infantry south. The enemy remained hidden, with just the beat of their drums a reminder of their presence and the occasional flash of the sun on steel spear points.

Jack remained on the tower, focused his field glasses on Moffat's mounted infantry and then swivelled to watch Baxter's foot soldiers slogging south. Baxter had them in a close column and opened into extended order once clear of the killing zone.

"Colonel Wahiba!"

"Sir!" The Egyptian's salute was as smart as any Royal Malvern.

"Major Baxter might have to retire in a hurry. I'd like a company of your men to support him. Choose your best officer."

Wahiba smiled and returned to professional expressionless. "Yes, sir. I'll take the company myself."

"I rather hoped you would," Jack said and appreciated Wahiba's smile.

He watched as Wahiba marched his company over the drawbridge, feeling a little uneasy about having the white-uniformed men as allies after recently fighting them.

Why not? Dammit, the Sikhs and Gurkhas were enemies once, and now they're the best we've got. We recruit half the Guides from the Pashtun tribesmen who shoot at us in the passes, and after centuries of enmity, we fought alongside the French in Crimea and China.

Moffat's mounted infantry was out of sight now, with even their dust plume fading away, and Jack concentrated on Baxter's diversion force and Wahiba's supporting company.

Zubeir's guns give him an advantage over us. If I can neutralise them, we have scored a notable victory.

Jack fretted on the roof of the tower, realised he was doing no good and withdrew to his quarters to attend to administrative matters. He found it too hot to concentrate, listened for musketry and toured the fort instead, finding fault with minor issues.

I can't look too concerned, or the men will get nervous. I must appear detached and confident.

A woman's voice sounded from the Malverns' B Company's barrack room. Jack frowned and pushed the door open.

"What the devil is going on in here?"

Three women stared at him. Two were village women, and the third was one of the dancers who had entertained him when he first arrived.

"What are you doing?" Jack asked in Arabic.

The dancer lifted the clothes that lay in front of her. "Dhobbying," she said. (Cleaning.)

"Dhobbying?" Jack repeated the word.

"Yes, sir." When the dancer smiled, her whole face lit up. "Donnelly Pasha tells us whose uniform to dhobi, and he gives us extra food."

"Does he indeed?" Jack said. "Does he give you anything else?"

When the dancer repeated Jack's question, all three women laughed.

Jack smiled. "I understand," he said and resolved to speak to Donnelly later. He had wondered how Donnelly managed to keep his uniform immaculate. He heard the sound of musketry.

"Keep up the good work, ladies!" Jack said, took a deep breath and strode to the tower. *Here we go again.*

CHAPTER TWENTY-SIX

The strength of any plan depends on timing
   Michel de Montaigne

"Which direction?" Jack asked the lookout on the roof.

"To the south, sir. I can't see anything except dust."

Jack focused his field glasses. About a mile distant, he saw Wahiba's Egyptian company marching steadily onward without any sign of trouble. Jack followed the desert for another mile and a half until he saw the curtain of dust.

Major Baxter had found trouble. I hope he doesn't lose too many men out there.

A breeze carried the crackling of musketry to Jack, and he swore, hoping the Egyptians would quicken their pace.

"Major Bryant, call the stand to," Jack said. "We might have to send out reinforcements."

"Yes, sir," Bryant said, and a few moments later, the shrill notes of the bugle ran out. The off-duty men ran to the parade ground, pulling on tunics and pith helmets, but each carried his rifle.

Colonel Wahiba had increased his pace, with the men

opening to an extended formation as the Malverns had trained them.

Jack checked to the north, hoping his mounted infantry were successful. He scanned the desert without success; there was not even a hint of dust. When he faced south again, Wahiba's Egyptians had altered formation to a double line and had taken a position on a small ridge.

"They've seen something we can't," Jack said and raised his voice. "Captain Jamieson! Take out C Company and support the Egyptians."

"Yes, sir!" Jamieson said and led the way, with his company marching behind him.

I hope I'm not sending my men out to be defeated in detail.

The distant dust cloud crept closer as the sound of musketry increased. *That's Baxter's men withdrawing.*

"Your plan worked, sir," Bryant said. "Baxter has drawn the enemy to him."

"So it seems, Bryant." Jack tried to appear imperturbable as if the possible death of a large portion of his command meant nothing to him.

Wahiba's Egyptians open fire, with the sound of their volley crisp and close. Gunsmoke rose above them, stagnant in the still air.

Baxter's company appeared through the dust, marching in a square and firing as they moved, which was a manoeuvre suitable only for well-trained infantry. Beyond the British, Jack saw the enemy, a moving mass of men with spears, shields, and swords. One side of the square fired again, with the gun smoke rolling before them and some of the Mahdists falling.

The Egyptians were static, with Jamieson's company hurrying to join them.

Jack was so engrossed in the unfolding battle that he barely heard the thud of a distant shell. He grunted when it exploded five hundred yards beyond the defensive ditch, raising a tall column of dust.

Swivelling, Jack saw Moffat and the mounted infantry galloping back, with a host of Mahdist cavalry a quarter of a mile behind. Beyond the cavalry, foot soldiers crowded around their artillery. Jack saw four spurts of smoke from the guns' muzzles. Three shots fell far short of the horsemen, and the fourth was wide and over.

Jack swore. So far, his stint at being a brigadier had not been successful. "Rawlinson!" he shouted to the artillerymen. "Are the enemy guns in range?"

"Not yet, sir!" Rawlinson said, and then ten minutes later, he shouted.

"They're in range now, sir!"

"Then blow the damned things to buggery!"

"Yes, sir!" Rawlinson leapt to the highest point in his earthwork. "Right, bombardier, let's show these bastards! Traverse right, raise the elevation!"

Jack left the gunners to do their job and concentrated on the infantry in the south. Baxter's forward company had joined Wahiba's Egyptians, while Jamison's supporting company had covered half the distance to them.

Moffat's mounted infantry trotted over the drawbridge, horses and men covered in sweat and dust.

Rawlinson fired another salvo, with both shells exploding above the Ansar's guns, showering shrapnel on the gunners.

"Get back out, Moffat!" Jack roared. "Harass the Mahdists, hit and run. Captain Rawlinson, keep firing!"

Moffat acknowledged, wheeled, and ordered his men outside.

Jack heard the double crack as the seven-pounders fired. Both shells exploded in front of Najumi's gun position, throwing up dust and spreading deadly shrapnel. Jack saw two Mahdist gunners fall and another running away.

"Common shell!" he shouted, but Rawlinson had already given that order. The seven-pounders fired again, with one shell landing twenty yards short and the other landing between two enemy guns, knocking one on its side and felling the crew. The Mahdist cavalry had reined up and was milling around the guns.

"Good shot!" Jack yelled.

Moffat's mounted infantry had turned withdrawal to an attack. They rode to within three hundred yards of the enemy artillery, fired a volley and drew back to reload. Jack nodded approval and turned his attention to the battle on the south side.

All three infantry units had merged and were firing volleys. As Jack watched, they formed a single square, immobile and wreathed in grey-white gun smoke.

Your men are holding well, Wahiba.

When the Mahdists advanced on the square, Jack only saw a confused mass of bodies surging outside the khaki-and-white. He heard the regular hammer of volley fire, and then the warriors fell back. The square moved forward, marching slowly toward the enemy and firing. The Mahdists began to fray, with men falling with every volley and the British and Egyptian infantry advancing step by stubborn step.

"Good move, lads," Jack approved. He watched until it was apparent the battle had turned in favour of the British and then switched his attention to the artillery duel.

The Mahdists had lost two guns, and the remaining two were retreating, with the British gunners and Moffat's mounted men harassing them across the desert.

"Traverse, right!" Rawlinson shouted. "Fire!"

Both seven-pounders fired again, and seconds later, Jack saw the twin columns of dirt and dust rise amid the retreating enemy.

"Good shooting!" Jack said.

"Sir!" Sarsens had run up the stairs to the top of the tower. "Permission to chase the enemy with the rest of my mounted infantry, sir?"

My mounted infantry?

"Are the men ready to ride?" Jack asked.

"Ready and willing, sir," Sarsens replied said.

"Very well, Sarsens."

"Thank you, sir!" Sarsens saluted again and ran downstairs, sweat-stained, and eager as a puppy. A few moments later, he led his men towards the retreating Mahdists under the arc of the British guns. He joined Moffat, and the combined force harassed the fringes of the enemy, advancing, firing, and retreating.

"Be careful not to hit the mounted infantry!" Jack warned the gunners.

"One last shot, sir," Rawlinson said, and the seven-pounders fired again.

With their eye in and the enemy moving on a fixed line, the gunners had improved their accuracy. Both shells exploded side by side, throwing one of the enemy's guns into the air.

"Good shooting!" Jack congratulated the gunners again as the dust and smoke cleared, and he saw the results.

The enemy crowded around the fallen gun, attempting to replace it on the carriage.

"Cooper!" Jack shouted. "Take your sharpshooters and fire at these men. Slow them down!"

The sharpshooters ran to the outer wall, eager to show their skill. They took their positions and the first shots cracked out within two minutes, with the bullets whistling across the killing area to the confused enemy ranks.

"They're still well in artillery range, sir," Rawlinson said.

Jack balanced his desire to end the threat of the enemy's artillery with his need to harbour his ammunition. "No," he said. "We might need the guns later if the Ansar launch a major attack."

"Yes, sir," Rawlinson gave reluctant agreement. "Cease fire, boys."

Sarsen's mounted infantry was breaking up the enemy's

flanks, shooting men, forcing the fringes to scatter, and kicking up a plume of dust as they hammered over the desert.

The sharpshooters fired again, targeting the officers as Jack had taught them. Jack raised his voice. "Shoot the gunners!" he shouted.

As the artillery smoke drifted away, only the sharpshooters' irregular, aimed crack shattered the silence. Jack saw one of the Mahdist gunners crumple to the ground, and the enemy cavalry form a protective screen around the remaining guns.

Sarsens' mounted infantry attacked again, closing to two hundred yards, firing, and withdrawing. After the artillery bombardment, the enemy could not face the double threat of the horsemen and the terrible accuracy of the long-range musketry. They were brave men dedicated to their cause, but civilians with weapons, not trained professional soldiers.

When one tribesman ran away, another quickly followed, and then a third. Jack knew that panic was like an epidemic disease. Once started, it spreads quickly, and even the bravest of men can succumb to it without seeming cause or reason. With the sharpshooters still picking off individual targets, and the mounted infantry pecking at their flanks, firing, and withdrawing, the Ansar broke and ran.

Follow them, Jack said silently, but Sarsens needed no orders. He had his men chase the retreating enemy, firing into the brown, one section firing and withdrawing to reload as another section took over. The result was a continuous trickle of casualties that spurred the men in front to greater speed.

"Lieutenant Rawlinson," Jack shouted down. "The enemy is on the run. Take your men and disable their abandoned guns. Bimbashi Mabruk will provide an escort." He wiped the sweat from his forehead with the back of his hand and found himself trembling with the nervous exhaustion of organising two simultaneous battles.

"Sir!" Major Bryant arrived. "I've ordered food for the men, and there's an Arab civilian who says he has an urgent request."

Captain Jamieson was behind the major, battle stained and triumphant. "Where shall I put the wounded, sir?

"I know you're busy, Brigadier, but do you have a moment?" Drummond asked with a bright smile.

Jack took a deep breath. Command looked exciting from a distance, but the constant barrage of demands was wearying.

CHAPTER TWENTY-SEVEN

Can anything be more ridiculous than that a man should have the right to kill me because he lives on the other side of the water and because his ruler has a quarrel with mine?
Blaise Pascal

Jack pored over the pile of paperwork that seemed to multiply each day. Even though the adjutant dealt with much of the administration, there still seemed sufficient to weigh down his desk. He lifted his pen, dipped the nib in the inkwell, shook off the excess ink and carefully signed his name to the next official form. Perhaps an army marched on its stomach, as Napoleon Bonaparte allegedly said, but it carried reams of paper on its back.

Fierce sunlight slanted through the window slats, highlighting motes of dust and the perennially circling insects. From the courtyard outside, Jack heard the barking sergeants installing soldierly discipline into the Egyptian infantry.

"You're improving," Sergeant Hanley allowed. "You have defeated the enemy in a few minor skirmishes." He walked up and down the courtyard. "By the time I'm finished with you, you'll be better than the Brigade of Guards!"

Jack glanced out the window to see Drummond standing in the shade of the wall, observing everything.

What the devil am I going to do with you, Miss Drummond?

"The first duty of a soldier is obedience!" Sergeant Hanley said and waited for the translator to project his words to the white-uniformed men. "And that means you do as the officers and non-commissioned officers tell you when they tell you and not when you feel like it!"

"Sir!" Donnelly knocked on Jack's office door and stepped inside. "The lookout reports that a rider's approaching the gate with a white flag."

"A flag of truce?" Jack stepped away from the desk, thankful for the interruption. "I'm coming, Donnelly!" He fastened his sword belt around his waist, checked his revolver was loaded and stepped from the stifling heat of his office to the glaring heat outside.

Mounting the tower, Jack lifted his field glasses.

"Over there, sir," the lookout pointed north, where a lone rider cantered in a spiral of rising dust. Jack could see the banner in the man's hand, with the white flag flapping in the wind of his passage.

"I see him," Jack said and raised his voice. "Saddle my horse! Open the gate!"

"I'll come too, sir!" Donnelly said.

"No," Jack shook his head. "That would show distrust, and I want to be open with Zubeir." He gave a wan smile. "Maybe he's offering to surrender to us."

Jack's attempt at humour failed as Donnelly shook his head. "I would not trust these people, sir."

"I know you wouldn't," Jack said. "Jamieson, have a section of men ready behind the parapet in case of treachery."

"I already have, sir," Jamieson, the duty officer, said.

Although Jamieson lacked the dash and fire of Sarsens, he was experienced and dependable. *Perhaps he will make major.* "Well done, Jamieson."

Mounted on Tinker, Jack passed through the Well Gate, clattered over the drawbridge, and rode forward. He stopped on a piece of rising ground, where he would appear taller than the messenger and allowed the man to come to him.

The rider reined up with his white Arab stallion tossing its mane. "I have a message for Brigadier Windrush and none other," he said in Arabic.

"I am Brigadier Jack Windrush," Jack said.

The man smiled. "*Assalaam alaikum*, Windrush." (May peace be upon you.)

"*Wa 'alaikum as salaam*" (and peace be upon you,) Jack replied.

"I have a letter for you, Brigadier," the messenger held Jack's eyes. "It is from my master, the Mahdi; peace be upon him."

"The peace and understanding of Allah on your master," Jack said.

The messenger looked surprised and handed over a rolled parchment tied with a silken cord.

"Thank you," Jack said. "Please tell your master I shall consider the contents and place a reply in a cleft stick one thousand paces in front of this gate. I shall mark the stick with a white flag, and any man is safe to remove it."

The messenger lifted a hand and said, "*Bifadl min Allah*- by the grace of God," turned his horse and cantered away. Jack watched him until his dust drifted to the ground and returned inside the Well Gate.

"Keep the gate open and the drawbridge down," Jack said. "Zubeir won't attack us until I have replied to his message."

"Do you trust him, sir?" Baxter asked.

"He is an honourable man by his lights," Jack said and returned to his office.

Untying the silken cord, Jack unrolled the parchment and called for Sergeant Deng. "Read that for me," he said. "Anything it says must remain confidential. Do you understand?"

"Yes, sir."

Deng knew Jack well enough to dispense with the usual preliminary salutations.

"Give me the gist of the meaning," Jack said, "until you reach the important part."

"I will, sir," Deng assured him. "The letter gives notice that the Mahdi has declared the power of God is upon him by the advice of Mahomet, the messenger of God."

Jack nodded. "Continue, Sergeant."

Sergeant Deng began to quote directly from the message. "And if anyone believes in the coming of a Mahdi, he will not suffer for confidence in one who has proved his Mahdiship by proper miracles. He who denies the Mahdi denies God and the Prophet."

"Many Moslems might think that is blasphemy," Jack murmured.

"Yes, sir," Sergeant Deng said. "This man is setting himself up as equal to the Prophet."

Jack nodded, "carry on."

Deng continued. "He who does not believe in him is a Kaffir, and whoever opposes him will be cursed in both worlds. Be it known that he does nothing except by the order of God and his Prophet, and the Jihad which he is waging against the Turks is by order of the Prophet."

Jack grunted. He understood that the Mahdi was leading the people of Sudan against the Egyptians, who the Mahdi saw as Turks as they represented the Turkish or Ottoman Empire.

We've blundered into a private war.

"Shall I continue?" Sergeant Deng asked.

"Yes. Paraphrase what doesn't matter to us," Jack said.

Deng smiled. "Yes, sir. The letter says the Mahdi will have future conquests of countries and religions and claims the Prophet has promised him constant victory. May I quote, sir? It helps to give the spirit and beliefs of the writer."

"Yes," Jack said, "quote if it helps."

"The letter says that the spirits of the Turks who have been slain will complain to God, saying, "Oh, God, the Mahdi has killed us without cause." But Mahomet himself then appears and says, "Your sins be on your own heads. My Mahdi warned you with full information and proof, and now the Mahdi is warning Brigadier Jack Windrush Pasha, the garrison and all the people of El Kutuk."

Deng paused for a moment to catch his breath.

"Continue," Jack said.

"If Windrush Pasha and the garrison and people of El Kutuk will not accept baptism by advice, and they must therefore be baptised by the sword — all save those who are under the mercy of God."

Jack looked up. "That's the direct threat," he said. "We have a choice to surrender or be baptised by the sword; I presume that means baptised in blood."

"Yes, sir. Zubeir is saying you must accept the Mahdi as the Prophet of God or die."

"Is there more?"

"Much more, sir. The writer talks about killing and burning the skins of the dead and gives details of past victories. Then he says, and I'm quoting again, sir: "The Mahdi intends soon to proceed to Egypt, for the soldiers in his Sudanese provinces have all surrendered.

Do not think we are afraid of you for waiting so long. We do not wish to kill you without cause, but if God wishes it, we will kill you in an hour. Do not boast that you have rifles and cannon. If we wanted these, we have taken sufficient from you. We await the reply to this letter so that you may be saved from the punishment of God. If you deceive us, we will, with God's permission, administer to you the baptism of the sword. Should you wish to treat send to us a man, when you will be under the protection of God and his Prophet."

"The baptism of the sword," Jack repeated the phrase. "Thank you, Sergeant Deng. I will consider my reply."

There can only be one reply, yet the villagers must have a choice.

* * *

Jack sat astride Tinker with Sergeant Deng and the Imam at his side. The people of El Kutuk gathered in the fort's courtyard and stared at him, wondering why he had invited them here.

"Thank you for coming," Jack began. "You might have noticed a messenger arrived from Osman Zubeir." He waited for the expected murmur to die down. "He told me that he intended to capture El Kutuk. I do not intend to let him have it."

The people looked at one another, some anxious, others defiant. Abu Bol lifted his rifle and shouted, "Allah Akbar!"

Jack continued, "Zubeir has promised that anybody who accepts the False Prophet as the true Mahdi will live, and all others with be baptised with the sword, which means he will kill them."

Jack waited as people in the crowd stirred uneasily. One man drifted away, and a child began to wail.

"As I stated before," Jack said, "anybody who wishes to leave El Kutuk to join the false prophet's army may do so. I will have the gate open from noon until mid-afternoon tomorrow."

Jack turned away. He had said all he intended to say. He had told the people what Osman Zubeir had said and given them a choice.

"Donnelly!"

"Sir!" Donnelly hurried up to him.

"Fetch me the letter that's on my desk. It's sealed with the name Osman Zubeir written on top in English and Arabic."

Holding the letter high so any Mahdist observer could see what he was doing, Jack rode out of the Well Gate. He wondered how many of Zubeir's men were watching him, stopped after a thousand yards, thrust a stick in the ground, attached his letter and returned to the fort.

Nobody tried to stop him.

"What did you tell him, sir?" Baxter asked,

"I thanked him for his kind offer and said if he wanted to

surrender to us or convert to Christianity, we would give him a friendly welcome."

Baxter smiled. "I doubt he'll agree to your terms, sir."

"No more than I will agree to his."

* * *

There was a slow trickle of people out of the gate, with men bundling up their families and possessions to leave El Kutuk. Jack watched them go, silently wishing them the best of luck.

"Is that the last?" he asked when a man hurried out with two wives and a collection of children.

"I think so, sir," Baxter said.

"Close the gate, put the bar in place and double the sentries. I'd guess that Osman Zubeir will attack tonight."

There was no attack that night. Instead, tom-toms beat slowly, and campfires flickered around El Kutuk.

"They're preparing themselves for an assault," Baxter said.

"That is possible," Jack said. "Ensure the men have a good breakfast tomorrow."

"I will, sir," Baxter said.

Jack nodded and walked around the walls, speaking to the sentries. The Egyptians stiffened to attention when he appeared.

"Stand easy, men," Jack said. "Is anything happening out there?"

"No, effendi," a stout sergeant replied. "It's quiet tonight."

Jack nodded and walked on. Abu Bol's militia was alert and pacing their section of the wall.

"If Zubeir will attack," Abu Bol warned. "He'll come soon. He'll have squeezed information from the people who left the village, and he'll know our defences."

"Fighting in the open desert and attacking a walled and defended town are two different things," Jack encouraged. "The Mahdists won't prevail against determined men."

Second Lieutenant Lang gave his opinion as he stared over the wall at the desert.

"With the Mahdi," Lang said, "*Aut bibat aut abeat* – you're either for us or against us. There is no neutrality or middle ground." He sighed. "We're all going to die here, sir."

"That is possible," Jack said. "That's part of the soldier's bargain, Lang. Now stiffen your back, and don't let the men hear such talk!" He walked away, hoping Lang's attitude was not common among the Malverns. *Has the isolation of El Kutuk affected my men?*

Now all we can do is wait and pray.

CHAPTER TWENTY-EIGHT

Beware of false prophets, which come to you in sheep's clothing, but inwardly they are ravening wolves.
   Matthew chapter 7, verse 15.

The horsemen came at dawn, riding slowly under a profusion of flags and banners. Thirty strong, they halted a hundred yards beyond the extreme range of the seven-pounders and within minutes, a large tent, more like a pavilion to Jack's eyes, sprang up, green and white and reflecting the sun's rays.

"What the devil are they playing at?" Jack asked.

"That must be somebody important," Baxter said. "Maybe Osman Zubeir or Wad-el-Najumi."

"Maybe so. Send a runner to Colonel Wahiba and see if he knows."

Drummond ran light-footed to the top of the tower. "I see you have a distinguished visitor, Brigadier."

"We have, Miss Drummond," Jack agreed.

"The Mahdi himself," Drummond said. "You are honoured."

Jack raised his field glasses. "So that's the Mahdi, is it? I wonder what he wants."

"He wants El Kutuk," Drummond told him.

"Well, he can't have it," Jack replied. He noticed Drummond's musing eyes on him and said nothing.

An hour later, a body of riders approached the fort, with banners fluttering and robes flowing above magnificent horses.

"Let them come," Jack ordered. "Nobody fire!" He stepped closer to the parapet so the riders could see him. They rode along the road and stopped outside the Well Gate.

"A message from the Mahdi!" one man shouted in Arabic. "He will meet Brigadier Jack Windrush in his tent."

Jack lifted a hand in acknowledgement. "Tell your Mahdi I will meet him."

The riders wheeled and galloped away.

Baxter frowned. "Are you going out, sir?"

"I am," Jack said. "I've wanted to meet the Mahdi for some time."

"It could be a trap," Baxter warned.

Jack did not feign his grin. "We'll soon see. I've never met a Mahdi before."

"Be careful, Brigadier," Baxter said. "I'll stand the men to and have the mounted infantry ready."

"Thank you, Baxter," Jack said.

Wearing his best uniform, with Donnelly at one side and an escort of Moffat and six mounted infantry, Jack rode Gonda from El Kutuk. A body of Arab horsemen met them five hundred yards from the Well Gate.

"I am Brigadier Jack Windrush," Jack said. "Pasha of El Kutuk."

"Come with us, Brigadier Windrush," the leader of the Arabs trotted to the green tent, where a body of men stood outside. Jack recognised Osman Zubeir in the centre and an older, bearded man he did not know.

"Abd-el-Rahman, Wad-el-Najumi," the bearded man introduced himself.

"Your name is known," Jack did not hide his respect. "You are a notable warrior."

Najumi smiled. "*As-salaam 'alaykum,* Windrush."

"*As-salaam 'alaykum,*" Jack replied.

Zubeir turned his smouldering eyes on Jack. "You may enter the Mahdi's tent," he said.

"I want Najumi's word that you will not attack my men," Jack said.

"You have my word," Najumi agreed.

Jack dismounted and stepped through the open flap.

The tent was surprisingly cool, with rugs on the ground and the sides open to the breeze. Three men sat at the opposite end. The man on the extreme left was tall and broad with the face and bearing of a warrior. He fixed basilisk eyes on Jack and kept one hand on his sword hilt. The man on the extreme right was younger and slender, with a neat beard and a face that could have been carved from a block of granite.

Both men would have stood out in any crowd yet faded into insignificance when Jack looked at the man between them.

There was no mistaking the central man was Muhammad Ahmad bin Abd Allah, the self-proclaimed Mahdi. He sat quietly with his patched jibbeh identical to that worn by his followers and a serene smile on his face, yet power seemed to flow from him.

Jack restrained himself from bowing. He felt as if he were in the presence of royalty and suddenly understood how this man, this boatbuilder's son from the back of nowhere, could exert such influence over such a large number of wild desert warriors.

The Mahdi was powerfully built, with broad shoulders and a head that seemed slightly too large for his body. He greeted Jack with a smile that revealed a vee-shaped gap between his teeth, a feature considered lucky among the superstitious in Sudan. Yet it was not the smile that held Jack's attention, nor the neat black beard or the three tribal slashes across his face, but the eyes. They were calm, brown, and sparkled as they surveyed Jack.

"Brigadier Jack Windrush," the Mahdi said. "Holder of the Victoria Cross and veteran of many wars."

"I am Windrush," Jack agreed. "And you are Muhammad Ahmad bin Abd Allah, known as the Mahdi."

The Mahdi inclined his head in agreement. He clapped his hands softly, and a pair of slaves appeared with glasses of cool water and sweetmeats. "You are safe in my presence, Brigadier Windrush."

"I know," Jack said sincerely. Despite this man's reputation, Jack knew he could trust his word.

"When will you surrender my village of El Kutuk to me, Brigadier?"

"My Queen entrusted me with the safekeeping of El Kutuk," Jack said. "Until she, or one of her representatives, orders me to leave, I will remain."

The Mahdi inclined his head. "I am the Mahdi, the successor to the Prophet, and my word is more important than any queen."

"That may be so, your Highness, but I have sworn loyalty to Her Majesty, and I cannot break my word."

The Mahdi's smile did not waver. He offered Jack a sweetmeat from the bowl in front of him. "I hope I can persuade you to change your mind, Brigadier Windrush. You have proved yourself an effective commander."

"Thank you." Again, Jack had to restrain himself from bowing. The Mahdi had that effect.

"When you join me, Brigadier, I will give you command of one of my armies," the Mahdi mused, with his smile unwavering and his bright eyes never straying from Jack's face. "I will not send you to fight the British or Turks." He selected a sweetmeat and chewed delicately. "No, General Windrush. You will lead one of my armies against King John of Abyssinia, and I will convert him to the true belief."

"Sir," Jack said. "I will not leave my allegiance to Her Majesty, and I will not surrender El Kutuk."

The Mahdi sighed. "Is it women you want, Brigadier? I can find you the pick of women and slaves."

"No, sir. I already have a wife."

The Mahdi tried another sweetmeat. "It is good to have a wife and better to have more than one. I have many, and so will you when you follow me."

Jack smiled. "Thank you for your kindness, sir, but my wife would not like to share, and nor would I." He altered his stance. "I will not surrender El Kutuk, sir, and will remain at my post until my senior commander orders me elsewhere."

"Then I must baptise you with the sword." The Mahdi continued to smile. "You may return. *Wafaqak Allah liltariq alsahih* - May God guide you to the right path."

"*Allah yarhamuk*, God go with you," Jack responded.

He bowed and backed out of the tent. *One must never turn one's back on royalty, and by God, that man has all the bearings of a king.*

Jack shivered. He did not know what power the Mahdi had, but he had filled his head with strange images. Jack could see himself leading an army of patched-robe warriors, charging under a green banner with the words of the Koran on his lips.

Allah Akbar!

"Come on, lads!" Jack mounted Gonda and walked slowly away. He felt his back twitch as he returned to El Kutuk, as though the Mahdi was watching him, or the Ansar were aiming their rifles. As soon as he entered the fort, he gave rapid orders.

"The Mahdi won't waste time. I expect him to attack us very soon. Baxter, feed the men and ensure there is water and spare ammunition. Jamieson, call up Abu Bol and the village militia. Colonel Wahiba! Have your men ready! Sarsens! Take the mounted infantry on patrol, but don't get heavily engaged. Major Bryant, double the standing pickets. Lieutenant Rawlinson, ensure the guns are ready. Lieutenant Hamilton, I think your Gatling will be required today."

The tom-toms had begun to throb before Jack finished speaking, a circle of sound around the village's perimeter, so the defenders did not know from which direction any attack might come.

As they did every day, Sergeant Anderson's pioneers were improving the ditches, removing any bushes or rocks that could give the enemy cover, filling in the dead ground and placing more stakes wherever possible.

Jack made it a point to acknowledge the pioneers, men whose work was often neglected but always essential.

The defenders waited behind the ramparts, searching for shade when Jack heard the crackle of musketry in the distance and then a shout from the lookout. "The mounted infantry are returning!"

Jack ascended the steps to the tower, trying to appear nonchalant while his heart pounded. He lifted his field glasses and focussed on the plume of dust where Sarsen's mounted infantry was withdrawing at speed, with the rearmost men turning to fire at so-far unseen pursuers.

"Is that another sandstorm?" Baxter pointed to the rising curtain of dust behind Sarsen's men.

"No," Jack shook his head. "I fancy that's the Mahdi's army."

Baxter focused his field glasses and waited for a moment. "I fancy you're right, sir. No wonder Sarsens is retiring. The Mahdi must have gathered every warrior from Suakin to Darfur and Berber to Fashoda."

"Pray convey my compliments to Lieutenant Rawlinson and ask him to hold his fire until he is sure of a target and then to aim for the enemy's leadership."

"Yes, sir."

The dust cloud expanded until it filled the entire northern horizon, with groups of cavalry leading a horde of infantry. Jack did not try to count the enemy but checked his defences were as strong as possible.

I know these officers and men. The Malverns are campaign-hardened and battle-tested, and the Egyptians have proved themselves. Now it all depends on discipline, courage, and musketry.

The mounted infantrymen were in the killing area, ensuring they remained on the marked safe path. Jack saw three empty saddles and two more men riding awkwardly and leaking blood.

"Good lads," he breathed, hating himself for sending them into danger so frequently. *Three more good men killed fighting for a territory Britain doesn't even want.*

The rearguard wheeled their horses around, halted, fired at an onrushing horde of Arab cavalry, and withdrew.

"Load with shrapnel!" Rawlinson yelled. "That group of horsemen! Fire!"

The seven-pounders fired, with one shell exploding over the pursuing horsemen and the other crashing into the middle. Jack saw a bloody swirl, with men and horses falling, legs kicking, manes flying, and swords and spears dropping. One of the standards vanished, and the mounted infantry galloped on, following the twists and turns of the safe route through the killing area.

The enemy cavalry reorganised and pushed on, now further behind.

"Open the gate!" Jack shouted. "Push out the bridge!"

The mounted infantry clattered over the bridge and through the gate, with Sarsens the last to cross. He stopped at the gate, waited until the infantry had dragged in the bridge, and fired a parting shot at the enemy.

The moment Sarsens was inside, Sergeant Trafford ordered the gate shut and the huge timber bar slotted into place. The pursuing cavalry pushed on, losing one man as the horse stepped on a spike.

"It's a shame for the horse," Wright said.

"Sergeant!" one of the guards on the wall shouted. "They're dismounting!"

"Shoot them!" the sergeant ordered, scrambling up the stairs.

The guards fired, worked the ejector levers, thumbed in a cartridge, and fired again as the Arabs left their horses to jump into the ditch. Too few to pose a threat, they achieved nothing and swiftly withdrew, leaving a scattering of bodies.

Far behind the advance force, the Mahdi's main body halted at extreme rifle range. They stood static as the tom-toms continued to thunder, and Jack scanned them through his field glasses.

"I guess ten thousand," he said.

"I'd say twelve," Baxter gave his opinion.

The Mahdi's infantry was dressed in the ubiquitous white jibbeh with square patches, with a turban on their heads. They carried shields and spears, although some had swords and others the rifles they had captured from the armies they defeated. Regularly spaced among them, groups of horsemen carried banners, either the green of the Mahdi or the black flags of the emirs, decorated with texts from the Koran. Rather than immediately charging towards El Kutuk, they remained static as the dust settled around them.

"What are they waiting for?" Baxter asked.

"I think they're trying to unnerve us," Jack said. "Corporal Cooper! Can your sharpshooters shoot that distance?"

"No, sir," Cooper replied calmly. "We've tested the range, and it's beyond accurate shooting. They'll have to come a hundred yards closer."

The drums stopped, with the harsh silence worse than the noise, and one of the Arab horsemen stepped forward. The others followed, taking their time, with the banners held high and the entire shifting mass moving in disciplined silence.

"Do you have the range, Lieutenant Rawlinson?"

"Yes, sir!"

"How many shells do we have left?"

"Fifteen common shells per gun, sir and twelve shrapnel!"

So few!

"Hold your fire. We can't afford to waste ammunition."

"We won't, sir!"

As the Ansar approached the edge of the killing area, one

horseman spurred forward. He jinked around the spikes, lifted his sword above his head and shouted, "Allah Akbar!"

"What's that idiot doing?" Baxter asked.

"Proving his bravery, perhaps," Jack suggested.

"Proving his stupidity, perhaps," Baxter retorted.

Jack expected the sharpshooters to open fire, but they watched, unsure whether to admire the rider's bravery or kill him. Jack shared their sentiments, for it was hard to shoot a brave man who had no hope of success.

The rider approached the ditch and shouted again, "Allah Akbar!" Sliding his sword into its scabbard, he lifted his spear from its rest beside his saddle, poised and threw it. The long shaft vibrated as it hissed through the air, and the point plunged deep into the baked mud battlement beside two British soldiers.

"Missed!" Private Brotheridge gave the expected reply. "You couldn't hit a bull's arse with a banjo!" He lifted his rifle and aimed without squeezing the trigger. "Now, bugger off home before you get hurt."

Drawing his sword, the rider began a circuit of the ditch, perhaps looking for a weakness or an opportunity to cross. When he reached the wall around the village, the Egyptian defenders set up a great hoot of derision, with one or two firing their rifles.

"The Gyppos don't like him much," Donnelly said.

"They know he'd kill them sooner than spit," Wright replied.

Jack heard Khalif give the order to fire, there was an irregular volley, and a moment later, the horse appeared, dragging the wounded rider. The man bounced on the rough ground, leaving a smear of blood that the sand soaked hungrily up.

"One down," Brotheridge sounded offhand.

"He was a brave man," Kerswell said.

"He was a bloody fool," Brotheridge gave his unforgiving reply.

The Mahdists set up a great cheer when the horse returned

with its bloodied rider. They lifted their spears, swords, and rifles in the air, chanted their war cry and began a slow advance.

"Here they come at last," Baxter said. "Now there's an appallingly solemn sight."

The fierce sun reflected from thousands of spear blades as the Ansar advanced steadily. Jack knew these warriors had defeated Hicks Pasha and Baker Pasha and were led by the same experienced commanders; they were veterans with a history of victory. As they closed, the drums recommenced their unsettling hammer, joined by a cacophony of human voices. Jack could not make out the words, but he knew the fanatics, the wild-haired men who roused the warriors to holy war, were goading them to attack. Beneath the frantic screeches, the warriors chanted their prayers, confident that Allah would welcome them to Paradise if they killed the Nazarenes.

"Come on then, you howling bastards!" Private Brotheridge shouted.

Kerswell stamped his boots on the walkway, sighted along the barrel of his rifle and grinned. "The same procedure as always, Brothers? If the Dervish kill me, you'll get my kit."

"And if they kill me, you'll get mine," Brotheridge agreed.

"Halloa, Donnelly," Wright nudged Donnelly with a sharp elbow. "Will you look after Nicky if I don't make it?"

Donnelly grinned. "I'll do that, Wheelie, and you look after Old Jack."

Jack wondered if Donnelly was comparing him to the Malverns' dog. *That's probably an honour.* He gauged the temper of his men. They had waited long enough in the oppressive heat and constriction of the village and now wanted to face their enemy and settle accounts with them.

"Lieutenant Rawlinson!" Jack shouted when the Ansar reached the first of his range markers.

The two seven-pounders immediately cracked out, with the shells exploding a few feet short of the range markers. Jack watched through his field glasses, knowing the artillery was short of ammunition but determined to cause as much damage as possible to the enemy before they got close.

When the shells exploded, the enemy increased their speed, and their yelling and shouting grew louder.

"There's bloody thousands of them!" Private Barr shouted. "Where's the bloody Gatling?"

"You've got a Martini," Sergeant Hanley put a hand on Barr's shoulder. "They've only got spears!"

"Sharpshooters!" Jack shouted when the Ansar reached the second black-painted range marker. "Fire when you get a target! Aim for the horsemen with the standards."

He hoped the sharpshooters could find the Mahdi or Osman Zubeir but doubted that the Mahdi would lead his army in person.

The sharpshooters fired slowly, aiming each shot. Scott exclaimed when he made a kill, keeping the score as if he were shooting pheasants in a British estate while MacLeod and Graham were silent. They were professionals, intent on doing the best possible job.

Jack saw a shell burst over a knot of cavalry, killing and wounding half a dozen men, but the Mahdi would not notice such numbers in his army of thousands. A warrior lifted a fallen standard, passed it to another rider, and the advance continued without a check.

Jack saw a warrior fall here and there as the sharpshooters added to their tally. Still, the Ansar advance continued, picking up speed as they approached the killing area. Jack watched them through his field glasses, waiting until they reached the white-painted range markers.

Now they're in the effective range of my men.

"Company commanders!" Jack raised his right hand. "At your discretion, fire!"

There was a slight pause and then a confused crackling from the Ansar as their riflemen opened fire. Jack saw some shots raise puffs of dirt from the defensive wall and one from the fort's battlements. His company commanders did not reply. Jack saw the men staring at the approaching enemy, rifles cuddled close to shoulder and cheek, hands ready on the triggers.

"C Company, fire!" Jamieson shouted, and sixty-eight Martinis crashed out. Jack imagined the heavy bullets spinning through the air and their hellish impact on the tribesmen's bodies. Gunsmoke rose, acrid, stinging, and ugly.

"D Company, fire!" Captain Regan ordered, and the company's fifty-three Martinis fired. Gunsmoke jetted out to lie in front of the wall and blanket the defensive ditch.

From his vantage point in the tower, Jack could see the entire outer perimeter of the defences, with the Mahdi's army advancing in a semi-circle, avoiding the south wall. Confident that the Malverns were well-handled and steady, Jack concentrated on the Egyptians guarding the east wall of the village. Colonel Wahiba had them in hand, and they fired steadily, with their volleys felling dozens of the enemy.

Abu Bol's village militia guarded the south wall, the strongest part of the defences because of a natural cliff outside. Jack had posted a half company of Malverns to stiffen the militia and had Moffat's mounted infantry as a mobile reserve, ready to reinforce whichever point most needed help.

The Ansar broke into a full charge, and the defensive fire was a continuous roar. Jack saw some warriors fall and writhe in agony as they trod on the half-hidden spikes, and others stopped to fire their rifles. Jack realised he had been under fire for some time as he saw spurts of dirt rising from the battlements around him. Something zipped past his head to crash against the flagpole.

"Their shooting is improving," Baxter said calmly.

"Maybe," Jack conceded. "Or perhaps they were aiming at the wall and shot high."

Baxter laughed and ducked as a bullet hissed past his face.

The artillery was firing over open sights now, hammering the Ansar with common shells and shrapnel. Each shot was causing terrible devastation, killing, maiming, and wounding, turning brave warriors into broken, maimed cripples. Pieces of men were scattered over the ground, ignored by the chanting, advancing warriors.

"There!" RSM Deblin pointed to a large group of warriors who had taken temporary refuge behind a tempting mimosa bush. "Can you hit that?"

"With my eyes closed, RSM," Cooper replied. He aimed at the small mark the pioneers had also left above the surface, smiled, and squeezed the trigger.

The heavy Martini bullet struck the detonator for the black gunpowder. The resulting explosion sent twenty pounds of old nails, pebbles and pieces of glass and scrap metal in a hellish circle.

"Oh, dear God!" Jack said.

Five Ansar warriors died instantly, one blown into fragments by the explosion. Five others were seriously wounded, with others shocked or knocked over by the blast.

Cooper raised the muzzle of his Martini and chuckled. "Now, that was a good shot!"

Jack nodded. His mines worked, yet the enemy continued to advance in their thousands. The defenders' fire was destructive, knocking down men by the score and carving great holes in the Mahdist's ranks, but for every man hit, ten more seemed to take their place.

"It's like a wall of steel coming towards us!" Lang yelled.

Jack saw the Mahdi's green banner twitch and jerk as British bullets punched holes in the silk. "Lower your sights!" he roared. "You're firing too high!"

With limited ammunition but a seemingly limitless number of the enemy, the defenders could not afford to waste bullets. Jack became aware of the sound as the attackers shouted and yelled their slogans, with the British defenders responding with curses and roars of encouragement. Augmenting the voices was the constant hammer of the Martini Henrys and the Egyptian and Ansar Remingtons. There were also the cries of wounded horses and frightened camels and the head-splitting hammer of the seven-pounders.

When Zubeir sent a strong force against the Well Gate, the Navy finally had the opportunity to show their skill.

"Shoot, lads!" Lieutenant Hamilton ordered, and the Gatling added its murderous chatter to the hellish cacophony and sliced into the attackers. Jack nodded with professional satisfaction as he watched the Malverns firing, reloading, aiming, and firing with calm efficiency. The fort and defensive wall blazed with gunfire, becoming frantic as the Mahdists passed over the killing area, losing scores of men without faltering.

Jack shifted his attention to the Egyptians, who were firing volleys as steadily as Guardsmen. Colonel Wahiba was walking along the wall, encouraging his men, sorting a jammed rifle here, stopping for a brief word with an officer there.

"Come on, my children," Wahiba shouted. "Fight like the men of old!"

Jack nodded; Wahiba's Egyptians were performing well.

"Sir! They're concentrating on the wells!"

Jack had expected nothing less. Water was the gold of the desert, and the Mahdi's men would be hard-pressed to survive with what they had outside. The only reason for the village's existence was the wells, a lifeline for desert caravans. Zubeir or Najumi had sent three separate forces toward the Well Gate. While the Gatling held one section back, the others charged across the killing area in two flanking attacks.

"Gunners!"

"We know, sir!" Lieutenant Rawlinson ordered his men to push his seven-pounders up the ramp to the wall walk. "Shrapnel, lads!"

The Mahdists were at the ditch, with the mounted men shouting encouragement, waving their swords, and throwing the occasional spear at the defenders. Lieutenant Jarvis ordered his platoon to fire a volley, then staggered and fell. Some of the men rushed to help until Sergeant Hanley snarled at them.

"Leave him to the doolie bearers! Shoot these Dervish!"

Some Mahdists climbed the wall, thrusting their spears into the mud bricks as the British had done with bayonets at Tel-el-Kebir three years previously. Hundreds crowded behind, yelling their slogans as they massed in the ditch. The spikes claimed a few, but there were always more, many more eager to kill a Nazarene to smooth their passage to Paradise.

Rawlinson watched calmly. "Fire," he said.

The double blast of shrapnel tore down the Mahdists, killing twenty men and wounding more.

"Fire!" Sergeant Hanley shouted, and his section fired, loaded, and fired again, hammering the survivors until their bodies piled into the ditch.

Jack fought his instinctive sympathy with the warriors caught by that terrible hail. "Send them back," he ordered as the Malverns cheered to see the Mahdists reeling.

"Effendi!" Bimbashi Khalif nearly pulled at Jack's sleeve in his agitation. "The enemy has made a lodgement in the south!"

CHAPTER TWENTY-NINE

To save your world you asked this man to die:
Would this man, could he see you now, ask why?
W. H. Auden

Jack swore. The Mahdi, or perhaps Zubeir, was more devious than he imagined. While holding Jack's attention with an assault on the wells, he launched an attack on the less well-defended south of the village.

"How many men?" Jack asked.

Khalif gestured weakly. "I don't know, effendi."

"I'm coming," Jack said.

The militia had fought hard defending their wall and now took up quarters in the houses, with the remains of the Malverns' half company formed up in the street, firing at an unknown number of Mahdists.

"Where's Lieutenant Pearson?" Jack asked.

"Dead, sir. So is Sergeant Fagan. I'm Corporal Brand." Brand was in his twenties and bled from a wound to the face. "We've got thirty-one men left and about two-thirds of the militia. The Dervish swarmed up the cliff like bloody monkeys, sir, and took us in both flanks."

"Hold them here, Corporal." Jack saw the near panic in the man's eyes. He turned to Khalif. "Fetch the mounted infantry."

"Yes, effendi." Khalif ran away, shouting as Abu Bol's militia opened an erratic fire from the roofs and windows of the houses.

"Fire!" Corporal Brand shouted. "Keep these files together!"

The Mahdists poured over the wall and into the village, screaming their slogans as they ran into the Malverns and militia's fire. Jack's previous experience of house-to-house fighting had been during the Indian Mutiny nearly thirty years before, and he remembered it as bloody and untidy.

Jack remained with the half-company. "Volley fire on my word," he ordered. He knew it would usually be better to order individual firing, but the Mahdists' advance had shaken these men, and they needed calm directions.

"Aim!" Jack shouted and pushed down the muzzle of one young soldier's rifle. "Aim low, lads!"

The militia was firing from the rooftops, yelling at one another as the Mahdists pushed up the street. Jack unfastened his holster and pulled out his revolver.

"Fire!" Jack shouted. "Reload!" He peered into the smoke, seeing the warriors continue their charge. "Aim! Fire!" Each volley brought down a dozen or more of the enemy. Mahdists' bodies tumbled in the dusty street, and their colleagues leapt over them, eager to kill the Nazarene. The enemy chanting rose in triumph, and Jack was sure he could smell their grease and sweat above the acrid stink of gun smoke.

"Reload!" The Mahdists were only twenty yards away now, with a few diverted to attack the houses the militia occupied. "Fix bayonets!"

The Malverns were swearing, one man praying as he clicked his bayonet in place. Corporal Brand glanced at Jack with beads of sweat hanging from his clipped moustache and a rip in his sun helmet. He gave a lopsided grin although his eyes were wild.

"Aim!" Jack said. There was no need to aim. A blind man

could shoot with the certainty of hitting one or more of the enemy. "Fire!" At close range, the large-calibre bullets were devastating. They knocked charging men backwards or passed through one man to kill the warrior behind. They tore off legs, arms and heads and sent a spray of blood into the air, through which the survivors continued to charge.

Jack knew he would never forget the Mahdists' spears. With their long staffs and heads like trowels, he had seen what damage they could do to a human body and knew the warriors were experts in wielding them.

"Load! Present! Aim! Fire!"

The warriors smashed into the thin khaki line, yelling their slogans. Jack saw one warrior leap in the air and plunge his spear into the throat of a British soldier, withdraw the blade even before he landed and thrust it a second time into the man's chest. The soldier was dead before his bloody body crumpled to the ground.

The soldier's backmarker screamed and lunged forward with his bayonet. He caught the warrior in the chest, but the blade crashed against a rib and bent double. The warrior looked at the young soldier and, despite the wound in his chest, poised his spear for a killing blow until Jack put two bullets in his head.

"Use your mate's rifle!" Jack ordered the shocked soldier with the bent bayonet. "He won't mind!"

The Malverns' line was crumpling, with men gasping and swearing as they fought toe-to-toe with the Dervishes. Corporal Brand held his Martini by the barrel and swung it like a club, panting with effort as he attempted to keep the enemy at bay. One bearded soldier was wrestling with an enemy, both men rolling in the dirt as another warrior waited with his spear poised.

Where the devil is the mounted infantry? If they don't come soon, it'll be too late!

The bearded soldier got on top of his man and began to

throttle him when the spearman poised to lunge. A young soldier, sobbing with fear, lunged with his bayonet and caught the spearman in the armpit. Both men screamed, and the soldier struggled to free his blade as another group of warriors ran up.

"No! Oh, God, no!" The young soldier dropped his rifle and backed away.

Jack fired into the mass of the enemy, unaware he was shouting as loudly as any of his men.

Another soldier fell with a spear in his stomach, and the khaki line took a step back and then another.

"Stand your ground!" Jack ordered. If the Mahdists broke through here, they would crash through the village and kill every man, woman, and child.

Is this where I die? A newly promoted brigadier fighting for an obscure village in a country we don't even want?

The volley came from Jack's left, and he heard a voice call in Arabic. "Another, my children! Give them another!"

He looked up to see Colonel Wahiba had occupied the houses on the left side of the street, with the white uniforms and red fezzes a welcome sight. Jack lifted a hand in acknowledgement, and Wahiba grinned in return.

With Wahiba's company pushing against the Dervishes' flank, the pressure on the remaining Malverns eased.

"Sir!" Moffat trotted up with the mounted infantry. "How can we help?"

"Where the devil have you been?" Jack snarled. "I sent Khalif for you half an hour ago!"

"Khalif is dead, sir!" Moffat reported. "He never reached me. The Mahdists broke through in the west, and we've been pushing them out. The artillery used the last of their shells blasting the Mahdists." He took a deep breath. "Where do you want us, sir?"

Jack reloaded his revolver.

We don't want Sudan; Egypt doesn't deserve Sudan, and men are dying for no good reason. Why doesn't Gordon get out of Khartoum, and we can turn our back on this place?

Jack realised that Moffat was waiting for his reply. "Push these damned Mahdists out of the village, Moffat."

"Very good, sir!" Moffat said. "Come on, boys! Follow your uncle Douglas."

Moffat led the mounted infantry down the village street, shooting every warrior they saw. Some MI carried the warrior's long spears, which they used like lances, stabbing at men on the ground. They had learned never to assume a Mahdist warrior was dead and that bayonets and swords lacked the length to reach a warrior lying prone.

Wahiba greeted Jack with a smart salute. "Do you wish my men to remain, Brigadier?"

"Yes, please, Colonel," Jack said. "You saved the day, I think. Could you leave half a company to hold the southern wall? The Malverns lost a lot of men."

"My soldiers will help the Malverns," Wahiba said.

"I'll leave this wall in your hands, Colonel," Jack said. "Corporal Brand will obey your commands."

"Yes, Brigadier," Wahiba said.

Jack realised that the musketry was fading away.

"Take over here, Colonel," Jack said and strode to the fort. *Don't run; don't allow the men to think you are agitated.*

From the top of the tower, Jack had a better view of the entire village and fort. On the north and south, the Ansar was retiring in good order, turning every few moments to fire a few shots at the village.

"We've repelled them," Baxter said.

"For now," Jack agreed. "I doubt the Mahdi will give up yet." He looked over the village street, the ditch, and the killing area, all littered with dead and dying men. "I want this place cleaned up," he said. "I want the dead decently buried." *In these temperatures, the dead will quickly decompose, attract flies, and spread disease.*

"Yes, sir," Baxter understood. "How about the wounded?"

Jack nodded grimly. "If they respond to our help, then, by all means, help them."

"If not?"

"Our priority is the lives of our men," Jack said. "Send out Moffat with a mounted patrol. I want to know the enemy's location and find me how many men we lost."

CHAPTER THIRTY

The first quality of the soldier is constancy in enduring fatigue and privation. Courage is only the second.
Napoleon Bonaparte

Moffat returned within the hour. "The enemy has withdrawn about four miles, sir."

"All of them?" Jack asked.

Moffat nodded, dripping sweat. "I believe so, sir."

Jack considered for a moment. "It's either a trap or something significant has happened."

"Yes, sir."

"Get some rest, Moffat," Jack said. "You'll be out again tomorrow."

Jack ordered Sergeant Anderson's pioneers to restore the defences and posted strong pickets around the village.

"Lieutenant Lang, take a party out and collect any weapons the Ansar has left behind. We need as much ammunition as we can get."

I didn't notice Lang during the latter stages of the fighting.

With the immediate danger gone, Jack concentrated on caring

for the wounded and ensured everybody, military and civilian, was fed.

"Sir," Sergeant Trafford saluted. "A messenger has arrived, sir. He's asking to see you in person."

"Bring him in," Jack said and stepped to the window to watch proceedings.

The messenger was a slender Baggara tribesman with a patient camel. He dismounted outside the fort and allowed two privates to search him before he entered the courtyard.

"What's this?" Private Brotheridge held up a small book the tribesman had up his sleeve.

"It's the Koran," Kerswell told him. "Their Holy book."

Brotheridge flicked through the pages. "I can't read this!"

"He can read it," Kerswell said. "Give it back to him."

"I'll stay close by," Donnelly said as Trafford escorted the tribesman to Jack's office.

"Thank you, Donnelly," Jack replied.

The tribesman entered Jack's office as if he owned the place. "Windrush Pasha?"

"That's me," Jack said, exchanging the customary polite Arab greetings.

"I have a message for you from Hook Pasha," the Arab said.

"Thank you," Jack said. The tribesman opened the Koran, extracted a slip of paper from the spine and handed it to Jack.

"Do you want a reply?" Jack asked.

"No, Windrush Pasha. I only require water for my camel and me and some fodder for the beast."

"Private Donnelly will ensure you have all you need," Jack said.

The message was in code, and Jack reached for his deciphering manual, taking pains to ensure his translation was accurate. Even one wrong syllable could alter the meaning of a brief message.

When he was satisfied, Jack read the message through, shaking his head.

Wolseley proceeding up Nile to relieve Gordon. Evacuate British and Egyptian forces from El Kutuk and join British forces.

Jack frowned. *That's a bit ambiguous. Which British forces? Wolseley's? Or Suakin. Is Suakin still under our control?*

Jack sighed, stood up and stepped to the window that overlooked the courtyard. The Egyptian NCOs were drilling a company of their regiment, their attitudes reflecting close companionship with the Malverns. Jack watched them for a few moments, noting that Abu Bol and some of the village militia were also present.

Wahiba's Egyptian soldiers have progressed in leaps and bounds. Damn it! We've achieved great things here.

"Major Bryant!"

"Yes, sir," Bryant replied so quickly that Jack guessed he had been waiting for the summons.

"Orders for the day, Bryant. I want a meeting of all the senior British and Egyptian officers at six tonight. Invite Abu Bol and the village militia as well."

"Yes, sir." Bryant hesitated for a moment. "What's happening, sir?"

"We're evacuating El Kutuk, Bryant," Jack said. "That's what's happening."

"Where are we going?"

"To find a British Army," Jack took a deep breath. "Read that," he handed Bryant the message and its translation.

"I see, sir," Bryant said. "I'll start making preparations."

"Thank you, Bryant." Jack knew how much organisation the move would take.

* * *

Jack gave the officers a few moments to settle as they gathered in the courtyard.

"Gentlemen," he said and waited for Sergeant Deng to translate his words. "I have been ordered to evacuate the village and march the British and Egyptian soldiers to safety." He saw the look of sudden dismay on the faces of the village militia.

"I have no intention of abandoning the good people of El Kutuk to the Mahdi or any of his lieutenants. General Wolseley is advancing up the Nile to relieve the siege of Khartoum, and I intend to take the garrison to meet him. I will also take as many villagers as wish to come."

Most of the officers appeared stunned. Abu Bol and some of the militia looked relieved yet worried.

"Are there any questions?" Jack asked.

"Where will General Wolseley be based, sir?" Baxter asked.

"I don't yet know," Jack said. "I only know he is heading upriver with a relieving army."

"The nearest point to the Nile is Berber, sir," Bryant said. "Do the Mahdi's forces not hold that?"

"As far as I am aware, the Ansar controls Berber," Jack agreed.

"Would we not be better heading towards Suakin?" Bryant asked.

"At present," Jack said, "I do not know if we still hold Suakin. We do know that Osman Digna operates between here and Suakin with his Hadendoa. I don't wish to lead a force that includes civilians through such dangerous territory on the off chance there might be a British garrison at Suakin."

"What if Wolseley does not make it, sir?"

Jack had considered that possibility. "Of one thing, I am certain," he said, forcing a smile. "The Mahdi will not stop Sir Garnet Wolseley."

When some officers cheered at Jack's words, he lifted a hand for silence. "We have a lot to do, gentlemen. I want both our regiments organised to leave with as much spare water as we can carry. I want to know how many civilians will come with us and who will remain behind. We will leave nothing the Ansar can use, not a broken bayonet or a single brass cartridge case!"

Aware that much of the administrative work would fall on

Bryant, Jack told him to find a couple of literate NCOs as assistants.

"Hanley's a good man," Jack said. "He'll be useful."

"Thank you, sir," Bryant said.

"Moffat!" Jack called the subaltern to him. "As you're the best desert hand in the garrison, I want you to find the fastest route between here and the Nile. Take out strong patrols and leave supply dumps every ten miles, food and especially water."

"Yes, sir," Moffat said. "I'll miss this place, sir."

"We're not away yet," Jack said. "Don't take any chances out there."

"I won't, sir."

Jack watched Moffat lead his mounted infantry from the fort with a long line of camels, each loaded with skin water bags. A few moments later, Drummond entered the stables and left with her camel, Ozzy.

Jack intercepted her. "Where the devil do you think you're going?"

"With Lieutenant Moffat," Explorer said. "I understand the desert better than he does."

Jack considered for a moment. Drummond had travelled the desert alone, and Moffat could find her helpful. "All right. Be careful."

Drummond smiled and drifted a hand across Jack's shoulder. "One must always be careful in the desert."

Jack waved Drummond on and returned to organising the evacuation, spending the remainder of that day in his office talking to villagers and working out details with his senior officers. They discussed the number of transport and baggage animals, water, and food they would need.

"It's going to be a long column," Baxter said.

"Not as long as some of the columns we've had in India, where camp followers made up a sizeable proportion of the total," Jack reminded. "We'll use our Indian experience here."

"Maybe so. How much will each civilian carry?" Bryant was writing screeds of notes.

They worked out the maximum weight of possessions each refugee could carry and how the column would march.

By late afternoon, over four hundred village inhabitants elected to travel with the British, and the remainder decided to remain in El Kutuk.

"Most of these people who choose to remain have lived in the village all their lives," Abu Bol sounded apologetic. "They'll accept the Mahdi as their leader if he allows them to continue living as they always have. It is the will of Allah."

"I will not try to influence their choice," Jack said. He stood up wearily. "Has Moffat's patrol returned yet?"

"Two minutes ago, sir," Bryant told him. "Here's Moffat now."

"Sir!" Moffat nearly ran to Jack. "We saw a huge cloud of dust, and when we investigated, we found about a third of the enemy marching away."

Jack felt some of his burden lift. "In which direction did they march?"

"South and west, sir."

"Towards Khartoum," Jack said.

I'll wager the Mahdi was withdrawing Wad-el-Najumi's warriors back to Khartoum. He'll have heard that Wolseley is on his way and wants to capture the city before the British relieve Gordon.

"Thank you, Moffat," Jack said.

With less of the enemy, it will be easier to slip away from El Kutuk. I wish I knew our objective, though. The Nile is a devil of a long river.

* * *

"That's four supply depots placed, sir," Moffat reported three days later. "They are at ten-mile intervals along the route."

Jack nodded. "The furthest is forty miles away," he said.

"That's right, sir," Moffat agreed.

"That will leave us around eighty miles to cover to reach the Nile, where we'll have fresh water." Jack looked up. "I am sorry, Moffat, but I want you for another expedition. How far can you ride unsupported?"

Moffat considered for a moment. "I could go further on camelback, sir. If I took fewer men and carried more water skins on camels."

Jack thought of the distance he had to take the garrison and four hundred civilians. "Do that, Moffat."

"Yes, sir," Moffat said.

It's always the best and brightest we send on the most dangerous expeditions. One day we'll find we've used up our supply, and we're left with the dull, unimaginative, and spiritless. When that happens, Britain will collapse, and the world will be poorer.

As Moffat carried water and supplies ever further along the route to the Nile, Jack prepared the garrison and civilians for the journey. "Only bring what you can carry," he advised. "If you have transport or a baggage animal, bring it along. Make sure you have water and food."

Jack checked the route to the Nile and ordered the most gifted artists in the regiment to copy out maps so each officer possessed one. He asked Sergeant Deng and Colonel Wahiba to have half a dozen maps written in Arabic and passed them to the Egyptians and Abu Bol's village militia.

"I want the mounted men to scout ahead and on the flanks," Jack said at his final officers' meeting before the evacuation. "The infantry will march with rifles empty but ready to use. The civilians will be within a cordon of infantry, and the militia will act as rearguard." Jack looked around the weary, sun-browned faces.

My Malverns are tired. They travelled straight from war in Afghanistan to another war in Egypt, garrisoned the country for over a year and then marched into a third war in Sudan. They are gaunt, weary, and ready for a rest.

Jack continued. "The mules will carry food, water, ammunition, and the villager's possessions. The camels will carry the sick, tired, and lame."

The officers, Egyptian and British, nodded.

Jack spoke slowly, with Deng translating for the Egyptians and villagers. "We will not leave anybody behind, British, Egyptian, or Sudanese. Everybody who leaves the village tomorrow will be with us when we arrive, or we'll bury them decently on the journey."

The officers nodded in agreement.

"We leave an hour before dawn tomorrow," Jack said. "Abu Bol, please ensure the villagers are ready."

Before he left the village, Jack paid a visit to the mosque. The Imam was inside, quietly praying.

"You are welcome to join us, Imam," Jack told him when the Imam had completed his devotions.

The Imam gave his gentle smile. "Thank you, Brigadier, but my position is with the people of El Kutuk."

"Zubeir will most likely kill you," Jack reminded.

The Imam smiled. "If that is the will of Allah."

"You're a brave man," Jack said. "If you reconsider, you will be very welcome."

"My place is here," the Imam repeated. "Go with God, Brigadier. We will not meet again."

Jack gave a slight bow. "*Assalamo alaikum wa rahmatullahe wa barakatohu.*

Peace be on you and the mercy and blessings of Allah."

"Thank you, Brigadier. *Wa alaikum salaam.* And peace be on you too."

Jack returned to the fort. He could do no more.

* * *

Despite all Jack's planning, it was an hour after dawn before the convoy straggled out of the village. Civilians were not as amenable to timetables as disciplined soldiers, and the militia ran themselves ragged, rounding up young families and elderly women. When the column finally left El Kutuk, the sun was well above the horizon.

"We'll have to push them hard to reach the first supply cache," Jack said.

"Yes, sir," Baxter agreed.

"*Acta est fabula*," Lang said, looking over the village. "It's all over."

"No," Jack shook his head. "We never intended to stay, Lang. We always planned to leave, with or without Gordon."

With the mounted infantry acting as scouts and guides and the militia picking up stragglers, Jack fretted over his charge. The convoy stretched over a mile, with baggage animals in the centre and the rising dust better than a flag to alert the enemy.

"We're very vulnerable, sir," Lang said. "We might have been better to leave all the civilians behind."

"No," Jack said. "When Zubeir takes the village, his warriors will murder anybody who helped us. Many of these civilians are the militia's families, and I won't leave them to the Ansar's mercy."

"We might all get killed defending them," Lang said.

Jack put an edge to his voice. "It's a soldier's duty and function to protect civilians. If we don't do that, what good are we?"

"Yes, sir," Lang said without conviction.

"Go and attend to your men, Lang," Jack said.

Jack had weighed the same factors when he decided to bring out the civilians. He balanced the possible loss of British lives against the chance of escorting hundreds of civilians to safety across the desert.

If he could find Wolseley's army.

Maybe the Mahdi has defeated Wolseley in battle, and I'm dooming all these people to die of thirst.

No! Jack shook his head. *The Ansar could not defeat Wolseley. I considered all the possibilities and made my decision. We continue.*

Riding to the rear of the column, Jack spoke to the militia.

"The civilians are slower than we are," Abu Bol told him. "Some may be regretting their decision."

"We've only ten miles to travel today," Jack said. "Try to keep them moving."

The first day was slow, with the dust irritating the civilians and some begging for water long before they arrived at the supply depot. The British and Egyptian soldiers plodded across the sand, some sucking date pips, others cursing, but all carrying their rifles and nobody dropping out.

Moffat had placed the first supply dump on top of a prominent ridge, and Jack ordered the pioneers to erect a zareba. "Take D Company of the Malverns and a company of Egyptians," Jack said. He looked over the milling crowd, with mules, camels, soldiers, and civilians.

Now I know how Moses felt. He was forty years on his journey, and I hope to finish in seven days.

Jack was surprised the following day when the civilians were only an hour late, and they left in the brisk coolness before dawn.

Abu Bol saluted with a broad grin. "I woke them early, sir!"

"You did well, Abu Bol," Jack told him and sent out Moffat on his perennial patrolling.

Moffat returned in a curtain of sand and threw a brief salute. "I found hoof prints on the ground ahead, sir."

"How many hoof prints and what kind?" Jack asked.

"Horses, sir and I estimate a couple of hundred."

"Did you see in what direction they were going?" Jack asked. Two hundred hostile cavalry could be dangerous to a slow-moving column and could easily gather more men.

"Westward, sir," Moffat said. "The same as us."

"Thank you, Moffat. Let's hope they keep going but look out for them."

"I will, sir."

"Take a strong patrol ahead to ensure the next supply dump is untouched."

"Yes, sir!" Despite the strained lines on his face, Moffat responded cheerfully.

"Avoid trouble if you can," Jack added.

"We will, sir!" Moffat said. Calling up a score of his riders, he pushed them forward, leaving a rising ribbon of dust to mark his passage.

Envying Moffat his youth and freedom, Jack pushed the column on. The journey was already telling on the civilians, who were moving more slowly and halting more often. Painfully aware of the distance they had to cover, Jack encouraged them.

"Keep moving, people!" He glanced at the surrounding desert, where the heat rose in shimmering waves. The camels plodded on, many carrying civilians, and Branley mustered the mules, talking to them, calling them by name.

"Come on, Clara, you can do better than that. Look at Amelia there; she never complains! Jasmin, that's the way, girl. Come on; I'll give you a hand."

Outside the civilians and animals, the infantry, British and Egyptian, trudged on, heads bowed under the lash of the sun, complaining, grumbling, and cursing the heat.

"We've only five miles to go!" Jack shouted, with sand grating in his throat. "Keep moving!"

That day passed in a nightmare of dust, heat, and exertion, as did the next. Jack nearly lost count of the days. Every night he held a conference with the officers and marked the column's position on the map. Moffat proved himself an expert at navigation by the stars and compass.

"Miss Drummond improved my skills," Moffat said, correcting Jack's dead reckoning on more than one occasion.

"I'll have to add her to the strength," Jack said and toured the zareba, checking they had left nobody behind.

The march continued, baking hot by day, biting cold at night. On the fifth day, when Tinker began to flag, Jack dismounted and rode Gonda, his grey Arab, and when he saw a mother carrying two children, he handed her the horse.

"Up you get," he said and walked on, with the hot sand seeping through the eyelets of his boots to chafe and irritate his feet.

"Sir!" Wahiba rode beside him. "Take my horse. It is not fitting that you should walk."

"I'll walk," Jack said. He felt the heat rising from the sand and smelt the rank human sweat mixed with the stink of camels and mules. "Keep moving." The sand slid beneath his feet, a camel snorted somewhere, and Branley was soothing one of his mules.

Keep moving, he told himself. *Put one foot after the other, lift them, keep your head up and march.* Although he knew he was in the Sudanese desert, in his mind, Jack was walking the cool green slopes of the Malvern Hills, with the glorious views over Herefordshire and Worcestershire. He could see his ancestral home of Wychwood Manor and the neighbouring Netherhills, with the welcome smoke spiralling from the multiple chimneys.

Jack stumbled, steadied himself, realised he was still in the desert and stepped on. He had a different perspective from ground level. Astride a horse, Jack could see over the heads of the men to the land beyond. Here, he blinked in the dust and saw only trudging legs, shuffling boots and the shoulders of suffering men. He moved to the head of the column, feeling the sweat break from his body and almost instantly evaporate.

"Brigadier!"

Jack looked up, dazed by heat and effort.

"Brigadier Windrush!" Alexandrina Drummond looked down on him from the back of a camel. "Mount up here."

"I can walk," Jack had almost forgotten Drummond's existence.

"No, Brigadier," Drummond said. "You must lead these people, so we need you to be fit and mentally alert. You must ride rather than walk, or we're all in danger."

"The lady's right, sir!" Donnelly pushed to Drummond's side. "I'll find you a camel."

"Take this one." Drummond patted Ozzy's neck. "You can't control the column from the ground."

"I won't ride while a lady walks," Jack protested.

Drummond shook her head at Donnelly. "Is he always this stubborn, Donnelly?"

"I can't answer that, Miss," Donnelly said.

"Sir!" Moffat shouted from outside the column. "Sir! Has anybody seen the Brigadier?"

"Here, Douglas!" Drummond shouted, and Moffat pushed his horse through the troops.

"Sir, Captain Sarsens sends his compliments, sir, and we've made contact with the enemy."

"Tell me more, Moffat," Jack demanded, trying to focus on the lieutenant with his head whirling.

"We were heading towards the final stores' dump, sir, when we saw dust rising on the left. Captain Sarsens sent me on reconnaissance, and I saw a dozen camels. I watched them for a while, and they rode into a wadi with a camp inside it."

"How many men?" Jack's mind cleared as he had a problem to solve.

"I'm not sure, sir. Hundreds at least."

"Very good," Jack said. "Where is Captain Sarsens now?"

"He's keeping a watch for the enemy, sir. He sent Sergeant Toner ahead with a section to the supply dump."

"Thank you, Moffat. Return to Captain Sarsens and tell him to continue to watch and let me know of any development."

"Yes, sir," Moffat turned his horse, pushed through the trudging infantry, and trotted away.

"You'll need your camel," Drummond said quietly. She dismounted smoothly and pulled the camel to a kneeling position. "His name's Ozzy, and he's well-behaved."

"Yes, Miss Drummond." Duty was more important than the comfort of a single civilian. Jack mounted and pushed to the head of the column. There were four miles to the final supply dump, and the civilians were dragging at the back. "Company commanders! To me!"

When the officers hurried to join him, Jack informed them of the situation. "Ensure your men are alert," he said, "and pick up the pace. If we're at the supply dump, we have more chance of fighting off an attack."

"Yes, sir." The officers returned to their men while Jack rode to the rear of the column and told the militia what was happening.

"Try and get the civilians to move faster," Jack said, "but don't cause any panic. I won't leave anybody behind."

"Windrush Pasha!" Abu Bol pointed to the west, where a ribbon of dust rose high in the air.

CHAPTER THIRTY-ONE

Away for we are ready to a man!
Our camels sniff the evening and are glad
Lead on, O Master of the Caravan:
Lead on the Merchant Prince of Baghdad.
James Elroy Flecker

Jack nodded. "That might be our mounted infantry," he said, with more hope than conviction. He sent word to his men to keep alert, ensured any straggling civilians were brought within the column and marched on.

The dust came closer, moving faster than Jack's column.

"Baxter," Jack called.

"Sir!"

"When you think it proper, have the men load."

"Yes, sir,"

Jack gave the same order to Colonel Wahiba, lifted his field glasses, and scanned the desert. He could not penetrate the dust but saw a slight ridge ahead, surrounded by mimosa bushes and with a solitary fig tree on the side.

"Head for that ridge," Jack ordered. "If whoever's making that dust proves hostile, we might need the height."

The civilians complained at Jack's course alteration, and some panicked at the approaching dust cloud.

"Keep them calm," Jack told Abu Bol. He glanced ahead, working out relative speeds and distances.

"Jamieson!"

"Sir!"

"Take out B Company, extended order and keep a watch on that dust. If they're hostile, keep them occupied until we set up a defensive perimeter on the ridge. Retire slowly towards us and keep close order if they attack you."

"Yes, sir."

Where the devil is Sarsens with my mounted infantry? He's my eyes and ears.

Jack watched B Company march out, the worn khaki-clad men barely visible against the scrub and sand, and hoped he was not sending them to their deaths.

The ridge was half a mile long, steeper on the northern side than the south, with a clear field of fire in every direction.

"This will do," Jack said. "Colonel Wahiba, place your men on the north and east. Baxter, I want the Malverns on the south and west. The sailors can stand at the south-eastern corner."

"How about us, sir?" the gunners asked.

"How much ammunition do you have?" Jack asked.

"None, sir, but we can fight," Rawlinson said. "If my lads can handle a mountain gun, they can fire a Martini."

"Stand by to replace any casualties," Jack said. "Egyptian or British."

"We're your men, sir," Rawlinson agreed.

When the dust came closer, Jack focused his field glasses. "Arabs," he said.

"How many, sir?" Baxter asked.

"I'm not sure," Jack said. "Hundreds rather than thousands." He passed over the field glasses.

"I'd estimate around eight hundred, sir," Baxter said, "and

with three banners." He grunted. "I've seen that banner before, sir, during the siege."

Jack recovered the field glasses. "Osman Zubeir," he said flatly. "He must have followed our dust."

Zubeir sat upright in the saddle with the banner immediately behind him, staring across the intervening desert at the British position.

"Bugler!" Jack rapped. "Sound the retire for Jamieson's company! Where the devil is Sarsens?" He scanned the desert without success.

When the bugle sounded, Jack watched Jameson's company withdrew in good order and slotted into their positions on the ridge. The men were panting and sweating with exertion.

"Sharpshooters!" Jack snapped. "Can your rifles reach that distance?"

Corporal Cooper screwed up his eyes. "No, sir," he said. "They're about three hundred yards beyond our range."

"How fast can you run, Cooper?"

"Fast enough, sir." Cooper looked confused.

"Fast enough to get back here from three hundred yards out with a hundred Dervish chasing you?"

Cooper grinned. "With a hundred of these devils chasing me, sir, I'd be back here quicker than a politician can tell a lie."

"Do you see that tall Arab on the white horse?"

"Osman Zubeir, sir?"

"That's the fellow. Take out your men and try to shoot him," Jack said.

"Yes, sir," Cooper said. He collected his sharpshooters and doubled forward, rifle at the trail.

Jack estimated Cooper ran nearly five hundred yards before he found a suitable location.

I think it was Wellington before Waterloo who said that army commanders had more to do than fire at each other. I disagree. If I manage to kill Zubeir, I'll have removed a serious threat.

"Lang," Jack said. "Cooper's men might have to return in a hurry. Get your platoon ready to move in support."

Lang started. "Yes, sir."

Cooper's sharpshooters seemed to be taking a long time to prepare themselves. Jack checked his watch; they had only been ten minutes.

Where the devil is my mounted infantry? It's not like Sarsens to let me down.

The first rifle shot sounded flat, and the puff of grey-white smoke rose slowly. Other shots followed swiftly, and Jack focused his field glasses, hoping to see Zubeir fall.

The black-and-green banner behind Zubeir jerked as a bullet slammed into the staff, and Zubeir and his immediate followers withdrew a hundred yards.

"Try again," Jack murmured.

As Cooper's sharpshooters fired, two groups of horsemen peeled from Zubeir's force and cantered forward, robes flying and dust rising from their hooves.

"Sound the retire," Jack ordered the bugler. "Lang! Take your men out to support Cooper."

Cooper's men fired a third time as the thin bugle notes trilled across the desert. Jack saw one of the enemy fall, but Zubeir was unharmed. The Arab cavalry pounded closer, racing across the desert as Cooper and his men fled back toward the British position.

Lang took a defensive position and fired a volley at long range, doing no damage. One group of Arab cavalry hesitated, and the other moved faster, yelling as they charged.

"Can I send out more men, sir?" Baxter asked.

"Not yet." Jack shook his head. "Lang can cope but have C Company ready." He watched anxiously as Cooper's sharpshooters raced the Arab cavalry. Lang had his platoon in hand, and when the sharpshooters slid behind him, they fired another volley and began a fighting withdrawal.

"Lieutenant Hamilton," Jack said. "Fire a burst at the cavalry."

Hamilton was waiting for the order, and his Gatling rattled on Jack's last word, with the bullets slicing into the closest of the Arab cavalry. Men and horses fell, and the cavalry withdrew, with one warrior firing his rifle. Lang arrived at the ridge without casualties, and Cooper reported to Jack.

"Sorry, sir, we didn't get Zubeir."

"You gave him a fright, Cooper, and sent them back," Jack said. "Now we'll see what Zubeir does."

"Sir!" Bryant looked agitated. "We have a problem, sir. Most of the water bags were leaking, and we've only about half a pint a man left."

Jack swore. He had a shortage of water, Zubeir hovering with an unknown number of men to attack him, hundreds of dependent civilians and his best officer and men were somewhere in the desert.

My first command as a brigadier, and I could have led my men to their deaths. Jack lifted his head. *Nonsense. The heat and strain are talking, not me. I can't allow the men to see me down.*

"Well done, lads!" Jack shouted. "We've outfaced one of the Mahdi's best generals and found ourselves a good defensive position. Now form a zareba and ration your water."

"Sir." Bryant looked unhappy. "What are we going to do?"

"Fight, Major Bryant," Jack said. "We're going to fight."

Jack toured the position. He knew his men were experts at making zarebas now and had all faced and defeated attacks by the Ansar, but the men liked to see a senior officer share their dangers and hardships.

"Brigadier Windrush."

Jack forced a smile. "Yes, Miss Drummond?"

"I heard that we are short of water."

"That's correct," Jack agreed.

"I may be able to help," Drummond said.

"Any help is useful," Jack said. "Do you know of a handy oasis, perhaps?"

"Better than that, Brigadier," Drummond said. "I know of a water source, not a hundred yards from where we stand."

"Where, Miss Drummond?"

"That fig tree holds about a ton of water," Drummond said. "It's unusual to see one this far north, so I can only imagine that the seeds fell from some wandering caravan."

"I don't give a damn how it got here," Jack allowed his stress to take over. "How can we get the water out?"

"By scaling the trunk and scooping out the water," Drummond told him. "It's quite simple."

"I'll need an active man for that," Jack said.

"You'll have a hundred volunteers," Drummond said with a smile. "Water is more precious than gold out here."

Drummond was correct. Some of the younger British soldiers proved adept at climbing up the tree, and Sergeant Hanley organised a chain that passed buckets and water skins to the man on top. Within twenty minutes, the civilians and animals were drinking fresh water. After an hour, the infantrymen were also drinking.

"Now, we're fit to fight the French," Jack saw new life surging through his men. "Thank you, Miss Drummond."[1]

Drummond gave a slight curtsey, with her gaze never straying from Jack's face. "You're doing well, Brigadier," she said softly. "We'll get to safety."

Jack recognised she was trying to help. "I know we will," he agreed.

Osman Zubeir did not come that day, and Jack settled on the ridge for the night to give his mounted infantry time to return. He posted double sentries, gave orders to awaken him if anything occurred and retired to his tent.

Distant gunfire woke Jack during the night, and he struggled from his bed to find most of the officers also awake.

Why's it always at night?

"It's coming from the west, sir." Baxter pointed to intermittent flashes in the dark. "I can't see what's happening."

"Whatever it is," Jack said, "it's well out of range. We'll sit tight."

"I could take out a patrol, sir," Jamieson volunteered.

"You'll remain inside the zareba," Jack ordered. "We've got enough men wandering around the desert like blasted nomads."

"Yes, sir," Jamieson said.

"Keep the sentries alert," Jack said. "Everybody else grab what sleep they can." He retired to his tent, affecting unconcern while his mind raced at the possibilities. Sarsens and Moffat could have bumped into Osman Zubeir and were now fighting for their lives. They could also have got lost in the desert. Jack lay on the charpoy with his stomach churning.

I can't lie here and do nothing but sending a patrol out in the dark might reinforce disaster.

Jack sat up.

"Donnelly!"

"Sir!"

"Fetch Gonda!"

"Very good, sir! Where are we going?"

"We're going to investigate that musketry. I want a dozen volunteers and twelve camels." Jack had made his decision.

"It will be hard to find a dozen men, sir. They'll all want to come," Donnelly said.

"I want Sergeant Hanley, Brotheridge, Kerswell, Wright, Cooper and Walters," Jack said. "If they volunteer." He picked his Afghan veterans. "Every man to wear a bandolier of ammunition."

"The men don't like wearing bandoliers, sir."

"Bring one for me, too," Jack said. *The men won't complain if they see me wearing the same as them.* "And bring a heliograph and Corporal Walters to operate it."

Jack knew his Afghan men would volunteer. They would grumble and complain, swear and glower, but when things were at their worst, they would be with him. That was the nature of the British private soldier.

* * *

Jack's patrol rode out with the stars already fading and the desert cold biting at their faces. The musketry continued, intermittent but distinct through the silence of the night. Then it ended, only to flare up again, the sound brittle, echoing and dying away, with the muzzle flashes less evident in the growing light.

"Canter!" Jack ordered and pushed his camel forward. He hoped there were no hidden holes in the sand or lurking parties of warriors.

Another sound drifted over the sand, men cheering.

"Royal Malverns!" somebody shouted and then, "Cry, Havelock! Let loose the dogs of war!"

It was the old battle cry of the 113th Foot, now the second battalion of the Malverns. Jack had not heard it for years and never expected to hear it again. He raised his voice in a roar. "Cry, Havelock! Come on, lads! They're ours!"

Jack's camel riders increased their speed, sliding over the desert sand.

"Royal Malverns!" Jack shouted, and a reply came from behind a sandy ridge. "Second Malverns!"

Jack reined up when a khaki-clad soldier rose from behind a rock in front of him.

"Where the devil did you spring from?" The man wore a captain's insignia.

"Where the devil did you spring from, sir!" Jack corrected.

"What?" The captain stared at Jack's dust-covered uniform.

"I am Brigadier Jack Windrush of the Royal Malverns," Jack became aware of more soldiers emerging from behind rocks and thorn bushes.

"My apologies, sir! I am Captain Hugo Entwhistle of E Company, Second Battalion, Royal Malverns."

"The 113th Foot," Jack said. "We heard your battle cry. What's the to-do?"

"We're on an extended patrol, and we encountered a party of Dervishes, sir." Entwhistle came to attention.

"Relax, man! We're not at Horse Guards here. Where is the enemy?"

"We've lost contact with them, sir."

Jack nodded. "The Ansar can vanish at will, it seems. Did you see anything of a mounted British patrol?"

"We heard firing to the north, sir. It might be a mounted patrol or some more of the river column."

"The what?" Jack glanced over at his men. "Spread out! Keep watch for the enemy!"

"The river column, sir. General Wolseley's sent down two columns to relieve Gordon in Khartoum, General Earle is leading the river column up the Nile, and Sir Herbert Stewart commands a column mounted on camels."

"We've been out of touch for a while," Jack said. "We're heading for the Nile with two battalions and four hundred civilians from El Kutuk."

"El Kutuk?" Entwhistle sounded surprised. "I thought Osman Zubeir captured that place months ago."

"He didn't," Jack said.

"We lost contact," Entwhistle said. "I'll pass on your location, sir."

"Do that," Jack said. "You said you heard firing to the north?"

"Yes, sir."

"Then that's where we'll head," Jack decided. "Where are you men based?"

"We're with the River Column, sir, but we'll join up with the Camel Column at the Fifth Cataract of the Nile, north of Berber."

Jack nodded. "We'll see you there, Entwhistle."

"Yes, sir."

"Osman Zubeir is somewhere around with around eight thousand men. I'd advise you to return to your main body and report what you've seen to your commanding officer."

"I'll do that, sir." Entwhistle saluted, called together his men and marched away.

Jack watched for a moment, glad to see his old regiment again, and then headed north.

We're only a few days' march from two British columns. There is hope yet for my civilians.

CHAPTER THIRTY-TWO

The man who can govern a woman can govern a nation
    Honore de Balzac

Jack headed north, deeper into the desert, with the men in an extended formation.

"Look for any signs, boys," Jack said. "Footprints in the sand, discarded equipment or anything that doesn't seem to belong."

Twice they heard musketry without being able to pinpoint the direction.

"This is frustrating, sir!" Sergeant Hanley said.

"It is," Jack agreed.

Jack sent scouts to investigate every outcrop of rock and clump of bushes and had the trumpeter sound reveille every fifteen minutes in the hope that Sarsens might hear. The brassy notes floated across the desert calm.

There was no response. The desert remained frustratingly empty, with a faint wind stirring the sand and a group of vultures circling above.

"Try again, bugler," Jack ordered.

"Yes, sir," the bugler said, put the instrument to his lips and sounded reveille.

"Who's making all that noise?" The man rode from the north, dressed in tattered khaki and local Arab dress. He glowered at the suddenly guilty bugler.

Jack wheeled Gonda to meet him. "I am!"

"Sorry, sir!" Moffat saluted. "I didn't recognise you."

"We've been searching for you for days!" Jack began, disguising his relief at seeing Moffat safe and well.

"Yes, sir. I'd keep the noise down, sir; Osman Zubeir's army is only two miles away. We've been trying to head him away from the column."

"Show me," Jack ordered and raised his voice. "Sergeant, you're in charge. Form the men into a defensive circle."

"Yes, sir," Hanley sounded weary as if the order was superfluous.

"This way, sir." Moffat wheeled his horse and rode north, with Jack a few yards behind and Donnelly in the rear.

Moffat rode to a long ridge, where the mounted infantry lay beneath the summit with their horses at their side. Sarsens was a little apart, scanning the landscape through his field glasses.

"It's the brigadier, sir," Moffat reported.

Sarsens wore an Arab headdress, like Moffat. "Good afternoon, sir. Did Moffat tell you what's happening?" he spoke quietly.

"You're skirmishing with Zubeir's army," Jack paraphrased Moffat's words.

"Yes, sir," Sarsens said.

"Where's Zubeir?"

"About a mile over there, sir," Sarsens jerked a thumb at the ridge.

"Show me." Jack inched to the crest, ensuring he was not on the skyline and raised his field glasses. Osman Zubeir's tents covered a wide area, with foot soldiers lying in groups and dismounted cavalrymen tending to their horses.

Sarsens lay at Jack's side. "I'd say about five to six thousand men, sir," he whispered.

"I agree, Sarsens," Jack said. "Our column is camped on a ridge a long day's march to the southeast. That's too close to Zubeir for safety."

"What do you intend to do, sir?"

"Avoid them," Jack said and gave Sarsens a quick evaluation of the situation. "We met a patrol of our second battalion. Elements of our army are gathering at the Fifth Cataract of the Nile, north of Berber."

Sarsens whistled. "What do you want us to do now, sir?"

"You will disengage from Zubeir's army and join the main column," Jack said. "We'll take everybody to the Fifth Cataract and join the army there."

Sarsens nodded. "We'll have to pass between the Mahdi's men at Berber and Zubeir's army," he pointed out.

"We will," Jack agreed. *That won't be easy with hundreds of civilians and slow-moving animals.* "Let's get back to the Malverns." He considered for a moment. "Leave Moffat and half a dozen men here to watch Zubeir. He can keep in touch with us through the helio."

"We don't have one, sir."

"I do," Jack said. "Corporal Walters will remain here with the heliograph. Gather your men."

The column was where Jack left it, well dug in behind a formidable zareba. Baxter looked relieved when Jack arrived with the mounted infantry.

"You found them, sir."

"Sarsens was trying to keep Zubeir from us," Jack explained. "Gather round, men," Jack invited the senior officers and informed them of recent developments.

Baxter nodded. "We're only two days' march from a British Army?"

"That's right," Jack said. "But we'll have to negotiate a passage between Berber and Zubeir," Jack said, "and that will take careful navigating and meticulous scouting. Sarsens!"

"Sir!"

"Relieve Moffat's outpost with fresh men and horses every six hours. Corporal Borway can replace Walters on the helio. Moffat will remain out there." *Moffat prefers the desert to regimental duties in the column.*

"Yes, sir."

"Do we tell the men, sir?" Wahiba asked.

Jack considered for a moment. "Yes. Tell them what's happening and how important it is to maintain our discipline. We expect the men to fight and die for us, so we'll show them respect."

Wahiba smiled. "Yes, sir."

Jack set off two hours before dawn the following morning. He retained the same formation, with the civilians and pack animal in the centre, Abu Bol's militia in the rear and the fighting regiments on either flank.

"Move slowly," Jack ordered, "And kick up a minimum of dust. We don't want to attract Zubeir's attention."

Drummond pushed her camel beside Jack. "Your Private Wright told me about Zubeir," she said. "Your regiment has some history with him."

"We have," Jack said. "We skirmished with him outside Kafr-ed-Daur, and he killed two of my men at Tel-el-Kebir."

Drummond nodded. "Wheelie Wright mentioned that. They were his mates."

"So I believe," Jack said. "Wright's been a bit of a loner since then, which isn't always a good thing in a fighting regiment."

"You know Wright?" Drummond sounded surprised.

"He's one of my men," Jack said. "A veteran of the Battle of Kandahar in Afghanistan and Tel-el-Kebir in Egypt. You'll notice he wears both medal ribbons."

"I'm surprised that a brigadier would know anything of a private soldier," Drummond said.

"I'm equally surprised that a relative of the queen should know his name and nickname," Jack countered. "Excuse me, Miss Drummond." He moved on, encouraging the tired and old, checking progress with his compass, and ensuring the column moved at a steady pace.

The mounted infantry formed a screen a mile from the column on either flank, watching for the Ansar. Jack sent Sergeant Toner to command the southern side, closer to Berber, and Sarsens the north.

Jack saw the heliograph's firefly flicker from the north, and a moment later, a galloping rider approached Jack. "I have a message for Brigadier Windrush!"

"Here!" Jack met the rider. "What's the message, Doncaster?"

"Captain Sarsens compliments, sir, and Lieutenant Moffat's sent a helio message. Zubeir's men are on the move!" Sweat had plastered desert sand to Doncaster's face.

"Thank you, Doncaster. Please ask Captain Sarsens to find out more." Jack was aware the heliograph was busy, with the light twinkling across the desert.

"I will, sir!" Doncaster returned to the mounted infantry as Corporal Borway approached Jack.

"Sir. I can read the message."

"Translate, please, Borway."

"Yes, sir. Lieutenant Moffat says he found some of Zubeir's men running loose and finished them with the bayonet rather than shoot. He scouted north and found Zubeir's army on the march."

Jack nodded. "Does Moffat say which way Zubeir is heading?"

"He's still signalling, sir." Borway screwed up his eyes against the glare. "Westward, sir, towards the Nile."

"Thank you, Borway."

Jack checked his map. They had twenty miles to the Fifth Cataract, with Zubeir's army only a few miles north.

"Gather round!" Jack called his senior officers together. "If Zubeir finds the convoy, he will attack and even if we beat him off, the civilians will be in danger."

"What do you propose, sir?" Baxter asked.

"We divert Zubeir's attention and rush the convoy to the Fifth Cataract," Jack said. He pointed to their destination on the map. "So far, we've danced to Zubeir's tune, parried his lunges, and acted on the defensive. It's time we took the initiative."

"Are we going to attack Zubeir, sir?" Jamieson asked.

"That's what we're going to do," Jack agreed. He saw Bimbashi Mabruk look concerned. "What's the matter, Mabruk?"

"My men are not used to attacking the Mahdi's forces," Mabruk admitted.

"Your regiment acted very well at El Kutuk," Jack pointed out.

"Defending and attacking are not the same, Windrush Pasha."

Jack agreed that sheltering behind a wall to shoot a man was vastly different from advancing over open ground. "How about you, Colonel Wahiba?"

"My children will fight in the open as well as they did behind a wall," Wahiba glared at Mabruk.

"Then that makes things simpler," Jack said. "I'll leave one company of Egyptians, the militia and one company of Royal Malverns with the convoy. The rest will keep Zubeir occupied." He nodded to Mabruk. "You will stay with the civilians, Mabruk, and Captain Jamieson with Lieutenant Lang will help, plus Lieutenant Hamilton and the seamen with the Gatling."

The Gatling was a cumbersome weapon, better suited for defence than attack and would significantly add to the firepower of the convoy. Jamieson had vast experience, while Lang disliked the desert and would push the convoy on to return to a more civilised environment.

"Lieutenant Rawlinson, you take your guns with the convoy and don't let Zubeir capture them."

"Yes, sir."

"Destroy them if you have to."

Rawlinson winced. The guns were his pride and joy. "Yes, sir," he said.

"Jamieson and Mabruk, push the convoy through and don't stop. If Zubeir attacks, fight him off and keep moving but don't leave anybody behind. Colonel Wahiba and I will divert his attention as much as possible."

I hope I'm doing the right thing. Splitting my force in the presence of the enemy is never wise, but if we stayed together, I'd be inviting civilian casualties.

* * *

The civilians watched with dismay as the bulk of their defenders headed north.

"Are you sure, Windrush Pasha?" Abu Bol asked.

"We'll divert Zubeir," Jack said. "If any stray Mahdists get through, you have a couple of hundred quality soldiers and some dedicated militia to see them off."

Abu Bol nodded. "Yes, Windrush Pasha."

"I depend on you to ensure none of the villagers is left behind."

"I'll see them to safety," Abu Bol promised.

"Take them away, Jamieson and Mabruk!" Jack shouted, turned Tinker, and trotted to the head of his brigade. Although part of him felt guilty about leaving the civilians, Jack felt his spirits lift. He was in command of a fighting unit; he knew his enemy and had a definite mission.

"I thought I'd come along with you, Brigadier." Drummond arrived at Jack's side. "I know the desert better than you do."

"As long as you keep out of the firing line," Jack did not hide his displeasure.

"I've been useful before," Drummond said.

"You have," Jack admitted. He forced a smile. "You saved us with the fig tree."

"I won't get in the road," Drummond promised.

Jack nodded, although he did not like the idea of a woman

involved in the fighting. He led the column at a fast pace, aiming to increase the distance from the civilians as quickly as possible.

I've made my decision and must stick to it. God help us all.

* * *

As the sun crept to its zenith the following day, Private Innes of the mounted infantry rode up to Jack. "Captain Sarsens' compliments, sir, and could you join him."

"Lead on, Innes," Jack ordered. "Baxter! You're in charge of the Malverns. Colonel Wahiba, please accompany me."

Sarsens had positioned his mounted infantry on the southern side of a kidney-shaped ridge, with two men on permanent lookout.

"Morning, sir," he greeted Jack laconically. "Moffat rode in ten minutes ago. Zubeir has camped two miles to the north, but he sends out an occasional mounted patrol. One of them noticed your dust."

Jack made an instant decision. "Call in your men, Sarsens. We're going to hit Zubeir's camp."

"When, sir?"

"Now, sir," Jack said. "Before he moves to investigate us. I want two men left on patrol and the rest with me."

Sarsens smiled despite the weary lines on his face. "Yes, sir."

"Colonel Wahiba, I'll leave you in command of the main force. Create a zareba around this ridge. Major Baxter will take charge of the Malverns while Captain Sarsens and I provoke Zubeir. If Zubeir decides to follow us, you'll stop him with volley fire."

Wahiba looked surprised for a moment. "Yes, sir."

"Ask Baxter for advice if you need it. He's a veteran of Afghanistan as well as here. You'll need an all-round defence with no gaps."

Am I correct in leaving an Egyptian in charge? Yes, Wahiba has proved himself, and if he oversteps the mark, Baxter has the experience to keep him right.

Jack watched Wahiba return to the main force, exchanged Tinker for the faster Gonda, ensured that Donnelly was behind him and consulted with Sarsens.

"Our objective is to keep Zubeir occupied, not to defeat him," Jack said. "So we hit and retire, attract his attention and draw him away from the convoy."

"Yes, sir," Sarsens understood immediately.

"It's time to use all that training at El Kutuk!" Jack said.

* * *

Zubeir's army was moving slowly, with infantry and cavalry mixed with camels and camp followers.

His scouts can't have reported our presence yet.

"Zubeir must be confident of his strength, sir," Moffat said. "He's not posted any flank guards."

"They're wide open," Jack agreed. "Hit them!"

He saw Sarsens' predatory grin and knew the man was a natural warrior.

"Right, boys!" Sarsens gathered his mounted infantry. "We've done this before. Sergeant Toner, take the left flank, Doncaster the right. The usual procedure, attack in two waves and don't leave any of our wounded for the enemy. Moffat will command the second wave."

Jack joined in the mounted infantry's initial attack, riding forward in extended formation with the dust rising around them. A glance around him showed that the months of fighting in the desert had transformed the mounted infantry into experts. The men were hard-faced professionals who rode their horses like centaurs and aimed each shot.

Sarsens and Moffat have trained them well.

At the sight of all the young, fit men, Jack suddenly felt very old. These MI were half his age and moved with the smooth precision of a team. Jack realised neither Sarsens nor Moffat needed him. They tolerated him because of his rank.

Sarsens led the first wave and Moffat the second. Sarsen's men poured into Zubeir's column, shooting at the cavalry, and wheeling around to return to the desert. As the Mahdists tried to recover and give chase, Moffat's second wave struck, attacking the infantry, and increasing the confusion. Both assaults killed a few men and galloped away, leaving corpses and chaos in their wake.

After months of similar manoeuvres, Sarsens did not need to order the first wave to reload. The mounted infantry rode back three hundred yards, stopped, thumbed in cartridges, and reformed. As Moffat's unit withdrew in open order, Sarsens' men passed through the gaps and returned to the attack.

"They're recovering!" Sarsens warned as a deluge of warriors ran to meet them. His men stopped a hundred yards short of the advancing Mahdists, aimed, fired, and circled away.

"Entice them," Jack ordered. "Lead them to the ridge. We can't allow them to find the civilians!"

"Yes, sir!" Sarsens said. "Open the ranks!"

Moffat's men were returning to the attack, carbines held in their right hands as they passed through.

"Careful, lads!" Sarsens warned. "They're prepared!"

Moffat raised an arm in acknowledgement, grinned and swept forward.

"Wait!" Jack pointed to the left. "Zubeir has countered!"

Zubeir had sent his cavalry in a wide outflanking movement, aiming to catch the British in the rear.

"I'll cover Moffat!" Jack yelled. "Fifteen men, ride with Sarsens; the rest come with me!" He wheeled to the left, kicking in his spurs. Zubeir's cavalry was galloping now, charging to cut the British force in half.

Jack advanced fifty yards and halted, allowing his men a few moments to catch their breath. He estimated the enemy was a hundred strong. "Fire at will!"

The mounted infantry responded, aiming, firing, and reloading with all the skill the NCOs had hammered into them over years of training. Mahdist men and horses fell in a tangle of flailing legs and screaming bodies. The Malverns fired fast and accurately, and Jack ordered them back when the Mahdists were thirty yards away. Faced with a continuous stream of bullets, some attackers pulled away while others tried to return fire.

"They're breaking, lads!" Jack shouted, firing his revolver into the mass. His shots struck home, sending a leading rider reeling back.

The Mahdist attack disintegrated. Only a few riders continued forward, with the experienced mounted infantry shooting the warriors down without pity.

"Well done, boys," Jack reloaded, ramming cartridges into his revolver. He watched the survivors flee back to Zubeir's force.

Sarsens had completed his attack, and Moffat's men were ready to return.

"That's enough," Jack ordered. "We've stung them and attracted their attention." He counted the men and found nobody missing. "Now we'll lead them a dance away from the civilians."

"The horses are getting weary, sir," Sarsens warned. "In an hour or so, they'll begin to flag."

Jack nodded. If the horses tired, Zubeir's cavalry would have the advantage. He checked his watch, calculating how much time had elapsed since he left Baxter.

"You're right, Sarsens. That would hand the initiative to Zubeir."

"The horses have enough left for a few more attacks, sir, and then we'll have to retire," Sarsens said.

Jack thought rapidly. "Thank you, Sarsens. We'll have a fighting withdrawal to Baxter."

"Yes, sir," Sarsens agreed.

They began a prolonged assault, riding toward Zubeir's men, firing and retiring, fraying the edges of the enemy force without inflicting significant casualties. Jack's study of military history told him that such tactics could be effective. The English Border prickers had destroyed a Scottish army at Solway Moss in 1542, and more recently, the Boers had adopted similar methods against the Zulu impis.

The pin-prick assaults were frustrating Zubeir's men, with their discipline eroding. Small parties charged at Jack's mounted infantry, allowing the British to cut them off and destroy them in detail.

"We're pulling them away," Sarsens shouted.

"Aye," Moffat yelled, "but my mount's about done."

Jack knew that Moffat was correct. He had pushed the horses hard for days, and they were tired. If Zubeir's cavalry pursued hard, with fresher horses and far more men, they would have all the advantages.

"One last attack," Jack decided, "and head for Baxter's position."

"Yes, sir!" Sarsens was panting, with sweat creating light streaks on his sand-and-gun smoke-covered face. Jack realised that all the riders were tired, some drooping in the saddles and others nursing minor wounds that would fester unless he got them to the surgeon.

"One final effort, boys," Jack shouted. "Follow me!"

The men checked their carbines, glanced at one another, and gave words of encouragement to their horses.

"Right, boys," Jack shouted and spurred forward.

The mounted infantry followed in a wedge shape, men readying their Martinis as they rode. They trotted over the hard sand, raising a cloud of dust, dodging the thorn bushes and rocks, alert for sudden ambushes.

Zubeir had reorganised his men, pushing the cavalry to the flanks to cover the infantry. A clump of standards thrust up from the centre.

"Follow me, men!" Jack shouted and roared the old battle cry of the 113th Foot. "Cry Havelock!"

The men spurred, not firing until they saw a target, spreading out to cover more ground, with Sarsens and Moffat in the lead. Jack held his revolver in his right hand, fired twice at a yelling Mahdist, and saw the man jerk back, then pushed Gonda on, looking for another target. Something screamed past his head, and three spearmen charged toward him. He aimed quickly, fired at the nearest man, and turned away.

The Mahdists seemed to be everywhere, some attacking and others reeling back as the mounted infantry fired into the mass or rode their horses like weapons.

Sarsens was yelling, directing his men, with Doncaster and Smith operating as a team, one firing while the other reloaded.

Jack saw the cluster of banners a hundred yards away, emptied his revolver in their direction and withdrew to load. All around him, the mounted infantry were firing, shouting, swearing, and reloading. The Mahdists quickly regrouped to counterattack.

"Bugler!" Jack shouted. "Sound the recall!"

A bullet sliced into Jack's pith helmet, knocking it sideways. He slid in his final cartridge as the bugler blasted out the recall.

The mounted infantry disengaged, with Moffat and Sarsens at the rear, marshalling their men.

"Back to base, lads," Jack shouted. "Moffat! Take six men as a rearguard! Sarsens, organise flank riders!"

They withdrew in formation, with the rearguard halting every few hundred yards to fire at the pursuing Mahdists. One of the men slumped in the saddle, nearly dropping his rifle.

"Are you wounded, Willis?" Jack reined up alongside. He could not see any blood on the man and realised he was suffering from heat exhaustion. "Give me your rifle." He took the man's weapon. "Hold on, son; you'll get a rest soon."

The sun was long past its zenith and dipped towards the western horizon, casting short shadows behind the mounted infantry.

"They're following us!" Sarsens warned.

Jack glanced over his shoulder. "That's the idea!"

Zubeir had mobilised his entire army to catch the irritating mounted infantry. The cavalry was in the van, with horsemen leading from the front and long-legged camels on the flanks. Behind the mounted screen, hordes of infantry followed, kicking up the dust as they ran. Jack felt the ground shudder with the passage of thousands of feet and hoped his brigade's defences could hold them.

"There's less than I thought," Sarsens gasped.

Jack nodded. The steady drip of casualties had weakened Zubeir's army, and others had lost heart and drifted back to their native villages. "Keep your boys moving, Sarsens!" He saw the kidney ridge in the distance, rising above the endless plain. "Watch for Willis; he's about done."

The Arab cavalry galloped, trying to cut off the mounted infantry. Jack swore. His men's horses were slowing down after their long day. He eyed the distance to the ridge.

We're not going to make it.

"They're in front of us!" Sarsens shouted as a line of men rose from cover directly in the mounted infantry's path.

Damnit! Zubeir's outmanoeuvred me!

CHAPTER THIRTY-THREE

Even the dreadful martyrdom must run its course
  W H Auden

Jack swore. With the Arab cavalry galloping on the flanks, a mass of infantry behind and an unknown force in front, he had led his mounted infantry into a near-impossible situation.

A voice rose from a wadi in front, speaking Arabic. "Volley fire, my children, and don't hit the British!"

"That's Colonel Wahiba!" Sarsens said.

"Wahiba!" Jack repeated. He saw a double line of white-uniformed soldiers seemingly rise from the ground and heard the synchronised crackle of a volley. The shots ripped past the mounted infantry to hammer at the Mahdist cavalry.

"Head for the Egyptian flank!" Jack shouted and led the way. Wahiba's men fired again, a rolling volley that covered the mounted infantry's withdrawal.

Some pursuing cavalry fell, and others pulled up at the unexpected ambush. Jack led his men around Wahiba's flank and reined in, counting his men.

"We lost Halloran!" Moffat shouted. "A Dervish bullet caught him."

Jack nodded. Any man's death was a tragedy, but there was no time to mourn. "Form up behind the Egyptians!" The kidney ridge was half a mile away, with the sun twinkling on bayonets.

Colonel Wahiba greeted Jack with a grin and a salute. "We thought you might need a hand, Windrush Pasha!"

"You were right, Colonel," Jack said. Zubeir's cavalry was already recovering from their surprise and reforming. "We'd best head back to the ridge."

"Yes, sir," Wahiba said. "Withdraw in sections, my children!"

The Egyptians worked well, one section covering the next, firing and moving, so they subjected the Mahdists to a near-constant crash of volleys.

"Guard the flanks," Jack ordered, "Moffat, take the Egyptian left; Sarsens, take the right."

The mounted infantry split in two and withdrew steadily, keeping the enemy back until they reached the ridge. When they approached the zareba, Sergeant Anderson hauled the thorn bushes aside to create a gap and hurriedly replaced the barrier when they were through.

"Welcome back, sir," Baxter said. "I see you've brought friends."

"One or two," Jack agreed. "Colonel Wahiba saved us."

Drummond peered at the mounted infantry and fluttered her fingers at Moffat, who responded in kind.

"The Dervishes are advancing!" Bryant shouted.

"Come on, children!" Wahiba roared. "Take your positions!"

Zubeir launched his whole force in a frontal charge, with the horsed cavalry on the left, camels on the right and infantry in the centre.

"No tactics this time," Baxter said. "And no artillery barrage."

Jack nodded. "Maybe he wants to overwhelm us by sheer aggression." He raised his voice. "Company commanders! Fire when they get to five hundred yards."

The British and Egyptian infantrymen had seen it all before.

They settled into position, hugged their rifles, licked dry lips, and waited for the word of command.

The Mahdist cavalry arrived first, and C Company of the Malverns swept them away with aimed volley fire. The men were unhurried, making grim jokes as they fired, reloaded, presented, aimed, and fired again.

The cavalry recoiled from C Company as the camel men ran at Wahiba's flank. The Egyptians treated them the same way, with controlled volleys that felled dozens of the attackers.

"Now for the infantry," Baxter said.

Jack calculated the numbers of infantry as they advanced. With the dust screening them, he could only guess at four thousand.

"They outnumber us three-to-one." Bryant had also been counting.

"That's not bad odds," Jack said.

"Baker Pasha's men outnumbered the Hadendoa," Bryant reminded.

Jack nodded, remembering the nightmare of Teb. "Corporal Cooper!"

"Sir!" Cooper shouted from the firing line.

"I want you and your men on the highest point of the ridge," Jack said. "Shoot at the leaders."

"Yes, sir." Cooper and his sharpshooters scrambled up the ridge.

Zubeir's men advanced at speed, chanting, with the spears and swords held high. Jack ran his gaze along the ridge. Baxter and Wahiba had arranged an all-round defence, strong at the flanks where the enemy might concentrate.

The defenders opened fire when the Mahdist infantry was five hundred yards away, with the sides of the zareba a mass of flame and gun smoke. The warriors charged bravely, dodging from cover to cover as they advanced in groups and as individuals.

The defenders' volleys crashed out, with the heavy bullets

ripping into the warriors' unprotected bodies, knocking men back and leaving gaps in the attackers' ranks. Despite the horrific casualties, the Ansar charge continued with yelling spearmen advancing against the massed muzzles of the British and Egyptian infantry.

"Brave men, these Sudanese," Jack muttered, shaking his head. "Back off, for pity's sake. You can't prevail against riflemen in a fixed position."

"Fire!" The command rang out around the perimeter of the ridge as company after company, British and Egyptian, opened up in flames and smoke. The Mahdists ducked, weaved, bobbed into cover, rushed forward, and fell under the relentless volley fire of trained infantry.

"They're not as aggressive as Hadendoa were," Baxter said. "We've taught them caution."

"They've lost a great many men," Jack scanned the advancing enemy through his field glasses. "I can't see their leaders."

"There, sir," Wahiba had joined them. "Left of centre."

Jack shifted his stance. "You're right, Colonel. I see them." A twist of dust had obscured the banners. They moved forward, the brave flags with the inspiring words from the Koran white on black and the near plain green flag in the centre. "I wonder if Cooper has noticed." Jack pushed Gonda up the ridge to the knoll where the sharpshooters congregated.

"Cooper," Jack said.

"I see them, sir," Cooper said. "We've tried a few shots but without success."

"Keep trying," Jack said.

"We will, sir," Cooper promised.

The musketry eased as the Mahdist attack failed, with the warriors recoiling without reaching the zareba where the hungry bayonets waited.

"Well done, lads!" Jack shouted as he returned to the senior officers.

"We're doing all right," Bryant said, "but we can't hold out forever. Our ammunition and water are running low." He forced a smile. "Time is on Osman Zubeir's side."

"The longer we hold him here, the better chance the civilians have of reaching safety," Jack said. He toured the defences as Anderson's pioneers strengthened the defences.

The Egyptians lounged behind the zareba, joking, and exchanging reminiscences, much like the British soldiers, and an Egyptian sergeant acknowledged Jack with a salute.

"We saw them off, sir."

"You did, Sergeant," Jack agreed. "How are your men bearing up?"

The sergeant glanced over his soldiers. "They're ready for the next assault."

"Good man, Sergeant."

Jack moved on and saw Bramley comforting his mules, and Wright petted Nicky. Sergeant Deng was talking to Donnelly, both standing in the ranks of the Malverns' A Company.

Jack looked up as the sharpshooters fired again, with the crack of the rifles breaking the silence. Jack had experienced that hush before as a battlefield fell strangely silent, a breathing space between bouts of slaughter.

"I got Zubeir!" Scott exulted and then swore. "No, I only hit his horse. The bugger's getting up again."

"He's got a charmed life, that one!" MacLeod grumbled.

"Maybe our bullets turn to water," Graham said.

Jack swore silently. Osman Zubeir was encouraging his men for another attack, giving orders to launch another frenzied assault.

"How many bullets do the men have left?" Jack asked.

"Six each," Sarsens replied, and the other company commanders responded.

"Ten per man."

"Twelve per man, sir."

"Only seven, sir."

Jack nodded. *We have sufficient ammunition to repel one more attack; after that, it'll be bayonets, rifle butts and boots.*

"Here they come again!" Baxter shouted. "Bugler, sound the alert!"

The shrill, brassy notes of the bugle thrilled across the ridge as Osman Zubeir ordered his men forward. With the sun swiftly sinking, the defenders found it hard to identify reality from shifting shadows.

"Don't fire until they reach three hundred yards!" Jack ordered. "Preserve your cartridges until you can't miss!"

Jack recalled the battle of Isandlwana when the poorly positioned 24th Foot ran out of ammunition, and the Zulus had annihilated them. He did not wish posterity to remember him as the man who had lost his brigade.

"Steady, there!" Jack called as one nervous man fired prematurely.

The Mahdists were trotting forward, yelling, with the cavalry on the left. They were four hundred yards away, half-seen in the fading light, a mass of warriors with upraised spears. Some fired captured Remingtons, with the shots screaming high or thudding into the ground.

"Steady!" Jack repeated. He drew his sword and raised it in a dramatic gesture all the men would see. "Steady!"

The Mahdists approached to within three hundred yards, with the cavalry and infantry level and the banners held aloft.

Cooper's sharpshooters fired again, yet Zubeir remained on his horse.

"That's him!" Wheelie Wright jabbed an urgent finger toward Zubeir. "That's the bugger that murdered Bull and Dusty!"

Jack thought of the carnage of Tel-el-Kebir, where Zubeir had killed Bullard and Miller, two of the Malverns' best men. He saw Drummond exchange a brief word with Wright, then concentrated on the onrushing Mahdists.

"Fire!" Jack ordered and swished down his sword. British and Egyptians fired together in a long ripple that stabbed into the charging warriors. The previous volleys had shredded the thorn bushes, denying the Mahdists' cover, so the musketry was more effective, yet still, they came on.

"I've never seen braver men," Baxter repeated the opinions of many British soldiers.

"Nor have I," Jack agreed, loosening his revolver. The British and Egyptians fired again, with Jack counting the volleys and calculating how much ammunition they had remaining.

Drummond scrambled to the marksman's knoll and spoke to Cooper. Jack frowned and followed.

"What's happening, Miss Drummond?"

"Your men don't seem able to shoot Osman Zubeir," Drummond said. "I wish to try."

As Drummond spoke, a bullet zipped past her head. She did not flinch.

"We're in the middle of a battle, Miss Drummond. Please allow Cooper to do his duty."

"I've been shooting since I was four years old," Drummond said. "My father taught me to shoot grouse, deer and partridge on the Perthshire moors."

Jack opened his mouth to blast Drummond when Scott gave a grunt and dropped his rifle.

"They've got me," he said, staring at a spreading red stain across his chest.

"Doolie bearers!" Jack roared, caught Scott as he fell and lowered him to the ground. "Doolie bearers! Dr Park!"

Drummond scooped up the discarded Martini, checked that it was loaded and adjusted the range slightly. She stepped to the summit of the knoll and, with Cooper and MacLeod watching critically, hugged the rifle to her shoulder.

"Be careful," Cooper warned. "It's got the devil of a kick."

Drummond nodded, sighted along the barrel, and squeezed the trigger. She rode the recoil well, and Jack pressed his field glasses to his eyes to see the result.

Drummond's bullet struck Osman Zubeir in the centre of his

chest, knocking him backwards in the saddle. He coughed blood, lifted a hand, and slid sideways just as Drummond and MacLeod fired again. Both bullets hit their mark, and Zubeir died on the spot.

"Fire!" Baxter roared, and D Company unleashed another volley. "That's the last of the ammunition! Fix bayonets!"

With Martinis and ammunition, the advantages lay with the defenders. When the cartridges were expended, the pendulum swung to the more numerous attackers with their long spears. Jack took a deep breath.

Goodbye, Mary. I'd like to hold you one more time. Take care of yourself.

"They're stopping!" Bryant shouted. "The Dervishes are stopping!"

The enemy attack faded away. Either they had lost too many men in their previous encounters with Windrush's men, or the death of Zubeir sapped their will, but only a few dozen men continued the attack. Colonel Wahiba pushed forward a company of his men, took the advancing Mahdists in flank and destroyed them.

Not in ones and twos, but in hundreds and thousands, the Dervishes were falling back. They turned and walked away from the battlefield, slowly fading into the desert night as the British and Egyptians watched, too exhausted to cheer.

"You did it, Miss!" MacLeod said, grabbing Drummond in an impromptu hug. "You killed the bastard!"

Drummond smiled and released herself. "Thank you, Davie."

"We've won!" Bryant said in amazement. "They're running away."

"They won't be back," Jack agreed. As he spoke, the sun set, sending darkness onto the ridge. "We'll remain here overnight and resume in the morning."

Dear Lord, we've done it. We'll be at the Nile tomorrow, and after that, it's a short march to the 5th cataract. We're as good as home.

CHAPTER THIRTY-FOUR

She's my pulse, she's my secret, she's the scented flower of the apple, she's summer in the cold time between Christmas and Easter
  Eighteenth-century Irish folk song

Jack stood on the banks of the Nile with a British zareba at his back and half a dozen men of the 2nd Battalion, Royal Malverns, on guard. The El Kutuk refugees spread out, most staring at the river in wonder, for they had never seen so much water before. Abu Bol and his militia clustered together, facing north, and wondering what the future held.

"Where's the River Column?" he asked. "I expected hundreds of boats here."

Redvers Buller emerged from behind the prickly barricade. "You've not heard the news, then?"

"What news?" Jack asked.

Buller grunted. "The River Column smashed the Mahdist armies at Kirkbean and Abu Klea. We won the battle but lost General Earle and that explorer, Colonel Burnaby."

"Burnaby was an adventurer," Jack said. "He could not live forever."

Buller nodded. "And the Mahdists broke the square."

"Again?" Jack asked.

"Again," Buller said. "There's worse news. We sent a small force ahead to contact Gordon in Khartoum but were too late. The Mahdi captured Khartoum and killed Gordon Pasha. It's a major blow to British prestige."

"*Fuit Ilium,*" Jack murmured. "Troy has been." The loss of Khartoum left him cold, except for the fate of the garrison and the citizens. "Britain doesn't want Khartoum anyway, and Gordon knew that."

"Indeed," Buller said. "We should have set out months before if we wanted to save Gordon. It's that old woman Gladstone's fault."

Jack thought of the thousands of dead and wounded, British, Egyptian, and Sudanese, in the bloody desert battles. What was it all about?

"No," he said. "It wasn't Gladstone's fault. Gladstone didn't want Britain sucked into a war in Sudan. It may have been Gordon's fault; he disobeyed his orders to evacuate Khartoum, but the real cause is far deeper. The Egyptians should never have invaded Sudan, and when they did, they should have treated the people decently."

Buller shook his head, smiling. "Maybe all imperial powers should treat their people decently. Britain is certainly not innocent."

"No," Jack remembered the carnage in the wake of the Indian Mutiny and the burning villages along the North West Frontier. "We're certainly not."

"Well, Windrush," Redvers Buller puffed smoke from his cheroot into the air. "You got here with your men and evacuated hundreds of civilians, which is more than the celebrated General Gordon managed."

"I did," Jack agreed. "It was a close-run thing, though. We had no ammunition left and very little food. More importantly, how will my people from El Kutuk get to safety without the boats from the river column?"

"It's all in hand, Windrush," Buller said. "We're only an outpost here. The remainder of the River Column is far downstream. We'll ferry your people to the main camp and then transport them to Aswan, the most southern city of Egypt," Buller said. "They speak the same language and share the same religion as the local people."

Jack nodded. "They'll be safer there than in Sudan," he agreed. "I'll leave it in your hands."

"Come into my tent," Buller invited.

After the austerity of the past few months, Jack found Buller's tent more like a palace, with a complete set of furniture and an extensive selection of wines.

"Champagne?" Buller offered.

"Thank you," Jack sunk into one of Buller's chairs and stretched his legs. He felt dusty, filthy, and tired, as if he had been travelling for months.

"The campaign is over," Buller said. "With Gordon and Khartoum gone, there's no point in continuing." He grinned. "We've given the Mahdi a few bloody noses, but we don't want his desert, so no glory or honours for you, I'm afraid."

Jack thought of his weary, gaunt men, battle-worn and hungry. He would have liked to lead them to Khartoum and victory over the Mahdi, but men could only fight and march for a limited time. The Malverns, and their Egyptian allies, had reached the end of their endurance.

"Where are we going?" Jack asked.

"Cairo for a start," Buller told him. "After that, I don't know."

"Cairo sounds good," Jack said. "My wife's in Cairo." He closed his eyes and was asleep before Buller could reply.

* * *

Jack stood to attention on the veranda of Shepheard's Hotel and saluted as the regiment marched past. Baxter was in front astride a black stallion and with his dress uniform pristine under the sun. Jack blinked away the tears as the men, sun-browned, weather-beaten, and gaunt, marched past with colours unfurled and bayonets bared.

It was not often that both battalions of the regiment, the Royal Malverns and the old 113th, were together on active service, and they had altered their route as a tribute to their one-time commanding officer. Jack recognised the faces as the memories returned, memories of the steaming forests of Burma, the bitter battles and winter of Crimea, and the nightmare of the Indian Mutiny. He remembered the friendships and dangers of the North West Frontier, crossing the River Pra to Ashantiland, the losses and bravery of Afghanistan, and the recent desert campaigns in Egypt and Sudan.

Jack recognised the men, Bryant the ever-efficient adjutant and Sarsens, a man who came of age in Afghanistan and was the best junior officer he had ever known. Jamieson was next, stolid and unimaginative but dependable, then Lang, glorious in his tailored uniform.

Jack ran his gaze over the men, with RSM Deblin the imperturbable, Sergeants Hanley and Trafford and Corporal Cooper, who could turn his hand to anything. The private marched past, veterans all, with Nicky at Wright's feet, Doncaster and Innes, the glowering Brotheridge and Kerswell. At the tail was Branley, out of step and his bootlace trailing, yet as much part of the regiment as the immaculate RSM.

Oh, God, I'll miss these men.

The second battalion marched behind the first. Jack knew very few of the men but recalled them from his early career. He remembered the 113th, the Baby Butchers, in Burma, Crimea and India, and felt himself gasping for breath as the old sensations returned.

We grew up together, the 113th and I.

Corporal Borway began to sing, and the rest joined in, roaring the words to disturb the Cairo night.

"Always victorious,
Glorious and more glorious,
We followed Marlborough through battle and war,
We're the Royal Malverns, the heroes of Malplaquet,
We carry victory wherever we go."

Jack found himself chanting the words, and then the song faded into the distance and his regiment was gone. He knew he might never serve with them again. They had bid farewell to their old commander and now returned to their barracks at the Citadel.

"Sit down, Jack," Mary's quiet voice broke his reverie. "Sit down." She placed her hand on his sleeve.

Jack stretched his legs under the table and listened to the fading drumbeat of marching men and then the sounds of Cairo. He pulled back his mind from distant wars and smiled at Mary. "This is the same table we sat at when we attended the ball."

"That's right," Mary returned his smile, her eyes gentle. "It seems like a hundred years since I saw you."

"It seems the same to me," Jack said.

Oh, God, I've missed you, Mary.

"You fought a few more battles," Mary said, "but do you know the most important thing? And something nobody will give you a medal for?"

"What's that?" Jack asked.

"You saved hundreds of civilians. That makes me proud of you."

Jack held her hand under the table as he felt renewed affection for his wife. "That means more to me than a dozen medals," he said.

Mary examined him, tilting her head. "You've lost a lot of weight."

"I'm sure I'll put it back on," Jack said. He lowered his voice. "I'm weary, Mary. I've done enough soldiering and seen too much death and suffering."

Mary looked worried, twisting her fingers around his. "What do you intend to do, Captain Jack?"

Jack shook his head. "I don't know. The army has been my whole life."

Mary smiled. "Have a few weeks off. You'll feel better after a rest, although I'll be glad to have you to myself." She leaned back in her chair as the sounds of Cairo drifted to them. "Did you hear about Arthur?"

"Arthur?"

"Arthur Elliot, your friend," Mary explained patiently.

"Lieutenant General Sir Arthur Elliot, VC," Jack said with a smile. "What's he done now?"

"He married Helen Windrush, your sister-in-law," Mary told him.

"That's a good match," Jack was not surprised. "Arthur's a fine man, and Helen will look after him."

"They're looking for somewhere to live," Mary said.

Jack lit two cheroots and passed one to Mary. "And?"

"We have three houses," Mary reminded. "Wychwood Manor, Netherhills, and the place in Berwick."

"Our son likes Berwick," Jack said. "I was thinking of giving it to him if you agree."

Mary nodded. "Of course, but that still leaves Wychwood and Netherhills." She waited for an answer.

"Wychwood has been the Windrush family home for centuries," Jack said and raised his head. "But Netherhills is ours, yours and mine, and the Windrushes disowned me." He drew on his cigar. "I think we should lease Wychwood to Arthur and have him and Helen as neighbours."

Mary smiled. "I hoped you'd say that. I never felt welcome at Wychwood." She blew out a ribbon of blue smoke. "Don't look now, Jack, but General Hook is coming."

Jack closed his eyes. "Does that man follow me? He always seems to know where I am."

General Hook beckoned to a waiter and ordered a bottle of

champagne and three glasses. "With ice," he said and sat opposite Mary. "I thought I'd find you here, my dear."

"Who do you have spying on us, General?" Mary asked.

Hook smiled. "Have you heard what's happened since you arrived in Cairo?" hook asked.

"I've not heard anything," Jack said. "I've tried to ignore the rumours and speculation."

"You'll know that Major Baxter is now Lieutenant Colonel of the Malverns," Hook said.

Jack nodded. "I saw him a few moments ago. He deserves his promotion."

"And Lieutenant Lang has asked to transfer to the Guards."

Jack grunted. "He'll do better parading around London impressing the women than sweating in some Empire hell-hole."

Hook nodded. "I heard he wasn't cut out for the Malverns. Your Lieutenant Moffat's a bit of a lad, isn't he?"

"Moffat?" Jack nodded. "One of the finest young officers I've ever commanded. He took to the desert like an Arab."

"He's handed in his papers," Hook murmured with a slight smile. "He and Lady Drummond are haring off into the wilderness, searching for some mythical oasis."

"Lady Drummond has a very strong personality," Jack said. "I wish her and Moffat well."

"So do I," Hook said. "They'll either become famous or turn native and remain in the desert."

Jack smiled. "Whatever they do, Lady Drummond will ensure they survive."

"Colonel Wahiba is now Brigadier Wahiba. We're using him to train up the Egyptian army," Hook said. "You gave him a glowing report."

"He saved us more than once," Jack said.

Mary interrupted. "That's all very interesting, but I don't think you've come here to give us an update on the military gossip, General."

"No," Hook looked up as the waiter returned with the champagne and poured three glasses. "The War Office has a vacancy for a Major General for South Western Command. He'll be responsible for the garrison forces, including the Royal Malverns, recruiting and training men from Cornwall to Herefordshire. It's a sinecure for an experienced man."

"Arthur Elliot would be perfect," Jack said at once.

"So would you," Hook said. "You can be home in Netherhills nearly every weekend."

"I'm not a major general," Jack pointed out.

In reply, Hook pulled a thick envelope from inside his jacket. "Yes, you are, Jack."

"What?" Jack ripped open the envelope and read the contents. He passed the document over to Mary's eager hands.

"It's true," Mary said, smiling. "You're a general, Jack."

"Congratulations, General," Hook said, smiling. "Will you take the job in South Western Command?"

Jack nodded as visions of the Malvern Hills came to him, the sound of blackbirds in the evening and nights of rest undisturbed by enemy fire. "Yes, sir," he said.

Mary sipped at her champagne. "I'll have to call you General Jack now," she said and lifted her glass in salute. "Congratulations, General Jack Windrush."

APPENDIX ONE

The Mahdi

Muhammad Ahmad bin Abd Allah (1844 – 1885) was one of a long list of Islamic religious leaders. Born at Latab Island into a family of boat builders from Dongola, Ahmad claimed to trace his descent from the Prophet Muhammad's grandson, Hassan. When the family moved to Karani, near Omdurman, the later Mahdi left the boat-building industry and turned to religion.

After extensive religious study, Muhammad Ahmad became known as a devout spiritual leader. In June 1881, Muhammad Ahmad claimed to be the Mahdiyya or Mahdi – the Muslim Messiah. His initial task was to expel the Egyptians – the Turks – from Sudan, then to conquer Egypt and ensure the whole world was Islamic.

When the Egyptian authorities responded by offering Muhammad Ahmad a government pension, he replied, "He who does not believe in me will be purified by the sword." Muhammad Ahmad withdrew to Kordofan and began an increasingly successful rebellion. In December 1881, the Ansar destroyed an Egyptian army 1,400 strong in the south. They continued their advance the following year by defeating 4,000

APPENDIX ONE

Egyptians in Kordofan, and the revolt spread. In January 1883, the Mahdi captured the town of El Obeid with six thousand modern rifles, plus artillery.

The Khedive of Egypt sent a British officer named Colonel William Hicks south with an ill-trained, reluctant Egyptian army. The result was predictable as the Mahdists massacred Hicks and his men. Eventually, the Khedive and the British, now in control of Egypt, sent General Gordon to Khartoum with orders to withdraw the Egyptian garrisons and abandon Sudan. Instead of leaving the city, Gordon strengthened the defences and held off the Mahdists for months. Eventually, as a relief expedition sailed up the Nile, the Mahdists captured Khartoum and killed Gordon.

The Mahdi died of typhus six months later, with his descendants retaining their hold on Sudan until 1898, when General Kitchener defeated them.

APPENDIX TWO

General Gordon

Charles George Gordon was born in Woolwich in 1833 into a military family. He joined the Royal Engineers as a Second Lieutenant in 1852 and participated in the Crimea War. Subsequently, he worked as a surveyor along the Turko-Russian frontier, and in 1860 he joined the British expedition in the war with China.

China was to give Gordon his reputation and his nickname. After participating in the capture of Pekin and the destruction of the Summer Palace, he helped the Chinese fight against a formidable rebel army known as the Taipings. He led a Chinese force known as the Ever Victorious Army, captured several walled towns and fought over thirty battles and skirmishes.

Back in the UK, Gordon worked on various engineering duties while also engaged in charity work. In 1873, Chinese Gordon, as he was now known, accepted a commission from the Khedive of Egypt to open up the southern part of Sudan. He worked tirelessly, established bases, and brought steamers for the Nile, but the extent of corruption and the slave trade depressed him. He returned to the UK but was back in Sudan in 1877, armed with greater powers over a vast area.

APPENDIX TWO

Three years later, the climate had damaged Gordon's health, and he left Sudan. After globetrotting with other endeavours, in 1884, the British government, feeling responsible for the Egyptian garrisons in Sudan, sent Gordon to Khartoum. His mission was to evacuate the garrison. He delayed, and the Mahdi besieged the city. The British government did not send a relief expedition for months, and it arrived only a couple of days after the Mahdi captured Khartoum, killing Gordon.

APPENDIX THREE

Nineteenth-century Female explorers

In theory, respectable women in the nineteenth century were demure, peaceable wives who remained at home and looked after the house, husband, and children. In reality, many women escaped these bonds. Some females sailed on deep sea voyages, owned shares in ships and worked as missionaries. There were also female travellers and explorers.

For example, Gertrude Bell (1868 – 1926) spent much of her life travelling in the Middle East. Fluent in Arabic, Bell was also a mountaineer and archaeologist. Gertrude Benham was another adventurer. London-born, Benham climbed mountains across the Americas and Africa, travelling alone or with local guides. She was the first woman to climb Kilimanjaro, and Truda Peaks in British Columbia is named in her honour.

Mary Kingsley explored West Africa, Elizabeth Mazuchelli travelled the Himalayas, and the amazing Hester Stanhope (1776 – 1839) was a pioneer of archaeology in the Holy Land. An aristocrat, she travelled disguised as a man and allegedly had various romantic affairs. Her *Memoirs* are fascinating reading.

Isabelle Eberhardt was another inveterate wanderer. The

French Foreign Legion named her "The Amazon of the Sands," among other things. Eberhardt was unique, born to emigrants in Geneva; she claimed no nationality, was fluent in at least six languages, dressed in male clothing and adopted Islam. She wandered North Africa and died tragically young.

THE WINDRUSH SERIES

Book One: *Windrush:*1851-1852 Young Jack Windrush is an ensign in the 113th Foot during the Second Burmese War.

Book Two: *Crimea*: 1854. Lieutenant Jack Windrush and the 113th Foot face the Russians at the Battle of Inkerman.

Book Three: *Blood Price:* 1855- 1856. Lieutenant Jack Windrush finds romance and danger as the Crimean War continues.

Book Four: *Cry Havelock*: 1857. Captain Jack Windrush and the 113th Foot become involved in the Indian Mutiny, and Jack discovers more about his history.

Book Five: *Jayanti's Pawns*: 1858. Captain Jack Windrush and the 113th Foot fight their way through jungles and treachery, with Jack meeting a Pashtun named Batoor and cementing his relationship with Mary.

Book Six: *Warriors of God*: 1863. Still a Captain, Jack chases gunrunners on the North-West Frontier of India and becomes involved in the Bunerwal Expedition.

Book Seven: *Agent of the Queen*: 1865-1867. Captain Jack Windrush is recruited as an agent to trace the Fenian Brotherhood. His travels take him to Scotland, Ireland and North America and the Fenian invasion of Canada.

Book Eight: *The City of Dreadful Death*: 1873-1874. Shipwrecked off West Africa, Major Jack Windrush and Mary become involved in the Ashanti War, where Jack finds himself leading a company of the West India Regiment.

Book Nine: *Beyond the Frontier*: 1878 - 1879. Major Jack Windrush and the 113th Foot follow General 'Bobs' Roberts into Afghanistan, where he meets an old friend and the Russians.

Book Ten: *Farewell to Afghanistan*. 1880. The Afghan War erupts again, and Jack fights at Maiwand and on the Kabul to Kandahar march.

Book Eleven: *A Ditch in Egypt:* 1882. Lieutenant-Colonel Jack Windrush and Mary are bound for the UK when trouble breaks out in Egypt. After a spell as a spy, he leads the Royal Malverns into various actions, with the war complicated by an Egyptian association with the Fenians.

ABOUT THE AUTHOR

Born in Edinburgh, Scotland and educated at the University of Dundee, Malcolm Archibald has written in a variety of genres, from academic history to folklore, historical novels to fantasy. He won the Dundee International Book Prize with *Whales for the Wizard* in 2005 and the Society of Army Historical Research prize for Historical Military Fiction with *Blood Oath* in 2021.

Happily married for over 42 years, Malcolm has three grown children and lives outside Dundee in Scotland.

* * *

To learn more about Malcolm Archibald and discover more Next Chapter authors, visit our website at www.nextchapter.pub.

NOTES

Prelude

1. A zareba was a thorn hedge used as a barricade or protection for a village or encampment.
2. Bashi-Bazouks: Irregular troops of the Ottoman Empire, notorious for indiscipline. The Egyptian authorities in In Sudan often used them as an armed police force.

Chapter 4

1. This incident happened as described, except for Jack's presence. The European officers were impressed with the boy's bravery.
2. Colonel Burnaby was a celebrated athlete, marksman and equestrian who had written a book about his travels in Central Asia, The Ride to Khiva. He took part in Baker's expedition in a private capacity.

Chapter 7

1. A camel did wander into Suakin during the siege, and some Egyptian officers wished to kill it, fearing it was a magical creature sent by Osman Digna to harm the garrison.

Chapter 9

1. Saint Barbara is the patron saint of artillerymen, and her feast day is the 4th of December.

Chapter 10

1. "Get to Freuchie!" – Freuchie is a small village in Fife in Scotland. When King James VI held court in nearby Falkland Palace, he is said to have exiled anybody out of favour to Freuchie. The insult is no longer used.

NOTES

Chapter 15

1. Griff or Griffin was a term used by British soldiers in India to describe a man new to the country.

Chapter 21

1. The Oasis of Zerzura is a long-standing legend. The first recorded reference dates to the thirteenth century, when it was said to be a city "white as a dove." Various accounts speak of a town packed with treasure and where a royal couple sleep. Black giants are said to guard the city. In 1853 a British Egyptologist named John Gardner Wilson revived interest when he reported that an Arab had located the oasis, and in 1930 Europeans formed a Zerzura Club in the continued search. If the oasis exists, it remains elusive to date.
2. Ibn Battuta (1304 – 1352) was a Tangier-born traveller. In 1325 he set out on a pilgrimage to Mecca and must have enjoyed travelling for he kept going. He visited the Middle East and East Africa as far south as Kilwa. From there, he sailed to India and returned to Morocco in 1349. He later visited Moslem Spain and travelled across the Sahara to Mali. He claimed, perhaps accurately, to have seen all the countries of the Muslim world.

Chapter 31

1. Charles Gordon encountered a similar tree near Al Fashir in Darfur.

Baptism Of The Sword
ISBN: 978-4-82415-550-4

Published by
Next Chapter
2-5-6 SANNO
SANNO BRIDGE
143-0023 Ota-Ku, Tokyo
+818035793528

3rd November 2022

CPSIA information can be obtained
at www.ICGtesting.com
Printed in the USA
LVHW100334221122
733724LV00033B/301